WULFRIK

A long, lean coil of scaly flesh slowly crushed the planks of the longship beneath its bulk. Azure above and with a white belly below, the monstrous serpent blended almost perfectly with the waves that crashed against it, only the contrast between itself and the wreck in its grasp allowing the men on the cliff above to see it. Here, both Norscans knew, was the killer of their ship, the monster whose thoughtless act of destruction had obliterated the greatest longship ever built by mortal hands.

More pointedly, the merwyrm had left them stranded, denied their only hope of escape from the trap they had been led into.

'What do we do now?' Broendulf raged, smashing his fist against his side in impotent fury. Another arrow clattered off the stones near his feet.

Wulfrik smiled coldly at the blond Sarl. 'The dragon or the elves,' he told Broendulf. 'The gods leave us small choice, but at least the serpent won't make a game of killing us.'

Wulfrik did not wait to see what effect, if any, his logic had upon the other Norscan. Clenching the blade of his sword between his fangs, the warrior flung himself over the side of the cliff.

WARHAMMER

· WARHAMMER HEROES ·

SWORD OF JUSTICE
Chris Wraight

WULFRIK
C. L. Werner

SWORD OF VENGEANCE
Chris Wraight

⟞ TIME OF LEGENDS ⟝

· THE LEGEND OF SIGMAR ·

Book 1 – HELDENHAMMER
Graham McNeill

Book 2 – EMPIRE
Graham McNeill

Book 3 – GOD KING
Graham McNeill

· THE RISE OF NAGASH ·

Book 1 – NAGASH THE SORCERER
Mike Lee

Book 2 – NAGASH THE UNBROKEN
Mike Lee

· THE SUNDERING ·

Book 1 – MALEKITH
Gav Thorpe

Book 2 – SHADOW KING
Gav Thorpe

A WARHAMMER NOVEL

WARHAMMER HEROES

WULFRIK

C. L. WERNER

BLACK LIBRARY

For Nick, who is always pointing out my mis-steps along the way.

A BLACK LIBRARY PUBLICATION

First published in Great Britain in 2010 by
The Black Library,
Games Workshop Ltd.,
Willow Road, Nottingham,
NG7 2WS, UK.

10 9 8 7 6 5 4 3 2 1

Cover illustration by Cheoljoo Lee.
Map by Nuala Kinrade.

© Games Workshop Limited 2010. All rights reserved.

The Black Library, the Black Library logo, Games Workshop, the Games Workshop logo and all associated marks, names, characters, illustrations and images from the Warhammer universe are either ®, TM and/or © Games Workshop Ltd 2000-2010, variably registered in the UK and other countries around the world. All rights reserved.

A CIP record for this book is available from the British Library.

UK ISBN13: 978 1 84416 892 7
US ISBN13: 978 1 84416 893 4

No part of this publication may be reproduced, stored in a retrieval system, or transmitted in any form or by any means, electronic, mechanical, photocopying, recording or otherwise, without the prior permission of the publishers.

This is a work of fiction. All the characters and events portrayed in this book are fictional, and any resemblance to real people or incidents is purely coincidental.

See the Black Library on the internet at
www.blacklibrary.com

Find out more about Games Workshop
and the world of Warhammer at
www.games-workshop.com

Printed and bound in the UK.

THIS IS A dark age, a bloody age, an age of daemons and of sorcery. It is an age of battle and death, and of the world's ending. Amidst all of the fire, flame and fury it is a time, too, of mighty heroes, of bold deeds and great courage.

AT THE HEART of the Old World sprawls the Empire, the largest and most powerful of the human realms. Known for its engineers, sorcerers, traders and soldiers, it is a land of great mountains, mighty rivers, dark forests and vast cities. And from his throne in Altdorf reigns the Emperor Karl Franz, sacred descendant of the founder of these lands, Sigmar, and wielder of his magical warhammer.

BUT THESE ARE far from civilised times. Across the length and breadth of the Old World, from the knightly palaces of Bretonnia to ice-bound Kislev in the far north, come rumblings of war. In the towering Worlds Edge Mountains, the orc tribes are gathering for another assault. Bandits and renegades harry the wild southern lands of the Border Princes. There are rumours of rat-things, the skaven, emerging from the sewers and swamps across the land. And from the northern wildernesses there is the ever-present threat of Chaos, of daemons and beastmen corrupted by the foul powers of the Dark Gods.
As the time of battle draws ever nearer,
the Empire needs heroes
like never before.

Northern Tribes under the Shadow of Chaos

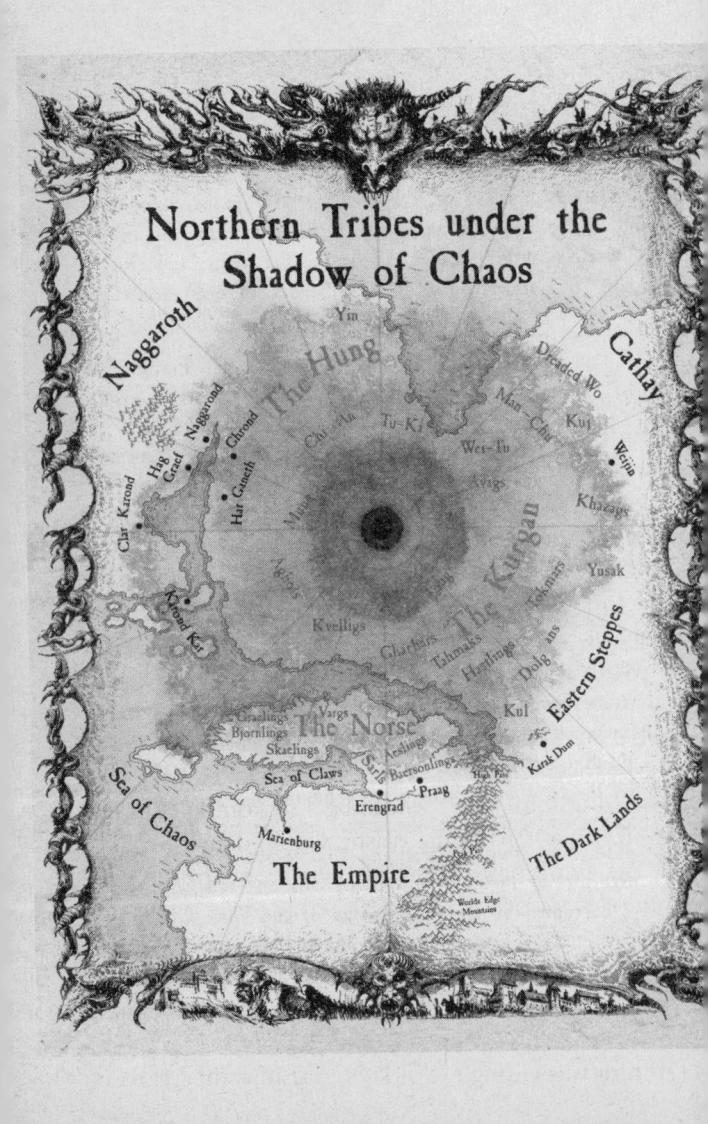

Prologue

THE WINTRY SKY was blemished by black stains that whirled and circled high overhead, their ugly squawks raining down upon the ears of the men below. The crows had gathered quickly, drawn by the smell of death in the air. A great murder of the scavenger birds had risen into the sky, betraying what the northmen had done to every eye within a hundred leagues.

Wulfrik glared at the croaking birds and spat against the rocky earth. It was a small betrayal beside what had come before it. The Norscan ground his fangs together, imagining the many ways his revenge would unfold. There would be a reckoning, and not all the daemons of the Wastes would deny him.

The northman turned his eyes from the heavens and stared back at the bleak terrain over which his enemies were even now stalking him. Tall, powerfully built even for the muscular breeds of Norsca, the skulls of his conquests dangling from the chains fastened to his armour, Wulfrik knew the mere sight of him was enough to strike terror into the hearts of lesser men. His bearded face pulled back in a grim smile that displayed his sharp fangs. He had taken his name from those fangs, teeth he had been born with and which belonged in the jaws of a wolf, not the mouth of a man.

His instincts were those of a wolf, the savage unthinking rage of a cornered beast. Wulfrik's foes were many and they had hunted him far across their bleak and sinister land. Warned by the circling crows or perhaps by treacherous magic, the elves had emerged from their watchtower to strike down the humans who had invaded their shores and defiled their sacred grove. The coastal fog that had cloaked the *Seafang's* crew from observation during their landing was gone, banished by some caprice of the gods.

The longship was his only hope for escape, anchored at the base of the towering cliffs that formed the shore of this eldritch land. The *Seafang* had borne Wulfrik and his warriors through the spectral sea between worlds to reach the strange land of the elves. It was the only chance he had to return to the realms of men.

Wulfrik's fist clenched tighter about the hilt of his sword. A Norscan did not fear death in the same way the weak southlings did. To die in battle was the greatest triumph most Norscans aspired to, a glorious death with blade in hand and his wounds to the fore. An end to make both gods and ancestors proud.

It was that promise which drew men to his banner, which made warriors from across Norsca and beyond flock to his side. Wulfrik felt no guilt when such men fell, for he knew that in their deaths they found the glory they desired. This time, however, there was guilt in his breast, the sharp stab of shame in his heart. The men he had left behind, strewn across the landscape like so much carrion, they had not died the glorious death of warriors. They had been felled like dumb beasts, struck down by elven arrows, killed before they could even see the enemy.

He had watched men die before in such cruel fashion, but always there had been reason for their deaths. This time, that reason was a lie – a lie that Wulfrik had insisted on believing. He had led them to this slaughter. The shame of their deaths was his. It was his punishment for trying to defy the will of the gods.

Wulfrik reached a hand to his thigh, ripping from his flesh the barbed arrow that had struck his leg. He threw back his shaggy head, roaring in pain as the missile was torn free. Contemptuously he snapped the shaft and threw the pieces to the ground. Again he threw back his head and roared, but this time it was a cry of challenge, not pain. Let the filthy elves come! He would face them and show them a finish even their cold hearts would remember!

A strong hand closed upon his shoulder. Like his namesake, Wulfrik spun about, snapping his fangs and striking out with his sword. A tall blond Norscan dodged back as the other warrior blindly lashed out at him, falling into a fighting crouch as he fell back. There was hate in the blond giant's eyes as he met the furious gaze of Wulfrik, but it was tempered by the man's own sense of shame.

'We can't make a stand here,' the huscarl said. 'They will cut us down as they did the others.'

Wulfrik sneered at the cowardly words of his comrade. Alone of his crew, the treacherous Broendulf had survived. 'If it is a choice between arrows in my belly or a knife in my back, I charge the bowmen and damn their sires with my dying breath!'

Broendulf's face flushed crimson as the champion spoke. For an instant, he considered answering Wulfrik's challenge. Among the Sarls, Broendulf had always been known for his sharp wits. They did not desert him now.

'If we die here, who is left to avenge your crew?' Broendulf asked. He saw doubt flash through Wulfrik's eyes. Emboldened, he pressed the point with words that were hateful to him even as they left his tongue. 'If you die here, who is there to protect Hjordis from her father?'

Wulfrik continued to glare at Broendulf. 'After the traitor is dead, we will finish this thing between us,' he growled. 'Hjordis is mine!'

Broendulf answered the champion with a cold smile. 'As you say, we will finish this thing between us. But not here.'

An arrow sizzled through the chill morning air, passing so near to Wulfrik's head that it disturbed his mane of crimson hair. The champion paused only long enough to spit in the direction of the unseen archer, then turned and began running across the barren ground, weaving from side to side in an effort to foil the aim of his enemies. Other arrows followed the first, rattling against the stones, striking sparks from the iron heels of the Norscans' boots.

Even with a half-dozen wounds peppering the champion's body, it was an effort for Broendulf to match Wulfrik's pace. However much he hated the man, Broendulf could not control the awe he felt in his presence. Wulfrik was truly a warrior who had been chosen by the gods; no simple mortal could match his endurance. He was like one of the bronze machine-beasts of the dawi zharr, untiring, indefatigable. Broendulf counted himself among the strongest warriors of all the Sarls, but beside Wulfrik, he felt as puny as a southling priest.

The cries of their pursuers grew nearer now. It was difficult to tell from the strange, almost melodious tones of elven speech, but there seemed a trace of panic in their voices. Wulfrik allowed himself a grim smile. The elves were afraid the men were going to escape. He allowed himself to concentrate on the cries. Even the curse of the gods had its blessings. For Wulfrik, that blessing was the Gift of Tongues. By focussing his mind, he could understand the speech of any creature, no matter how strange. Often he would use this eerie talent only to challenge his foes in words they could understand, but it had its other uses.

As he listened to the cries of the elves, Wulfrik's smile dropped. They were not afraid the men would escape. The elves were only afraid they would not be able to catch them alive. During the chase it seemed they had decided that the rest of the Norscans had died too swiftly. With Wulfrik and Broendulf, the elves intended to take their time.

Humans were not the only creatures who had a concept of revenge.

The cause for the elves' concern thrust itself upon Wulfrik with such suddenness that he nearly pitched over the edge. The northman charged across the rocky grade, unheeding of its gradual rise, unaware of the jagged cut that had sheared away its side as cleanly as though by the Blood God's axe. His feet teetering upon the crumbling lip of the cliff, he watched pebbles kicked up by his approach sail out into empty air. For an instant he stared into the dark waters of the sea, watching its waves smash against the breakers far below. Then Wulfrik regained his balance and steadied himself at the edge of the cliff.

The craggy shoreline stretched away in either direction as far as Wulfrik's keen gaze could see, rising from the blue sea like a great white wall. Mammoth rocks, curled and twisted by the ravages of brine and wind, leered from the depths, huddling about the feet of the cliffs like a mob of mongrel half-kin. Faintly, the northman could see the distant shores of barrier islands, their bleak stone shores little more than a black smear upon the horizon. Wulfrik scowled at the forbidding islands. If half the tales told in the sagas were true, there would be no respite from his enemies even if he could reach the forsaken spits of rock.

Broendulf was beside him a moment later, gasping for breath and staring with horror at the angry sea below. 'Where's the ship?' he moaned, gesturing at the breakers with his axe.

Wulfrik pointed to a jumble of shattered wreckage

being pounded against the rocks. 'It seems our anchorage wasn't as secure as I thought,' he growled. Suddenly the champion's eyes went wide with shock. 'Mermedus's rutting eel!' he exclaimed as he spotted the thing slithering across the ship's broken hull.

A long, lean coil of scaly flesh slowly crushed the planks of the longship beneath its bulk. Azure above and with a white belly below, the monstrous serpent blended almost perfectly with the waves that crashed against it, only the contrast between itself and the wreck in its grasp allowing the men on the cliff above to see it. Here, both Norscans knew, was the killer of their ship, the monster whose thoughtless act of destruction had obliterated the greatest longship ever built by mortal hands.

More pointedly, the merwyrm had left them stranded, denied their only hope of escape from the trap they had been led into.

'What do we do now?' Broendulf raged, smashing his fist against his side in impotent fury. Another arrow clattered off the stones near his feet.

Wulfrik smiled coldly at the blond Sarl. 'The dragon or the elves,' he told Broendulf. 'The gods leave us small choice, but at least the serpent won't make a game of killing us.'

Wulfrik did not wait to see what effect, if any, his logic had upon the other Norscan. Clenching the blade of his sword between his fangs, the warrior flung himself over the side of the cliff.

Chapter One

ENORMOUS, MAN-LIKE, THE huge tracks gouged the barren face of the snowfield, a black line fading into the howling gale. Pressed so deeply into the ice that bare rock shaded their depths, the prints made a clear trail even in the driving snow. It would take hours for the tracks to be covered. Long before then, Jokull would lead his captain to his prey.

The Norscan hunter whipped the scaly, lash-like appendage that grew from his left shoulder against his beard, knocking frost from the thick black hair. Jokull shivered beneath the heavy furs he wore, casting anxious eyes at the land around him. For days they had climbed the jagged slopes until Jokull thought they must be at the roof of the world, and still he could see the grey shapes of even higher peaks looming behind the falling snow. Much higher and surely they would be crushed beneath the feet of the sun when the Blood God's hunt chased it across the morning sky! The vision made the hunter tremble and place the little bone icon of the Skull Lord between his teeth. He could feel the iron staples fastened to the talisman stab into his gums, could taste the coppery tang of blood in his mouth. The gods of the north were angered when prayers did not come with offerings.

Wailing like the frozen wraith of a Kislevite witch, the winds swirled and crashed around Jokull. Spitting the bone icon from his mouth, he could see the blood covering it freeze into icy mush as the talisman dangled around his neck. The men of Norsca were used to the brutality of winter and the savagery of the elements, but even an experienced woodsman like Jokull felt oppressed by the harshness of these snow-swept mountains. It was as sinister and hostile a place as anything the skalds sang of in the sagas.

Jokull lifted his bow, the fingers of his right hand – the one that hadn't been changed by the gods – rubbing the feathers fitted to the arrow nocked against the string. Black feathers, crow feathers, feathers hungry for the taste of meat. The hunter placed great faith in such feathers, trusting them to speed the arrow to its target. With such arrows he had brought down snow bears and ice tigers and more than a few men when the hunting season faded into the time of war. Now, however, the hunter's faith in his weapon wavered.

Surely no clean beast would dwell in such a blighted place. The cold was like a gnawing thing that chewed through fur and cloth and skin to seep down into the bones of a man. The wind was a howling torment more furious than the gales upon the Sea of Claws, driving the snow like a thousand daggers into the face of any bold enough to stand against its fury. The air was thin and poor, like the breath of a frozen grave. A man's lungs gasped for it, gulping it down in desperate shudders but never drawing in enough to satisfy his body.

No clean beast would live in such a place, Jokull decided. He cocked his head as he fancied he heard a deeper howl sound behind the wind. His skin crawled as he heard the sound repeated, even more distinctly, from the higher peaks. Again the cry came, this time from further ahead, a low, growling sound that slowly rose into a piercing shriek. There was an unmistakable note of threat in the cries, a threat that made Jokull glance back the way he had come. How far was it to the ship, he wondered, and could he reach it before the crying things decided he had ignored their warning?

The hunter shook his head and spat a blob of blood into the snow. He could not deny the fear he felt but he did curse his foolishness. There was no going back. The way back was closed to him. It had been ever since he signed on to the crew of the *Seafang* and swore a life-oath to her captain. There was no retreat for the men of the *Seafang*, only victory or death. Their captain made sure of that.

The thought made Jokull smile. However terrible the creatures of the mountains were, he would bet his beard that his captain was worse. Jokull had only believed half of the stories told about the captain of the *Seafang* when he joined her crew. Now he knew better. He had seen trolls butchered like sheep by his captain, watched as daemons cringed before him and begged for mercy. He had been there when the fleshless wight of Jarl Unfir rose from its cairn only to have its bony back broken across the captain's knee.

Wulfrik the Wanderer was a name spoken of in awed whispers, and with good reason.

He looked back, willing his gaze through the falling snow. Beyond the flurry, he could see the grey figures of the crew marching in his steps. Even as a shadow veiled by snowfall, Jokull had no trouble picking out Wulfrik. There was an aura of almost palpable menace that exuded from the man, a sense of wrongness about him that compelled even as it horrified.

The master of the *Seafang* stomped through the snow, emerging from the flurry to glower at Jokull. The hunter was a big man, but Wulfrik towered a full head above him. Heavy furs cloaked his ogrish frame, while a hairy cape cut from the scalp of a giant billowed about his shoulders. With every step, Jokull could hear the rattle of bones and chains rise from the champion as Wulfrik's gruesome trophies clattered against the armour he wore beneath his furs.

Jokull lowered his bow, a cold more piercing than the snowstorm running through him as he considered that Wulfrik might decide a readied weapon meant a challenge. The champion had a brutal way of answering challenges. Jokull would rather face Jarl Unfir again than cross blades with Wulfrik.

The champion chuckled at Jokull's unease, his laughter sounding more like a wolf worrying at a bone than the sort of sound a man should make. Wulfrik's thick crimson beard parted, exposing his fearsome smile. Until he smiled, an observer might think Wulfrik's body untouched by the gods, what the weak men of the south would call 'uncorrupted'. But the instant he bared his teeth, the change was there for all to see. Wulfrik's teeth weren't teeth, but long sharp fangs, fangs of a beast, not a man. When he was drunk, Jokull had seen Wulfrik bite through iron with those fangs. One day, the champion swore, he would be strong enough to do the same to steel.

'Why have we stopped, weasel-slayer?' The question, when it came, did not rise from the hulking Wulfrik, but from a tall blond Sarl standing just behind the champion. The Sarl was a contrast to Wulfrik, his chiselled features presenting a face that was more becoming than the champion's fearsome countenance, yet still possessing formidable strength: Broendulf the Fair, one of the most renowned warriors in all the holdings of the Sarls.

'I don't like these tracks,' Jokull said, making a point to address his words to Wulfrik and not the surly Broendulf.

'I don't like anything that keeps me out in these Tchar-cursed mountains, but you don't hear me complaining,' Broendulf snapped at the hunter.

'Worried all this snow is going to scar those girly cheeks of yours!' laughed an ashen-haired reaver, his leathery skin darkened to the colour of ale and his right leg a mass of ivory-hued bones bound together with steel chain. A fleshless skull grinned where the reaver's knee should have been. Bitten off by a kraken during a misadventure on the northern seas, Arngeirr's leg had been replaced with the bones of the man who had caused the accident. Even without any skin on it, some said they could see the family resemblance when they looked at the skull of his father.

'You should grow out your beard!' cackled another warrior, running a hand banded in steel through the wiry black hair that covered his face from chin to eyelash. The hairy Norscan's eye vanished behind a lewd wink. 'Gives the wenches something to keep hold of!'

'The only wench you ever kept hold of said "oink", Njarvord!' another of the warriors snarled. The man, his shaven head covered in tattoos, drew a curved sea-axe from his belt and brandished it as the hairy Njarvord rounded on him. 'You know the rule, Baerson! First spills blood tastes the captain's sword!'

What little flesh showed past Njarvord's thick beard flushed crimson. His armoured hands clenched tight at his sides, the muscles in his arms bulging with frustrated violence. 'One day, I'll make you eat your words, Haukr,' the warrior promised with a menacing growl. 'One tooth at a time.'

Wulfrik noticed the squabbling of his men. He was not so detached that he was not aware of the tension and anger growing inside them. Even for men as accustomed to hardship and cold as the hardy stock bred in Norsca, the mountains were an ordeal. But that ordeal was nearing its end.

'Why don't you like these tracks?' Wulfrik suddenly asked.

It took a moment for Jokull to realise the question was directed at him. The hunter waved his tentacle at the steady line of tracks in the snow. 'They're too straight, too direct,' he said. 'Not like something just minding its own self. Not like something knowing it was being hunted and trying to get away. These feel slow and careful, like something that knows where it is going and why.'

Wulfrik nodded his head in agreement. 'Indeed they should,' he told the hunter, his voice rising in a soft roar so that the rest of his crew could hear him. 'The offering we stalk knows we are here and has for some time.' He gestured with one of his gnarled, hairy hands to the snowy ground all about them. 'There are rocks here to either side of this trail, rocks sturdy enough to hide the passing of many large beasts.'

One of the Norscans came forwards, staring hard into Wulfrik's savage face. Alone among the crew this grizzled old warrior would dare to look at their captain in such a fashion. Alone among men, would Wulfrik allow him to do so.

The old warrior was of the Sarls, a veteran marauder named Sigvatr. In his time, Sigvatr had been many things: war-chief, mercenary, bear-hunter, pirate and slave. Of all the things he had been, Sigvatr took the most pride in being the mentor of Wulfrik Worldwalker.

Sigvatr had been there, that night after the Battle of a Thousand Skulls when Wulfrik had made his drunken boast. He had been with Wulfrik long before and often warned the champion against his hubris. Now, the champion did not forget the man whose advice he had once spurned.

'The beast leads us into a trap,' Sigvatr said. It was not a question.

Wulfrik's fierce smile showed beneath his beard. 'The offering will not escape,' he said. 'Nothing chosen by the gods can escape,' he added in a bitter growl.

THE CRIES GREW louder and more frequent the deeper into the mountains the small band of men pressed. Echoing strangely off the icy rocks, twisted by the howling wind, there was no way to determine distance or direction when the screams sounded. Only the uncomfortable fact that the calls came not from one creature but from many could be learned from the cries. It was a fact that fed the fear growing in each of the Norscans. Ferocious in battle, unafraid of death when it stared at them from across a sword, the warriors now felt dread. The eerie sensation of being stalked by an unseen, unknown enemy was new to them. In their own lands, in the mountains and fjords of Norsca, they would at least have known the ground they fought upon and taken strength from that knowledge. Here they felt as far from their homeland as if they had been drawn up into one of the moons.

Only Wulfrik gave no sign of fear. What terror could the world hold for a man who had been cursed by the gods themselves?

But caution was not the same as fear. Wulfrik was wary as he pushed his body through snow that now came up to his knees. He did not turn his eyes away from the shadowy slopes of the high peaks; his ears remained trained upon the wailing cries that echoed behind the wind. Like his teeth, his senses had been sharpened by the gods. No eyes untouched by the gods could have seen the grey shadow plummeting down the side of the mountain or heard the soft rumble that rolled behind the howling wind and shrieking beasts.

'Run, dogs!' Wulfrik roared at his men. 'Run or sleep in the Crow God's larder!' The champion pitted deeds against words, turning and sprinting back down the trail with the ferocious speed of a charging bull. The other Norscans blinked at him in surprise then hurried to follow their overlord. Anything that could make Wulfrik turn tail was no such thing that any of them wanted to risk meeting.

The soft rumble was no longer masked by the wind. It grew into a groaning clamour, taking strength with each passing breath. The ground shuddered as though from the steps of a titan. Ice cracked and crumbled from the rocks, snow shivered upon the ground. One of the Norscan warriors dared lift his eyes to the high peaks. He screamed in terror as he saw a great shadow, like the hand of a malignant god, reaching down for them, blotting out the night sky.

The scream spurred the warriors on, urging their pounding hearts to greater effort. The heavy snow about their feet seemed to drag on them, sucking them down like a swampy morass. Men struggled desperately to press on, knowing that each passing instant brought a terrible doom rushing down upon them.

As the last of the starlight was darkened by the growing shadow a colossal bellow resounded through the mountains. To the Norscans it sounded like the mightiest wave ever dredged up from the Sea of Chaos had come smashing against the earth. They could feel the impact quivering through their bones, knocking many from their feet. The air was filled with frost, an icy cloud that danced and swirled like flames rising from a fire. Some of the men choked as the frozen mist was sucked into their panting lungs.

Wulfrik turned as the echoes of the avalanche died away. Grimly he pushed his way back through his exhausted warriors, turning his eyes again to the high peaks. His fangs gleamed in the returning starlight. The valley had been obliterated in the slide, great mounds of snow rising amid broken boulders and the splintered trunks of trees snapped like twigs before the avalanche. An icy pall, like frozen smoke, drifted slowly across the devastation. The champion studied the havoc, appreciating the unbelievable force his enemy had loosed against him. He did not look aside when he heard steps behind him.

'How many?'

Sigvatr's face was twisted into a grimace. 'At least six, and Bjornn's leg is broken.'

'Then say seven,' Wulfrik told the old warrior. A calculating fire blazed in the champion's eyes. 'That will leave enough.'

'Enough for what!' raged a furious Njarvord. 'All of us were nearly killed in that avalanche!' The hairy Baersonling clenched his fist tight about the huge double-axe he carried. 'You seem like you were expecting this!'

Fangs shone in Wulfrik's smile. 'Have a care, Njarvord. I can afford to lose seven. I may decide I can lose eight.' The champion's smile became a full snarl. In an instant, his sword leapt from its orc-skin sheath. Njarvord backed away timidly from the dull black blade, his nervous eyes locked on the skull dangling from the sword's hilt.

Wulfrik had already dismissed the outraged warrior from his thoughts. He was listening instead to the sounds of the mountain. The wailing cries were silent now. In their place there was only the occasional clatter of stone or the crash of falling ice.

'Dogs of Norsca!' Wulfrik bellowed at the scattered marauders. The warriors forgot their hurts and fatigue, compelled by the force in Wulfrik's voice to heed his words. 'The bones of your brothers lie buried in the snow, far from the halls of their ancestors! The beasts that visited such craven death upon your comrades come now to feast upon their still-warm flesh! You run when I tell you to run,' Wulfrik snarled. 'Now fight when I tell you to fight!' The champion raised his sword high above his head, starlight shining across the murderous edge of the blade. The skull tied to its hilt seemed to direct a mocking grin at the ragged warriors.

There was no time for the minds of the marauders to think about Wulfrik's words. A hulking shape rose from the snow bank beyond the Norscan champion, a great white figure of claws and fangs twice as tall as the champion. With a fearful roar, the hairy beast leapt for Wulfrik, its talons spread to rake the man's flesh from his bones.

In a single motion, Wulfrik spun, ducking beneath the sweep of the monster's claws. He thrust his sword into its hurtling bulk, letting its own momentum help to skewer it upon his blade. The leathery, ape-like face of the creature grew flush with pain, its amber eyes becoming wide with agony. The beast tried to pull itself off the champion's sword, but Wulfrik wrapped his hand in the creature's shaggy white fur, dragging it back down the blood-slick blade.

The monster shrieked again, slashing at Wulfrik with its claws. The heavy talons shredded the outer layer of furs the champion wore but scraped uselessly against the armour beneath. Its own blood bubbling from its jaws, the white beast leaned down, trying to bite the human's sneering face. Wulfrik twisted away from the desperate attack, in the same motion ripping his sword from the beast's body. The monster collapsed with an earth-shivering impact, flopping obscenely in a pile of its own entrails.

The *Seafang's* crew gave voice to a fierce cheer as they witnessed the fearsome prowess of their captain. Doubts about the leadership of their master were forgotten as the spirit of battle overwhelmed them. With the example of Wulfrik before their eyes, with his vengeful words still in their ears, the warriors did not hesitate when they saw more hairy monsters charging down the slopes. Shouting the black names of their gods and ancestors, the Norscans took up their weapons and rushed to meet the oncoming monsters.

For a moment, Wulfrik felt pride swell in his chest, the pride of a leader who exults in the valour of those he leads. Then the darkness inside him rose up to smother the sensation. The champion's face became stern, callous. He did not care anything for these men. He could not. He had to wield them as he wielded his sword, without thought or compassion. It was the only way he could ever hope to appease the gods.

Cold fury swelled within Wulfrik as the pain of all that he had lost filled him. The gods didn't do anything in half-measures. When they claimed a man, they claimed everything he had – or hoped to have.

The champion brought his boot smashing into the face of the beast writhing on the ground. The impact snapped its head back, breaking its neck like a stick despite the thick layers of muscle and fat that surrounded it. Wulfrik stalked away from the quivering corpse, his steps as unhurried as those of death itself.

Yhetee. Wulfrik could not say how he knew that was the name for the beast, any more than he could say how he knew that these were the Mountains of Mourn. Thoughts seemed to simply place themselves in his brain, bestowing upon him such knowledge as he needed. He knew it was the work of the gods, this strange knowledge, for the thoughts only came when he was hunting the offerings they demanded of him. A shaman of the Kurgan tribes had called Wulfrik blessed, saying he had been granted the 'Gift of Tongues' by the gods. The shaman hadn't been able to explain more, even when Wulfrik began burning the toes from his feet. He hadn't been able to say where the thoughts came from, or how to make them stop.

Wulfrik wiped the icy blood of the yhetee from his sword and glared at the snowfield where his warriors made their stand against the shaggy white monsters. The avalanche had filled the valley with snow, making it difficult for the men to move. With every step they sank to their hips in the soft slush, fighting to keep their balance. The yhetee, despite being nearly twice the height of a man and many times as massive, manoeuvred over the snow with contemptuous ease, their great bulks capably supported by their huge feet and widely splayed toes. Wulfrik was reminded of Varg seal-hunters and the snow-shoes they wore when plying their trade.

The yhetee did not quite outnumber his men, but they did not need strength of numbers in their favour. Each of the beasts was many times as powerful as a man, and as if their fangs and claws were not enough, many of them bore crude axes fashioned from tree limbs and ice. When one of the howling monsters charged a marauder, the icy edge of its axe cut as cleanly through the man's neck as any steel blade. Another Norscan had his axe and the arm that held it chopped in two by the sweep of a yhetee's crude weapon.

At the same time, Wulfrik's warriors managed to fell some of their foes. A screaming yhetee, four of Jokull's arrows sprouting from its hairy hide, fell to Broendulf's blade. Njarvord threw himself into the fight with the vicious madness of a berserker, hacking at the foe he had chosen with such ferocity that when it at last stumbled and fell it was little more than a dripping mass of bloody meat. Arngeirr, the sinister reaver from the sea, slashed his way through the yhetee with murderous skill, his kraken-tooth sword carving through the beasts with the same horrible efficiency as their own icy axes. Only the reaver's infirmity held him back, his bone leg slowing him as he hobbled through the snow.

Wulfrik savoured the fray, enjoying the smell of battle. Almost, he was tempted to throw himself into the melee, to lose himself in the joy of fighting as he once had. No, he decided, he was past such things now. Before, if he fell, he would only lose his life. Now there was much more to lose and much more to risk. Kings and warlords could only punish a man to the point of death. Gods could visit damnation upon even those safely in the halls of their ancestors.

Ignoring the sounds of battle raging all around him, Wulfrik cupped his hand to his mouth. The Gift of Tongues, the tortured shaman had called that part of Wulfrik's curse. It was his uncanny ability to instantly know and speak the language of any enemy. It had allowed him to curse and threaten the Kurgan in the shaman's own dialect, it had allowed him to do the same to an orc warboss and a Bretonnian earl and even a thane of the dwarfs. Even the voices of beasts were not unknown to him when the gods desired such things as an offering.

Wulfrik raised his voice in a sharp, ululating howl, a piercing shriek that clawed at the winds and boomed off the mountains. Many of the yhetee paused in the fighting to stare at him in bewilderment and wonder, their primitive brains recoiling at the sight of a man who could shout such abuse in the shriek-scream that served them as a language.

A furious wailing roar thundered from the snow-swept night. It was a sound to freeze the blood, like the snarl of winter itself. There was savagery and hate in the sound, the pure hate of the primitive, unburdened by thought or reason. It threatened agony and promised horror, that cry. The force behind the howl would offer no clean death. It would rip the belly and devour the guts of its prey while life yet pulsed through its foe's veins.

Wulfrik's challenge had been answered.

The other yhetee retreated as a great grey shape ploughed across the snowfield, abandoning their melee with the Norscans to avoid drawing the wrath of their own leader. One marauder, too slow to follow the example of the monsters, found himself in the path of the charging beast. He had time to scream once before the grey creature's slashing claw opened him from neck to groin.

Wulfrik steadied himself as the monstrous thing came rushing at him. A cold, fatalistic calmness quelled the stirrings of fear that churned his belly. It was the deadly courage of a man who knows there is no retreat, only triumph or destruction. Of such men, the sagas are made, though they are seldom alive to hear their tales sung.

The monster hesitated as it drew near Wulfrik. It was a massive yhetee, twice again as tall as any of its kin, its hair darkened by age to a dull silvery grey. Its claws were sheathed in the same steely ice as the axes of the younger yhetee and its fangs were like ivory sabres jutting from its jaws. There was wisdom and intelligence in its black eyes, enough reason to know when it was being hunted and to draw its hunters into its own trap. Enough imagination to be suspicious of this little man who stood so boldly before its fearsome charge.

Wulfrik lifted his face and stared into the greyback's eyes. From his lips came a feral grunt, the most base insult the language of the yhetee could offer.

The greyback shrieked in rage, its bestial temper overcoming its reason. The monster lunged at Wulfrik, the murderous claws lashing out. The champion did not trust his armour against the frozen talons of the greyback. Instead of standing against the monster's attack, he threw himself forwards and rolled beneath the yhetee's powerful arms. The black sword licked out, slashing across the monster's belly.

The greyback howled. Its powerful foot lashed out, kicking Wulfrik in the chest. He was thrown back, tossed across the snowfield like a boulder flung from a catapult. The champion crashed into the snow, sinking several feet into the soft icy ground. Snow collapsed in upon him, crashing down around him in a frozen mantle.

Wulfrik clawed at the snow, trying to find purchase, trying to gain a solid enough grip to free himself from an icy grave. Every effort brought more snow collapsing into the hole.

Suddenly a great paw smashed down through the roof of Wulfrik's prison. Talons of ice closed about his chest, coating his armour in hoarfrost. The Norscan could feel his blood turning to slush, could feel the breath freezing in his lungs. He struggled to free himself of the withering clutch, but the talons would not relent.

Slowly, Wulfrik was lifted from the snow. The greyback glared at him as it held him clenched in its claws. The yhetee swayed on its feet, its other paw pressed against the wound Wulfrik had slashed across its belly. Dark blood bubbled between its talons, staining the snow about its feet.

The greyback's ape-like face pulled back in a fierce grin. There was enough resemblance to something human about the yhetee's face that Wulfrik could tell it was gloating over its victory.

Fires of rage burned away the ice in his veins. Roaring, Wulfrik twisted his body, ignoring the sharp pain as his own armour tore his flesh. Sword gripped in both hands, the champion turned himself enough to bring the blade chopping down into the greyback's wrist.

Wulfrik crashed into the snow as the yhetee dropped him. This time his impact was only enough to sink him to his waist. Quickly the champion rose, ready to fend off the monster's next attack. His sword licked out as the greyback's claw slashed at his head. Sparks danced from his sword as ice and steel scraped against each other. Wulfrik could feel the shock of the impact rumble through the bones of his arms but he managed to retain hold of his weapon.

The greyback staggered away, snarling threats at the man who had crippled it. Wulfrik could see now that the cut across its belly was not deep, though the wound continued to bleed. The real injury the monster had suffered was where he had hacked into its wrist. The greyback's claw dangled from only a few tendons, looking as though it must fall off each time the monster moved.

Wulfrik waved his sword at the monster, daring it to attack. The mocking challenge did not need to be shrieked in the howling speech of the yhetee. Slapping its chest with its good claw, the goaded greyback rushed the Norscan.

Again, the beast proved itself more than a simple animal. Only a few feet from Wulfrik, it paused in its charge to dig its foot into the snow. This time when the monster kicked out at the man, a white sheet of snow flew into his face, blinding him!

The instincts of a hundred battles made Wulfrik dive away rather than try to wipe the ice from his eyes as another man might. The marauder hurled himself from the path of the onrushing greyback, throwing himself into the snow. Even so, the yhetee's claw slashed near enough to him to catch the heavy cape he wore. The icy claws of the greyback cut through the giant-scalp as though it were cheesecloth, the tangled tatters dangling from its talons like a knight's pennant.

Wulfrik rose to meet the yhetee's next charge. Shielding his eyes from another shower of snow, he was able to dodge the claw as it came whistling at his head. Rolling low, he brought his blade raking across the greyback's ankle, cleaving its foot from its leg.

Shrieking, the greyback crashed into the snow. Wulfrik did not give it a chance to rise. Screaming a war cry only a little less savage than the howls of the yhetee, he leapt upon the struggling beast. Steel crunched through bone, stabbing through the yhetee's horned skull to impale the primitive brain within. The greyback made one furious effort to fling the champion off its back. Then it uttered a mewing whimper and its body collapsed back into the snow.

Wulfrik wrenched his sword free from the greyback's head. One foot planted upon the gory mess, he raised his bloodied weapon high and shouted into the night.

'Skulls for the Skull Throne!'

THE DEATH OF their leader put the remaining yhetee into a full rout. The beasts fled back into the high peaks, their wailing cries piteous and mournful as they withdrew into their icy refuges.

For the men who stood victorious, it was enough that the monsters were gone. In the aftermath of battle, they gathered about their master and watched him perform a sombre ritual.

The head of the greyback was cut from its body and cleaned of flesh. Once prepared, Wulfrik took possession of it. The champion was silent as death as he carried the trophy towards a raging fire Sigvatr had coaxed into life with whale oil and cloth stripped from the dead. Bowing to each of the eight points of the flame, Wulfrik held the inhuman skull above the fire.

'Glory and horror to the Blood God, whose Rage shall devour the world! An offering to honour my debt!'

Wulfrik dropped the skull into the fire. Instead of

smouldering like a normal bone, the skull cracked and crumbled, disintegrating into a fine red mist. The stench of boiling blood rose from the crimson smoke. Wulfrik turned away from the flames, wiping his hand in the snow.

'It is done?' Sigvatr asked the champion when he returned from making his offering.

'It is done,' Wulfrik told the grizzled warrior. 'The hunger of the Blood God is appeased. At least for a time.'

'The gods have mighty hungers,' Sigvatr said.

'They are gluttons,' Wulfrik corrected him, casting a spiteful look at the flames. 'Will they ever have enough?'

Sigvatr shook his head in sympathy. It was an old sorrow Wulfrik expressed, a sorrow that had been with him ever since that terrible night after the Battle of a Thousand Skulls. 'Many men would envy the favour the gods have shown you,' he said. Wulfrik followed the old man's gaze to where his warriors were encamped.

'Most men are fools,' Wulfrik snarled, storming away from his friend. The thought that any man would look at what the gods had done to him as some kind of blessing was one that made his blood boil. He knew it was what made men so eager to join his crew. He couldn't understand how anyone could be so blind.

Jokull came running from the camp, a great mass of fur held in his arms. The hunter bowed as he approached Wulfrik. Smiling, he held out the heavy mass of fur to the champion. 'I saw the beast ruin your cape, war-chief,' Jokull said. 'I thought it only fitting that it should provide you with another.'

Wulfrik took the heavy fur from the hunter. It must have taken some nerve for the man to steal back to the battlefield and skin the greyback. The champion could admire that kind of valour, but he felt only contempt for anyone who thought he could bribe his favour with presents. Wulfrik's boot kicked into Jokull's knee, spilling the hunter into the snow.

'When I desire new raiment, I'll ask for it,' the champion growled. He didn't look down as he marched past the fallen hunter. The man would either learn his place or he would over-reach himself. Wulfrik hoped it wouldn't come to that. He could tell just from the feel of it that the cloak Jokull had made was a good one.

Conversation faded as Wulfrik stalked back into camp. The champion let his steely gaze sweep across the gathered marauders. They had spent a day resting and recovering from the battle. They should be grateful for their captain's indulgence.

'Kill the wounded, gather the names of the dead,' Wulfrik told his crew. 'We march to the *Seafang*. It is time we put these mountains behind us.'

The champion turned away, marching back down the mountain, following the path they had climbed when they had made their ascent. The meaning was not lost upon the Norscans. Without Wulfrik, none of them would ever leave these mountains, and Wulfrik would brook neither argument nor delay.

The screams of the Norscan wounded did not linger long.

Chapter Two

THE SURVIVORS OF Wulfrik's crew stood in silence upon the icy deck of the *Seafang*. Men of Norsca were not like the weak southlings. They did not cower in fear at the thought of magic or scream in terror when a sorcerer cast a spell. To them, such things were as natural as the turning of the seasons and the passing of the moons. Magic was but another creation of the gods.

Even these hardened men of the northlands felt a chill slither down their spines as they considered the magic they would soon behold. Many of them had experienced it several times, but never did they lose their awe of it.

Great, snow-capped peaks rose all around the longship, vanishing into the cloud-swept sky. The lake upon which the *Seafang* rested was more a thing of ice than water. No river or stream fed into the lake, no passage by which mortal hands could have rowed the vessel to its mooring. She might have been plucked from the sea by the hand of a capricious god and set down again in the glacial lake.

To the men who stood in silence upon the *Seafang*, that was precisely what had happened. Only the power of the gods could have brought the ship into the mountains. Only the power of the gods could bring her back again.

Wulfrik stood at the prow of the ship, his powerful arms folded across his chest, the grey fur of the yhetee cloak snapping about his shoulders as the wind rolled across the ship. Sternly, the champion watched as Sigvatr ushered the men of the crew forwards. With undisguised malice, Wulfrik studied each man as he brought the sharp edge of his knife slashing across their palm.

Each man pressed his bleeding hand against the carved dragon head rising from the prow. Under Wulfrik's wary gaze, each man waited, watching as the wood absorbed his blood. Then the warrior would step back, allowing another to take his place and repeat the ceremony.

After all his crew had pressed their bleeding hands to the figurehead, Wulfrik's expression softened, a triumphant gleam in his eye. He unfolded his arms and stared at the ranks of his gathered warriors.

'Your blood is weak,' Wulfrik told his men, his voice booming like thunder across the *Seafang's* deck. 'The gods have no taste for it.' The champion smiled, displaying his fangs. It was as well for the warriors that none of them was favoured by the gods. If one of them ever showed he was able to evoke the ship's magic, the next instant would find Wulfrik's sword buried in the man's belly.

'The wolf lets the dogs hunt with him,' Wulfrik

laughed. 'But only until they think they too are wolves.'

The champion brought his knife raking across the palm of his hand. He clenched his fist, letting blood trickle from his cut hand. 'This is the blood the gods have chosen,' he told his warriors. 'This is the strength they honour!'

Wulfrik spun around, slapping his hand upon the horned forehead of the dragon. Immediately a tremor ran through the ship. Shields rattled against the hull, masts creaked overhead, links of armour jangled upon the hauberks of the crew. A smell like bubbling pitch swept across the deck, bringing tears to the eyes of every man. Slowly at first, then more rapidly, thick grey mist began to stream from the mouth of the wooden dragon. Smoke or fog, the grey mist spread swiftly across the lake. In a matter of minutes, a wall of smoke engulfed the *Seafang*, cutting her off entirely from all sight of the lake and the mountains beyond.

'To oars!' Sigvatr roared at the awestruck Norscans. The warriors scrambled onto the benches that lined the deck. Quickly they gripped the thick oaken oars and set the blades slashing into the icy water of the mountain lake.

Sigvatr glanced back to the prow of the ship. Wulfrik still stood beside the figurehead, but now he held a sword in each hand. Fiercely, the champion watched the billowing wall of smoke. Sigvatr shuddered to think what might be staring back at the hero.

'Row, dogs!' Sigvatr snarled at the crew. 'Row or rot

in the belly of the gods!' He raised a heavy iron rattle, shaking it viciously, hoping the sound would ward away the evil spirits he knew were closing in upon the ship.

Gradually the *Seafang* began to move as the efforts of the crew tore her free from the ice that had closed about her. The grinding shriek of cracking ice drowned out the grunts of the straining Norscans. The ship began to move forwards, piercing the smoke that surrounded her.

New sounds replaced the crack of ice and the howl of mountain winds. A dull rasp, like the sizzle of a new-forged sword, rumbled through the fog, crashing about the hull of the *Seafang* like an avalanche of sound. Dark shapes flittered through the smoke, hazy apparitions that pawed at the fog like moths beating against a lantern. Screams and wails could be heard rising from the smoke, growling cries that each man knew he heard not with his ears but with his soul. Bestial and malignant, the Norscans knew that it was death to answer those cries, yet a perverse temptation clawed at each warrior's heart, urging him to self-destruction.

'Father!' one burly Norscan shouted, throwing down his oar. Before Sigvatr could stop him, the warrior rose up onto his bench and threw himself over the side of the ship. In an instant, he was lost to the fog. A piteous scream exploded from the fog, and in its echoes was heard the giggle of hungry things.

'Keep those scum at the oars!' Wulfrik growled. The champion stabbed one of his blades into a black shape that pressed in upon the ship, nearly piercing the veil of smoke which surrounded her. The apparition was splattered by the piercing steel, flying apart in little blobs of darkness that quickly merged into a new shadow before sinking back into the fog.

The death of the lost warrior brought more and more of the shadows converging upon the ship. Soon the grey smoke was turned black by their pressing shapes. As the veil grew thinner, burning eyes began to gleam from the darkness, staring hungrily at the *Seafang's* crew.

'Row!' Sigvatr shrieked, banging his sword against the ship's mast, waving the iron rattle over his head as though it were the standard of a king. 'Row until your hearts shrivel and your bellies burst! Row! Row! Row!'

The crew strained to keep time to the frantic banging of Sigvatr's sword. They fought to keep their eyes focussed upon the deck, upon the back of the man before them or upon their own feet. Anything to keep from gazing at the veil beyond the ship. It was more than eyes that could be seen there now. Things were taking form as they started to penetrate the fog, things with wings and claws and dripping fangs. Eagerly the slavering daemons fought their way towards the ship.

No longer did Wulfrik stand at the prow of the ship. The champion raced across the deck of the *Seafang*, slashing his swords at the furies hungry for the souls of his crew. Wherever his blades lashed out the daemons relented, slinking back beyond the veil. But as soon as he turned to fend back another clutch of inhuman spirits, the furies would return, gnawing at the fog.

Suddenly, the darkness was gone, banished by a cold, wintry light. The sharp smell of brine replaced the mephitic stink of daemon ichor. A stiff sea breeze wafted across the deck, invigorating the gasping men who crouched over the oars.

Wulfrik laughed and sheathed his swords. Boldly, the champion rushed back to the prow of his ship and set his boot upon the dragon's wooden neck. He pointed his bleeding hand at the rolling waves which now embraced the *Seafang*. As the wisps of fog parted, there could be seen an expanse of dark water, wind-whipped waves splashing against the longship as the sea rebelled against the *Seafang's* sudden intrusion into her domain. A distant shore with towering peaks loomed in the distance, rising from the clammy ocean and splitting the stormy sky with snow-swept summits.

'Today we cheat the daemons of their supper!' Wulfrik roared in triumph. His keen eyes detected the sharp cliffs of Norsca's jagged shore. To the rest of his crew, their homeland was nothing but a purple smudge on the horizon.

'Do you know where we are?' Njarvord asked his captain between gasps for breath.

Wulfrik closed his eyes, threw back his head and sniffed the air. For the champion, the smell was as familiar to him as the back of his own hand. A jubilant expression filled his face. 'No more than a day's sailing from Ormskaro,' he told the hairy Baersonling. He glared sternly across the deck at his warriors.

'But you'll make it there in half that time.'

* * *

ORMSKARO WAS NESTLED within one of the fjords cut into the coast of Norsca. Like some beached leviathan, the town sprawled upon the shore, stretching up into the cliffs and the flatlands beyond. The deep waters of the fjord made Ormskaro a perfect harbour for the fleet of sleek dragonships anchored off her beach. A flotilla of fishing scows timidly picked their way between the warships, bound for the open sea.

The town itself was a confusion of earthen longhouses and timber mead halls. The wattle huts of thralls squatted beside the stone keeps of jarls without pattern or reason. Animal pens spilled out into the muddy streets, their denizens roaming at will through the settlement, their owners trusting to the brands burned into their hides to secure their property. The tents of traders and craftsmen were nestled in little clumps wherever space permitted, gaudy banners proclaiming the nature of their wares and services. Close to the shore, upon a great timber platform, whalers busied themselves sectioning meat from an immense black whale while others drained oil from the carcass.

High upon the slopes that overlooked the fjord, a palisade of enormous logs formed a wall, sectioning off the entire summit of the hill. Behind the palisade, a second wall rose, this of cut stone, all but obscuring the great tower of granite it surrounded.

Wulfrik smiled as he saw the wall and the tower. The tower was ancient beyond the memory of men. Some whispered that it had been built by that race of giants who ruled Norsca before the birth of the gods.

Others said it had been raised by the gods themselves to mark the land. The oldest skalds claimed it was not a tower at all but rather the backbone of the father of all dragons, cut down by the Blood God's own axe.

Whatever its beginnings, the tower had become the seat of Ormnir, the great king of the Sarls. He had made it his fortress and founded the town of Ormskaro to provide a home for his warriors. From Ormskaro, the Sarls became a mighty people, among the strongest of the northmen. When the great army of Asavar Kul marched against the weak kingdoms of the southlings, it was Ormnir's grandson Ulgra Trolleater who led the Sarls into battle. From the burning husk of Erengrad his warriors brought back enough stone to raise the wall around the tower – an enduring testament to their victory over the Kislevites.

The smile turned to a sneer as Wulfrik thought of the current master of the tower of Ormfell. King Viglundr was a pathetic shadow of his illustrious predecessors. Generations of kings like Viglundr had squandered the might of the Sarls, allowing other Norscan tribes to grow strong. The soft kings of Ormskaro had grown content with their riches and thought no more of conquest and the joy of battle. They used their wealth to bribe their enemies where once they would have used their swords to bring them low.

Viglundr was such a king, a schemer and plotter with no taste for war. Well did Wulfrik know the Sarl king's mind. Had he not fought a war while Viglundr sat safe behind his walls?

'Is that a king's throat you crush?' Sigvatr asked Wulfrik in a low voice.

The hero tore his eyes away from the distant tower. He stared down at his hands. So fiercely had they been gripping the neck of the figurehead that splinters of wood had pierced his flesh. Wulfrik scowled at the old warrior, uneasy that Sigvatr had read his mind so well.

'Have the men make port,' Wulfrik told his friend. 'We will take on provisions, refit the *Seafang* and gather crew to replace those we lost in the mountains.'

'And what will you take from Ormskaro?' Sigvatr pressed, a note of caution behind his words.

Wulfrik turned his eyes back to the tower. This time it was sadness, not hate, that coloured his vision. 'So long as the curse of the gods is upon me,' the champion said in a sullen whisper, 'there is nothing I dare take from Ormskaro.'

Wulfrik turned and marched away, climbing down into the hold of the ship. Sigvatr watched his friend go, sympathy in his eyes.

'But you'll still go see her,' the old warrior said in a quiet voice. 'However much pain it causes you.'

THE MUDDY STREETS of Ormskaro were teeming with people as Wulfrik made the long climb up to the king's hill. Fur-clad trappers from the high mountains, the skins of beaver and fox dangling from the poles they carried; armoured bondsmen, their shields bearing the device of their lords; weathered fishermen, their skin burned to the consistency of leather; doe-eyed dairy maids, their arms grown strong from the milk jugs they carried; all of these and more passed the champion as he marched through the settlement. From the lowest house thrall to the richest huscarl, they were careful to step aside as the famed hero walked past. Even the sheep and swine that prowled the streets scurried from Wulfrik's path, squealing with fright as the champion's scent reached them.

Wulfrik gave no notice to the town around him. It was more unreal to him than the fog-wraiths that had tried to devour his crew. Since the gods had touched him and laid upon him their terrible curse, he had no part in the ways of men. Once he had marvelled at the delights Ormskaro had to offer and had thought it the greatest town in the land. Now those same delights mocked him and filled his heart with bitterness.

There was only one thing that could give him solace, if only for a few precious hours. He could leave the provisioning of the ship to Sigvatr and Arngeirr. Both had the wit and experience to know what would be needed before they set upon their next voyage. It would take time for those who would join his crew to gather; he could see to their trials on the morrow. For tonight, Wulfrik would try to forget voyages and battles, gods and curses.

For tonight, Wulfrik would try to remember what it was to be a man and not a hero.

Entry to the great hall of Ormfell was a privilege Wulfrik had earned after the Battle of a Thousand

Skulls. As his fame spread, even the boldest huscarls would be loath to confront the terrible champion. Even so, Wulfrik noted a hesitancy on the part of the warriors as they opened the gates to him and conducted him into the tower. There was an uneasiness about the men that went beyond their awe of the hero. Stalking through the stone corridors of the tower, he found that even the king's servants averted their eyes and hurried from his approach.

As he neared the great hall, Wulfrik found one man who did not turn away at his advance. Alone among his crew, the blond reaver Broendulf enjoyed the hospitality of the king. Before joining the *Seafang's* crew, Broendulf had been captain of Viglundr's household guard, a mighty huscarl in his own right. Wulfrik was not surprised to find that Broendulf had come to speak with his sovereign. What was surprising to him was the look of anxiety on the reaver's face. Broendulf glanced about the corridor, looking to see that there was no one else present. Cautiously, he met with his captain.

'Be wary,' Broendulf warned in a low voice. 'Viglundr is plotting something.'

Wulfrik favoured the fair-faced warrior with an amused look. 'He knows better than to scheme against me,' he said. 'Viglundr knows I saved his crown.' Wulfrik patted the skull tied to the hilt of his sword. 'He won't forget that.'

'It is not his memory but his ambition that should worry you,' Broendulf cautioned. 'The tower is filled with Aeslings this night.'

'Aeslings?' Wulfrik repeated, only half believing

what he'd heard. 'Since when do the Sarls play host to their enemies?'

Broendulf's face was twisted with contempt. 'Few of us may question the mind of a king, whatever madness may grip it.'

Wulfrik bared his fangs as he stared down the corridor at the oaken doors of the great hall. He clapped his hand upon Broendulf's shoulder. 'That explains the cold looks of Viglundr's huscarls. It must be an embarrassment for Viglundr to play host to both the Aeslings and the man who took their king's head. I am indebted for your warning.'

'Perhaps it would be best to wait for Viglundr's guests to leave,' Broendulf suggested.

Wulfrik snorted at the thought. 'Perhaps Viglundr needs to be reminded who he owes his crown to. If I disturb his other guests, they are welcome to ask me to leave.' The gleam in the hero's eyes made it clear how easy his removal from the tower would be.

'Someday you will seek a fight you will not walk away from,' Broendulf said, shaking his head.

'The Aesling isn't born who could cross swords with me,' Wulfrik laughed. 'My saga won't end on some Aes axe. The gods aren't so merciful.'

Hearing the melancholy in Wulfrik's voice, Broendulf knew it was best if he left the champion to ponder his troubles alone. Wulfrik did not like others to see him when his sorrow came upon him.

Broendulf had only taken a few steps before he found himself restrained by Wulfrik's clutching hand.

'Have you seen her?' Wulfrik said, eagerness in his voice.

The reaver was quiet, considering how he should answer his captain. Broendulf did not know if it was more cruel to let Wulfrik torture himself with his impossible hope. He knew too well the pain of a love that could never be. It was the reason he had joined the crew of the *Seafang* and the bond that joined his doom to that of the Wanderer.

Broendulf felt Wulfrik's fingers tighten about his arm. He stared at the champion, then turned his eyes to the doors of the great hall. Wulfrik released his grip and marched quickly down the corridor.

Broendulf turned and walked away before Wulfrik reached the doors. However desperate the hero was, there was no chance for his cherished hope. The gods had seen to that. Even Viglundr understood that fact. But Broendulf knew it would take more than cold reason to make Wulfrik understand. He wasn't sure if Wulfrik's tenacity made him pity the man or envy him.

What he did know was if he had the champion's strength, he wouldn't let anything hold him back. Not the cruelty of the gods and not the schemes of King Viglundr.

THE GREAT HALL of Ormfell was a vast chamber at the very centre of the fortress. Its stone walls were lost beneath the trophies which adorned them. The hides of strange beasts, the shields of fallen champions, the bloodied banners of vanquished armies, all of these surrounded the great hall, making of it a gallery of the Sarl people's triumphs over their foes. The bones of a great behemoth, the monster named Morrgawr in the sagas and more commonly called Shipcracker, hung suspended from the timber ceiling fifty feet above the floor. The slaying of Shipcracker had been the deed which earned Ormnir the title of king and which had allowed Ormskaro to thrive and prosper. Many heroes had tried to end the behemoth's rampage, but it had been Ormnir's spear which had brought the beast to ruin.

In the middle of the hall, surrounded by bearskin rugs and rich carpets plundered from the cities of Araby, the throne of Ormfell dominated the room. Twelve feet high, carved from the jawbone of Shipcracker, the throne was inlaid from crest to foot with plates of gold and studs of sapphire and jade. The luxurious furs of ermine and ice tiger were heaped upon the royal seat and at its feet rested a stool of silver and silk.

Almost lost amid the finery of his throne was King Viglundr himself. The king was a tall man, his long hair faded by age into a steely grey, his plaited beard adorned with golden combs and ruby beads. Though humbled by time, there was yet a powerful body beneath Viglundr's royal robes. In his youth, he had earned his father's favour by breaking the necks of his seven brothers with his bare hands. Years later, he had sent the old king to his barrow in the same way.

No coward, King Viglundr. His dislike for battle was a practical one, for he preferred to win by subtlety what others sought to take by the sword. It was said he bore the mark of the Raven God upon his heart, and few who became trapped within the coils of his plots doubted the Trickster's touch.

Wulfrik had learned long ago to be careful in his dealings with Viglundr. It took a keen eye to pierce the mantle of deception he wore and discover the truth behind the mask.

As he boldly entered the great hall, Wulfrik noted the slight narrowing of the king's eyes. No other sign of displeasure did Viglundr show, for his expression at once became amiable and excited. Wulfrik was reminded of a vulture waiting for a tiger to leave its kill so it could swoop down and glut itself.

'The mighty Wulfrik returns to us!' Viglundr announced, rising from his throne and extending his arms in welcome. 'Word reached us that the *Seafang* was spotted in our waters. Happy is the news that your hunt was successful and you come back to us unharmed!'

Wulfrik could feel Viglundr studying him as the king spoke, as though checking to be certain the champion was indeed unharmed. Any sign of wound or weakness, and the king would be quick to exploit it.

'The Blood God has been given his prize,' Wulfrik announced. 'The hunger of the gods has been sated.'

'At least for a time,' Viglundr added, a thin smile on his face as he sank back into his throne.

Wulfrik ignored the subtle reminder of his curse. He cast his eyes across the hall. It was more crowded than usual, and not because Viglundr had expanded the circle of bodyguards and sycophants that made up his court. There were a number of Aeslings present as well, pale-skinned marauders from the northern reaches of Norsca. Wulfrik found his gaze drawn momentarily to a black-haired Aes with gaunt features and jewelled rings about his fingers. There was no mistaking the hate in the dark Aesling's eyes.

Quickly Wulfrik forgot all about the Aeslings. Looking past the dark-haired marauder, he saw a cluster of women conversing in hushed tones. They turned coy looks his way, then shyly whispered to one another. In the midst of the maids there was one who did not look away, a tall, lissom woman dressed in a flowing gown of wolfskin, her golden hair twisted into long coils that hung to her waist. Her youthful face flushed with colour as she caught Wulfrik's attention, a twinkle shining in her lustrous azure eyes.

'Hjordis,' Wulfrik called to her, his voice almost catching in his throat. He started to walk towards her when the commanding voice of Viglundr made him turn back towards the throne.

'We have not dismissed you, Worldwalker,' the king said, disapproval in his tone. 'We might believe you more interested in our daughter than your king.'

Rounding on the ruler of Ormskaro, Wulfrik let his hands drop to the hilts of his swords. 'I call no man my king,' he told Viglundr. 'Such was the reward of victory,' he reminded the rest of the court, his fingers tapping against the skull tied to one of the swords. He turned his eyes back to the princess. 'Among other promises that were made.'

Viglundr at first turned pale at this brash reminder of his debts, then quickly composed himself. He waved aside the bodyguards who had started to close upon Wulfrik. Perhaps if the champion had been injured in his last voyage...

'We do not forget our debts,' Viglundr told Wulfrik. 'Ormskaro, indeed all the tribes of the Sarls owe you much. But there is a limit to our indulgence.'

'Maybe I should have made war in the name of Torgald instead of Viglundr,' Wulfrik snarled, his fingers still tapping the skull dangling from his sword.

'Do all the Sarls speak such impertinence to their king?' shouted a voice from the crowd. Wulfrik turned his head, unsurprised to find it was the dark-haired Aesling who had spoken. 'Among the Aeslings, we know the respect due a king!'

Fangs bared, Wulfrik grinned back at the marauder. His fingers closed around the tether binding the skull to his sword. Maliciously, he pulled it taut, holding the skull out for the Aesling to see. 'I also know how to respect an Aesling king!' he taunted.

The words stabbed home like a dagger. Shrieking in rage, the dark-haired Aesling drew the sword from his belt. Before he could fling himself upon Wulfrik, his retainers grabbed hold of him and pulled him back.

'No, Prince Sveinbjorn!' they cried out, fear in their voices.

Sveinbjorn fought to free himself of their grasp. 'I have heard the stories of your voyages, Wulfrik Whore-son!' the prince raged. 'I call them what they are: lies! Draw your blade and meet your ancestors, sea-worm!'

Slowly, Wulfrik drew his sword from his belt. He glanced at the men holding Sveinbjorn back and laughed. 'Whenever your nurse-maids will let you play.'

The last barb was too much for the retainers. One of them released the prince. Drawing his own axe, the warrior rushed at Wulfrik, a war cry howling from his lips. With the fury of a berserker, the marauder brought his weapon flashing at Wulfrik's head.

Wulfrik twisted aside as the axe came hurtling down. Moving with the grace and speed of a panther, the champion swung his body around, side-stepping the Aesling's charge. A blur of steel, a splash of crimson, and the Aesling toppled to the floor, his body folding back upon its spine where Wulfrik's sword had slashed across his belly.

Sveinbjorn relented in his efforts to escape his retainers. His pale features turned a sickly colour and his tongue licked across suddenly dry lips. There was terror in his eyes as he saw Wulfrik stalk towards him.

'Enough!' Viglundr's outraged roar thundered across the hall. He pointed a trembling finger at Wulfrik. 'Whatever services you have performed for me in the past, barbarian, they will not excuse the murder of my guests!'

Wulfrik sneered at Sveinbjorn. 'The Aeslings are welcome to collect their wergild anytime they have the stomach for it.'

The humiliated prince glared at Wulfrik, then ripped free of his retainers. Sheathing his sword, he marched from the hall. The other Aeslings quickly followed their prince in retreat.

'It seems I won't have a chance to kill any more of your guests,' Wulfrik said, turning back to the throne.

Viglundr quivered with rage. 'You forget your duty to me.'

'You forget yours to me,' Wulfrik answered, casting a sideways glance at Hjordis. 'I was promised riches, rank, the privileges of a king…'

'All these you were given,' Viglundr snarled.

'And I was promised the hand of your daughter,' Wulfrik finished. 'King Torgald is dead,' he announced, his fingers tapping on the skull. 'But I have not been paid for the killing.'

Cruelty filled Viglundr's expression as he leaned forwards from his throne. 'It was not our boasting tongue that brought the curse of the gods upon you,' he reminded Wulfrik. His face softened into an expression of regret and pity, though there was still malignance in his eyes. 'How can we give our daughter to a man such as you? Marked by the gods, cursed by them to wander the world to slay in their name? What manner of life would that be for a princess?' Viglundr smiled to see that his words brought the champion pain.

'You speak of our duty to you,' the king persisted. 'But what of your duty to Hjordis? Should she stay here forever waiting for you, waiting for a man despised by the gods? Must she grow old and wither, husbandless, childless, because you were too proud to free her from an impossible promise?'

Wulfrik felt his chest tighten, a coldness that was worse than the ravages of the yhetee. 'It is not pride that binds me to Hjordis,' he said.

Viglundr kept the triumph he felt from his face as he heard the champion's confession. 'You cannot keep her,' he said. 'If you do love our daughter, you must release her.

'Why would you force her to share your curse?'

THE KING'S LAST words echoed through Wulfrik's brain like thunder. Viglundr was right, he had no reason to force Hjordis to share his curse. Doomed to wander the world, killing men and monsters in the name of the gods. That was not the life he would have Hjordis share. She was better here, in her father's castle, surrounded by the riches of Ormskaro.

The image made Wulfrik sicken. However much he tried, he couldn't let her go. He wouldn't let her go.

The sound of footsteps in the hall behind him brought Wulfrik spinning around. His sword was already half from its sheath before he saw that his stealthy assailant was a shapely young princess with long blonde hair.

'I might have killed you,' Wulfrik growled, slamming the blade back into his belt.

Hjordis placed her soft hand on Wulfrik's scarred, leathery fingers. 'Am I so ghastly that I frighten the great Wulfrik?'

'You might have been an Aesling assassin,' Wulfrik told her.

The princess cocked her head and smiled at him. 'Who says I'm not?' Her expression became serious, contemplative. 'Prince Sveinbjorn is a handsome man and noble in his manners. A woman might do much worse than take such a man for a husband.'

Wulfrik snorted in amusement. 'That sounds like your father talking.'

'Oh yes, most certainly,' Hjordis sighed. 'He's been urging me to marry that reptile for the last fortnight. Fear of you is the only thing that's kept him from forcing me into it. Somehow he thinks you won't burn down Ormskaro if the whole thing is my decision instead of his.'

Hjordis cried out as Wulfrik's hands clamped around her arms. 'I'd make all Norsca a smoking crater if you were taken away from me! I'd kill every damn Aesling that ever crawled out of its mother if they—'

'Be careful of your boasting,' Hjordis warned. She regretted her words when she saw the pain that sprang into Wulfrik's eyes. She quickly diverted his thoughts, squirming in his grip.

'You're going to leave marks,' she scolded Wulfrik. Rubbing her arms as he released her, she fretted over the stains his fingers had left on her gown. 'You might have stopped to wash before coming here. I don't even want to know what kind of things you've been touching while you were gone.'

'Only some ice-giants,' Wulfrik told her. 'I killed their king. Cut all five of his heads clean off.' A sharp look from Hjordis made Wulfrik think better of continuing the tale.

The princess rubbed at the stain Wulfrik's fingers had left. 'This is never going to come off. I'll have to get a new one before my father sees and asks indelicate questions.' A sly smile spread across her face as she glanced at the hero. 'You should help me pick one out,' she suggested.

'And what about Viglundr?' Wulfrik asked.

'He'll be busy all night trying to apologise to the Aeslings,' Hjordis said. 'I think we could pick out a dress by then.'

'Maybe not,' Wulfrik warned her. 'I've been at sea for two months.'

Hjordis laughed and led the champion by the hand down the corridor. 'Where is your caution now? This could all be a trick to leave you so weak and tired that Sveinbjorn will only need a dozen warriors to overcome you.'

'I'll take my chances,' Wulfrik assured her, kissing the back of her neck.

Chapter Three

THE FEEBLE LIGHT of the Norscan sun was just starting to peek beneath the heavy furs shrouding the tower windows. Hjordis awoke slowly, stretching her body and sighing contentedly. She smiled as the warmth of the bed tried to lull her back to sleep. She rolled onto her side, half-tempted to submit to the enticing lure. As she moved, her arm fell into the warm emptiness beside her.

Hjordis blinked her eyes in confusion, then heard once more the sound which had awakened her. She sat upright, letting the bearskin blanket tumble from her body. Her eyes stared into the darkness. Only faintly could she pick out the figure standing at the foot of the bed, buckling armour about his brawny frame.

'You rise early,' the princess said, her words not quite spoken before a terrific yawn overcame her.

'There's much to be done,' was Wulfrik's gruff response.

The content smile she was wearing faded. Hjordis crawled across the length of the bed, pressing herself against the hero's armoured back. The cold mail sent a shiver through her naked flesh, but it wasn't so cold as the fear that trembled in her heart.

'Another of your dreams?' she forced herself to ask.

Wulfrik abandoned the vambrace he had been tying about his arm, tossing the piece of armour across the room. He sank back into the embrace of the princess. 'Always the dreams,' he told her. 'Always the dreams. When will the gods stop sending me these visions? When will they relent? How much do they expect a man to suffer before it is enough to appease them?'

Hjordis leaned over Wulfrik, pressing his head against her bosom. She ran her fingers through the wild tangle of his hair. 'You must have hope.'

'I saw a town,' Wulfrik continued. 'Some southling place. The walls were of stone and a river ran through its gates. Buildings were burning, the dead strewn like seed in the streets. The wailing of children filled the air and there was an ugly light in the sky. A great voice spoke, crying out: "For the Lord of the Winds, the last breath is given!" Then the earth shook with the laughter of vultures and I saw myself among the dead.'

A shiver of absolute terror ran through Hjordis as she heard Wulfrik relate the apocalyptic dream. It was easier for them to discuss the things as though they were only dreams, of no more substance than any other nightmare. But they both knew better. Wulfrik's dreams were not his own. They were visions sent by the gods, a portent of things that would come to pass. They were a part of his curse, guiding him to the offerings the gods demanded of him.

Never before, though, had Wulfrik seen himself in one of these visions, much less seen his own corpse. It sent a wave of horror pulsing through Hjordis's veins. In their cruelty, perhaps the gods had answered all of the hero's questions.

'What will you do?' Hjordis asked, her voice little more than a feeble croak.

Wulfrik pulled away from her so he could stare into her eyes. 'I'll see Agnarr and ask him to interpret the dream,' he said, making it sound almost inconsequential. 'Then I'll supervise the choosing of new men for the crew. If Sigvatr hasn't finished outfitting the ship, I'll have to help him rumble some of the traders. Then it'll just be the small matter of dragging my men out of the mead halls and whore-huts. I hope I don't have to kill any of them this time.'

The champion looked hard at Hjordis. His forced joviality hadn't fooled her; there was still a troubled expression in her eyes. He ran his thumb against her cheek, trying to tug her face into a smile. After a few tries, the smile became genuine.

'Tchar take all of them!' Wulfrik exclaimed, pushing Hjordis onto her back. 'They can do without me for a few hours yet!'

THE SEER AGNARR lived in a strange little shack crouched between a smithy and a storehouse for salted fish. Unlike its neighbours, the shack hadn't been built from timber and stone, but was made entirely from whale bone, the splintered ribs of a dozen beasts lashed together with stout cords to form a weird, ramshackle shelter. For the entirety of their length, each bone was richly carved with scenes drawn from the sagas. Wulfrik had heard that if a man studied the carvings for too long they would change, and that some of the carvings depicted things not yet chronicled in the sagas. He wasn't sure he believed such stories. There were always tales being told about the strangeness of seers. Even so, he made it a point never to look too closely at the engravings.

The interior of the seer's home never failed to evoke a sense of uneasiness in Wulfrik. The air was always colder than outside, whatever the season. There was a crude sort of ceiling stretched overhead to keep out the rain, but even in all his travels, Wulfrik could put no name to whatever scaly beast had once worn such a craggy skin. Oddments of every shape hung from hooks set into the scaly hide so that moving anywhere inside the shack required an effort not unlike that of an explorer forcing his way through a jungle. Dried bats, the desiccated shells of mammoth spiders, stagnant weeds that smelled like blood and looked not unlike severed fingers, the mummified husks of crocodiles, such were the arcane bric-a-brac of the seer.

Wulfrik pushed his way past a string of goblin bones and a rope made from the intestine of a manticore, manoeuvring into the heart of the dwelling. An eerie blue flame smouldered in a circle of skulls, beckoning the warrior forwards. He found it unsettling that the flame should burn so brightly yet do nothing to ease the chill of the place. He glanced at the floor around the fire, then sat down upon a pile of wolf pelts some distance from the flame. As he sat down, an insane gibberish accosted his ears, the idiot babble of a tiny batrachian daemon locked inside a silver cage. The thing eyed him with malicious, multi-faceted eyes and licked its long talons with too many tongues.

The hero threw a stone at the noxious creature, smiling when he heard it growl its displeasure. Wulfrik hoped Agnarr wouldn't keep him waiting long. From past experience, he knew the daemon's gibberish would start to make his head swim after a time. If he had to suffer from a headache, he'd prefer to induce it on his own with a few barrels of mead.

The idea turned sour almost as soon as it occurred to him. A few barrels of mead had been the cause of all his troubles. After the Battle of a Thousand Skulls, with King Torgald's head tucked under his arm, Wulfrik had celebrated the victory. Along with the arms and armour of the Aeslings and their allies, Wulfrik's army had captured their supplies. Whatever his other vices, Torgald had not scrimped in maintaining his troops and Wulfrik's warriors enjoyed a victory feast worthy of the sagas.

How hollow that celebration felt now, for it had brought doom upon Wulfrik and tainted his glory. The hero had feasted with his men. No man had fought more fiercely than he in the battle, now he vowed no man would outdrink him in victory. Using the skull of King Torgald for his cup, Wulfrik had matched his words with deeds. It had taken four entire barrels of mead to put him under the table, a feat that impressed even the ogres.

Before the mead overwhelmed him entirely, however, the drunken Wulfrik had started to boast of his exploits. Before he was done, he'd killed every monster in the Wastes twice and personally boxed the ears of three southling emperors. It was his final proud boast that had doomed him. He claimed that he was the equal of any warrior in the mortal world or in the realm beyond flesh.

The gods enjoy punishing hubris.

That night he'd had the first of his visions. A dark shape stole upon him in his dreams, a shadow blacker than night. It was an emissary of the gods, it told him. The gods were displeased with his proud words. However, it amused them to allow Wulfrik the opportunity to prove his arrogant boast. In his dream, he saw fantastic worlds, places he could recognise only from the dimmest legends. He saw cities built from bones and the soaring towers of the elf-folk. He saw the vast underground warrens of the ratkin and the jungle temples of the dragon-folk, the ramshackle fortresses of orc kings and the gilded halls of the dwarf lords. The putrid palace of the Plague Lord rose from the muck of his nightmare, its walls crafted from the wailing bodies of the damned. The dead halls of Nagashizzar, silent with the dust of centuries, made his soul cringe in terror.

Such would be Wulfrik's hunting grounds. He would wander the world, seeking battle to prove himself the equal of any warrior, mortal or spirit, living or undead. He would make offerings to the gods he had offended, offerings the gods themselves would choose. When he failed – and the dark emissary left no question he would fail – the gods would take great delight in torturing his soul through eternity.

Wulfrik might have believed the vision nothing but a drunken nightmare had it not been for the changes that had been visited upon his body. He bore the brand of the gods in his flesh, marked not by one, but by all the Great Powers. His tongue had become an inhuman thing, sharp and fluted like that of a bird and he found he could speak any language, however strange to him. The Gift of Tongues, the Kurgan shaman had called this strange power.

The first offering he was to make came to him in a dream. He was to kill the tomb lord Khareops and sacrifice its shrivelled entrails to Wormking Nurgle. The dream even told him where he would find Khareops. The creature's tomb was far to the south, in the wastes beyond Araby: a voyage only the boldest northmen ever attempted. It was a voyage that would take even a fast ship many months to make.

And this was only the first of the tasks the gods would have of him.

Wulfrik would have despaired then but for his old friend Sigvatr. The grizzled warrior remembered hearing about a 'sky-ship' crafted by the Skaeling witch Baga Yar, a ship that could sail anywhere in the world in the blink of an eye. It was the kind of extravagant legend Wulfrik had always discredited, but it was the only hope he had of beating the curse.

It took all of the treasure he'd won from Torgald and all the gold Viglundr paid him for defeating the

Aeslings to bribe the warriors he'd needed to assail the fortress of Baga Yar. In the end, the witch had been consumed in her own cauldron after Wulfrik's sword removed her arms. Two hundred warriors had died fighting the crone and her daemons, but victory had been his. The other treasures in the witch's fortress he left to his followers; the only thing Wulfrik wanted was her magic ship.

Seafang he had named the vessel and quickly he learned how easily fables can lie. It was not flight that allowed the ship to speed its way across the seas. Instead the *Seafang* would fade from the mortal world to sail upon phantom tides in that realm known only to gods and daemons. Such was the horror of the ship he had taken for his own.

'A man may forge his own doom.'

The voice was like the croak of a raven, at once thin and guttural. Wulfrik turned around to find the seer Agnarr limping through the menagerie of oddments. He was old, so old that even the elders of Ormskaro could not remember him as ever being young. His head was hairless and wrinkled, like a turtle's egg, his face like dried parchment across the bones of his skull. Eyes frosty with blindness stared vacantly from Agnarr's colourless face. The seer wore a heavy sealskin robe, the bisected head of one of the creatures framing his shoulders. He leaned heavily upon a staff carved from troll bone and behind him he dragged the twisted abortion of his left foot. It was more a shapeless mass of flesh than anything else, though there was some affinity to the webbed foot of an albatross about it.

'I have tried,' Wulfrik answered the seer gruffly. There was no need to introduce himself. Agnarr did not need sight to know things. Whenever he visited the seer, he had the impression that Agnarr knew everything he was going to say before he said it.

'Perhaps you have already succeeded,' Agnarr said. The seer turned and shook his staff at the imprisoned daemon until it was quiet. Then he unerringly picked his way to a mouldy pillow with tattered bits of lace clinging to it – some gift he'd received from another seafaring reaver long ago.

'Who could have called upon you the eye of the gods, if it was not you yourself?' the seer continued.

'That isn't the life I want!' Wulfrik snarled.

Agnarr fixed his sightless eyes upon Wulfrik. 'It is the life you have made for yourself. Few men would be resourceful enough to outwit the gods. Few would have been strong enough to survive their challenges. The name of Wulfrik has spread to all the steads of Norsca, his fame has been recorded in the sagas.'

'To hell with fame and glory!' Wulfrik smashed his fist against the floor. 'I want my life back!'

'Why?' Agnarr asked, genuine bewilderment in his voice. 'You have achieved what mighty lords squander armies and slaughter nations to win for themselves. The gods gaze down upon you! Your flesh bears the mark of their favour! You have been gifted to serve them as few mortals may ever hope!'

Wulfrik bared his fangs at the blind man. 'The last prophet who told me this curse was a gift spent a long time dying,' he warned.

'And how long will you take to die?' Agnarr's

question lashed out at the hero. 'How long will you fight against the will of the gods, and to what end? To marry some wench, sire a clutch of offspring.' The seer chuckled darkly. 'Perhaps steal her father's throne? Bah! What are women and offspring and thrones? Dust and less than dust!' He wagged one of his withered fingers at Wulfrik. 'The gifts of the gods, these are the rewards a man keeps forever. The rewards of love and greed and ambition, these rot with a man in his grave.'

'I want them just the same,' Wulfrik growled. 'I did not seek this curse…'

Agnarr nodded his head. 'Yet it found you just the same. Sometimes the feet walk a path the head does not know.'

Wulfrik rose from the pile of wolf-skins. 'I did not come here to be told to accept my doom.'

Agnarr waved his hands at the champion, motioning for him to sit down. 'You came so that I might interpret your vision.'

'Seldom has one come upon me so soon after a voyage,' Wulfrik said. He made no effort to hide the anxiety he felt. 'Is… is this… how they are… to be… now?' The thought was horrible to him, that he would sail the world for the rest of his days, moving from one hunt to another, without rest or respite.

'I cannot say,' the seer admitted with a shake of his head. 'I can only try to discern the will of the gods from your vision.'

'I saw myself among the dead,' Wulfrik shuddered. It was not the idea of death that frightened him, but the awful fate that would await him in the world beyond.

'Through our lives, we are all of us many men,' Agnarr told him. 'Sometimes the gods conspire to destroy one of these selves without killing the body. When that happens, a new self arises to command the flesh.' The seer tapped his bony chest. 'Sometimes it is in a man's power to destroy his self on his own.

'For the rest of your vision, I can say little,' the seer said. 'The signs are clear enough. The offering the gods have chosen is to be offered to Great Tchar, the Raven God. That you will find the sacrifice in the lands of the southlings is obvious too.'

'But who?' Wulfrik demanded. 'Where? The Empire of the southlings is a vast land to stalk nameless prey.'

Agnarr lifted his hands to his eyes, rubbing at the corners of their sockets. 'I do not know. There is something wrong. Before your visions have been as clear to me as if I had had them myself. This time is different. It is like trying to peer through a thick fog. Shapes and shadows are there, but more I cannot see. But a place once seen, why must it have a name to be found?'

Wulfrik scowled at the seer's inability to tell him more. Irritably, he snapped a gold band from around his arm and tossed it onto the floor beside Agnarr's feet. 'I always come here looking for answers, but I always leave with more questions than I came with.'

'That is because you do not like the answers you are given,' Agnarr scolded him. 'The gods answer every prayer, but few are wise enough to understand when the answer is "no". You might ponder that.'

'I'd rather find a barrel of mead and a plateful of roast horse,' the champion confessed.

'Then I wish you good appetite,' Agnarr said. 'Remember your dream, and listen to it. Otherwise I fear we shall not speak again.'

Wulfrik had been shoving aside the tangles of dried eels and withered herbs on his way from the seer's hut. Now he froze, a chill running down his spine. He spun about, tearing his way through the maze of oddments. 'What did you say, ghost-caller? What do you mean?'

'More questions when you've been given answers,' Agnarr's croaking voice laughed.

Wulfrik fought his way towards the voice, anger swelling up inside him. Savagely he tore strings of sea shells and eagle eyes from the ceiling. Then the hair rose on his arms as his hand connected with the bony curve of the shack's outer wall. He was certain he had retraced his path exactly, yet he'd reached the far side of the shack without passing through the opening at the centre. He turned about, still able to see the blue light of the fire.

Again Wulfrik bulled his way across the shack. He would find Agnarr and get straight answers from him if he had to choke them out of the seer!

This time when he crossed the hovel, Wulfrik found himself blinking in the sunlight, the sounds of the smithy and the smells of the warehouse welcoming him back into the mortal world.

A GREAT CROWD was already gathered when Wulfrik made his way to the Bloodfield. A training ground for Ormskaro's warriors and a place where Sarl youths would prove their manhood in fierce contests, the large plateau overlooking the sea was no stranger to the sounds of combat and the smell of blood. One corner of the plateau, however, was different. It was not devoted to the warriors of Ormskaro or the Sarl tribe. It was a place of death and slaughter that went far beyond the trials of youths and the training of warriors.

It was called the Wolf Forest, and it served one man. That man was Wulfrik and it was in this place he would choose the warriors fit to join his crew.

Whenever Wulfrik returned to Ormskaro it would mark the beginning of a festival for the Sarls. There would be grand feasts and much dancing and singing. But the highlight of the festival would not be in the mead halls but in the Wolf Forest. Here, every freeholder, bondsman and huscarl in the town would gather to watch as the fiercest warriors in Norsca did battle that they might join the crew of the *Seafang* and earn the glory of following Wulfrik on his voyages.

For months the warriors would come. Great hairy Baersonlings and crafty Skaelings, twisted Vargs and dour Graelings, all would make their way to Ormskaro to test their strength and prove themselves mightier than their foes. They would gather and they would wait, waiting for this day, the day when they would enter the Wolf Forest.

Wulfrik took his seat at a long table set a few yards from the forest. He set down the platter of grilled walrus he had carried with him onto the plateau, then slid the barrel of mead tucked under his arm next to it. He smiled at Sigvatr as the old warrior nodded, clearly impressed by the combined display of balance and strength.

'I'd like to see you do that again after you empty the barrel,' Sigvatr quipped.

'Only if you watch to see I don't walk off the cliff,' Wulfrik said, pointing a thumb over his shoulder at the sheer drop that marked the seaward side of the plateau. He glanced across the crowd that had gathered to watch the testing. It seemed to him that most of Ormskaro had surrounded the Wolf Forest. Even Viglundr was in attendance, surrounded by his huscarls and Aesling guests. Wulfrik made a point of waving at Sveinbjorn. The Aesling prince grew pale and sank into his heavy bearskin cloak.

'A good turnout,' Sigvatr commented. 'A lot of the crew even showed up to watch. Though Haukr probably did so just to make wagers on who will win.'

Wulfrik slammed his fist into the barrel of mead, smashing open its top. 'Don't be glum, grey-beard. If they're all here then it will be easier getting them back on the ship when we leave.'

The remark made Sigvatr look twice at his captain. 'So soon? We only made port yesterday.'

Wulfrik took his silver drinking horn and dunked it into the mead. 'Maybe I should tell the gods to wait then,' he grumbled, taking a long drink.

'You've had another dream?'

The champion grimaced, spitting the liquid from his mouth. 'It tastes bad enough without your chirping,' he complained. 'Of course I've had another dream!' Wulfrik stared back at King Viglundr's table, this time locking eyes with Hjordis instead of

Sveinbjorn. He gave the princess a lewd wink and chuckled when he saw colour rush into her cheeks. 'I've as much longing to stay here a few weeks as any of the crew.'

'They won't like it,' Sigvatr said. 'Kaetill's holed up in a longhouse with all five of Jarl Svanir's daughters and Njarvord is down in one of the mead halls trying to outdrink three steelmongers from Kraka Drang.'

'Kaetill better hope we find him before Svanir,' Wulfrik said. 'As for Njarvord, the sea air will help clear his head after those dwarfs put him under the table.' He looked back to Viglundr's table. Anger flashed through him as he saw Sveinbjorn leaning across the table to speak to Hjordis. Wulfrik's hand clenched into a fist, crumpling his drinking horn.

'How many jackals have come this time?' Wulfrik growled at Sigvatr.

'Almost a hundred,' Sigvatr told his captain. 'We only need twenty-three.'

Wulfrik wiped up the mead that had splashed onto him when he ruined his silver horn. 'We'll take thirty,' he decided, sucking the mead from his fingers. 'But we'll go through them all today.'

Once again there was surprise in Sigvatr's expression. 'We usually give them a day to recover before matching them again.'

Wulfrik directed a black look in the direction of the king's table. 'If they want to share my glory, then they don't need a rest.' The champion tore a strip of meat from his platter and gestured at the Wolf Forest. 'Send the first set in,' he ordered.

Sigvatr stood and unrolled the vellum scroll he

carried. He glanced down the list of names, selecting two at random. 'Tjorvi Tjorvisson of the Graelings and Garek Spearbreaker of the Sarls!' he shouted.

As soon as Sigvatr spoke, the noise of the crowd faded to a quiet murmur. The two warriors whose names had been called stepped forwards, their friends banging swords against shields in applause as they stalked towards the Wolf Forest. Gamblers scurried about making last-minute wagers and giving new odds now that the opponents were known.

Both warriors hesitated as they approached the Wolf Forest, their minds turning to the stories they had heard about the death and carnage the place had seen. They were bold men, however, and quickly overcame their misgivings. One of them would be victorious, one of them would not. Such was the way it should be. Drawing their axes from their belts, slipping their arms through the loops of their shields, the two northmen grabbed the ladders set at either end of the arena. They climbed to the narrow platforms set twenty feet above the plateau and gazed across at their foe.

Between them stretched the Wolf Forest, a maze of round wooden posts sunk into the plateau. The top of each post was just wide enough to accommodate a man's foot and spaced far enough apart that a man could step from one to another. The process wasn't an easy one, however, for the posts weren't sunk to a uniform depth, each varying slightly from the others. Beneath the posts, stretching all along the length of the Wolf Forest, the ground was littered with sharp wooden stakes. The Crow God's Teeth, the stakes had been called, for they were smeared with dung and offal to ensure a lingering death to any who felt their bite. A man who fell from the posts would have nowhere to go except onto the stakes.

The warriors stared at each other, then took their first trembling steps out onto the posts. As soon as their feet left the platforms, a raucous roar erupted from the crowd. Instantly the warriors raised their shields, trying to protect themselves from the barrage of stones, vegetables, fish bones and broken pottery that flew at them. The friends of each warrior attacked his opponent with concentrated volleys of rubbish while the gamblers directed their ire against whomever they had wagered against.

Under the assault, the two northmen struggled to keep their footing. At the same time, each tried to move forwards, to come to blows with his enemy. The roar of the crowd grew more intense as the men closed the distance, and the barrage became limited only to the odd stone and crab shell as the warriors came within reach of one another. Bracing their feet as best they could, the two fighters chopped at each other with their axes, now turning their shields to the effort of warding off the attack of their opponent.

Tjorvi, a scarred youth with tattoos covering his bald head, drove his axe at Garek's knee only to have the iron rim of the Sarl's shield intercept. The Graeling was almost overbalanced as his axe was driven down, teetering for a terrible moment as he leaned out over the stakes.

Garek was a brawny whaler with metal rings studding his arms and a bronze crescent piercing his nose. He tried to exploit his enemy, slashing the edge of his heavy axe across Tjorvi's back, trying to drag him off the posts.

Tjorvi cried out in pain as the axe tore through his armour and bit into his flesh. The Graeling stumbled to his left, only narrowly catching his footing. Garek pursued his enemy, chopping at him even as he tried to regain his balance. Tjorvi blocked the blow with his shield. There was a violent crunch as Garek's axe hacked into Tjorvi's shield, splintering it.

Tjorvi snarled at his attacker, flinging his arm wide. Garek's trapped axe shifted with the shield and the Sarl's eyes went wide with alarm as he realised his predicament. Hastily, he brought his own shield down to intercept Tjorvi's attack.

Instead of lashing out with his axe, however, Tjorvi threw all of his weight into his shield. Garek, instinctively maintaining his grip on his axe, shifted to the right. It was a delicate matter of balance and momentum that allowed Tjorvi to overcome his foe. With a practised move, the young Graeling slipped his arm out from the loops of his shield. The sudden loss of Tjorvi's weight arresting the shield's motion caused Garek's shifting body to overbalance.

The Sarl shrieked as he realised his mistake. He released his trapped axe an instant too late to save himself. Like a clam dropped from the beak of a gull, Garek fell from the posts and slammed into the waiting stakes below.

'A NASTY TRICK,' Sigvatr observed as the triumphant Tjorvi descended from the Wolf Forest. 'I think he deliberately used a weak shield to trap his enemy's axe.'

Wulfrik picked a strip of meat from between his teeth and shrugged. 'A feeble trick if his enemy had had a flail. We'll see how he fares the next time out.' The champion returned his attention to his mead, trying to capture what he could with his crumpled drinking horn. So fixated was he on his labour that he didn't hear Sigvatr call out the next two combatants.

He also failed to notice the approach of the Kurgan until he was standing right beside him.

The Kurgan was a short, sparsely built man, his skin possessing the dusky hue common among those who dwell in the northern Wastes. His stringy hair was frosty white and his beard was braided into a long coil that made it seem some tenacious serpent had bitten his chin and refused to let go. He wore a simple leather hauberk and mammoth-fur leggings, and about his body he wore a heavy horsehair cape.

All of this Wulfrik noticed in a glance, for as soon as he began to study the stranger, his eyes were transfixed by those of the Kurgan. The man's eyes were a deep, piercing blue and glowed like foxfire with an inner light. Looking into those eyes was like staring into an ocean abyss or gazing upon the limitless expanse of the night sky. Wulfrik felt a wave of vertigo grip him and quickly closed his eyes.

'You are Wulfrik Worldwalker,' the Kurgan said, inclining his head towards the champion.

'It doesn't take a sorcerer to know that,' Wulfrik said, rubbing his eyes. 'The lowest thrall in Ormskaro could have pointed me out for you.'

The stranger laughed, the sound somehow reminding Wulfrik of breaking glass. 'Of course, of course,' he said. 'The fame of Wulfrik is known to us even in the far north.' The Kurgan stepped closer to the champion, leaning on a tall staff fashioned from silver and studded with polished agates. At the head of the staff was a fist-sized orb of sapphire, an exact match for the eerie eyes of its owner.

'I am Zarnath of the Tokmars,' the stranger introduced himself, slapping his chest with his hand. 'I have come to offer a service to the great Wulfrik.'

'Then you may add your name to my list.' There was more than annoyance in Sigvatr's tone as he regarded Zarnath. 'Though I think few will risk their silver on your chances of success.'

Zarnath stared up at the combat raging atop the Wolf Forest. His thin features became twisted with repugnance. 'I am a shaman, the voice of the gods. You would subject me to such indignity?'

'A shaman worthy of joining my crew would have little to fear from the Wolf Forest,' Wulfrik said.

The shaman smiled at Wulfrik. 'I do not wish to join your crew,' he corrected the hero. 'I said I have come to offer a service to you.'

'What manner of service?' Sigvatr demanded, his eyes narrow with suspicion.

Zarnath did not even favour the old warrior with a glance but kept his attention fixed upon Wulfrik. 'I can break the curse that binds you,' the shaman said.

At once Wulfrik leapt to his feet, his powerful hands closing upon the Kurgan's shoulders in a fierce grip. 'You dare mock me?' he roared.

The shaman's expression remained placid. 'I did not journey across the Wastes simply for a jest,' he said. He waited until Wulfrik removed his hands before continuing.

'As I said, your fame has spread even to the campfires of the Tokmars. We have heard of the feats of the mighty Wulfrik, doomed to wander the world forever, fighting to prove himself to the gods.'

'You said you could break the curse,' Wulfrik reminded the shaman in a threatening growl.

Zarnath smiled at him. 'Indeed, such knowledge is known to me. It is within my power to break the doom the gods have placed upon you.'

'Then do so,' Wulfrik snarled impatiently. He did not believe the Kurgan's claims, but he could not quell the stirrings of hope rising within him.

The shaman spread his hands in a helpless gesture. 'It is not so easy. There are things I must have to perform the ritual that will free you. Things, I fear, only you can provide me.'

'He's trying to play you for a fool,' Sigvatr warned Wulfrik. 'He wants you to steal some treasure for him and then he'll be gone like a lamb in a wolf's den.'

'I could have found thieves among my own people,' Zarnath said, fixing his eerie gaze on Sigvatr. Despite his stubborn effort, the old warrior could not help but turn away. A slight smile pulled at Zarnath's face as he won the contest of wills. 'But to seize the artefacts I must have to free Wulfrik from his doom will require a great hero.'

'And if you do not mean to run off with these

artefacts, what price is it you expect to earn?' Sigvatr persisted.

Zarnath stood straight, his eyes hooded as he announced the reward he would have from Wulfrik for ending the curse. 'I want the *Seafang*,' he told the warriors.

Sigvatr sputtered in outrage, his hand closing about the Tilean poniard thrust beneath his belt. He would have lunged at the Kurgan for making such an outrageous claim but for the hand Wulfrik pressed against him.

'You demand a high price,' Wulfrik growled at the shaman. 'There is no ship in the world as fine as the *Seafang*. The magic bound into her is the mightiest I have ever seen. It would cause me great pain to part with her.'

'Would your curse cause you any less pain?' Zarnath objected. 'Free from the curse of the gods, you would not need the *Seafang's* magic as you do now. There would be no more hunts to the hinterlands of the world whenever the gods demanded it. You would be released from that claim upon you.'

'Very well,' Wulfrik told the Kurgan. The very immensity of the price Zarnath demanded gave the champion cause to believe he could do what he claimed to do. 'You end my curse and the *Seafang* is yours.'

Sigvatr gasped in shock. 'Wulfrik! Do not provoke the gods further by trying to cheat them!'

Wulfrik rounded on his friend, fury burning in his eyes. 'I will do what I must to free myself from this curse!' he growled. 'If that means cheating the gods, then that is what I will do!'

'The Kurgan is playing you for a fool,' insisted Sigvatr. 'At least confer with Agnarr about this. See what one of our own seers has to say about it. Don't blindly accept the word of an outlander shaman!'

Still fuming, Wulfrik settled back into his seat. He had to admit that Sigvatr was right. It wasn't smart to provoke the gods without good reason. He would speak with Agnarr about Zarnath's claim.

'My condolences,' Zarnath said, his voice humble. The shaman bowed to the two warriors. 'Gathered here to watch your contest, you have not heard. The seer Agnarr is dead. The imp he kept broke free of its cage and turned upon him. When his neighbours found him, the daemon had chewed his face right down to the bone.

'All it left of him were his eyes.'

THREE DAYS AFTER the trials of the Wolf Forest, the *Seafang* sailed. A great crowd gathered to watch the longship leave. But no eyes watched her departure more keenly than those studying her from atop the now-deserted plateau of the Bloodfield.

King Viglundr smiled as the ship sailed down the fjord and at last was lost to sight. Still smiling, he turned to the Aesling prince standing at his side.

'I will begin preparations for the wedding,' Viglundr told the prince.

Chapter Four

THE SEAFANG HAD just slipped out of sight of Ormskaro when Wulfrik called Zarnath to him. The hero didn't care to exhibit the manner in which his ship made its unnatural voyages lest such powerful magic frighten the Sarls and deny him a safe port on his return. Or lest such a display would excite the desire of some watching sorcerer to claim the *Seafang* for his own. Such an ambition had drawn a Kurgan shaman across half the northern Wastes. Wulfrik knew there would be others much nearer to home who would be no less interested in his ship.

The secret of the *Seafang* was his alone. No one else knew how to bind it to his will and bring it safely through the realm of the gods. Wulfrik intended to keep it that way.

'Hold out your hand, Kurgan,' Wulfrik told Zarnath as he joined the champion at the prow of the ship. 'I need a bit of your blood.' The hero drew a steel dagger from his belt.

Zarnath stared hard at Wulfrik, his eyes narrowed with suspicion. He started to back away, but found his retreat cut off by the brawny figures of Broendulf and Kaetill. The shaman's hands clenched tight about his staff, his head turning from side to side like a trapped beast.

'You wanted to know how Wulfrik controls the ship,' Sigvatr said from where he stood beside the champion. 'First he must see the quality of your blood. It's that, or we throw you over the side right now.'

His face pulled into a sour expression, his hands still clutched tightly about his staff, Zarnath relented and approached the champion. Sigvatr grabbed the Kurgan's left hand, pulling it free from the staff. Before the shaman could pull back, Wulfrik brought the edge of the knife slashing across his palm. Zarnath gasped in alarm, wrenching his injured hand from the champion.

'Now let the ship taste your blood,' Wulfrik said, pointing at the carved figurehead. 'Let the *Seafang* know what kind of man sails upon her.'

For a moment, Zarnath hesitated, his eyes burning like cobalt fires. He glared at Wulfrik and Sigvatr, searching their faces for any hint of duplicity. The sound of steel being drawn behind him alerted him to the uneasiness of the crew. A normal man displaying fear wouldn't have disturbed them, but they were uneasy when that man was a shaman with magical powers they didn't understand. They would react quickly and brutally if Zarnath made a wrong move now.

'You can still choose the sea,' said Wulfrik. 'It is a long swim back to Ormskaro, but even a Kurgan should be able to manage it.'

Zarnath scowled at the jest, but Wulfrik's taunt eased his mind somewhat. Timidly the shaman strode to the wooden dragon. A last suspicious look at Wulfrik, and he slapped his bleeding hand down upon the dragon's snout. He let his palm rest there for only an instant, then hurriedly backed away. Wulfrik and the older members of his crew watched the figurehead carefully as it absorbed the shaman's blood.

'Bind your hand, outlander,' Wulfrik said. 'I won't need any more of your blood. At least not today.'

Wulfrik nodded his head to Sigvatr. The old warrior began barking orders at the crew, repeating the ritual Zarnath had just undergone. Zarnath watched the process as he bound a strip of leather across his bleeding palm. It did not take the shaman long to deduce the sort of rite he had undergone.

'Blood magic,' Zarnath hissed under his breath, a shudder passing through him. He glowered at Wulfrik. 'It is a blood ritual,' he repeated.

Wulfrik kept his eyes on the crewmen as they slowly stepped to the figurehead and clapped their hands onto its snarling face. 'I know that it is magic that can only be evoked through blood,' he answered. 'You wanted the secret of the *Seafang's* power, there it is.'

Zarnath studied the warriors as they marched to the wooden dragon and came away again. 'But nothing is happening. It is doing nothing with their blood. I would be able to sense it if the ship was drawing power from them.'

'It is well for them that it is so,' Wulfrik said. 'If the

ship showed interest in any man's blood, I would gut him like a dog. No ship can serve two captains. That is even more true for the *Seafang* than any other.'

The shaman nodded in understanding. 'That is how you evoke the *Seafang's* power. The ship responds to your blood, but only your blood. Perhaps because you are the one who killed Baga Yar.'

'Maybe,' agreed Wulfrik with a shrug. 'I only know that I can send the ship through the veil between worlds and bring her out again wherever I command her to go. I do not know it is only my blood the ship wants. Hence this test at the start of each voyage.'

'But it might be tied to your blood alone,' Zarnath mused.

Wulfrik bared his fangs at the Kurgan. 'You think you have made a poor bargain, sorcerer? Agreed to help me only so you can win a ship you can never use?'

Zarnath backed away from the champion's threat, his hands closing reflexively about his jewelled staff. 'No, no!' protested the shaman. 'Our compact remains. I will help you break your curse. After the *Seafang* is mine, there will be time enough to unlock the secrets of her enchantments.'

'My men will be watching you, Zarnath,' Wulfrik growled, unmoved by the Kurgan's assurances of loyalty. He nodded his head to the longship's mast. Perched in the rigging, his bow resting in his lap, his eyes fixed on the shaman, was the hunter Jokull. 'The first sign of treachery, and they will kill you. Whatever magic you call, one of them will kill you. Unless I do it first.'

Wulfrik let the threat linger in the air, holding Zarnath's eerie gaze this time. The shaman needed no further proof of the conviction behind his murderous oath.

'Where are we sailing to?' Wulfrik asked the shaman.

Zarnath smiled nervously, grateful for the change in subject. 'The relic I require is a torc crafted from ruby. It is called the Smile of Sardiss, an ancient artefact of the Hung warlock-kings. For centuries it has fallen through the fingers of many owners, but for the last hundred years it has been worn by the dwarf lord Khorakk.'

Wulfrik lifted his hand, silencing the shaman. 'I need to know only one thing, Kurgan: where this ship must sail.'

Zarnath bit his lip at the brash interruption, colour rising to his face. 'Khorakk rules in a place called Dronangkul, a stronghold of the dwarf folk...'

The champion waited to hear no more. He brought his dagger slicing across his raised hand, then clenched his fist until beads of blood dripped through his fingers. With firm steps, he marched to the figurehead, slapping his hand upon the dragon's snout. Grey smoke began to billow from the wooden jaws, quickly expanding into a thick fog which completely engulfed the ship.

'This relic had better be where you say it is, sorcerer,' Wulfrik warned as he bound his hand with a strip of cloth. 'As you will soon see, there are worse seas where a man can be thrown overboard.'

* * *

86 C. L. Werner

THE RIVER UPON which the *Seafang* found herself when she emerged from the fog was a stagnant, lifeless thing. Red water sloshed against the hull like warm syrup, clinging to the wood with tar-like streamers of muck. A filthy smell, like hot copper mixed with burning skin, assailed the noses of the northmen. The banks of the sluggish river were littered with jagged piles of slag, slimy bones and puddles of yellow filth.

Wulfrik pinched his nose against the stench and gazed out across the shores of the river. To the south as far as the eye could see was a vast marshland, its brambles and weeds twisted by the polluted waters of the river. To the north was a barren land of sand and rock. He turned about, seizing Zarnath by the front of his robe.

'What trickery is this?' the champion snarled. 'I have seen the halls of the dwarf lords, made war against their thanes and taken from them both glory and gold! This stinking wasteland!' He glared at the tainted river dirtying his ship with its loathsome touch. 'No dwarf would live in such a place!'

'But they do,' insisted Zarnath, trying to free himself of Wulfrik's choking hands. 'This is the River Ruin. To the north is the Desolation of Azgorh, where dwell the dawi zharr.'

'The fire dwarfs?' The question came from Stefnir, a hulking axeman who had lost one eye and half of his face to a troll's acid. Stefnir was one of the few Aeslings among the *Seafang*'s crew. 'My people have had dealings with them. We trade skins and slaves to them in exchange for armour and weapons. They are a hard, cruel people and devious in their ways.'

Wulfrik laughed at the implied warning. 'We were hardly going to ask them for the torc,' he said as he released Zarnath. The hero nodded thoughtfully as the shaman massaged his bruised neck. 'This dwarf who has the torc…'

'Khorakk,' the shaman said.

'Khorakk. This place he lives in…'

'Dronangkul,' Zarnath supplied the name. 'It means something like "fortress of iron" in the dwarf tongue.'

Wulfrik let his fangs show as he glared at the shaman. 'I don't want to know what it means, just where it is.'

The shaman studied the bleak landscape to the north. He could see some stunted hills in the distance. After a moment of consideration, he pointed his staff at the nearest of the hills. 'There,' he said.

'I don't see anything,' Wulfrik told him.

'Their fortress will be behind the hills,' Zarnath assured the champion. 'Even the dwarfs would have little stomach for the river's stink. The hills would provide them shelter from any wind bearing the smell to them.'

'That I can believe,' Wulfrik said, clenching his nose tight again. He turned and bellowed at Sigvatr. 'Half the men stay with the ship. The rest go with me inland.'

'I'll leave ten of the new men on the ship,' Sigvatr said. 'Kaetill can be in command until we get back.'

'*We?*' Wulfrik asked, raising an eyebrow.

Sigvatr smiled at his captain. 'I've killed a lot of

things in my time, but never a fire dwarf. I don't want you bragging about how tough they are without seeing them for myself.' The old warrior's smile darkened and he darted a glance at Zarnath. 'You should take him along too.'

The shaman glared daggers at Sigvatr. 'I brought you here,' Zarnath argued. 'Getting the torc is your business.'

Wulfrik growled at the short Kurgan. 'I'm hardly going to leave my ship in the hands of a sorcerer who has already told me he wants it for himself. No, Zarnath, you brought me here and now you're going to stay right by my side. That way anything that happens to me, happens to you first.'

THE DESOLATION OF Azgorh lived up to its grisly name: a barren landscape of bleached sand and windswept rock, even the few patches of cactus which sprouted from the blasted earth were withered and sickly. The sun blazed down from a cloudless sky, a fiery tyrant that was impossible to reconcile with the feeble light of the northern day. After the cold of Norsca and the freezing ravages they were subjected to in the Mountains of Mourn, the crew of the *Seafang* was ill-prepared for the infernal heat. Their skin burned, their faces darkening to a blistered red. This was no such land as any of them had seen before. It was a place damned by mortal and god alike, a blighted hell with neither mercy nor pity for those foolish enough to enter it.

Several times, Wulfrik considered slitting Zarnath's throat and heading back for the ship. Only the hope the shaman had given him held him back. He had come this far. There would be time enough to settle with Zarnath after the curse was broken.

Jokull came dashing back through the ranks of Norscan warriors. The hunter, as usual, had been scouting ahead of the main group, studying the lay of the land. His excited manner made it clear he'd found something. Any hopes that he'd spotted the dwarf stronghold were dashed by his first words. 'We're not alone,' Jokull said. 'I found a few tracks in the dirt. Paw prints. Big ones,' he added for emphasis.

'Even the Hound of Khorne would find poor feeding here,' Broendulf argued, overhearing the hunter's report.

'Look for yourself, then,' Jokull snarled back. 'Unless years of being pampered in Ormskaro have addled your eyes as well as your wits.'

Other warriors joined the argument, siding with Jokull or Broendulf as the mood took them. The speed and vehemence with which they entered the fight was evidence of how much the barren desert was preying upon their nerves. Wulfrik let them vent their anxiety. If it looked like someone might get killed, he'd put a stop to it.

Turning away from the arguing warriors, Wulfrik gazed across the windswept, rocky cliffs. They were weird, barren things, formed into towering hoodoos, soaring archways and flattened mesas. The dark shadows playing across the sides of the eccentric rock formations indicated unseen gullies and ravines cutting between them. Wulfrik could imagine the rat's nest of dry canyons and caves worming their way between the eroded hills. It occurred to him that they might use the gullies to cross the wasteland unseen. If he had any definite idea where the dwarf stronghold was, he might risk getting lost among the rock pillars and barren hills in order to maintain the element of surprise.

As he looked across the weird cliffs, Wulfrik saw that the element of surprise was already lost. He saw the source of the tracks Jokull had found. Spread out across the span of one of the arches were three dark shapes. Eyes less sharp than those of the champion might have missed them, unable to tell them apart from the rock. To Wulfrik, however, they were clear enough: three great wolves, beasts the size of a pony. Each wolf had a rider upon its back. At such distance it was impossible to tell what sort of creatures they were, but Wulfrik knew goblins would often use huge wolves as steeds. If not for the stench of the river, he might have been able to pick their scent from the wind, though it was just as possible the goblins, or the animals they rode, were canny enough to keep downwind of their prey.

'Jokull is right,' Wulfrik's stern growl silenced his arguing men. 'We're not alone.' The hero indicated the distant shapes observing them from the cliff. It was only when the riders moved, perhaps made uneasy by the attention they were getting, that any of the Norscans spotted the watchers.

'Who are they?' Sigvatr wondered aloud.

'Scavenging goblins,' Njarvord spat. 'Only their slinking kind go around riding on the backs of curs!'

'Then we'd best make sure they don't get a whiff of you,' Haukr snickered. 'They might smell that dog you were spending your gold on in Ormskaro.'

Njarvord balled his fist and made for the tattooed seaman. 'Ilga's twice the wench your mother is, you ship-rat!'

Haukr drew a curved fishing knife from his sleeve, arresting the big Baersonling's advance. 'I said she was,' he chuckled. 'My mother would have settled for silver to warm your bed.'

Sigvatr pressed between the two warriors, pushing them apart. 'Enough!' he snarled at them. 'The smell of blood might be just the thing they need to bring them down on us.'

'I doubt it,' Arngeirr said. The one-legged reaver took a swallow of kvas from the Estalian brandy flask he carried. Wiping his stinging lips, he elaborated on his thought. 'Any tribe of goblins living here can't be doing too well. Goblins have little stomach for a fight unless they have numbers on their side. These lice might follow us, but only to see if we drop anything. They won't attack.'

Wulfrik considered the one-legged reaver's words, then shook his head. 'We won't count on that,' he told his men. 'Keep your shields ready and a hand near your blades. If they do decide to attack us, they'll try to weaken us with arrows first. Form a shield wall if they do. Force the little rats to come in close.'

'We should also watch for them to come from behind.' The suggestion came from Tjorvi, the sneaky Graeling who had proven his cunning during the trials of the Wolf Forest. 'There's no place better to stab a man than where he isn't looking,' he explained when he felt the eyes of the other Norscans on him.

THE ATTACK CAME during the night. Wulfrik had seen their watchers a few times throughout the day, observing the Norscans from the high cliffs. He suspected there was an even bigger company of riders sticking to the gullies between the rocks. The lack of overt aggression might have eased another man into a sense of security. He could imagine some foolish southling being lulled into believing the riders were content simply to watch, that they offered no real menace.

Wulfrik knew better. He had fought the horse-nomads of the Hung and knew the treacherous fighting style of that faithless folk. The riders following them were only waiting for that moment when they would be at their most vulnerable. The attack would come during the night, when the Norscans made camp.

There was nothing he could do to curb the rise of the moons, but Wulfrik did his best to upset the plans of their enemies by ordering a forced march through the night. If the riders were timid, this unexpected change might be enough to send them slinking back to their lair.

In a way, the champion was pleased to find his enemies weren't complete cowards.

With the moon of Mannslieb only half-full and its companion just an ugly splotch of sickly light upon the horizon, darkness held the Norscans in its black grip. Wulfrik snarled down any effort to light torches. He was more concerned about the light ruining the night vision of his men than the extra speed they could muster if they could see where they were going. He kept Jokull ahead of the column, hoping that the wily hunter could find some sign of their foes.

Even with such precautions, when the attack came, it came without warning. The silence of the night was suddenly broken by the thunderous howling of wolves from the darkness before them. It was the concentrated roar of an entire pack, a sound almost deafening in its fury. The cries of the beasts completely masked whatever noise the iron-headed arrows made as they came shooting out of the night. The first the Norscans were aware of the assault was when several men in the front ranks cried out in alarm.

Heavy armour and the poor archery of their foes protected Wulfrik's men from the first volley. The poorly crafted arrows failed to pierce the chain hauberks and heavy hide armour of his warriors; only two were injured in the barrage. The Norscans left them where they fell, closing together and linking their shields to defend against a second volley.

Arrows clattered against the shield wall for several minutes. As the howling of the wolves faded, thin voices could be heard arguing in the darkness. They were strange, whispery voices, their words more like a nail scratching against a piece of pig iron than any human speech. Wulfrik could understand them, one benefit of the curse he'd brought upon himself.

The ambushers were arguing about what to do now that their volley of arrows had failed to terrify the humans and send them running. One gruff-voiced attacker was demanding that his comrades mount their wolves and break the shield wall with a concentrated charge. Wulfrik smiled as the chieftain tried to evade the accusation he wouldn't be leading the charge by claiming he had to stay behind and make sure everything went according to plan. The argument persisted until there was a sharp cry and the most vocal voice raised against the chieftain was silenced.

'Whatever they do,' Wulfrik warned his warriors, 'we hold our ground. Tjorvi! Jokull! Keep your eyes on the rear! This scum wants to push us back. I have a feeling that means they have friends waiting for us back there!'

The Norscans shifted position so the scouts Wulfrik had appointed could shift to the back of their formation. The two men had barely reached their posts when the wolves started howling again. A tremor ran through the ground as the ambushers charged the northmen.

Once again, arrows clattered against the heavy shields of the Norscans. This time, however, the missiles flew at them sporadically rather than in a concentrated volley. One of the warriors cried out as an arrow grazed his face, but otherwise the arrows failed to inflict any damage. Wulfrik called out to his men, warning them not to let the random fire distract them.

His warning had just been given when the first

wave of their enemies rushed out of the darkness into the feeble moonlight. Wulfrik considered he had underestimated the size of the wolves when he judged them to be like ponies. The beasts were more on the order of full horses, their shaggy grey pelts clinging to lean, hungry frames. Foam dripped from their fangs, bloodlust blazing in their eyes, as they lunged at the humans. There was the crash of heavy bodies smashing against the shield wall, the growling fury of wild beasts as fangs bit into wood and steel, as claws scrabbled against armour.

Claws and fangs were not enough to break the Norscans' defence. Even the impact of the huge wolves was rebuffed by the support of the men behind the front line of warriors, pushing their comrades back when they would have faltered.

No, claws and fangs were not enough to break the shield wall. But it was not claws and fangs alone that assaulted the men. A motley array of iron cudgels, axes and swords struck at the men while iron-tipped spears stabbed at them from above their shields.

Upon the backs of each great wolf was a grotesque rider. Wulfrik had underestimated the size of the wolves, now he found he had made the same mistake with their riders. They were the size of a man, though with a lean and snaky sort of build, far larger than the goblins he had thought them to be. There was an undeniable kinship to the small monsters though as these creatures shared the same green, leathery skin as the goblins Wulfrik had faced in the past. He might have taken them for orcs, but for the overall thinness of their limbs and the sharpness of their features.

Wulfrik brought his sword slashing down at the snarling face of one of the creatures. The blade bit through the leather cap it wore, crunching deep into the skull beneath. The monster's face pulled into a rictus, exposing the sharp little fangs which filled its oversized mouth. The dying creature slumped against the back of its lupine mount as Wulfrik ripped his sword free. The wolf beneath the greenskin struggled to shrug the creature's dead weight off its back, snapping at the dangling arms. It was only for an instant that the wolf was distracted, but it was enough for Wulfrik to stab the point of his weapon into the animal's chest. The wolf yelped, leaping straight up, then crashed onto its side and flopped in the dust.

Almost immediately another rider rushed in to take the slain greenskin's place. This time Wulfrik attacked the wolf first, dropping low and slashing at its hind legs as it pounced at the shield wall. His sword chopped clean through the beast's leg, spilling both it and its rider to the earth. Wulfrik kicked the snapping jaws of the beast, then drove his sword across the neck of the greenskin struggling to climb out from under the wolf.

Hobgoblins! That was what these greenskins were. Wulfrik realised he had heard of these monsters from Kurgan traders. There were supposed to be a great many of them in the lands surrounding Cathay. Not as large or fierce as orcs, they were supposed to be cunning and sneaky, with a gift for dirty tricks and sneak attacks.

'Jokull!' Wulfrik roared. 'Start loosing arrows to our rear!'

'But I can't see anything!' the hunter objected.

'Just do it!' the champion shouted. He didn't have time to waste explaining his reasoning. With two dying wolves and two dead hobgoblins at his feet, Wulfrik had drawn the attention of his attackers. Slinking cowards at heart, the hobgoblins made no effort to close with him. They would spur their wolves straight towards him, then loose arrows from their bows. The concentrated fire forced the champion to shelter behind his shield, ducking low as the iron-tipped missiles clattered against it.

Sharp, inhuman shrieks sounded from the rear of the Norscan column. They were ghastly, grating sounds, but Wulfrik could understand them. A second group of hobgoblins had been sneaking up on them in the darkness, using the charge of the wolf riders as a distraction to cover them. Clearly the chieftain's plan had been to push the men back into whatever ambush the other group of hobgoblins had prepared. With the Norscans stubbornly holding their ground, however, the greenskins had abandoned their plan. They were too greedy for loot to abandon the attack though, and had left their places of concealment to steal upon the men unobserved. Jokull's blind shots made them believe they had been seen.

As Tjorvi had said, stabbing unsuspecting men in the back was appealing to the greenskins. A straight fight wasn't. Arguing and cursing, the second mob of hobgoblins retreated back into the darkness.

The cowardice of their comrades at first enraged the wolf riders. They redoubled their attack against the shield wall with such fury that two northmen were dragged down by the wolves and another was cut down by a hobgoblin axe. A horrible moment passed when it looked as though the greenskins might penetrate the wall.

Shouting a fierce war cry, Njarvord threw himself into the gap, laying about him with his blade. Broendulf rushed to the berserker's side, guarding him with his shield as the hairy Baersonling hacked down his enemies. The craven hobgoblins, horrified by the bloodthirsty madness of the berserker, quailed before the assault. Savagely they kicked and slapped their bestial steeds, cursing and pleading with them to break off the attack.

Suddenly the night was banished by a brilliant, flaming light. Wolves yelped in pain and hobgoblins screamed in terror as a ball of glowing blue fire smashed down upon them from the darkened sky. Three wolves fled across the desert, their fur smouldering as they ran. Their burning riders writhed on the ground, wailing in agony.

Wulfrik risked a glance over his shoulder. The same blue light was blazing at the very centre of the Norscan formation. Zarnath held his jewelled staff high over his head, as though trying to thrust it through the sky. The stone set into its head was glowing with magical energies as the shaman invoked his sorcery. A second blazing ball of light hurtled down from the night sky, smashing into the faltering hobgoblin attack.

Hurling epithets on the heads of the northmen, the hobgoblins broke away. Their wolves whining in fear, the monsters vanished back into the night as suddenly as they had come. Behind them they left their dead and dying.

'A fine trick,' Wulfrik told Zarnath as he turned away from the shield wall.

The shaman slowly lowered his staff. There was sweat dripping from his forehead, blood dripping from his nose, but the Kurgan managed to smile in acknowledgement of the compliment.

'You might have worked your magic sooner,' snarled Sigvatr. The old warrior was tying a rag about a cut along his forearm. 'These devils killed six of our men before they were driven off!'

'He raises a point,' Wulfrik said, fangs gleaming. 'The hobgoblins were already beaten. A poor time to decide to enter the fray.'

There was challenge and suspicion in Wulfrik's tone.

'I could not be sure the monsters didn't have a wizard of their own,' Zarnath said. 'I had to be ready in case they did. Only when their attack faltered was it clear to me they had no such help to draw upon.'

Wulfrik nodded, his anger appeased by the shaman's reasoning. Sigvatr's anger, however, was far from spent.

'The attack ruins our chance of catching the dwarfs by surprise,' the old reaver said. 'Stefnir tells me the fire dwarfs use these creatures as soldiers. The ones that attacked us may have been a patrol from

Dronangkul. Even now they'll be riding back to tell their masters about us!'

Zarnath smiled and shook his head in disagreement. 'Hobgoblins are sneaks and cowards by nature. The only things they respect are strength and fear. They serve the dwarfs because they fear them, not from any bonds of loyalty or blood. If they had defeated us, they would have crowed about their victory to their masters. But they lost here. The dawi zharr are famed for their cruelty, and their temper. No, these hobgoblins won't report their failure. They'll slink back to their holes and try to pretend this never happened.'

'If you're wrong, we'll be walking into a trap,' Sigvatr snarled.

'Then we walk into a trap!' Wulfrik told his friend. 'And we'll walk out again! If these dwarfs think they can keep me from what I want then they are bigger fools than the hobgoblins! I'll spill every drop of their blood before I leave this place empty-handed!'

'And what of our blood?' Sigvatr demanded.

Wulfrik fixed him with a cold gaze. 'To break this curse, I'd spill every drop of that as well.'

Chapter Five

A GREAT GAPING pit marked the site of Dronangkul, looking as though it had been gouged from the earth by a titan's axe and then left to fester. The place could be smelled long before it could be seen, a fiery, metallic reek almost as bad as the stench of the River Ruin. Great towers of blackened basalt and walls of stone surrounded the approaches to the pit. A wide road, its course flanked by gibbets, marched down from the wastes beyond the stronghold to end at the huge iron gates which guarded the entrance to the site.

From their vantage point in the rocky hills overlooking Dronangkul, the northmen could see the layout of the dwarf outpost. The entire northern wall of the pit was given over to a vast open mine. An army of slaves attacked the wall, pounding away at it with hammers while sneering hobgoblins whipped them with lengths of chain. There didn't seem to be any humans among the slaves, but rather a motley collection of goblins and orcs of every size and shape. Even Wulfrik had to grudgingly respect anyone tough enough to beat obedience into an orc.

Some small distance from the open mine squatted a huge stone building. Fluted towers rose from the roof of the structure, great chimneys that belched black smoke into the sky. Lines of slaves pushed heavy carts laden with ore into the building. Wulfrik decided it must be some kind of foundry, an observation reinforced by the copper flumes which emptied from one of the outer walls to flush out waste. The flumes disgorged their contents into a vast sump-pond. The slurry of industrial muck in the sump looked every bit as foul as the polluted river, with great blocks of slag jutting up from the morass and a green fog of noxious gas drifting just above the surface.

The dwarfs, at some point, had built dams to restrain the sump, but clearly had lost interest as the mine workings had expanded. A steady stream of pollution was sloshing over the lowest side of the pond, pouring down into the excavations below. A great, mucky pool of the slush was growing in the deepest part of the pit, a system of crude catwalks and wooden bridges criss-crossing the toxic lake. The hobgoblins who whipped slaves across these pathways had heavy rags tied across their faces and thick goggles over their eyes. Their charges, however, had to protect themselves as best they could by holding their breath and keeping only one eye open.

Wulfrik soon saw why the dwarfs had allowed the polluted lake to grow. Watching the lines of slaves being herded across the bridges, he saw the pit where they were held. Situated on the other side of the lake, any escape or revolt would have to use the bridges to have any chance of success. These points could be easily controlled from a few key positions and at each of these chokepoints a wooden tower had been raised. Hobgoblins stood guard in each tower, manning the ramshackle bolt-throwers mounted upon the roofs.

Turning away from the mine and slave pen, Wulfrik studied the upper tiers of the pit. A large area was given over to colourfully painted hide tents, looking like nothing so much as the bivouac of a Kurgan tribe. The bone-strewn kennels of giant wolves made it obvious the encampment belonged to nothing human. Still, the size of the camp surprised Wulfrik. He would have expected many more hobgoblins given the number of slaves down in the mine.

Above the hobgoblin camp, looming over it like the castle of a southling lord, were the homes of the dwarfs themselves. Guard towers of basalt flanked the causeway leading up from the foundry and the mine. The sentries Wulfrik could see patrolling the battlements were shorter than the hobgoblins but far broader and more powerfully built. They wore heavy armour crafted from scales of steel and heavy plates of bronze, their faces locked beneath metal helms. Even from a distance, Wulfrik could see the long black beards of the dwarfs, the hair curled into heavy ringlets. The hook-headed axes the dwarfs carried looked especially vicious, capable of lopping off a man's arm as neatly as a dandelion-head.

Past the towers was a cramped cluster of stone buildings, crushed together as though their presence in the outpost had been an afterthought. Each of the buildings bore a bronze glyph above its entrance, each different from the next. The Gift of Tongues gave Wulfrik no facility to decipher writing; he was unable to decide if the bronze runes denoted the trade of the inhabitants, their clan allegiance or perhaps the mark of some guild affiliation. Between the clustered buildings there rose covered storehouses, their floors piled with iron ingots. Small groups of slaves with dwarf overseers worked in the storehouses, sometimes removing new ingots from carts drawn up from the foundry to pile onto the floor, at other times loading ingots into big wagons drawn by teams of black oxen. Once full, the wagons would slowly head for the outer gates of the stronghold, heading out along the road through the desert.

Towering over everything else in the outpost was the ziggurat: a huge structure masterfully crafted from immense blocks of basalt, adorned with runes cast in gold, its summit capped in spiked turrets of steel. For many minutes, Wulfrik watched the ziggurat, studying the squads of dwarf warriors marching from its bronze doors.

There was a great deal of activity in the stronghold, activity that boded ill for the Norscan's quest. He turned his head and again considered the main gates of Dronangkul. Here the activity was even more distinct. Mobs of wolf riders were leaving the outpost, prowling back across the desert. Near the gates, he could see several dwarfs crucifying an especially large hobgoblin. As they finished their grisly labour, they lifted the pole to which the greenskin had been nailed and set it upright in a hole to one side of the road. A gang of hobgoblins pointed at the crucified prisoner and laughed at his fate. One of them ripped the leather cap from his head and threw it into the prisoner's face. Then, with a flourish, he put on an extravagant iron helmet adorned with horns to replace the discarded cap.

'So much for them not saying anything about us,' Sigvatr observed, scowling at Zarnath.

'Looks like one of them decided ratting out his chief was a good way to advance his own position,' Broendulf said, gesturing at the scene playing out at the gates. He looked over at Wulfrik. 'What do we do now?'

'We go in,' Wulfrik answered, eyes never leaving the dwarf citadel.

Sigvatr blinked in disbelief. 'There's no glory in suicide,' he told Wulfrik. 'They're on the alert, waiting for us!'

Wulfrik shook his head. 'I did not come this far to turn back,' he warned his friend. 'I'm going in there. I'm going to find this Khorakk and I'm going to take the torc from his corpse.'

'They're waiting for us!' Sigvatr insisted.

'No,' Wulfrik corrected him. 'They're looking for us.' He pointed at the large company of wolf riders loping off into the desert. 'That lot is riding back to where we fought their friends. They'll try to pick up our trail there. That gives us a day at least before they get there and then follow us back. While the wolf riders are gone so is the better part of their garrison.'

Stefnir frowned at the champion's reasoning. 'The

dwarfs won't fall as easily as their hobgoblins. I've seen them. They're tough, nasty bastards who don't run from a fight.'

Wulfrik grinned at the Aesling. 'Then we'll give them something else to fight.' He turned and faced Broendulf. 'You always said you were the best climber in Ormskaro,' he told the huscarl. 'Now you'll have the chance to prove it. Take Jokull and a few others who think they can make the climb. There's a crevice at the lip of the pit right over the slave pens.'

'You want us to climb down and free the slaves?' Broendulf asked. The Sarl looked doubtful of the idea. 'What makes you think they'd help us? You can't trust an orc.'

'You can,' Wulfrik told the fair-faced warrior. 'You can trust an orc to charge right at his enemy and try to kill it.'

Sigvatr disapproved of the idea. 'They'll never make it past those watchtowers. And if they did, the dwarfs could just cut the bridges.'

Wulfrik patted his old friend's shoulder. 'Exactly!' he boomed. 'The dwarfs will have to cut the bridges! They've sent most of their hobgoblins off to look for us, so they'll have to deal with the slaves themselves. Every dwarf that goes down to stop the orcs is one less standing in my way.'

'Even if your plan works, we'd need to find Khorakk in a hurry,' Sigvatr pointed out. 'We have no idea where he is.'

'But we do,' Wulfrik assured Sigvatr. 'He'll be holed up in his citadel. I've been watching the dwarfs. The ziggurat is where they are all going to get their orders.

If Khorakk's the one running things here, then that's where he is.'

'Okay,' persisted Sigvatr, 'but how do you know he won't head down into the mines when we free the slaves?'

'What glory is there in killing slaves?' Wulfrik asked. 'Dwarfs are not so different from men in that regard. They thrive upon glory in battle. Khorakk will leave putting down the slaves to his underlings.' He looked at Stefnir. 'Does that sound right to you?' The Aesling nodded his head in agreement.

'That still leaves getting into the ziggurat,' Arngeirr said. The reaver gestured with his false leg at the thick bronze doors guarding the outpost's main gate. 'We'd need a battering ram the size of the *Seafang* to break those down.'

'I have something better than a battering ram,' Wulfrik told him. He waved his hand in the direction of Zarnath.

The shaman had been sitting in silence since the discovery that his prediction about the hobgoblins had been wrong. Now he gave a sudden start as he felt all eyes fix upon him. His hands tightened about his staff as he rose to his feet. An azure glow burned in his widened eyes.

'Time to make amends for your mistake, sorcerer,' Wulfrik said.

Zarnath backed away, holding his staff in front of him as though to ward off a blow. Wulfrik laughed at his fright.

'I need you to bring down yon gates,' the champion told him, nodding at Dronangkul.

A look of horror swept over the shaman's face. For an instant, his body trembled. After a moment, however, he composed himself. 'You want me to use my magic to throw open the gates?'

'If it is strong enough,' Wulfrik growled. The shaman's display of fear had diminished his confidence in Zarnath's powers.

The Kurgan's head bobbed excitedly. 'Oh, yes! Yes!' he assured Wulfrik. 'I can bring down the gates! I can turn them into vapour and scatter them to the winds! I can melt them into the earth! I can–'

'Just open them,' Wulfrik said, turning away to explain the rest of his plan to his warriors.

He didn't notice the smile that flickered across Zarnath's face as he walked away.

Broendulf looked down on the slave pens from the edge of the pit and decided he'd never brag about his climbing skills again. The walls of the pit were jagged enough to offer plenty in the way of handholds, but they were weak and prone to crumbling as soon as any weight was put upon them. The pit hadn't been eroded by any natural process but had been excavated by generations of slaves. The walls still bore the marks of their picks and were pock-marked with deep craters. Some sections had tiny holes drilled into them, scars left from where the dwarfs had been ready to blast instead of dig.

The fissure Wulfrik had selected from the hill proved to be an excellent choice. For much of its length it was curled in upon itself, hollowed out like a rotten log. If the bottom was as thin as the upper reaches of the tube, Broendulf thought they would be able to easily smash their way through the side once they reached the ground. The most important thing was the concealment the fissure offered. One of the watchtowers was uncomfortably close to where the men needed to go.

They had waited for night before sneaking to the pit, though Broendulf wasn't certain how much help the dark was to them. The wolves would be able to smell them if they got far enough away from the chemical reek of the sump, and the hobgoblins seemed more than capable of seeing in the dark. The dwarfs might have been a bit less used to the darkness though, although the evidence of this made Broendulf's skin crawl. From the towers guarding the causeway and the main gates of the stronghold, thick rays of light emanated, bursting from huge eyes of frosted glass. He could see the dwarfs working the weird devices. The eyes were fastened to steel posts which the dwarfs would pivot to bring the glaring beam of light swinging around. Whatever the rays struck was illuminated as though caught beneath the sun. Throughout the long march across the desert, Stefnir had regaled them with stories about the devilish machines the dwarfs built. Now Broendulf was prepared to believe the Aesling's tales.

'Jokull, the rope,' Broendulf whispered to the hunter. They'd managed to avoid the few hobgoblins they'd seen patrolling the edge of the pit, but there was no reason to think there weren't more they hadn't spotted. The huscarl took the rope from Jokull and began tying it fast about his own waist. Grimly he checked the tightness of his knots, then tossed the end of the rope back to Jokull. 'Loop it about yourselves,' he told the other warriors. 'Measure out five feet of slack. As we climb down, each man goes one at a time and only as far as the slack allows. If one man loses his grip, the others will be able to stop his fall.'

Arngeirr quietly pounded a steel stake into the ground, winding the tail of the rope about it and making it fast with a complicated seaman's knot. The one-legged reaver hobbled over to the edge of the pit. 'A fair way down,' he said, spitting over the side.

'Too late to turn back now,' Broendulf chastised him. He'd argued with Arngeirr to stay with Wulfrik's men, but the reaver had insisted climbing down a cliff wouldn't be half as hard as shimmying up a mainmast in a storm. Moreover, he objected to Broendulf's insistence that his sword accompany the huscarl into the pit unless he went with it. Arngeirr's kraken-tooth blade was the keenest among the crew, capable of shearing through solid rock. Broendulf wanted that blade with him in case the hobgoblins weren't obliging enough to give him the keys to the slave chains.

Broendulf tugged at the rope again, testing how securely the stake held. Nodding in approval, he turned to lead the descent into the fissure.

A sudden crimson flash filled the sky, freezing Broendulf where he was. For a terrible moment, he thought Zarnath had set his magic against the gates too soon. Looking in the direction of the dwarf settlement, however, he discovered his mistake.

Cold dread drained all of the colour from his face.

Above the ziggurat, blazing in the night sky, a monstrous flaming head hung suspended. Broendulf could pick out gigantic horns and a long beard and eyes that burned like dragonfire. A terrible voice boomed across the sky, its words crashing like thunder against their ears. He couldn't understand what the voice said, but he didn't need to to know fear.

'Hashut,' Jokull whispered, recalling the name Stefnir had given for the god of the dawi zharr.

The hunter's terror firmed Broendulf's resolve. He glared back at the fiery head. 'Our gods are stronger,' he said, curling his fingers into the sign of Tchar the Trickster. As he did, the giant, ghostly head vanished, disappearing as suddenly as it had sprung into existence.

Below, the pit echoed with the terrified wails of goblins and orcs. The clamour boded ill for the success of their mission. They might free the slaves only to find them too frightened to fight their masters. Broendulf shook his head in disgust. Such was a problem he could worry about later. For now, the wailing provided a perfect cover for any noise they might make in their descent.

The climb down into the pit was a tense struggle to maintain both stealth and speed. Throughout the first part of the climb, Broendulf kept expecting the weird light-casters on the towers to shift in their direction, catching them helpless in the open. If that happened, there would be no place to hide. They would be left with the grisly choice of trying to climb back and no doubt being shot down by the arrows of the hobgoblins, or dropping into the pit and breaking their necks.

Broendulf gave thanks to his ancestors that the eerie beams of light never shifted in their direction. The dwarfs were more interested in illuminating the slave pens and the mine itself than searching the walls of the pit. The huscarl was struck by the idea that the dwarfs were so used to the idea of slaves trying to break out of the stronghold that the concept of someone trying to break in was alien to them. He wondered if perhaps the thought had occurred to Wulfrik and if the hero hadn't based his entire strategy upon it. He knew the sudden, impulsive way the champion's mind worked, but there was usually a foundation of strategy involved in his decisions.

The northmen felt marginally safer once they had descended to that part of the fissure protected by the outward-curving side of the wall. At least the threat of being caught by one of the beams was removed. In its place, however, they found the increased danger posed by the walls themselves. The rock here was even worse than that above, flaking and crumbling at the slightest touch. Several times one of the Norscans lost his hold as the wall disintegrated beneath his fingers, only the rope binding him to his fellows preventing a headlong plummet to the floor of the pit.

Each time they knocked loose a few stones and sent them clattering down into the pit, the northmen froze. Almost timidly they waited to hear the whispery voices of hobgoblins raised in alarm. No cries answered the cascade of rocks, however. Either the wailing of the slaves was enough to drown out the noise or the walls were in such bad shape that loose stones rattling down into the pit were a common enough occurrence that the hobgoblins took no interest.

It was with a sense of relief that Broendulf reached the bottom and untied himself from the line. Soon the rest of the warriors joined him at the base of the fissure, cramping the narrow cavity. There was a small opening at the base of the hollow tube, just big enough that the Norscans could crawl through. Jokull took the lead, worming his way under the lip of rock and out into the pit. A long moment passed before the hunter tugged on the rope, giving his comrades the all-clear.

Broendulf and the other warriors hurried to join Jokull, Arngeirr awkwardly bringing up the rear, his bone leg held out stiffly as he crawled. The men knew how long it had taken them to climb down the fissure. Wulfrik was depending on the cover of night to sneak up to the outpost's walls and the distraction of the freed slaves to cover his own attack. Over an hour had already been spent making the descent, time the warriors could ill afford. Broendulf was almost thankful he couldn't see the horizon from the bottom of the pit, fearful that even now the first glow of dawn might be rising in the east.

The men quickly took stock of their surroundings. The fissure was situated in a particularly dilapidated section of the pit, the ground strewn with rocks and boulders that had fallen from the walls, confirming Broendulf's suspicion that falling rocks were no novelty to the denizens of the pit. Bleached bones protruding from beneath some of the bigger rocks told why slaves were no longer kept in this area.

Creeping among the rocks, the Norscans studied the slave pen. Broendulf couldn't decide if the slaves numbered in the hundreds or the thousands, so tightly were they herded together. The area in which they were kept was so restricted the slaves didn't have room to sit, but were forced to remain standing at all times, leaning upon each other when sleep overcame them. They were mostly orcs, huge ape-like greenskins with ugly, fanged faces and massive knots of muscle, though a not inconsiderable number of goblins were also scattered amongst the herd. These small monsters, similar to the hobgoblins but about half their size, tried their best to keep from being trampled by the big orcs.

Iron chains circled the left ankle of each slave. A hundred slaves might be shackled to a single chain, the long coffle doubling back upon itself so that the chain formed a long loop. Both ends of the chain were secured to a steel plate bolted to an enormous block of basalt. Looking at the black block of stone, Broendulf judged there must be a dozen such chains fastened to it.

Only a few hobgoblins monitored the slaves, keeping close to the block of basalt. Perched atop the rock, sprawled upon a high-backed chair, was the master of the slave pens. Broendulf had fought dwarfs before, but never had he seen one as ugly and vicious-looking as the villainous creature sitting in the chair. He was dusky-skinned, with his black beard pulled into long coils and festooned with the severed ears of goblins and orcs. His face was stamped with the marks of cruelty and avarice, his mouth distorted by the bestial tusks jutting from his lower jaw. He wore a suit of scale armour, a mesh of interlinked bronze that resembled the skin of a fish. Across the dwarf's lap rested a murderous-looking device with a wide, bowl-like mouth attached to a slender wooden stock. Broendulf had seen the guns of other dwarfs and recognised the object as being some sort of kindred weapon.

'If anyone has the keys, it'll be Ear-taker there,' Arngeirr said.

Broendulf nodded in agreement. 'Then we'll just have to make sure he's the first to die.' He looked over at Jokull, nodding at the hunter's bow. 'Think you can hit him from here?'

Jokull stared intently at the dwarf slave master, gauging the distance. 'I think so,' he decided.

Broendulf looked anxiously at the dark sky overhead. How much time did they have left, he wondered? Grimly he shook his head. He didn't know. That meant he had to assume the worst.

'Send him to his inbred ancestors,' Broendulf growled.

Jokull lifted his bow, aimed and loosed in one smooth motion. The arrow sped straight and true, but even as it streaked for the dwarf's head, the slave master was leaning forwards to bark an order to one of the hobgoblins. Instead of piercing the dwarf's skull, the arrow glanced off the steel skullcap he wore.

Instantly the dwarf was dropping down from his

seat, crashing to the ground beside the boulder. Frantically he glanced in every direction, trying to discover from where the attack had come. His eyes narrowed with fury when he saw the Norscans hiding among the rocks. Spitting some curse in his own guttural language, the dwarf raised his weapon, pointing the wide mouth at the men.

There was a loud crack followed by a thunderous roar and a brilliant flash of light. Broendulf winced in pain as he felt his arms and face torn by what felt like a fistful of gravel. He could see that Jokull and the others were likewise scratched by the blast. The huscarl snickered at the sorry results of the dwarf's attack. He didn't understand how the force of the shot had spread out over the distance or the havoc the blunderbuss could cause at close quarters.

Boldly, Broendulf emerged from the rocks and charged at the dwarf. The other Norscans followed his example, shouting a fierce war cry.

The slave master smiled at the rushing humans. Savagely he snapped orders to his hobgoblins, punctuating the command with a particularly violent threat. Reluctantly, the hobgoblins drew their weapons and ran forwards to intercept the northmen.

His face still twisted with sadistic anticipation, the dwarf hurriedly began pouring powder and shot down the muzzle of his blunderbuss. The hobgoblins would buy him the time he needed to recharge the weapon.

This time the humans would be in a better position to appreciate its performance.

* * *

WULFRIK GLARED UP at the black walls of Dronangkul. If he could have burned a hole through the thick basalt with his eyes, the entire stronghold would have come crashing down. Locked away inside the fortress was something he thought he'd never have again.

Hope.

The champion watched the sentries patrolling behind the spiked battlements with a murderous eye. Up close he could appreciate the degeneracy of these dwarfs. They were twisted, vile caricatures of the dwarfs he had fought against in the Worlds Edge Mountains. Where the other dwarfs had displayed a martial pride the Norscan could respect, these dark kindred had a sneaky, duplicitous air about them. Observing the dwarf warriors on the walls, Wulfrik could see that they handled their weapons capably enough, allowing their heavy axes to rest against their shoulders in a fashion which was a perfect balance between comfort and readiness, but there was an emotionless precision to their motions, like a clockwork toy from Kraka Drak. Theirs was a skill at arms born from years of drill and training, not from a life on the battlefield.

At the same time, Wulfrik would not make the mistake of thinking these creatures to be timid and untried after the fashion of southling soldiers. Their scaly armour was festooned with all manner of grisly trophies, from severed ears to mummified hands. Many of the dwarfs wore helms that appeared to be bronzed skulls. No, these were no strangers to death. Far from it. The fiends appeared to revel in death with sadistic enthusiasm. But there was a difference between facing a worthy enemy in a fray and slaughtering vanquished foes. Wulfrik judged these dwarfs had little experience with the former.

Certainly they were arrogant in their might. After dark, the Norscans had crept through the desert to within a few hundred yards of the stronghold. In all that time, they had encountered only a few easily dispatched hobgoblins patrolling outside the gates. The dwarfs themselves did not stir from their fortress, so secure in their minds that they left such chores to their lazy minions. Even the weird daemon-lights mounted on the towers never strayed beyond the stronghold, the dwarfs directing their rays instead down into the mine and slave pit.

The dwarfs could not conceive an enemy attacking them, and that was the great weakness Wulfrik intended to exploit. By the time the dwarfs were fully aware of their mistake, Khorakk would be dead and his torc well on its way back to the *Seafang*.

'Your sorcery had better be strong enough, Kurgan,' Wulfrik growled at Zarnath. He pointed at the immense gates. The northmen were stretched out across the desert, their bellies in the sand. Zarnath was forced to lift his head to follow Wulfrik's gesture.

'My power is equal to the task,' the shaman hissed back. 'After that, it is your sword that will be tested.'

'You think we will leave you out here while we do all the fighting?' Sigvatr scoffed. 'No, witch-father, you'll be right there with us.' The old warrior emphasised his point by letting his hand close about the hilt of his blade.

The shaman's eyes crackled with blue light, glowing in the darkness as anger flared up inside him. 'Then we had better pray your friends have released the slaves. We will have no chance at all if the dwarfs are not busy elsewhere.'

'Broendulf will not fail me,' Wulfrik said. 'He knows I will feed his spleen to the vultures if he does.'

The champion's menacing words seemed to provoke a response from the denizens of Dronangkul. The northmen turned their faces from the stronghold as a fiery light blazed into life above the black ziggurat. When they looked back, a ghostly head, gigantic and formed of swirling flame, glowered from the night sky. A thunderous voice boomed down from the heavens, sending icy fingers of fear coursing through the hearts of the warriors.

Wulfrik felt his stomach clench in terror. He had heard Stefnir's stories about Hashut, the Dark Father of the dawi zharr. Alone among his men, he could understand the harsh words the thundering voice spoke: I watch what you do.

No wonder the dwarfs were so confident behind their walls! They were protected by their dark god! Against mortals and monsters, daemons and wraiths, Wulfrik had proven his valour and his courage, but what hope did he have against a god?

Anger roared through Wulfrik's body. What hope did he have? The only hope, the hope of breaking the curse that kept from him all that he desired! Other gods had inflicted the curse upon him; he would not let another deny him his only chance of escaping his doom.

120 C. L. Werner

'Dark Father of the fire dwarfs!' Wulfrik bellowed at the fiery phantom. 'I am Wulfrik, and I will cut your burning eyes from your face! Your children are greedy maggots and your lands are not fit for an ox to shit in! I defy you, you burned-out gargoyle! Here stands a man, and he dares you to stand in his way if you have the–'

Sigvatr pulled at Wulfrik's leg, trying to drag his friend back to the ground. He could not understand the words the champion was shouting, for they were uttered in the same harsh speech as that which the voice of thunder had spoken, but he could tell from the tone the sort of things the hero was saying. Nothing, beast or man, could fail to rise to Wulfrik's challenges when they were made. Now, his friend's despair and pride had caused him to challenge a god!

The other northmen were equally aware of what their leader was doing and their horror was no less than that of Sigvatr. Two men rose to their feet and sprinted across the desert in pure terror. Njarvord bowed his head and commended his spirit to his ancestors. Haukr pulled a knife from his boot and began to crawl towards Wulfrik, murderous determination in his eyes.

After the apparition spoke, a great wailing sound rose from Dronangkul, the sound of thousands of voices moaning in fear. It was a frightening sound in its own right. The Norscans knew the voices came from the slaves of the dwarfs. Anything that could make an orc cry out in terror was something a man would do well to fear.

Wulfrik relented in his blasphemous calls. At first, his warriors thought that even the champion had been struck dumb with fear. Then they thought that the Dark Father had answered his challenge, striking the hero's mind with madness.

Wulfrik threw back his head and laughed, laughed until it seemed his voice must crack. The champion spat into the dust as he watched the fiery head fade from the night sky. More frightened for his friend than before, Sigvatr tugged at Wulfrik's leg. The hero kicked at him, forcing him to let go.

'Sheep,' Wulfrik growled, staring angrily at his men. 'You should all go back to your mothers and leave the fighting to those worthy of calling themselves warriors!' He gestured angrily at the ziggurat and the empty sky above it. 'Do you think that was their god? Are you all such fools? It was a trick! Some foolishness these devils have concocted to frighten orcs and goblins! And you vermin are no better,' he added with a snarl.

The champion's insults made the northmen feel ashamed, as he knew the hard words would. Shame would make them forget fear. From shame would grow anger, anger against those who had tricked them. Wulfrik wanted that anger, for he would use it to slaughter his way to Khorakk's throat.

He did not bother to tell his warriors why he knew the vision was a lie. Wulfrik did not think they would be reassured if he told them he knew the head was some kind of trick only because the god did not answer his challenge.

Zarnath lifted himself off the ground, brushing the

dirt from his clothes. 'Yes, it was a trick,' he said, tapping his forehead with a long finger. 'I would know if it was a real sending from the gods. The vision was false, a trick and a lie! The dwarfs have devil-lamps upon the ziggurat they point into the sky to create the semblance of their god and a great bronze horn through which they create his voice.'

'That information might have been nice to know before I soiled myself,' Stefnir snarled. For a moment, the Aesling looked ready to attack the shaman, but the Kurgan's eyes were glowing again and such an overt reminder of his sorcery made the warrior think twice.

'What if Broendulf doesn't know it's a trick?' Sigvatr wondered aloud. 'If they don't free the slaves, we won't have our diversion.'

Wulfrik continued to glare at the ziggurat. 'Then we won't have our diversion,' he hissed through clenched fangs.

Chapter Six

BROENDULF DROVE HIS sword through the chest of a snarling hobgoblin, then pushed the squirming carcass off the blade with his foot. As soon as the corpse was free, he spun around and blocked the hooked dagger of another hobgoblin. The slinking cowards had an almost preternatural ability to creep up on a man from behind, as the huscarl's scarred armour could attest. The would-be backstabber bared its yellowed teeth at the warrior and tried to sink a second dagger into Broendulf's belly.

The Norscan grabbed the hobgoblin's wrist before the blade could reach him. He strained with his enemy for a moment, then caught a sudden motion from the corner of his eye. Snarling at the knife-wielding greenskin, Broendulf twisted his body to the side. Without warning, he released the hobgoblin's wrist. The creature yelped in surprise as it suddenly lurched forwards. The dagger sank up to the hilt in the gut of a second hobgoblin, the monster Broendulf had spotted trying to circle around and brain him from behind with an iron club. While the fratricidal hobgoblin stared in surprise at its dying comrade, the northman smashed his knee into its back. The hobgoblin spilled to the ground, cracking its jaw against the helm of the greenskin it had killed. Before the stunned creature could rise, Broendulf split its skull.

Around him, the fight was starting to peter out. The hobgoblins, used to bullying half-starved slaves restrained by chains, didn't have the stomach for a real fight. They would swarm over the northmen, then desert their comrades when the fighting went bad. A half-dozen of the monsters were on the ground already, with several more sneaking off into the rocks to lick their wounds. The rest wouldn't last much longer.

Vargr, a stout Sarl axeman, lopped the arm off one of the hobgoblins fighting him, laughing like a madman as dark blood sprayed across his face. The grim sight was too much for the other two hobgoblins opposing him. Almost falling over each other, the greenskins fled. Vargr shook his axe at them and charged in pursuit.

Broendulf started to run after the northman, but some premonition of danger made him delay. The hobgoblins were running back towards the basalt block. He could see the dwarf slave master standing at the base of the rock, the wide-mouthed gun raised to his shoulder. The huscarl shouted a warning to Vargr.

The warning came too late. Again there sounded the crack and boom of the dwarf's weapon. This time, however, the burst of shrapnel found a much closer target. The two hobgoblins and the man chasing them were knocked off their feet, hurled back as though smashed by a giant's fist. Their bodies crashed to the ground in tatters, their flesh shredded by the mass of shot fired by the blunderbuss.

The dwarf laughed heartily at the gory spectacle, then pulled the powder horn from his belt. His eyes narrowed with disgust when he saw how few of his hobgoblins were still in the fight. Cursing, he threw down his blunderbuss and turned to flee before the vengeful Norscans could catch him.

An arrow whistled out from the rocks and stabbed through the slave master's knee as he turned. The dwarf crashed to the ground, grabbing his leg in pain. He shouted for his hobgoblins to help him, but most of the wretches had already fled.

Ripping a curved scimitar from his belt, the dwarf lunged at the first northman he saw. The slave master's crippled knee gave out as he put weight on it and he fell, the outflung scimitar scraping against his enemy's leg.

Arngeirr chuckled gruesomely, tapping the morbid length of carved bone attached to his hip. 'You're too late,' he told the dwarf. 'There's nothing there.' Still chuckling, he brought the razored edge of his blade shearing through the dwarf's back. The kraken-tooth sword bit clean through armour, flesh and bone.

The sight of the slave master's body being cut in half was too much for the few hobgoblins still lurking about. Throwing down their weapons, the craven creatures dashed for the bridges, shrieking an alarm to the watchtowers.

'We don't have much time,' Broendulf warned Arngeirr as he ran to the reaver's side. The huscarl dropped down beside the slave master, searching the dwarf's body for anything that looked like a key.

'Even if you find one, there's no place to put it,' Arngeirr said. He gestured at the basalt block with his sword. The heavy chains were bolted into a weird, box-like mechanism with a complicated arrangement of levers. On his voyages, Arngeirr had once seen a puzzle box a Hung raider had stolen from a Cathayan trader. The device fastened to the chains looked even more complex.

Broendulf smashed his fist into the dead slave master's face. 'Crow God rot all these damn dwarfs!' he snarled in frustration. 'We don't have time to play games!' His eyes narrowed as he looked at the chains. 'Think you can cut through those?'

Arngeirr thrust the point of his sword into the ground. He spat into his palm and rubbed his hands together, moistening them before taking up his blade again. 'Just watch me.'

The kraken-tooth blade struck the heavy chains just above the devilish puzzle lock. Two of them snapped under the blow. Broendulf cried out in triumph. Arngeirr braced his feet and aimed another blow at the chains.

Across the slave pit, the orcs and goblins watched the northmen in silence. Terror of the fiery god of the dwarfs was still stamped upon their brutish faces. Many of them glanced anxiously up at the ziggurat, as though expecting the head of Hashut to blaze up into life again and smite the little men attacking the chains.

'They don't exactly seem grateful,' Jokull commented, joining the other northmen. The hunter held his bow at the ready, but it was towards the bridges that he kept the weapon aimed. The thin, whispery voices of hobgoblins could be faintly heard. It would only be a matter of time before the creatures gathered enough reinforcements to dare a return to the pit.

'Aye,' Broendulf cursed. 'The dwarfs have whipped all the fight out of them.'

More chains snapped as Arngeirr continued to chop at them. The men could hear them rattle as they fell slack. In the more distant parts of the slave pit, they could hear thick, guttural voices shouting. The packed mob of greenskins shifted, moving with the mindless surge of a herd of sheep. Through the press of goblins and orcs, several huge brutes swaggered.

'Looks like a few of them don't think so,' Jokull said as the monsters approached the basalt block. They were not unlike the orcs, big apish creatures with muscular builds, short legs and long arms. Only a stump of a neck supported their thick-skulled heads, massive jaws jutting out from their inhuman faces. There was a gleam of murderous intelligence in the beady eyes of the huge brutes, something that set them apart from the frightened herd of slaves as much as their leathery black skin.

The black orcs stared at the men who had freed them. For a tense moment, the Norscans thought the monsters would attack. As Jokull had said, gratitude wasn't exactly something greenskins were known for. The dark-skinned beasts grunted to each other in their savage tongue. Broendulf wished Wulfrik had come with them, if only to understand what the orcs were saying.

One of the black orcs stomped towards Arngeirr. Before the one-legged northman could react, the orc planted a huge hand against his chest and shoved him away from the basalt block. The reaver half-raised his sword to defend himself as he staggered back. The black orc grinned back at him, almost daring him to attack. A sharp bark from one of the other black orcs made the brute desist. Sullenly, the monster turned to the block. Its powerful hands closed upon those chains Arngeirr had not broken.

Broendulf watched in amazement as the black orc snapped the iron chain with its bare hands. The brute didn't even pause to draw in breath after it broke the chain, but instead leaned over a second and repeated the process.

A shadow loomed over Broendulf. The huscarl turned his head to find the biggest of the black orcs standing over him. The monster's eyes stared into his own, an unmistakable challenge in the orc's gaze. Broendulf swallowed his pride and backed away from the brute. It wasn't fear but practicality that made the northman retreat. They were in the pit to free these beasts, not fight them.

The black orc snorted in amusement as it watched Broendulf retreat. Then the brute turned away, staring out over the mass of huddled slaves. The orc's brutal voice rose in a furious bellow as it hurled abuse at the cowed greenskins. Other black orcs moved among the mob, cracking skulls and kicking shins, providing physical reinforcement for the words of the new warboss.

'He'll have them worked up into a frenzy in no time,' Arngeirr said, taking a swallow of kvas from his flask. The reaver glanced towards the bridges. There was no mistaking the sound of armed bodies rushing down the wooden platforms. 'And none too soon.'

Broendulf nodded. 'We'd better get back to the fissure,' he told the other northmen. 'It's a long climb and this isn't our fight.' He observed the way the slaves were quickly forgetting their fear and roaring their war cries as the black orcs encouraged their thirst for carnage and vengeance. The dwarfs would have a hard time putting down this uprising, even with their toxic lakes and watchtowers.

As the thought came to him, Broendulf winced as a bright light shone down into the pit. The first beam was quickly followed by others. The dwarfs had turned their daemon-eyes upon the slave pit. Fully illuminated by the beams, the huscarl was staggered by the sheer numbers of greenskins packed into the slave pens. So were the dwarfs in the stronghold. Only a moment after the lights shone down into the pit, a metallic shriek wailed throughout Dronangkul as the dwarfs sounded the alarm.

'Come on,' Broendulf ordered, ducking behind the basalt block to avoid the searching beams of the daemon-eyes. 'We've done what we came to do.

'The rest is up to Wulfrik.'

THE SHRIEKING ALARM was what Wulfrik had been waiting for. Waiting outside the walls, the northmen had seen the lights on the towers concentrate down into the pit, and they had heard the savage war cry of the slaves. But it was the alarm the champion had wanted to hear. Now he could see dwarf sentries rushing along the battlements, leaving their posts to reinforce the lower gates along the causeway. If they were still upon the heights overlooking Dronangkul, he was certain they would see ranks of dwarf warriors marching from the ziggurat to put down the revolt. Even if they would have preferred to leave the chore to the hobgoblins, the dwarfs had sent too many of their minions out into the desert looking for Wulfrik and his warriors. The dwarfs would be compelled to do their own fighting this time. And in so doing they would leave their outpost ripe for an assault.

Wulfrik counted out the minutes, judging how long it would take the dwarfs to mobilise and march down into the pit. He would allow for their short legs and heavy armour, give them extra time to open the causeway gates and close them again behind the warriors. The longer he gave the dwarfs to descend into the pit, the longer he would have to reach the ziggurat before they could react to his attack.

A sword in each hand, Wulfrik turned to his men. 'Die well,' he told them, 'because the gods *are* watching.' He shifted his gaze to Zarnath, his fangs bared. 'Your magic had better be all you claim it is, Kurgan,' he growled.

Wulfrik ignored the shaman's reassurances. Facing the stronghold once more, the champion threw himself forwards, sprinting towards the walls. Not all of the dwarfs would be gone from the walls, and even if they were, once the gates came down the entire stronghold would know it was under attack. The champion intended to be inside the ziggurat by the time the dwarfs could organise their defences.

Two hundred yards, then a hundred, then fifty. The black walls of Dronangkul drew closer and closer with every heartbeat. Wulfrik could hear his men panting as they ran beside him. There were no war cries, no shouts of battle and fury. That would come later.

The dwarfs noticed the men rushing at them from the black of night when the Norscans were only twenty yards from the walls. Wulfrik saw the sentries above the gates reel back in shock as they spotted them. One of the dwarfs lifted a bronze horn to his lips, blowing a solemn note to alert the rest of the stronghold. The others hefted blunderbusses and aimed at the men converging on their position.

Before the dwarfs could fire, the gate was rocked by a tremendous blast of blue fire the size of an ox-cart. Hurtling down from the night sky, the burning sphere smashed into the metal gates with the force of a rockslide. The entire wall seemed to rise up from its foundations then slam back down against the earth. The dwarfs were knocked off their feet, several screaming as they fell from the battlements to smash their skulls upon the ground below.

Smoke billowed from the gates, metal bubbling where Zarnath's spell had smashed into them. The basalt walls were cracked, great chips crumbling from the ravaged stone. Yet the sturdy architecture of the fire dwarfs was as robust as that of their western kin.

The barrier held, defying Wulfrik to breach them.

From the heavens, a second ball of fire coalesced, even bigger than the first. It left a trail of shimmering blue flame as it shrieked out of the darkness. This time when the fire slammed into the walls, they did not simply jump, they buckled. Immense blocks of stone were thrown high into the sky, and screaming dwarfs were tossed through the air like autumn leaves. The great gates of Dronangkul collapsed, slamming against the ground as they were ripped from their foundations, crushing the dwarfs who had rushed to reinforce them with iron beams.

Now Wulfrik did raise his voice in an exultant war cry, a roar of primal, savage abandon that was taken up by each of his warriors. For the moment, the desperate odds he challenged were forgotten, and even the hope of breaking his curse was absent from the hero's thoughts. There was only the thrill of battle, the lust for blood and triumph. Wulfrik leapt through the shattered gateway, smashing his boot into the face of a trapped dwarf trying to crawl out from under the fallen gates, thrusting his sword through the chest of a stunned guard who stumbled into his path.

'Khorakk!' Wulfrik howled, his voice echoing through the cramped alleyways of the dwarf settlement. A bearded guard wielding a great axe charged at him, then sank to the earth as Wulfrik's sword removed his arm at the shoulder. 'Khorakk!' the champion roared again.

Wulfrik was thrown from his feet as something slammed into him from the side. Air rushed from his lungs as he crashed against the stone steps leading up into the gatehouse, sparks flaring before his eyes as his head cracked against the hard basalt. He could feel the earth quiver as whatever had struck him came charging after him. The champion recovered his wits as a wickedly sharp axe came flashing down towards his face.

The northman kicked up with his legs, locking his boots about the descending blade, arresting its downward sweep. Powerful even by the standards of the Norscans, Wulfrik felt his entire body shudder at the effort of holding back the axe. He ground his fangs together, bracing his back against the steps as he threw his entire body into the effort.

'I'll make your skull a chamber pot for Thegn Khorakk!' a gruff voice snarled in the debased Khazalid of the fire dwarfs.

Wulfrik felt the axe start to move, forcing his legs to bend. Slowly, inexorably, his foe was proving the stronger. In a matter of seconds, the axe would come slashing down and split his head in two.

Growling like his namesake, Wulfrik twisted his legs, trying to wrench the axe from his enemy's hand. His foe laughed at the feeble effort. Certain his enemy was concentrated fully upon driving the axe through his face, Wulfrik released his hold.

The axe came chopping down, but before it could strike, Wulfrik's own sword was flashing across one of the hands behind the axe. Fingers flew in the wake of Wulfrik's blade, dwarf blood fountaining from the mangled hand. Gripped only in one hand now, the axe's momentum was diverted. Instead of cleaving through the northman's head, the blade scraped against the step six inches next to him.

Wulfrik sprang at his stricken foe, lashing out at him with the swords gripped in either hand. The crippled enemy retreated before the fury of the champion's attack. Wulfrik saw now that his adversary wasn't a dwarf at all, at least not completely a dwarf. From the waist upwards, he resembled the guards he had butchered on entering Dronangkul, even sharing the same scale armour and thick black beard curled into long coils. From the waist down, however, the creature was more like a bull, standing upon four muscular legs that each ended in an iron-shod hoof. The courtyard beyond the gate was filled with more of the dwarfs, many of them already locked in combat with Wulfrik's men, but this creature was the only one of his kind the hero could see.

The champion took a step away from the centaur and laughed. 'Was it your father or your mother who was a drunk?' he mocked in the beast's own debased Khazalid.

The centaur blinked in surprise to hear his language spoken by a human. Then the nature of what Wulfrik had said contorted the creature's face into a mask of pure rage. 'Barbarian pig! I'll braid my beard with your entrails! I am blessed by the Father of Darkness!'

'Then it was your mother who couldn't hold her ale.'

Fury overwhelmed the bull centaur. He forgot the axe in his hand, forgot the warriors he had brought with him from the ziggurat to protect the gate. The centaur's nostrils flared, his hooves stamped the ground. Like a blood-mad bull, he threw himself at the jeering man who had dared to insult both his ancestry and his god.

Wulfrik dived from the path of the charging centaur. The champion's laugh stabbed into the monster more keenly than any blade. Shaking his head in rage, the centaur turned around and made a second charge.

The northman was ready for the centaur this time, however. His dive from the onrushing brute became a sideways roll along the centaur's path. Wulfrik's swords slashed into the monster's legs, hewing through muscle and tendon. The centaur crashed onto his side, sliding across the ground, bowling over dwarfs and Norscans before skidding to a stop against the ruined wall.

Wulfrik rushed after the crippled monster, caving in the face of a dwarf who got in his way, disembowelling another who thought to stop him with a fang-edged axe. The champion reached the centaur as he was struggling to stand, trying to use the wall to support his ruined body. Wulfrik brought the edge of his sword biting through the centaur's arm, shearing it off at the elbow. The monster shrieked in pain and crumpled to the ground.

A loud explosion made Wulfrik spring away from the dying centaur. The champion spun about, swords at the ready. He smiled grimly when he saw Sigvatr standing over the corpse of a dwarf, a smoking blunderbuss lying beneath the guard.

'I wanted to keep the fight fair,' Sigvatr said, nodding towards the bull centaur.

'Then you should have let that backshooter bring a few of his friends to help,' Wulfrik growled. He glanced across the courtyard. Several of his warriors were down; whether they were dead or wounded he didn't much care. The dwarfs themselves were in full retreat.

The reason for their flight revealed itself quickly. From the towers on the causeway, lights were turned upon the courtyard. Immediately, there was a frantic burst of activity on the tower roofs. Dwarfs scrambled around a pair of artillery pieces. At first Wulfrik thought they might be like the cannons used by dwarfs in other lands. However, there was something incredibly sinister about these machines. They seemed to glow with some infernal power of their own, thick iron chains lashing them to great turnstiles sunk into the towers. He recalled Stefnir's claims that the fire dwarfs had a way to bind daemons into metal.

The dwarfs on the towers removed heavy tubular devices from racks and stuffed them down the yawning mouths of their artillery. Shielding their eyes by lowering the visors of their helms, the dwarfs touched flame to their weapons. A burst of blazing light, a snarl like the belly-growl of a bear, and the weird cylinders flew from the artillery. They streaked towards the courtyard, sparks streaming from their hollow ends. One of the rockets smashed into the outer wall of the stronghold, punching almost clean through before becoming stuck. It sizzled there for a moment, then exploded in a burst of fire and poisonous gas.

The second rocket smashed down into the courtyard itself, glancing off the basalt flagstones and spinning crazily about. Northmen fled before the runaway missile, leaping up stairs and clinging to walls to avoid its crazed movement. At last, the sparks leaping from the rocket's end sputtered out and it became still.

Wulfrik glared at the weird weapon, then at the towers above the causeway. He could see the dwarfs feeding more of the strange rockets into their artillery. 'Kurgan!' Wulfrik shouted. He raged across the courtyard, looking for the shaman. He smiled grimly when he saw Tjorvi leading Zarnath through the shattered gates.

'I need your magic again!' Wulfrik snarled at the shaman. He pointed his bloody sword at the distant towers. 'Stop them before they shoot at us again.'

Zarnath leaned weakly against his jewelled staff. 'Breaching the gates has sapped my powers. I must rest.'

'Rest when you're in hell!' Wulfrik snapped. 'Stop those vermin or I'll cut you down right here!'

Zarnath's eyes blazed with blue fire, his face twisting with hate. His expression softened when he felt steel against his ribs.

'You heard the captain,' Sigvatr hissed in his ear. The old warrior put enough pressure on his blade to break the shaman's skin. Zarnath shuddered as he felt his own blood trickling down his side. Reluctantly, he bowed his head.

Throwing wide his arms, Zarnath raised his staff. Arcane words even Wulfrik could not decipher rasped across the shaman's lips. The fire in his eyes slowly faded, gathering instead within the gemstone at the head of his staff.

Streams of lightning crackled from the head of the staff, sizzling into the rack of rockets upon the roof of the left tower. Several of the dwarfs were caught in the lightning storm, screaming in terror as their bodies were scorched by the electricity. Others, seeing the target of the malevolent magic, flung themselves from the turret, more willing to risk the fall to the causeway far below than remain upon the roof.

Zarnath's spell did its work quickly. The entire roof of the turret vanished in a pillar of fire and poisonous gas as the violence of the lightning caused the battery of rockets to explode. The dwarfs in the other tower abandoned their posts, scrambling with indecent haste down the trapdoor leading into the structure's interior. The northmen laughed at the frantic terror of the dwarfs.

'Sigvatr!' Wulfrik barked. 'Take half the men and secure the lower gate! Keep the dwarfs penned up down below as long as you can. If you strike out now while they're hiding from the Kurgan's sorcery, you may have a chance!'

The old warrior shook his head. 'My place is with you,' he told Wulfrik.

'Your place is where I damn well tell you it is!' Wulfrik yelled. 'Get your arse down there and hold the gate!'

Sigvatr held his ground, staring into his friend's eyes. At last he relented, calling out the names of the warriors he would take with him. The last man he called was the shaman. Wulfrik shook his head.

'I want the Kurgan with me,' he told Sigvatr. 'I might need him if I have to knock down any more doors.'

Sigvatr scowled at Zarnath. 'Just don't take your eyes off him,' he advised.

Wulfrik turned a fanged grin on the shaman. 'I don't intend to,' he warned Zarnath.

Seeing further argument would get him nowhere, Sigvatr and his warriors dashed down the broad road leading to the lower gate. There was no telling how quickly the dwarfs would rally from the violent destruction of the rocket battery. The northmen knew better than to squander the opportunity their confusion presented.

'To the ziggurat!' Wulfrik called to his men. He cast a last glance at Sigvatr leading the warriors in the other direction. If things went wrong, at least there was a chance his old friend would be able to get out and make his way back to the *Seafang*.

WULFRIK TURNED AWAY and led the way down the road to the ziggurat. He didn't see Zarnath gazing at the men rushing to the causeway, or the hate in his eyes as he stared at Sigvatr. He didn't see the small, toad-like creature that dropped from the sleeve of the shaman's tunic and grovelled at the Kurgan's feet.

Zarnath pointed his finger at Sigvatr's back. 'That one,' he hissed.

The fanged imp muttered a peal of insane gibberish and loped after the old warrior.

The shaman wiped the slime from his arm where

the imp had lain. Quickly he followed after the northmen. It wouldn't do for one of them to double back looking for him and discover what he had done.

Besides, Wulfrik might need Zarnath's magic when he reached the ziggurat, and the last thing the shaman wanted was the champion to fall for want of a few spells.

Chuckling at his own jest, Zarnath hastened his steps as the sounds of battle reached his ears.

Chapter Seven

WULFRIK CHARGED DOWN the wide roadway leading to the base of the ziggurat. His skin crawled as he passed the morbid ranks of statues lining the path, stone effigies of dwarf warriors with axes raised. As he glanced at them, Wulfrik noted that the silent sentinels were not wholly the work of chisel and hammer: real bones were plastered into hollowed sections of the guardians, a skull grinning from beneath the stony helm of each statue. The bones were those of dwarfs, but whether the dawi zharr intended the gruesome display to honour their own dead or defile those of their enemies, he could not say. It was enough for him to be reminded of the black hearts of his foes and the cruelty he could expect from them if he failed.

The champion half-expected the statues to leap into life as he passed them. Running down the road, he kept glancing back at them, watching them for some sign of motion. He could see his warriors doing the same, clearly victim to the same unsettling premonition of lurking menace. Njarvord succumbed to the sensation, attacking one of the statues with his axe, hacking slivers of rock and bone from one of the sentinels before throwing himself full against it and pitching it to the roadway. The statue cracked as it struck the road, collapsing into a heap of rubble.

Njarvord's attack encouraged the other northmen to lash out at the grim statues. Even Wulfrik felt the impulse to fling himself upon the closest of the guardians and smash it into dust. He was raising his sword to chop at stone ankles before he realised what he was doing.

Angrily, Wulfrik lifted his sword high and shouted at his men. There was some subtle sorcery woven into the statues, some insidious magic that antagonised any who trespassed within their influence. The statues protected the ziggurat by provoking fear in the minds of their enemies. Lesser men would have fled screaming from the stronghold. Norscans were made of sterner stuff. Instead of running, they fought back. But in doing so, they allowed the statues to fulfil their purpose. Attacking unfeeling stone, spending their strength, dulling their blades upon rock and bone, the warriors were weakening themselves. Worse, they were giving the defenders of the ziggurat the time they needed to muster their own troops.

'The Crow God's pox on all your manhoods!' Wulfrik cursed his men. 'Forget the gargoyles! There are foes of flesh to be slain!'

The champion's furious words fell upon deaf ears. Goaded by the baleful emanations of the guardians, his men were enthralled by their own violence. Their attacks became a frenzied assault, axes and swords smashing over and over into each statue as it was cast down from its pedestal. The urge for destruction consumed the northmen as they pulverised the sentinels with mindless abandon.

If there had been any doubt that some fell magic was sealed within the statues, Wulfrik settled the question when he drove his sword through the first of his warriors he encountered. Pierced through the breast, the Sarl axeman crumpled to his knees, coughing blood into his beard. The man's eyes didn't even focus upon the face of his killer. Instead, he crawled back to the statue he had been attacking, pounding his fists against the unyielding stone.

Wulfrik kicked the dying wretch and glared at the rest of his men. They were oblivious to the killing of their comrade, fixated upon their maddened assault on the statues. This was how the dwarfs protected their temple, with trickery and magic! Wulfrik could well imagine the effect the sinister statues would have upon any orc slaves thinking to storm the ziggurat.

But slaves did not have magic of their own.

'Zarnath!' Wulfrik called, storming back along the roadway. He hesitated when he saw a dark figure emerge from one of the alleyways connecting to the road. For a moment, his eyes locked with the murderous black orbs of an armoured dwarf. The dwarf's beard pulled up in a scowl when he saw that Wulfrik had resisted the magic of the statues. Raising a crooked scimitar, he shouted at the Norscan.

The dwarf did not get a chance to repeat his cry.

Snarling his fury, Wulfrik lunged at the sneaking murderer. Scimitar and sword crashed together in a shriek of bladed steel. The dwarf spat obscenities as the northman forced him back into the alley. He made a great show of giving ground before Wulfrik's attack.

Wulfrik didn't fall for the dwarf's ruse. He'd been able to understand the little killer's shout. It had been a call to arms, a warning to other lurkers that they would have to strike the men on the road quickly before any more of them broke free of the spell. He knew that the dwarf had friends close by, probably waiting in the darkness of the alleyway.

Leaning in close to the dwarf, Wulfrik locked his fingers in the coils of his enemy's beard. Pulling savagely, he ripped a fistful of beard out by its roots. The dwarf cried out in pain, staggering back in shock, one hand instinctively flying to his injured face. His eyes went wide with horror as he felt the damage he'd suffered.

'You look better as a beardling,' Wulfrik mocked the dwarf in his own language. The northman gestured at the fuming dwarf with the clump of black hair he held in his fist. 'But I wouldn't wipe a goblin's arse with this oily trash,' he grinned, tossing the torn beard back into the dwarf's face.

It was an inarticulate scream of rage that propelled the dwarf towards Wulfrik. It was an inarticulate groan of agony that ended his charge. Side-stepping the dwarf's flashing scimitar, Wulfrik brought his sword slashing through the ambusher's midsection. Designed to withstand the crushing impact of picks, hammers and orcish fists, the dwarf's scale armour did little to dull the cleaving stroke of the blade. Dark blood streamed from the dwarf's belly as he pitched face-first onto the ground.

Wulfrik leapt away from the dead dwarf, retreating from the alleyway where he could now see other soldiers emerging. Turning his head, he could see other dwarfs stalking from the shadows of the buildings, converging upon the road and the ensorcelled men oblivious to the danger.

'Zarnath!' Wulfrik roared again. He ducked behind one of the statues as a dwarf pointed a blunderbuss in his direction. Whatever magic had gone into its construction, the guardian was solid enough to protect him from the blast of shot. The same could not be said for the warrior who had been dulling the blade of his axe against the unyielding stone. The man was thrown by the impact of the blast, his body ripped apart by the iron shrapnel. For a pathetic moment, the ragged remains tried to rise and assault the statue once more, then the dying man fell and was still.

Wulfrik sprang from behind the statue, lunging at the dwarf with the blunderbuss before he could reload his weapon. A second dwarf, this one armed with a hooked axe, tried to intercept the enraged champion. For his effort, the soldier was rewarded with a cleft shoulder and a smashed face. The gunner looked up from his arming of the blunderbuss in time to see Wulfrik's sword chopping down at him. He squealed in terror, then collapsed as his face was split by the descending blade.

'Zarnath, you Kurgan cur!' Wulfrik howled. 'Break the spell on my men! Break it or I'll strew your guts from here to Araby!'

He could see the shaman further down the road, standing just beyond the first rank of stone sentinels. There was, about the way the Kurgan's head whipped from side to side, the air of a cornered animal to Zarnath. Wulfrik could see the indecision on the man's face as he wrestled with the urge to flee. The Norscan cursed once more the cowardice of all sorcerers. He reached down, ripping the blunderbuss from the dead fingers of the dwarf at his feet. Angrily, he threw the empty weapon at Stefnir, nearly striking the Aesling in the head. The close call was enough to snap him from his attack against one of the statues.

'Get the shaman!' Wulfrik ordered when Stefnir turned his way. The champion had no time to see if Stefnir would be able to carry out his command. Another pair of dwarfs were rushing at him from the darkness, gleaming axes in their hands and revenge in their eyes. Wulfrik snarled at them and braced himself to meet their attack.

Across the road, a large group of dwarfs were systematically cutting down the bewitched Norscans, laughing wickedly as their axes dismembered the defenceless men.

The slaughter ended in a burst of crackling energy, a sphere of white-hot light that engulfed the murder squad. The harsh voices of the dwarfs rose in screams of agony as the ball of lightning sizzled through their bodies. Sparks exploded from the dwarfs' armour; cinders fell from their burning beards. Flesh melted into the hafts of axes and eyes boiled in their skulls. Those few dwarfs outside the discharge of the spell fled back into the safety of the alleyways, wailing in horror.

Wulfrik kicked the severed head of his last foe, sending it rolling after the retreating dwarfs. 'Don't forget your friend!' he mocked the routed guards. He watched the dwarfs to ensure himself their fright was genuine and not some further deceit. Satisfied, he marched down the middle of the road. The surviving Norscans had abandoned their mad attack on the statues, instead leaning against their bases, breathing heavily as they tried to recover from their frenzied exertions. Wulfrik kicked and scolded the warriors he passed, demanding they get back on their feet. However far the dwarfs ran, he knew they would not go far. Besides, there were the dwarfs who had marched into the pit to consider. If those soldiers returned from the causeway there was little chance of fighting their way through them.

Wulfrik's hand tightened about his sword as he approached Zarnath. The shaman was trembling, blood dripping from ears and nose. The glow in his eyes was only a dim flicker. The hero didn't think it was possible, but Zarnath looked even more exhausted than the men he had passed on the road.

'The shaman let loose seven kinds of hell on them,' Stefnir boasted. The blackened bruise on the Kurgan's cheek showed the method he had used to convince Zarnath to fight.

Wulfrik glowered at Stefnir and sneered at the panting Zarnath. 'It would have been helpful if he'd helped sooner. Many dead men wouldn't be if he'd done his job.'

Zarnath was too tired to fit any emotion into his voice. 'I have told you. I must conserve my powers. No man may wield the winds of magic with impunity. Each spell takes a toll upon the body. I must have time to replenish my strength, to compose my mind.'

The shaman's plea made no impact upon Wulfrik. 'You can rest after the torc is in my hands,' he told Zarnath. The champion's face was twisted with contempt. 'It was you who led me here,' he reminded him. 'Without the torc, all this has been for nothing.'

Zarnath shook his head vigorously. 'I can't!' he pleaded. 'I must have time to rest and recover my powers!'

Wulfrik's hand clamped tight upon the Kurgan's shoulder. 'You are worthless to me without the torc,' he growled. 'But perhaps the torc can help me without you. What one sorcerer knows, another sorcerer can learn.' He turned and snarled at Stefnir. 'Bring the shaman. If he blinks wrong, tickle his spleen with your axe.'

THE NORTHMEN HURRIED down the road, warily watching the path for any more traps. The stone sentinels they passed stared at them in silence, their magic now only an uneasy whisper in the back of their minds. The dwarf soldiers, if they had lingered, kept out of sight, making no effort to stop the men. The warehouses and workshops of the outpost dwindled as the ground around the road narrowed. On one side the black wall of the stronghold pressed close against the road. At the other, the ground vanished entirely, leaving that side of the path open to the mine below: a sheer drop of half a mile into the darkness of the pit.

Ahead, Wulfrik could see the ziggurat. The base of the tower was immense, large enough to accommodate all of Ormskaro and its harbour. From the heights overlooking Dronangkul, he had failed to appreciate just how large the structure was. The walls of black basalt looked thick enough to withstand the rage of a shaggoth, the engraved bronze doors which fronted the ziggurat big enough that the *Seafang* might have easily sailed between them at full sail with her mast raised.

Strangely, the turrets set upon each tier of the ziggurat were empty. Wulfrik had ordered his men to form a shield wall as they advanced, expecting that the dwarfs would have gunners or bowmen stationed above the gates. That they did not set the champion's mind whirring. Had they really sent so many of their troops into the mines to quell the riot, or was this merely evidence that they had some new devilry planned?

Wulfrik studied the bronze gates, feeling his skin crawl as he stared at the grisly depictions of captives being fed into the fiery mouth of a gigantic bull. Stefnir said the dawi zharr worshipped their god by pushing sacrifices into bronze ovens cast in the shape of bulls. To find the motif repeated on the doors of their temple was a symbolism even Wulfrik did not fail to recognise.

The champion turned away from the doors and stared at Zarnath. The shaman's eyes went wide with horror and he shook his head in protest.

'I still don't have a battering ram,' Wulfrik told the shaman. He nodded to Stefnir and the Aesling pushed Zarnath forwards. 'I'll have these gates down,' he promised the shaman.

Before he could threaten the Kurgan further, Wulfrik's words were drowned out by the thunderous blast of horns. The entire road shook as a deep rumble shivered through it. The men could almost feel giant gears turning beneath their feet. Wulfrik spun about, watching in amazement as the great doors slowly opened.

From beyond the doors marched a column of grim figures. From head to foot they were encased in heavy armour of blackened steel, their horned helms cast in the image of fanged bulls. Plates of black marble veined with gold reinforced the armour on their arms and legs. Over their beards, sheaths of bronze gleamed in the starlight. The long axes they carried were curled like crescents with a long spike set at the tip of the axe-head and a barbed hook protruding from the back of the weapon.

The dwarfs did not hesitate when they saw the men standing before their gates, but continued to advance in a silent, forbidding column. At their flanks, small knots of lightly armoured dwarfs followed the heavy infantry, fingering a vicious assortment of whips and mancatchers. Their intentions were clear to every man who saw them.

Wulfrik was about to order his warriors to fall back,

then engage the dwarfs in the comparative security of the settlement where the narrow alleyways would force the heavy infantry to break formation and engage the northmen as individual fighters rather than as a unit. Even as the command was on his lips, Wulfrik saw that the way back had been closed to them. The rumbling the men had felt in the ground had been caused by machinery buried under the road. Under the power of these hidden mechanisms, the road behind them had been raised, swinging upwards like a Bretonnian drawbridge, forming a sheer wall behind them and cutting off any chance of escape.

The grim dwarf warriors halted just a few feet from the northmen, standing at attention with such solidity that they might have been carved from the same stone as the sentinels. Their eyes glared at the men from behind the masks of their helms, but not a sound rose from any of the armoured dwarfs. In stark contrast, the small groups of slavers began hooting and jeering at the northmen, promising all sorts of grisly tortures once 'the immortals' pounded them into submission.

Even the slavers fell silent, however, as a rider emerged from the depths of the ziggurat. He was an especially loathsome example of dwarf, his black beard dyed with streaks of crimson, his hands encased in a dazzling array of rings. His squat body was swathed in purple robes upon which flickering flames had been woven. The dwarf's eyes were hidden behind a veil of silver thread which depended from the brim of a tall helm of gold adorned with bloodstones. The face beneath the veil was burned, grey scar-tissue covering most of the bulbous nose and making one cheek resemble lumpy porridge.

More imposing than the hideous dwarf was the beast he rode out from the gates. It was a creature the likes of which Wulfrik had never seen in all his travels. In shape it was not unlike some great black bull, but from its back immense leathery wings were spread, fanned out like the pinions of a dragon. The tail was long and thick, more like that of some giant reptile than a beast of the field, and at its tip was a mallet-like knob of bone. The monster's hind legs ended in steel-shod hooves, but its forelegs were tipped by hand-like paws, each finger ending in a long claw sheathed in steel. The head of the beast was an even more ghastly mixture of dwarf and bovine than the centaur Wulfrik had killed, immense horns curling away from a black, leathery face with a curly red beard. With every breath, the creature exhaled a cloud of greasy smoke that sparkled weirdly as it swirled about the beast and its rider.

The dwarf brought his strange beast to rest and stared at the tiny band of northmen. A kick to the lammasu's side and the dragon-like wings retracted, folding upon themselves and curling against the monster's ribs. 'You powerful for have survive overlong,' the dwarf called out. He used a strange patois of goblin languages. Wulfrik felt his blood boil when he realised it was the same tongue the dwarfs used when they deigned to address their many slaves. 'Lay down weapon and live.'

'You are Khorakk?' Wulfrik demanded, spitting the

words in the speech of the dawi zharr. He felt Zarnath's terrified fingers clutching his arm.

'Do not make light of this dwarf,' the shaman said. 'He is a sorcerer.'

Wulfrik frowned as he heard Zarnath's words. 'I've been told you are not Khorakk,' he growled.

'Thegn Khorakk is lord of Dronangkul,' the sorcerer sneered. 'He does not waste his time with slaves.' The dwarf raised a heavy hammer and pointed it at the northmen. 'Do you surrender?'

Wulfrik glared back at the sorcerer. 'Do you always ride out on your mother's back to greet visitors?'

The sorcerer's face turned crimson. For a moment, he was physically stunned by the temerity of Wulfrik's insult. In that moment, the immortals were likewise caught unawares. The champion pounced upon the dwarf warriors, stabbing the tip of his sword through the mask of the first immortal he reached. The dwarf crumpled in a screaming heap, blood spraying from his ruptured eye.

The other northmen threw themselves at the dwarfs with a viciousness that would have impressed the orcs down in the slave pit. Few things were more guaranteed to steel the soul of a Norscan than the threat of being another man's thrall. It was a fate only lesser breeds of men would resign themselves to, men who cared nothing for the judgement of gods or ancestors. Death upon the axes of the immortals was at least an end that might make their ancestors proud.

* * *

THREE IMMORTALS CROWDED Wulfrik, fending off the champion's attacks with their heavy axes. Disciplined warriors, the dwarfs worked in unison to overwhelm the champion, two of the immortals using their axes to block Wulfrik's blows while the third moved in for the kill. The tactic might have worked had their sorcerer been less enraged.

The ground at Wulfrik's feet began to glow with a crimson light. It was the only warning the northman had, but it was enough. Flinging himself at the immortals with a reckless disregard, Wulfrik escaped his peril an instant before the ground exploded in a gout of steaming magma. The unexpectedness of his leap caught the dwarfs unprepared, the fiery explosion shaking them from their feet.

Wulfrik landed atop the armoured dwarfs, snarling like an animal as he hacked at their prone bodies with his swords. The heavy armour resisted his blades but at the same time hindered the dwarfs as they tried to defend themselves and regain their feet. At last the champion gave up trying to cut his way through their armour. Reversing his hold on his swords, he brought the spiked pommels smashing down into the masks of their helms. Ruthlessly, Wulfrik smashed the steel masks, pounding them out of all semblance of shape. Blood erupted from the grilled vents in the mouths of the masks. The dwarfs thrashed in agony, trying to knock the Norscan off them.

A sheet of black fire licked across the northman and his foes. Safe within their heavy armour, the black fire worked no harm upon the immortals. Wulfrik, however, was flung back by the blast, his skin steaming, his hair falling in singed clumps from his scalp. One of the protective talismans the champion wore about his neck fell to the ground in a molten lump, its magic consumed as it absorbed the force of the malignant spell.

Upon his lammasu, the dwarf sorcerer chuckled. His hand burned like an ember as he pointed his crooked finger in Wulfrik's direction. The three immortals painfully regained their feet and groped about for their axes. 'Leave enough of him to feed the belly of Hashut,' the sorcerer commanded.

If the sorcerer said anything else, the words were drowned out by the tremendous wind that suddenly shrieked down across the road. Even upon the Sea of Claws, Wulfrik had never felt such a furious wind. The tempest tore at him with malevolent determination, as though a thing of emotion as well as force. He could hear men and dwarfs crying out in fear as the gale smashed into them.

The fury of the wind only grew more terrible. Wulfrik felt himself being ripped from the earth by invisible talons. Shrieks tore at the air as struggling bodies were pushed inexorably to the lip of the pit. A dwarf slaver tore at the road, scrabbling desperately for a handhold to arrest his motion. His efforts were futile. Screaming, the bearded slaver was the first to pitch over the side and hurtle into the blackness of the mine.

He wasn't alone for long. Other slavers and their human foes were blown over the edge. The immortals, weighed down by their heavy armour, made an effort to hold their ground, but they too were unable to resist the power of the tempest. Their steel-shod boots scraping deep scratches into the stone, the immortals slowly slid towards the pit.

Wulfrik concentrated his strength into a single effort. Tossing aside one of his swords, he gripped the other in both hands. Lifting it high, he stabbed the blade deep into the road. He wrapped his arms around the embedded sword, bracing his feet against the burning edge of the magma pool conjured by the dwarf sorcerer. Groaning with effort, Wulfrik struggled to resist the tempest's pull.

Through the gale stalked the dwarf sorcerer. The villain seemed impervious to the tempest, the winds rolling harmlessly about the flanks of his monstrous steed. The lammasu growled, a roar that sounded uncomfortably like the speech of the dwarfs themselves. Grinning, the sorcerer kicked the beast's sides. In response, the lammasu's great wings snapped open. Like some giant vulture taking wing, the lammasu rose into the air.

The sorcerer didn't seem aware of Wulfrik now. Both the dwarf and his steed were focussed upon something pressed against the pivoting wall opposite the ziggurat's gates. Wulfrik could see Zarnath standing beside the wall, wind whipping about him, his eyes blazing with power. The jewel at the head of his staff was burning with such intensity that sparks flew from it. He could see streams of blood rolling down the shaman's cheeks like crimson tears. It didn't take a seer to know that Zarnath had conjured the windstorm, or to appreciate the toll such mighty magic was taking on him.

That his tempest had struck friend as well as foe was something that, perhaps, the Kurgan had not intended. Accident or intention, Zarnath's magic had betrayed him. The windstorm was having no effect upon the dwarf sorcerer and his steed. At the same time, the spell had sent most of those who might have defended the shaman plummeting to their destruction in the pit.

Laughing spitefully, the dwarf sorcerer raised his hand, curling his fingers into a strange pattern. 'I bring you death, human dog!' the sorcerer cackled. From his hand, a flare of black flame shot down at Zarnath.

The windstorm died as the flames wrapped around the shaman's body. For an instant, the Kurgan was lost to sight. In the next moment, a stream of lightning shot out from the midst of the flame, narrowly missing the hovering lammasu. Zarnath strode through the fire, his clothes dropping from him in burning tatters. He glared up at the dwarf. In one hand, Zarnath held a glass vial. Wulfrik could smell the tang of star-stone as the Kurgan crushed the vial in his hand. There was a cruel smile on the shaman's face as he licked the oily green liquid from his palm. The fires in his eyes, having faded to a flicker, now exploded with blinding violence.

Wulfrik knew what Zarnath had done. He had seen such a thing before, deep within the swamps of Tilea when the gods had sent him to kill a chief of the ratkin. There had been a horned ratman who had chewed upon a piece of star-stone. Immediately he had been consumed with sorcerous power, unleashing such devastating spells as to bring the entire cavern crashing down upon them all.

From the shaman's splayed fingers, a shower of fiery stones shot towards the sorcerer. Zarnath's magic seemed to curl around the weird exhalations of the lammasu, but several stones sped past the edges of the shimmering cloud. The burning stones punched through the membranes of the beast's leathery wings. Roaring, the lammasu dropped from the sky, crashing heavily against the road. Wulfrik could tell from its howls that it was in pain, but far from dead. The quaking of the ground and the violent appearance of another geyser of magma made it clear the sorcerer had survived as well.

The jewel atop Zarnath's staff shattered as he wove a barrier of magic to protect himself from the molten rock the sorcerer had called up from the earth. The loss of his focus didn't seem to diminish the shaman's hideous vitality. Instead he seemed to swell with even more power. Lightning exploded all around the Kurgan, whipping about him like the flaming tongues of a hydra. The lammasu snorted in fear, limping away from the crazed Kurgan. The sorcerer upon its back kicked and cursed at the beast, ordering it back into the fight.

Wulfrik didn't know how long Zarnath could hold out against the sorcerer and his beast. To try and help the shaman was out of the question. Anyone trying would be incinerated by the wild energies billowing about the Kurgan's body. Only the lammasu's strange exhalations allowed its rider to withstand that stream of death.

Zarnath would fend for himself or he would die. Wulfrik had more important things to do. He gazed across the roadway, watching injured dwarfs hobbling back towards the gates. He saw a few survivors among his own men as well. Tjorvi was dashing among the sprawled bodies of the immortals, thrusting a dagger beneath their bronze beard-sheathes and slitting their throats with sadistic glee. Haukr was sawing rings from the fingers of a dead slaver while Stefnir pursued some of the injured dwarfs, chopping at them with an axe he had lifted from one of the immortals. Njarvord, lost in one of his rages, was beating the crushed skull of a dwarf against the ground, oblivious to the mash of blood and brain it left every time it smacked against the road.

Wulfrik planted his feet to either side of his sword. Straining every muscle in his body, he wrenched the blade free. 'To me, heroes of Norsca!' he bellowed. The few survivors of his warband turned and stared at him. Wulfrik gestured at the ziggurat where the great gates stood open and unguarded.

'In there we will find our doom,' Wulfrik told his men. 'If it is to be our end, then let us make it one that even the gods will envy!'

His men lifted their voices in a fierce war cry. Mustering their strength, the warriors followed their leader into the yawning mouth of the ziggurat. Only Wulfrik hesitated, casting a last look back at Zarnath and the dwarf sorcerer.

The shaman knew the secret of the torc. If he abandoned Zarnath, he might never find another man who knew the secret. The Kurgan might be his only hope of breaking the curse.

Wulfrik snarled and shook his head. The torc was the key to breaking the curse. If he had the shaman and not the relic, then he had nothing. He would gain only a useless death and an eternity of shame if he tried to help Zarnath. All he could do was find Khorakk and take the torc from him. That was the hope he had to cling to now.

Chapter Eight

Njarvord bore the fleeing slaver to the floor, the dwarf's tusks snapping as his jaw cracked against the black stone. The dwarf struggled to push the northman's heavy bulk off him. Hurling curses on the slaver, the Baersonling grabbed the sides of the dwarf's head. The powerful warrior pulled the slaver's head back savagely, snapping his neck like a rotten stick.

'I thought the idea was to catch one alive and make it show us where the boss dwarf is hiding?' Haukr muttered. His annoyance at Njarvord's unthinking bloodlust wasn't quite enough to keep him from going through the slaver's pockets when the Baersonling stepped away from the corpse.

Haukr's bitter words sobered Njarvord. The bearded marauder turned an uneasy eye towards his captain.

Wulfrik didn't even glance in Njarvord's direction. 'I already have a trail to follow,' the champion growled. 'So long as none of you kill the dwarf I need you can wash this place in their blood for all I care.'

There was an eerie intensity in Wulfrik's eyes as he stalked past his men. Some of the Norse tribes spoke of the 'weirdsight', a premonition granted to those who have stared too long into the realm of the gods. Seers and witches were said to possess the ability to see into the future and allow that knowledge to reshape the present. It was a power that had toppled kings from their thrones and brought victory in war. Mighty as they knew Wulfrik to be, endowed with strength and endurance beyond most men, his warriors had never before suspected he might be possessed of the weirdsight.

The thing which guided Wulfrik was much simpler than the spectral powers of warlocks and sorcerers, though equally intangible. A wounded dwarf, a survivor of Zarnath's amok magic, had retreated back into the ziggurat. Several had done so, as Njarvord's last victim could attest, but this particular dwarf had left some of his blood behind him at the gate. Since fleeing, the dwarf had bound his wound, staunching the loss of blood. But he could not eliminate the scent he left behind so easily.

Like a wolf in the forest, the champion was following that scent now, focussed upon it with such fixation that the rest of the world had faded from his perception into a half-real place of shadows and whispers. Wounded, frightened, with his enemies at his heels, the dwarf would flee to a place of safety. Where would be more logical for him to go than to seek protection from his overlord? Follow the scent and find Khorakk, such was the wisdom Wulfrik had chosen to guide him.

The halls within the ziggurat were built from heavy basalt blocks, ground and sanded to an almost mirror-like sheen. No torches lit the black passages; instead light came from polished plates of obsidian set into the walls. Like black mirrors, the plates stared from their settings, an infernal crimson glow emanating from their depths.

Haukr and Tjorvi tried to pry one of the plates free when they had first discovered them, but quickly lost the appetite for such plunder. There were things behind the obsidian mirrors, things trapped inside the dark gleam, things that scratched at the glistening surface. It was the endless hate of the trapped daemons which produced the hellish light within the ziggurat. The two looters didn't need Stefnir to tell them the dwarfs were mad to create the obsidian mirrors, much less adorn the halls of their citadel with them.

The architecture itself was built in a ponderous, overwhelming fashion. Perhaps to compensate for their small bodies, the dwarfs had built their temple at titanic scale. The main corridor proved every bit as wide as Wulfrik had judged it to be when the great gates had opened. A fleet of longships might easily have sailed through the ziggurat's main hall were it somehow flooded. The archways which stretched overhead were like the stone ribs of a vanquished god, their weight pressing down upon the men even when the ceiling climbed from fifty to a hundred feet. The side passages which opened off from the main corridor at regular intervals were big enough to herd oxen down, and each was guarded by a massive door of bronze and iron. The faces of bulls were engraved into each door, the mouth of each face an open cavity through which a dwarf gunner might thrust the deadly barrel of a blunderbuss.

The northmen braced themselves each time they passed one of the doors, taking shelter behind their shields until they were beyond the menacing portals. Wulfrik snorted in contempt. This Khorakk was both soft and arrogant. He'd sent all of his troops down into the mines to subdue the slaves, keeping only his elite soldiers behind. Then, so sure of the strength of his immortals and the magic of his sorcerer, he'd committed all of his warriors to crushing the invaders at his gate. A Norscan king might do the same, but he would glory in the fight. He would march with his warriors, not dispatch them like thralls upon an errand while remaining behind in his palace.

Wulfrik would enjoy showing Khorakk the price of his hubris.

Deeper into the ziggurat the men crept. The trail of the wounded dwarf never wavered, keeping to the main corridor. Soon, the warriors could see an angry, fiery glow at the far end of the hall, a smouldering brilliance more sinister than the crimson light of the daemon-mirrors. A stench of sulphur and boiling pitch slithered through the air, stifling the breath of even the hardy Njarvord. It was like the molten breath of a mountain, a vapour of brooding malignance older than blood or memory.

The marauders hesitated, feeling the oppressive menace rising the closer they came to that diabolic glow. The tiny voice of their fear whispered to them, warning them to go no farther. Alone, the warriors would have obeyed their fear. But they were not alone. Even as they hesitated, Wulfrik strode onwards. There was no fear in his eyes, only the pitiless determination that had brought all of them so far. It was the fearlessness that had made Wulfrik a hero, a warrior whose sagas were sung across all the freeholds and steadings of Norsca. It was the unfaltering courage that made men risk their lives to sail with him, for the men who followed Wulfrik were lauded as heroes in their own right. By following Wulfrik, these men laid claim to a glory they would never win by themselves, a glory their ancestors could envy.

Some things are more powerful than fear. When Wulfrik marched towards the heart of the ziggurat, his men were at his side.

AT THE END of the massive hall was a room that could only be described as colossal. Only the craft of a people like the dwarfs could have shaped stone in such a fashion. Immense walls converged upon one another, like a reversed image of the tiered steps of the ziggurat's exterior. No beams or buttresses supported the mammoth construction; no archways interrupted the staggering vastness from floor to ceiling. Like a hollow hill, the great temple yawned between the basalt walls, a thousand feet across, nearly again the distance between its floor and ceiling.

Huge columns flanked the hall, forming the backs

of gigantic statues which combined the worst aspects of dwarf and bull, gargantuan brethren to the creature Wulfrik had killed at the gates of Dronangkul. The walls were everywhere adorned with obsidian mirrors before which were piled the skulls of goblins and orcs and other creatures, the crimson glow of the plates casting weird shadows upon the crumbling bones.

The whole scene was lit by volcanic fires, canals of molten rock that flowed across the floor to converge in a great pool of magma at the very centre of the hall. Suspended a few inches above the pool was a huge stone platform upon which stood a giant bronze statue cast in the image of a dwarf-faced bull. The belly of the idol was open and beneath its ribs dangled a nest of steel shackles. Barrel-like machines rested to either side of the idol, squatting like noxious toads in its shadow. Fore and aft, the machines ended in ugly nozzles, each nozzle fitted to a short hose of dragonhide.

The purpose of the machines was beyond the ability of the northmen to guess, but the function of the crystal lamps sitting at each corner of the platform was obvious to Wulfrik. These were the lights the dwarfs had used to create the ghostly face of their god in the sky above the outpost. A monstrous curling tube of brass gave evidence whence the god's voice had sounded.

Directly above the platform, far overhead, the ceiling of the temple was open, the first flicker of day washing out the stars. Immense chains extended from each corner of the platform to connect with enormous gears set into the roof of the ziggurat. Again, it was not hard for Wulfrik to discern their purpose. The platform was the altar of their god. Through their machines, the dwarfs could bring that altar down inside their temple or raise it up to the top of the ziggurat. Why they should do such a thing, whether it was some strange ritual Hashut demanded of the dwarfs, Wulfrik neither knew nor cared.

As he cast his gaze across the temple, studying its environs, Wulfrik noted the cluster of dwarfs standing upon the platform. Some were the ragged slavers who had survived the battle at the gate, others were bald dwarfs with scarred faces who wore red robes and bronze breastplates. Wulfrik decided they were monks or priests of some sort, servants of the dwarfs' Father of Darkness. It was the other dwarf upon the platform who interested him.

Wulfrik decided he had been hasty naming the sorcerer at the gate as the most loathsome dwarf in creation. The specimen upon the platform was hideous enough to sicken a jackal. His head was squashed and flat, his ears large and mismatched. His nose was a bulbous knot of hairy pimples and his eyebrows were thick enough to be braided. His black beard hung from a sharply pointed chin in oily locks, gaudy combs of diamond and ruby strung through them in the most haphazard way. Behind the rings of his beard, Wulfrik could see the blood-red hue of Khorakk's torc reflecting in the fiery light of the temple.

The dwarf thegn hadn't been so idle as Wulfrik had supposed. Instead of the rich robes of a pampered king, Khorakk was encased in a heavy suit of plate armour which drastically increased both his height and his bulk. There was no fright in the thegn's eyes when he saw Wulfrik enter the temple, not even surprise, only an amused sort of disgust.

'You led them here,' Khorakk's slithery voice rasped as he turned towards one of the slavers. Before the slaver could react, Khorakk's armoured hand reached out and closed about his head. Steam puffed from vents in the armour's elbow and shoulder as Khorakk crushed the slaver's head into paste. 'How inconvenient,' the thegn said. With a flick of his hand, he sent the slaver's body pitching into the molten fire beneath the platform.

The abrupt violence of the slaver's death was quickly followed by more bloodshed. The bald dwarfs turned on the other slavers, piling on them, dragging them to the floor of the platform. Some of their number seized heavy steel hammers, raising the mattocks and pulverising the faces of the struggling captives.

'The ugly one is mine,' Wulfrik snarled at his men, baring his fangs. 'I suggest you remember that.'

The northmen raced across the mammoth hall, leaping over the shallow canals of fire. The dwarfs stared back at them, seemingly unconcerned by the nearness of their enemies. Khorakk's hideous face pulled back in a smug look of arrogant victory. He nodded to one of the bald dwarfs.

'My immortals will be back soon enough,' Khorakk said. 'They will attend to this rabble.'

At Khorakk's gesture, the bald dwarf pulled a lever

jutting from a box-like contrivance standing at one corner of the platform. In response, the chains began to withdraw, pulling the platform and its occupants towards the roof of the ziggurat.

Wulfrik glared up at the retreating dwarfs and shook his sword. 'Khorakk! Fatherless mongrel of a vulture!' The violence in the champion's voice sent his words thundering through the cavernous temple. 'Your ancestors were oathbreakers and kinslayers! Small surprise their descendant doesn't have the guts of a jackal, much less a man!'

Uttered in the harsh tones of the dwarf tongue, Wulfrik's scathing challenge cut at Khorakk's pride. The dwarf would have liked to reach the roof of the ziggurat, then have the floor of the temple flooded with magma. He'd risen far by being petty, vicious and above all careful. The human's words, however, stung him in a way that went beyond reason, touching the primal essence of his being. He did not know about the Gift of Tongues, but he felt its power when he turned towards the bald dwarfs and ordered the platform to descend.

'Manling,' Khorakk snarled at Wulfrik. 'I will feed your spine to Hashut – if I can find it!' The dwarf thegn clenched his fist and a curved blade shot outwards from the heavy vambrace on his arm. He gestured menacingly at the Norscan with the sword-like weapon. 'You'll cry to your gods before I'm done!'

'I'll cry now,' Wulfrik called back at him. 'I asked my gods to send me a worthy foe, not the village idiot!'

Khorakk's face turned red as anger swelled up inside him. For a moment, it seemed the dwarf would hurl himself from the platform, so great was his wrath at Wulfrik's mocking tone. He was used to respect and fear, demanded it from all who stood in his presence. He would not suffer temerity from this barbarian!

While the platform was still a few feet from the floor of the temple, Khorakk lunged at Wulfrik. Jets of steam hissed from pistons fastened to the thegn's armoured legs, the machinery endowing his leap with force far beyond that of mere flesh. The Norscan scrambled as Khorakk's body came crashing down at him, clearing the dozen yards between himself and his prey in the blink of an eye. The dwarf smashed into the floor with such force that the basalt block cracked beneath the impact. Coiled wires fitted into the steel legs absorbed the shock of his violent descent, allowing Khorakk to recover immediately from his leap. The dwarf's crooked blade flashed out at Wulfrik, glancing across the champion's scalp as he ducked beneath the sudden assault.

The dwarf's armour made him taller than Wulfrik and about as massive as a troll. When the hero's sword stabbed at him, Khorakk laughed, the blade scarcely scratching the thick marble breastplate.

'Where is your bragging now?' Khorakk growled, pursuing his attack on the northman. The steam-powered arms of his armour gave the dwarf incredible speed, his blade slashing at Wulfrik as though it were crafted from lightning. Only the rage-ridden clumsiness of Khorakk's attack allowed the hero to defend himself, dodging and weaving his body as the crescent blade sliced at his body.

In dodging the blade, however, Wulfrik exposed himself to the dwarf's other hand, the steel gauntlet that had crushed the slaver's skull. The metal fingers ripped at him, cutting through his armour as though it were Cathayan silk. Shreds of mail dangled from Khorakk's hand when Wulfrik squirmed out of the dwarf's tightening grip. Blood rose to fill the deep gouges the thegn's talons left across the northman's chest.

Wulfrik snarled in pain, staggering back as Khorakk flung the tatters of his armour into one of the fiery canals. The dwarf's legs spewed jets of steam as he pressed his attack and forced the hero to give ground before him. Khorakk glanced about him to ensure himself that he would not be flanked by the barbarian's comrades.

The other humans were busy fighting the robed acolytes. Each of the bald dwarfs had seized a heavy hammer and followed their thegn into battle. The northmen were shocked to find that their foes were women. Dwarf mothers too old to produce children, their only purpose now was to defend the temple of their unforgiving god. They wielded their hammers with the maddened zeal of fanatics, the burned stumps of their tongues wriggling in silent cries of hate. Seldom had the veteran marauders ever battled foes who fought with such crazed disregard for their own lives as these viragos.

Khorakk's hideous face grinned as he saw the dwarf harridans take down one of the humans, bringing him low with a bone-crushing blow to his leg. The thegn wasn't overly concerned that two of the acolytes had died on the northman's blade to get that close to him. To his thinking, the barren viragos were almost as worthless as a hobgoblin in the grand scheme of things.

The dwarf's momentary distraction as he watched Stefnir fall before the acolytes gave Wulfrik the opportunity he had been watching for. Clenching his fangs, Wulfrik suddenly sprang at the gloating thegn. His blade scraped across the steel gorget the dwarf wore, failing to find the weak join between neck and breastplate. As his sword turned, Wulfrik twisted his hand, slamming the crosspiece into Khorakk's face. The dwarf howled in pain as his ugly visage was smashed into bruised wreckage.

'Swine! Dog!' the thegn swore, raising a hand to shield his face while swiping blindly at Wulfrik with his blade. Khorakk cursed again as the hero ducked beneath his sweeping steel to slash at the cables and pistons fitted to his legs. Screaming steam exploded from ruptured lines, venting across the floor in a boiling cloud. Wulfrik retreated from the steam, his flesh scalded by the burning vapour.

Khorakk stumbled back, the injured leg of his armour sluggish and jerky in its movements. As the cloud of steam jetting from the pipes dwindled, the dwarf's leg lost all of its remaining flexibility, at last becoming completely immobile.

'You'll suffer for that!' the thegn promised. He pressed his hand against a stud affixed to his breastplate. Puffs of smoke vented from the armour around his neck as two steel hinges sprang into motion, raising a horned helm from where it had rested against the dwarf's back and lowering it over his head. Khorakk's hate-ridden eyes glared from behind the grilled visor set into the helm's golden mask.

Wulfrik ran his hand across his bleeding scalp, flicking scarlet beads onto the dwarf's mask. 'Too late to spare your looks,' the northman said. 'They looked like troll vomit before I touched them!'

The dwarf thegn rushed at Wulfrik, chopping at the champion with his curved blade. The crippled leg of Khorakk's armour made the attack clumsy, almost unbalancing him as he struck. The northman rolled with the blow, letting the edge of the blade pass inches from his heart. As he rolled, he turned, driving his sword full-force against Khorakk's helm. The sturdy helm resisted the blow, but the gilded mask, its strength compromised by extravagance and hubris, crumpled. Khorakk cried out in shock as the dented slats of his visor were thrust inwards, almost crushing his eye.

Half-blinded, Khorakk slapped at a second stud fitted to his breastplate. From his right forearm, a steel plug suddenly popped free from the end of a pipe. Wulfrik had assumed the pipe was another piston designed to give the dwarf extra strength in his arm. Now he learned its real purpose. The dwarf clenched his fist. In response, a jet of fire exploded from the mouth of the pipe, billowing out at his foe in a sheet of flame.

Wulfrik leapt from the path of the fire, sliding across the floor. His momentum carried him to the very brink of one of the canals, the miasma of the bubbling magma singeing his beard. The hero didn't have time to consider how close he had come to destruction. As he arrested his slide, he threw himself to one side. Fire from Khorakk's armour blasted the floor where he had lain, the stones glowing red with heat as the flame played across them.

Awkwardly, Khorakk turned, trying to catch the agile barbarian in his sights. Unable to see through the left side of his helm and unable to bend his right leg, the hunt became an exercise in frustration for the thegn. A stream of curses echoed from his helm as he alternately cut at Wulfrik with his blade and shot at him with his fire-thrower. The curses faded into a gloating chuckle when the slow chase caused Khorakk to turn towards the ziggurat's main hall.

'You are doomed, barbarian!' the thegn laughed. 'My immortals are coming back, and against them you have no hope!'

Wulfrik did not need Khorakk's words to tell him more dwarfs were coming. He could smell the immortals as they rushed down the hall, feel their rage in their scent. Not many of them had survived Zarnath's spell and the attentions of Tjorvi and the others afterwards, but enough of them had endured to overwhelm the remaining Norscans.

Wulfrik ducked beneath another blind sweep of Khorakk's blade. Before the dwarf could turn his fire-thrower in his direction, the northman brought his sword sweeping down in a double-handed stroke that had all of his strength behind it. The blackened sword did not strike at Khorakk's blade, but at the metal housing behind it. The housing crumpled beneath the impact, springs snapping as the metal around them was crushed. Khorakk's blade wobbled against his arm, loosened from its fittings. When the dwarf struck back at the hero, Wulfrik's sword crashed against it, knocking it free and sending it bouncing into one of the molten canals.

'You're right, dwarf,' Wulfrik snarled at Khorakk. 'I don't have time to play with you any more!' Howling like an animal, the champion lunged at Khorakk's legs. His sword crashed against the pistons set into the thegn's still-functioning leg. The blade failed to work the same kind of havoc it had before, only a small spray of steam rewarding his effort.

The real impact of his attack was upon the dwarf inside the armour. Half-blind, his blade gone and with one leg already crippled, Khorakk appreciated how vulnerable he would be if he lost full control of the other. Fear gripped the overlord's dark heart. He turned away from Wulfrik, stiffly dragging his injured leg after him. As he retreated, he cried out to the dwarf acolytes for aid. Wulfrik was forced to ignore his quarry as a pair of hammer-wielding viragos rushed him. A low sweep of his sword slashed across the knees of one of the acolytes, spilling her to the ground in a bleeding heap. The second nearly caught him with an overhanded strike of her hammer, but when the blow failed to connect, the wizened old virago found herself staring at her own body as her head rolled across the temple.

'Stop the thegn!' Wulfrik roared at his surviving men. The marauders were scattered across the temple, defending themselves as best they could against the remaining viragos. Even so, they answered their captain's call, extricating themselves from their enemies to charge the retreating Khorakk.

Wulfrik could see Khorakk's goal. The thegn was making for the platform. Once there, he would be able to raise it to the roof of the ziggurat and escape. Even if he was able to fight his way clear of the immortals, Wulfrik knew his chances of catching the fleeing thegn would be poor. Those chances became worse when a stream of black fire erupted across the temple, narrowly missing Wulfrik's head.

The immortals were not the only ones who had survived the battle with Zarnath. Stalking down the hall was the dwarf sorcerer and his lammasu. The sorcerer and his beast looked the worse for their experience, the lammasu's wings tattered, one of its hind legs painfully curled against its side. But without a warlock of his own to fight them, Wulfrik knew even a weakened sorcerer was enough to finish his warband.

The only hope lay in using Khorakk's own escape route. Wulfrik wasn't going to die when he was so close to victory.

'Make for the platform!' he howled to his warriors. Wulfrik matched deeds to words, rushing towards the heart of the temple. He could see Khorakk limping onwards. The thegn stopped a dozen yards from the platform, his armour groaning and creaking as the pistons in its legs shuddered into action. Like some steel locust, Khorakk sprang from the floor of the temple, flinging himself up onto the dais. The dwarf landed badly, his damaged leg buckling under him and throwing him onto his side.

Wulfrik could see Khorakk was still moving, however, lifting himself with his arms. There would be only a matter of moments before the thegn reached the mechanism which controlled the platform. The northman's heart was hammering against his chest, his breath burning in his lungs by the time he reached the platform. Already in motion, he flung himself at the rising dais, his hands catching the edge. Below him, Wulfrik could feel the blistering heat of the molten pool. Had his hands missed the platform, the pool of fire would have been his tomb.

As the dais continued to rise, Wulfrik lifted himself onto the platform. He could see Njarvord and Haukr running towards him to help him up. Angrily he waved them away, pointing a fist at Khorakk. 'Just make sure he doesn't get away,' he told them. He retrieved his sword from its sheath, glaring murder at the thegn.

Khorakk glanced up at the roof of the ziggurat, then glared at the approaching northman. 'Hashut damn your bones, barbarian!' the dwarf growled. His armoured hand tore one of the crystal eyes from the side of the platform. There was a ghastly shriek, something like purple smoke flashing from the ruptured mechanism. Khorakk ignored the freed daemon. Lifting the heavy mass of bronze and crystal over his head, the dwarf hurled it at Wulfrik.

Wulfrik threw himself forwards as the cumbersome missile crashed against the platform, causing the entire dais to sway. His leap carried him just beyond the crystal eye as it rolled past him and over the edge of the platform. He could hear the sizzle as it splashed into the magma below.

More curses streamed from Khorakk's mouth. The dwarf took a lumbering step towards his foe, raising the arm equipped with the fire-spitter. Suddenly the thegn took a cautious step back.

'Watch out for the beast!'

The alarm came from Tjorvi, who like Wulfrik had only just managed to catch the edge of the dais as it rose above the temple. Slower to climb onto the platform, the Graeling had seen the frustrated immortals shaking their fists at them from the floor below. He had also watched a monstrous shape lift into the air in pursuit of the retreating dais.

Wulfrik dropped to the floor of the platform as he heard the warning. Claws swept through the empty air above him, the stench of brimstone and sulphur filling his nose, shimmering smoke clouding his eyes. Instinctively, Wulfrik rolled onto his back, slashing with his sword at the lammasu looming over him.

The monster reeled back, roaring in pain, one of its paws savaged by the champion's keen blade. The beast snarled down at him. Over its shoulder, Wulfrik could see the sorcerer's bloodthirsty grin.

Before either monster or sorcerer could strike, each found himself engaged from a different quarter. The pair had fixated too fully upon slaughtering Wulfrik, forgetting for the moment their other focs. They soon had cause to remember Njarvord and Haukr as the two warriors drove their axes into the lammasu's black hide. Haukr's blade cleaved deeply into the monster's leathery wing, smashing through the finger-like bones and ripping the membrane. Njarvord's hacked through the monster's flank, biting deep into its side. The beast reared back, forcing the sorcerer to forget about casting hexes as he struggled to stay mounted. The massive, club-like tail whipped around, smashing into Njarvord, flinging him like a ragdoll across the platform to crash into the side of the idol. The hollow statue rang like a bell from the impact of the marauder's body.

Haukr backed away from the raging lammasu, using the weird machines mounted beside the idol to duck behind as the beast swept its claws at him. Tjorvi jabbed at the monster with his own axe, trying to keep it distracted and divide its efforts between the two men.

Wulfrik left his warriors to keep the lammasu occupied. He had not forgotten Khorakk and knew that the thegn still posed a formidable threat in his own right. Backed into a corner, the dwarf might not care overmuch if he caught his own minions in a blast from his fire-thrower.

The thought gave Wulfrik another idea. There was a cruel smile on his face as he scrambled away from the lammasu and hurled himself towards Khorakk. The thegn was waiting for him, clenching his fist and sending a sheet of flame shooting from his armour at the charging hero. Khorakk imagined Wulfrik had made the last mistake he would ever make. The dwarf's fire would either immolate him or force him off the side of the platform. Either way the barbarian would burn.

The fire did drive Wulfrik off the side of the platform, but that was as the champion had planned. The northman sheathed his sword and lunged forwards, hurtling out over the side of the dais. As he leapt, his arms reached out, catching the chain fastened to the corner of the platform. Wulfrik felt his entire body shudder, felt the hot steel of the chain bite into his palms, but his grip held. The moving chain lifted him up and above the dais. Using the momentum of his leap, Wulfrik spun his body around and launched himself at Khorakk.

Like a bolt cast from a ballista, Wulfrik smashed down into Khorakk's chest. Striking from the dwarf's blind side, he caught the thegn completely by surprise. Believing Wulfrik had fallen down into the temple, a vindictive chuckle had been bubbling behind the dwarf's golden mask. Now the chuckle collapsed into a grunt of pain as Khorakk's heavy armour crashed onto his back.

Sprawled across Khorakk's chest, Wulfrik drove a dagger into the join between the armoured shoulder and his left arm. The Norscan sawed the edge across the tangle of pipes and cables until something broke and a jet of steam spurted out into the gloom. He wasn't sure if he'd cut the dwarf inside the armour. At the moment, he didn't care.

Wulfrik set his legs against the dwarf's left arm, hoping he'd damaged it enough that he would be able to pin it in place. Viciously, he seized Khorakk's right arm with both hands, straining to raise it. He could feel the dwarf struggling to pull free, pistons throbbing as they drove the armour's mechanisms.

It took every ounce of his strength to hold the arm.

And aim it in the direction he wanted.

The lammasu had ripped apart one of the machines flanking the idol. Oily chemicals spilled from the ruptured machine, spilling across the beast. Wulfrik could see the dwarf sorcerer crawling through the mess. Thrown at last from the raging monster's back, the sorcerer was frantically trying to get to safety, dragging his legs behind him as though they were lumps of granite. Wulfrik grinned to see the dwarf's panic.

Snarling, Wulfrik seized Khorakk's hand and forced the gauntlet to close into a fist. He could feel the thegn's fingers break as one by one he made them close. When the hand tightened into a fist, a stream of fire would shoot from the pipe fitted to the dwarf's forearm.

'Get clear of the idol!' Wulfrik shouted to his men. Haukr and Tjorvi saw the reason for their captain's warning. Hastily they pulled the stunned Njarvord back with them. On the ground, the sorcerer uttered a desperate wail of fright, pawing at the platform in a frantic effort to clear the pool of chemicals.

At his shout, the lammasu swung around towards him. Its face was similar enough to that of a dwarf for Wulfrik to enjoy the expression of horror it wore. The dragon-like wings snapped open, but Haukr's axe had ended any hope the lammasu had of flying away.

'Burn!' Wulfrik growled as he made Khorakk's broken hand tighten into a fist.

The flame shot across the platform, washing over the lammasu and igniting the pool of chemicals it was standing in. The monster shrieked, the entire dais shaking as its huge body writhed in agony. Its legs were columns of fire, patches of its black hide burning like hot coals where the chemicals had splashed across it. The beast's sorcerous breath did nothing to quench the fires consuming it. Screaming in pain, the lammasu bolted across the platform, making one last pathetic effort to take wing as it hurtled over the side.

The lammasu's screams were soon echoed by its master. The dwarf sorcerer had crawled through the chemicals, and as he retreated he'd left a trail behind him like some giant slug. The same fire that consumed the monster raced along the trail of chemicals to find the crawling sorcerer. He flailed like a living torch as the flames licked at his robes and scorched his flesh. He was still screaming when Njarvord walked over to him and crushed the dwarf's throat with his boot.

DAWN WAS GLOWING in the east, illuminating the desolation around Dronangkul. From the roof of the ziggurat, Wulfrik could see across the desert for hundreds of leagues. He fancied he could even see the black ribbon of the River Ruin somewhere to the south, though it was impossible to see the *Seafang* from such a distance.

The champion fingered the ruby torc he had ripped from Khorakk's neck. It felt like no other treasure he had even stolen. Was that because he sensed its power, or was it because he knew what it could do?

Zarnath was dead, the dwarf sorcerer and his beast

would have seen to that. But there had to be others who knew what the shaman had known! Among all the witches and sorcerers of the north, there had to be one who could unlock the power within the Smile of Sardiss.

Wulfrik would find the warlock who knew that secret. Then he would be free to wed Hjordis and become king of all the Sarls. His sons would be greater still, lords of all Norsca! So mighty even the gods would tremble at their deeds!

A black splotch upon the grey strip that marked the road to Dronangkul snapped Wulfrik from his dreams of the future. Somehow the plight of the dwarf outpost had become known. At such a distance, the splotch looked like so many swarming ants, but the northman knew it for what it was: an army. Even if they could keep the dwarfs trapped down below the causeway and track down those still lurking inside the ziggurat, they could never hold against such a force.

Nor did Wulfrik have any desire to. His men might have liked time to plunder the outpost, but he had what he'd come for. All that was left was to climb down and collect Sigvatr and his men from the lower gate.

That, and one other thing.

Wulfrik turned back to the platform. Khorakk's armour lay strewn across the roof of the ziggurat. It had taken some effort to pry the ugly dwarf from his shell. His curses had been such that Wulfrik had finally gagged the venomous overlord. Now he dangled from the shackles fitted into the belly of the idol.

Wulfrik didn't know how the remaining machine worked. Somehow the dwarf priests must have used it to heat the idol and roast the offerings trapped in its belly. He had, however, seen how readily the pungent chemical took to fire. Walking over to the machine, the hero nodded to his men. As one, the surviving warriors brought their axes chopping down into the nozzles. The released chemical sprayed across the idol. Khorakk struggled frantically in his bindings as the liquid splashed across him, his screams muffled by his gag.

Fangs gleamed in the growing dawn as Wulfrik smiled at the thegn. Grimly, he planted the point of his sword against the stone base of the dais.

'I wonder if you'll give Hashut indigestion,' Wulfrik said, scraping his sword across the stone, sending sparks flying into the puddles of chemical splashed about the idol.

Chapter Nine

WULFRIK AND HIS warriors hurried down from the ziggurat's roof. From their vantage point, they could see that the gate at the causeway had been breached. Sigvatr and his men had held the dwarfs back for some hours, but now the vengeful creatures and their hobgoblin minions marched back into the upper reaches of the outpost, scouring every shadow for some sign of the invaders.

The champion watched the progress of the monsters with a sickened heart. He hoped that Sigvatr had abandoned the gate before his retreat was cut off. Wulfrik felt a stab of pain as he thought about the old reaver. Sigvatr was his closest friend and confidant, a sword-brother who had fought by his side long before the Battle of a Thousand Skulls. After all they had been through, he had come to think of the elder warrior as being indestructible, a man who could not be killed. Watching the dwarfs reclaim their outpost, for the first time Wulfrik felt fear for his friend.

'They've cut us off,' Haukr spat, glaring at the

armoured dwarfs forming into ranks before the stronghold's shattered main gate.

'No need to go so far for a fight,' Tjorvi snarled. He pointed the blade of his axe at the dark figures closing around the bridge below. The immortals looked battered after being on the receiving end of Zarnath's sorcery, but none of the men staring down at them could doubt the dwarfs were still ready for a fight.

Wulfrik grunted as he considered the dwarf warriors. 'They're hungry for revenge, not battle,' he decided. 'Otherwise they'd be climbing up here to get us right now. They'll wait for the other dwarfs to join them, then swarm over us in numbers.' The champion's teeth gleamed in a cunning smile. 'We have some time yet.'

'Time for what?' objected Tjorvi. 'To let our ancestors know we're coming?'

The champion glowered at the Graeling, his intense gaze bringing fear onto Tjorvi's face. Wulfrik waited until he saw the last flicker of challenge wither inside the warrior. Tjorvi was new, his first voyage with the *Seafang*. Wulfrik did not begrudge a man his mistakes, so long as he learned from them. Next time Tjorvi tried to panic his crew, Wulfrik would gut him like a fish.

Wulfrik turned away from his cowed follower. He circled around the roof of the ziggurat, walking past the smouldering idol. He paused beside one of the winches. Without hesitation, he brought the edge of his sword crashing down into the heavy chain. A second blow and the dais began to sag in one corner. A third strike of his sword and the chain was broken.

Wulfrik sheathed his blade and grabbed the severed end of the chain. Bracing his feet, he tugged violently at it, studying how securely it was fastened to the roof. A wide grin was on his face when he turned back to his men.

'Let the dwarfs wait for us at the gate,' he told the marauders. 'Let their beards go grey and their axes turn to rust.' Wulfrik wrapped a length of chain around his arm and stalked towards the edge of the ziggurat. Understanding dawned on the faces of his warriors when he threw the heavy chain over the side. Instantly the chain still fixed to the winch began to unspool, following the line as it fell. Faster and faster the chain unwound, hurtling to the ground far below.

Ground on the outside of Dronangkul's walls.

When the chain grew taut, Wulfrik again tested the strength of its moorings. The dwarfs of the Dark Lands built just as sturdily as their kin in Norsca and the Worlds Edge Mountains. The chain held, resisting Wulfrik's savage efforts to pull it free. The northman nodded in satisfaction.

'While they watch the front, we slip out the back,' Wulfrik told his men. He laughed when he noted the disappointment on Njarvord's face. 'It is a long hike back to the *Seafang*,' he warned. 'You may yet get your chance for a fight. But at least it will be a fight on our terms, not the dwarfs'.'

Grimly, Wulfrik seized the chain and began to rappel down the sheer side of the ziggurat. For men accustomed to climbing the craggy sides of Norscan mountains with their bare hands, the descent was absurdly easy. Having observed the outpost from afar, they knew the impossibility of anyone within the stronghold being able to observe what transpired atop the ziggurat. The dwarfs would learn of their escape only when they climbed to the top of their temple to look for themselves.

By that time, Wulfrik hoped, they would be far away. There was something greater than a glorious death in battle driving him now. With Khorakk's torc in his possession, he felt for the first time there was a real chance to escape the curse the gods had laid upon him. Even without Zarnath's knowledge, he was certain the torc was the key to his release.

Then he would claim Hjordis's hand and her father's place as king of the Sarls.

THE MARAUDERS QUICKLY left Dronangkul behind them, making for the base of the cliffs overlooking the outpost. It had been agreed before the assault on the stronghold that those who survived the attack would regroup beneath the cliffs before making the long trek back to the River Ruin. Flush with their escape from the ziggurat, the spirits of the northmen fell when they did not see any of their comrades waiting for them. Again, Wulfrik's mind turned to the dark possibility that Sigvatr had fallen trying to hold the causeway. The champion regretted not leaving his old friend behind to guard the Seafang. A bitter smile flashed across his face as he imagined how violently Sigvatr would have protested being left behind.

'We had almost given you up for dead,' Broendulf's voice suddenly called out. Wulfrik and his men looked up to see the Sarl emerge from hiding, his blade at the ready. Arngeirr limped out from behind another boulder, his kraken-sword dark with greenskin blood. Standing atop one of the rocks, Jokull had his bow at the ready.

Wulfrik nodded respectfully to the warriors he had sent into the pit to free the slaves. 'The ancestors will drink to your valour,' he told them. 'The diversion worked. You drew most of the dwarfs down into the mines to subdue their slaves.'

Broendulf chuckled and ran a thumb along his cheek. 'I'd rather drink to our valour myself! My ancestors can find their own ale!' The huscarl's expression grew serious, his eyes studying his captain before continuing. 'Your quest was successful?' he asked at last.

Wulfrik drew the ruby torc from his belt, holding it up high for his men to see. The marauders licked their lips like hungry dogs, sight of the necklace exciting their natural greed. Such a necklace would bring a small fortune to the man who brought it back to Ormskaro's traders. Thoughts of wealth quickly faded as the northmen remembered who it was that had laid claim upon the torc, and why.

Jokull was the first to recover from the fascinating gleam of the necklace. 'Now Zarnath can break your curse?'

Angrily, Wulfrik shoved the torc back beneath his belt. 'The Kurgan fell,' he said. 'His magic wasn't equal to that of the dwarfs.'

'Then this has all been for nothing?' Arngeirr snarled, swaying uneasily on his bone leg.

'I'll find another warlock!' Wulfrik snapped. 'Kharnath's blood! Witches are thick as lice in the Wastes! One of them will know what Zarnath knew!' He slapped a fist against the pouch containing the torc. 'Getting this is the key. Somebody will know the door it fits.'

The marauders were silent, waiting while their captain's anger abated. They had their own ideas about how easy it would be to replace Zarnath, but each valued his own life too much to express those doubts to Wulfrik. Like a wolf with a bone, the hero was clinging to the hope the shaman had given him. None of the northmen wanted to lose a hand trying to take that hope away from him.

Wulfrik suddenly stared intently at the rocks behind Broendulf. The champion's hand fell to his sword, his eyes narrowing with suspicion. 'Who's back there?' he growled at Broendulf.

The huscarl stepped aside, allowing Wulfrik a better view of the cliff. 'Sigvatr and some of the men,' he said with a shrug. He caught Wulfrik's arm as the champion rushed forwards. 'Sigvatr was wounded,' Broendulf warned. 'Badly.'

Wulfrik pulled away from the huscarl. Rounding the pile of boulders he found two of the warriors he had left at the causeway kneeling beside Sigvatr. The old war-chief was sprawled on the ground, a rock under his head. His armour had been stripped away, one side of his neck swaddled in a crude compress of wool and leather. Sigvatr's breath came in ragged gasps, a crimson trickle oozing from beneath the bandage.

Quickly, Wulfrik was beside his old friend. He winced in sympathy as he saw Sigvatr's pained eyes, the grimace of agony that twisted his face. 'How did this happen?' the hero demanded.

The two marauders tending Sigvatr looked nervously at each other. 'We don't know,' the braver of them answered. 'One moment we were all holding the dwarfs at the gate, with Sigvatr bellowing orders at us. Then we heard him cry out. When we turned away from the gate, we found him lying slumped against the wall.'

'We... we brought... him out... as quick...' the other marauder stammered, fear filling his eyes.

Wulfrik turned in disgust before the warrior could finish explaining. Leaning over Sigvatr, he reached for the bandage over his friend's neck. He would see for himself what had brought down his war-chief.

Sigvatr's hand closed about Wulfrik's own, trying to pull his reaching fingers away. His clutch was as feeble as a newborn's, trembling with effort. There was a desperate, pleading quality in the dying man's eyes.

Gingerly, with such softness as he could manage, Wulfrik pulled Sigvatr's hand away. Again he reached for the compress, pulling it back by the corner. The champion's face became pale as he gazed upon the hideous wound beneath the bandage. He had expected the gory work of axe or blunderbuss; what he had not been ready for was the gruesome sight he had actually found. Sigvatr's neck had been bitten through by some fanged fiend, a great gouge torn from his body by vicious teeth. He could see vertebrae poking from the wet, dripping meat, a filthy blue venom mingling with the dark arterial blood gushing from the savaged veins. Horrified, Wulfrik pressed the bandage tight again.

Tears fought their way into his eyes as Wulfrik regarded his dying friend. He struggled to keep them from falling. He didn't want Sigvatr's last memory of him to be one of weakness.

'Wulf,' Sigvatr whispered, his voice a moist croak. 'Did... did...'

'Yes,' Wulfrik answered, displaying the torc for his friend. 'I took it from the dwarf and burned him in his own oven! They'll not soon forget us here!'

Sigvatr tried to shake his head. His eyes pinched closed in pain. 'No... No... Don't... forget! Mustn't!'

'They won't,' Wulfrik promised. 'Wherever they sing the saga of Wulfrik, the name of Sigvatr will also be known!'

Gritting his teeth, blood streaming across his shoulder, Sigvatr struggled to rise. 'Traitor!' he croaked. 'Mustn't... Agnarr... knew. Can't... cheat...' The old warrior's body stiffened and he slumped against the ground again. Wulfrik leaned close as words bubbled up from Sigvatr's lips. 'Beware... traitor...'

Wulfrik laid his hand on Sigvatr's dead face, shutting the pained eyes gazing blindly at him. In death, there was still an air of agony about his friend's expression. Wulfrik felt a fury such as he had never known blaze up inside him. When he rose from Sigvatr's side, his face was pulled back in a snarl, fangs gleaming.

'He spoke of traitors,' Wulfrik growled, glaring at

the warriors who had brought Sigvatr from the stronghold. 'How can it be that my friend lies here dead while you two live? How can it be that he was struck down and you did nothing to defend him?' The champion paced after the marauders as they retreated before him. 'He was standing near enough for you to hear his cry, yet you did not see what did that to him?'

The two marauders retreated before the menacing approach of their captain. Around them, Broendulf and the others drew their weapons, cutting off any chance of escape.

The warriors' protests of innocence fell on unheeding ears. A sword was in each of Wulfrik's hands when he closed upon them. 'I will not consign Sigvatr's body to the flame without dogs to lay at his feet,' the champion hissed. 'Even if they be cowards and curs!'

One of the marauders rounded upon Wulfrik, charging madly at him with a heavy flail. In a single fluid motion, Wulfrik caught the steel chains of the marauder's weapon upon his left sword. As the warrior reflexively tried to pull his weapon free, Wulfrik plunged his other sword into the man's side, burying the blade to the hilt in his ribs. The stricken northman collapsed, his body quivering as life fled through his wound.

The surviving marauder screamed in terror, throwing down his axe, making a display of his empty hands. There was no mercy in the gaze Wulfrik fixed upon him. Sobbing in fear, the man turned, tried to break through the cordon established by the other

Norscans. Pitilessly, Njarvord kicked the marauder in the stomach. Haukr grabbed the man by the hair, throwing him back towards Wulfrik.

'Pick up a weapon,' the champion snarled at the marauder. The man stared at his axe lying on the bloodied ground, then shook his head in protest, trying again to retreat from the enraged Wulfrik.

'Coward,' Wulfrik spat in disgust. He tossed his swords away, disarming himself. He waved at the retreating marauder, beckoning him to attack. Again the warrior eyed his axe lying on the ground, then at his captain's empty hands.

Shouting a ragged war cry, the marauder sprang forwards, ripping his axe from the earth. Furiously he brought the blade chopping down, seeking to bury it in Wulfrik's chest. Contemptuously, Wulfrik sidestepped the attack, his powerful hands locking about the marauder's arm. The champion's grip tightened, then he wrenched the marauder's arm around, breaking it at the elbow.

The surge of pain stunned the marauder. He tried to pull himself free of Wulfrik's clutch, but the vengeful champion would not be denied. Baring his fangs, the fierce hero grappled with the crippled warrior. Clawing fingers sought the marauder's face, gouging deep into his eye sockets, blood streaming down the man's tortured visage. Wulfrik shifted his grip, seizing the sides of the man's head. A single brutal twist and the marauder's neck snapped. Wulfrik pushed the coward's corpse away with revulsion.

'Put those curs at Sigvatr's feet and find something to burn,' Wulfrik told his men.

'Is that smart?' Broendulf asked. 'The dwarfs will see the smoke.'

Wulfrik glared at the huscarl. 'Sigvatr will be paid the honours due to him if it brings every dwarf and goblin in this damned land upon our heads!' The champion clenched his fist beneath the fair-faced Sarl's chin. 'I'm sure he won't mind three dogs at his feet.'

Broendulf blanched at the hero's threat. He had seen his captain take reckless chances before, but always from pride or ambition. He had never seen Wulfrik acting from grief before, never seen such blind fury take hold of the champion. It was something that chilled the huscarl's bones.

Keeping their misgivings to themselves, the Norscans began gathering dead brush from the base of the cliff to fashion a bier for Sigvatr's pyre.

THE POLLUTED BANKS of the River Ruin stretched before the weary eyes of the northmen. It had taken them days to recross the desert, hiding from the biggest of the hobgoblin patrols, fighting the smaller ones in order to steal the water and provisions they carried. Not a man among them did not bear some scar from their ordeal. They had dared the Dark Land to destroy them and it very nearly had.

Now, as they saw the foul river and the lonely ship anchored in its filthy morass, a thrill of triumph swept through the men. They had braved a deadly and hostile land, fought horrific foes, overcome overwhelming odds and emerged victorious. Great battles and worthy deeds to thrill the hearts of their kinsmen, to fill the songs of the skalds. Glory to honour their ancestors and earn the esteem of the gods themselves. The men who sailed upon the *Seafang* paid in blood and suffering for the right to be called heroes, but they knew nothing of worth came easy. As they marched towards the river, their minds turned to the welcome they would receive when they returned to Ormskaro, the feasts that would be held in their honour, the gifts King Viglundr and his jarls would bestow upon them, the lithe maidens eager to invite them into their bowers.

Around him, Wulfrik's warriors laughed and boasted about what they would do when they returned to Norsca. Their captain did not share in their talk, his mind turned to a scorched patch of desert just beyond the walls of Dronangkul and the blackened bones he had left behind. The dwarfs, it turned out, had not investigated the smoke from Sigvatr's pyre. Crafty and underhand, the dwarfs had stayed behind their walls, suspecting some subterfuge. They were content to wait for the reinforcements marching towards the stronghold before investigating the fire. Wulfrik had bet the dwarfs would display such caution when he ordered Sigvatr's pyre lit.

Though gamble or not, Wulfrik would not have done differently. He would not have left Sigvatr's body behind to be picked over by the hobgoblins and scavenged by their wolves. Death and damnation would have claimed him before he allowed such a miserable end for his friend's bones.

Bitterly, Wulfrik swatted the skull of King Torgald

tied to the hilt of his sword. If he had never made his drunken boasts after killing the king none of this would have come to pass. He would already be wed to Hjordis. He would be a great chief of the Sarls, ready to claim Viglundr's throne when the king passed. And Sigvatr would still be alive.

Shouts of greeting sounded from the ship as Wulfrik and his surviving warriors drew near. Kaetill leapt down from the deck of the ship, sloshing through the polluted shallows to greet his captain.

'Gods be praised!' Kaetill yelled as he drew near the warriors. 'We thought you were all dead!'

'Others have made that mistake before,' Wulfrik growled, stalking past Kaetill. He nodded towards the ship. 'Is she ready to sail?'

Kaetill hurried after his captain. 'Yes, we've kept her ready since you left. After the tales Stefnir told about the fire dwarfs, we wanted to be ready to leave in a hurry.' He turned his eyes away and hung his head in shame. 'We were going to follow the river south. It's supposed to empty into some sort of sea down there.'

'It is well for you that you had spine enough to stay,' Wulfrik said. 'No man steals my ship and brags about it later.'

'We thought you were dead,' Kaetill insisted, his voice turning defensive. He glanced about at the haggard warriors marching behind Wulfrik. 'Aren't we going to wait for the rest?'

'There's no one else coming,' Broendulf told him. 'Victory doesn't come cheap,' he added when he saw the shock on Kaetill's face.

Wulfrik suddenly stopped on the bank of the river,

staring up at the *Seafang*. Spinning around, he seized Kaetill by the throat. 'Who told you we were dead?' he demanded.

Kaetill's trembling hand pointed back at the ship, his finger indicating the same figure Wulfrik had focussed on. 'The... the shaman...'

Snarling, Wulfrik pushed Kaetill away. Lunging into the water, he trudged through the filth until he reached the *Seafang*. His fist tightened around the rim of a shield fastened to the hull, using it to lift himself out of the polluted river and onto the deck of his ship. Like his namesake, Wulfrik pounced upon the deck, fangs bared. Steel rasped against leather as he drew his swords. The Norscan crew backed away from their furious captain. Wulfrik didn't even glance at them, his burning gaze fixed upon the short, white-bearded Kurgan standing beneath the mast.

'Make peace with your gods, kin-eater,' Wulfrik snarled at Zarnath.

The shaman raised his hand in a placating gesture, his face betraying no sign of alarm. 'You survived,' he said, surprise in his voice. 'Few men could have.'

'Few men did,' Wulfrik spat, stalking towards the Kurgan. 'Now you'll join the others.'

Zarnath took a step back. The shaman pulled back his horsehair cape, displaying the charred wreck of his arm. 'There was nothing to be gained by my staying. The dwarf sorcerer and his beast were too powerful for me. Tell me, would my death have helped you in any way?'

'It will make me feel a lot better,' Wulfrik said.

Worry appeared for the first time in the shaman's

eyes, spoiling the affected serenity of his face. He continued to back away from the vengeful champion. 'You have captured the Smile of Sardiss,' he said. 'I can sense that the torc is in your possession. Now I can begin the ritual that will free you of your curse.'

'No thanks. I can find another warlock to help me.'

A cold smile stretched across Zarnath's face. The shaman stopped retreating from Wulfrik's approach. 'How long do you think that will take, great slayer? Five years? Ten? Will the gods wait while you try to cheat them, or will they demand further offerings? Perhaps so many that you will never have a chance to hunt for a sorcerer with the wisdom to help you.'

Doubt wormed through Wulfrik's mind. The champion lowered his swords as indecision took hold of him. His thirst for revenge withered before the possibility that Zarnath was right. The shaman's next words crushed the last embers of Wulfrik's fury.

'How long will Hjordis wait for you?'

Angrily, Wulfrik slammed his swords back into their sheaths. His fists clenched in impotent rage. 'I'll give you another chance, horse-cutter,' Wulfrik hissed through clenched teeth. 'But if you abandon me in battle again, I'll feed your flesh to the eels.'

Zarnath's expression was again serene, a mocking gleam in the blue fires of his eyes. 'Of course,' the shaman said. 'I would be a fool to play false with the great Wulfrik.' He extended one of his withered hands towards the fuming hero.

Wulfrik shook his head, a cruel laugh whispering

past his fangs. 'I'll keep the torc with me, Kurgan,' he said. 'It'll make me feel better that way.'

Zarnath shrugged, backing away from the champion. He shifted his attention to the side of the ship, watching as Broendulf and the others clambered over the side. 'I imagine we will be returning to Ormskaro,' he said. 'Preferably before the dwarfs come down on us for their own revenge.' The shaman nodded at the desert sky. Far in the distance a great shape could be seen hovering, circling over the trail Wulfrik and his men had left behind. To his men, it was just an indistinct blur, but to Wulfrik's keen gaze, the shape resembled a monstrous winged bull, a metallic gleam shining from its back. It didn't take Zarnath to tell him the gleam was from the armour of a rider, nor that the winged bull was another of the dwarf's sinister creatures.

'To oars!' Wulfrik bellowed at his men. He drew a knife from his belt, sliding the blade across his palm. 'We sail for home!' he shouted as he strode towards the figurehead, blood dripping from his clenched fist.

Chapter Ten

THE REALM BETWEEN worlds slowly faded away, the ethereal fog surrounding the *Seafang* vanishing as the longship returned to the world of men. The grey, overcast skies of Norsca were a reassuring sight to the northmen after the fiery skies of the Dark Lands. Many of the men rushed to the sides of the ship, dipping their helms into the cold waters of the fjord, cleansing the muck from the River Ruin from their bodies.

Wulfrik stood at the prow of his ship, his hand resting upon the scaly forehead of the wooden dragon, the jewelled torc clenched in his other fist. He had risked much and lost much to secure the relic. The pain of losing Sigvatr was a scar that would be a long time in healing. He was determined that his friend's sacrifice would not be in vain.

Gazing out across the icy waters of the fjord, Wulfrik could see the streets of Ormskaro climbing up the slope. He noted with perplexity the snow covering the roofs, the boats pulled up along the shore. He had experienced the hazards of voyaging into the border-realm before, never certain where or when the *Seafang* would return to the world of mortals.

The only constant was Ormskaro. Always he could lead the ship back to the one place he might call home. Sigvatr had once told him that the heart was a better compass to a man's needs than his mind. Wulfrik felt the old warrior had been right. His love for Hjordis was stronger than the malicious trickery of the border-realm. It was a beacon that guided the *Seafang* unerringly through the daemon seas, bringing her safely home again.

Hjordis! How long had he been away? How much time had the border-realm stolen from him on this voyage? Was it only weeks they had been gone? Months? Years?

Wulfrik shuddered at the possibility. Viglundr would not have been idle in his absence. The king sought alliance with the Aeslings. Without the threat of Wulfrik's fury to restrain him, Viglundr would have already married Hjordis off to the Aesling prince Sveinbjorn. Every day he was away from Norsca would have emboldened Viglundr, made the king wonder if the troublesome hero would ever return.

His fist tightened about the relic he held, the rubies digging into his fingers. He would not be cheated by the scheming old king! It was for Hjordis he had led the Sarls into battle against Torgald and brought down upon himself the curse of the gods! It was for Hjordis he had followed Zarnath's lead and made the journey into the Dark Lands! It was for Hjordis he had led Sigvatr to his death! King or no,

Viglundr would suffer if he tried to cheat him now!

Wulfrik's nostrils flared as a rich, savoury smell was blown across the *Seafang's* decks. It was the smell of roasting steer, the scent of boiling seal, the aroma of cooked mutton. There was a sound borne upon the wind, the distant bellow of horns, the clamour of drums.

'There are banners flying from the tower!' Jokull called down from his perch atop the *Seafang's* mast. 'I see the standards of Aeslings!'

The news brought a murmur of alarm among the crew. Their thoughts were of invasion and conquest. Wulfrik, however, knew better. 'Do they fly alone, or with the banners of the Sarls?' He felt pain flare through his heart when Jokull told him the flags of the Sarls were displayed beside those of the Aeslings. He glared at the distant slopes of the fjord, cursing Viglundr under his breath. Turning his back on Ormskaro, he marched along the ship's deck, barking orders to his crew, commanding them to make ready the storm sails.

Wulfrik strode to where Zarnath sat with his back against the oaken kerling supporting the ship's mast. The shaman looked up when he sensed the champion staring down at him. As soon as he did so, Wulfrik grabbed him by the front of his tunic, lifting him to his feet.

'Whistle me up a wind with your magic, Kurgan,' the champion growled. Zarnath tried to pull free of his clutch but Wulfrik only tightened his grip. 'Wind, witch-man!' he snarled. 'Speed this ship back to Ormskaro or the eels feed well this night!'

Submissively, Zarnath nodded his head. He could feel the rage in Wulfrik's grip, hear the fury in his voice, see the barely restrained violence in his eyes. No words would be enough to reason with the man. To even try would be to risk a sudden and brutal death.

The shaman walked to the stern of the ship, facing towards the mast where the northmen made fast the sturdy woollen storm sail. He could feel Wulfrik's impatient eyes upon him. Zarnath shuddered under his horsehair cape. It was an effort to focus his thoughts upon his magic, even more of an effort to wait until the crew had secured the sail.

Zarnath's arms spread wide, blue fire flaring from his eyes. Thunder rumbled through the darkened clouds, lightning flashed about the distant mountains. An icy shower rained down upon the *Seafang's* decks. The shaman drew a deep breath, sucking the frigid air into his lungs. Those watching him thought his body must burst from the air being drawn into it, yet still the shaman persisted.

At last, Zarnath released the breath he had taken, expelling it in a gagging cough. As he did so, a great gale rushed down upon the longship. The storm sail snapped in the sudden wind, propelling the *Seafang* across the fjord like a loosened arrow. Some of the marauders clung to their benches, hiding their faces in fear. Others shouted and laughed, revelling in the speed of their vessel.

Wulfrik neither hid nor laughed. Standing again in the bow of the ship, his hand upon the dragon's brow, the hero's eyes fixed upon the stone tower rising above Ormskaro.

* * *

THE GREAT HALL of Ormfell was filled with the laughter of a celebratory throng. Skalds played upon their whale-bone harps, singing of the great deeds of Ormnir and the kings of the Aeslings. Freeholders feasted upon platters of steaming meat borne through the hall by southling thralls. Drunken jarls shouted bold boasts about their great deeds, testing their strength against one another by splintering wooden shields with their fists.

Seated within the carved jaws of Shipcracker, King Viglundr nuzzled the neck of a semi-clad Graeling thrall, his body shaking with a lewd chuckle as he spilled Bretonnian wine across her breast. The Sarl king glanced aside at the ivory seat set beside his throne, scowling as he noted the miserable face his daughter wore. 'This feast is to celebrate your betrothal,' Viglundr told her. 'Try to enjoy yourself.'

Hjordis glared back at her father. 'I enjoyed myself the last time I was betrothed. You remember, Father, when you promised me to Wulfrik. He brought you the head of that animal Torgald...'

Viglundr dashed his drinking horn to the floor, kicking the slave-girl from his knee. 'You'll not speak of that again!' the king warned, wagging his finger at the princess. 'We have more to gain with the Aeslings as our friends than we ever could with them as enemies.'

'You have more to gain,' Hjordis said acidly. 'What do I gain? A husband I do not love, a scheming coward who lets others do his fighting for him?' Her pretty face pulled back in a sneer. She turned her head and looked across the hall to where Sveinbjorn and his retainers were huddled around a wicker cage, wagering on the outcome of a fight between weasel and fox. The groom's arm was wrapped about the waist of a buxom thrall, ignorant of the mead spilling from his drinking horn. 'I can see why you favour him. You have so much in common.'

The king's fingers seized Hjordis's chin, digging cruelly into her soft skin, bending her neck back. Viglundr's mouth curled in a sneer. 'It is enough that I *do* favour Sveinbjorn!' he hissed. 'I am your king and you will obey me! I've indulged your insolence long enough. You will marry Sveinbjorn and cement my alliance with the Aeslings.'

Hjordis struggled free of her father's clutch. 'You would not dare this if Wulfrik were here,' she hissed, fury in her eyes.

Viglundr leaned back and smiled condescendingly at his daughter. 'He's dead,' the king declared, his voice devoid of sympathy. 'Dead and rotting in whatever hell that Kurgan led him into.' He snapped his fingers, waving a thrall to bring him more wine. 'For six turns of the moons there has been no sign of him or his ship.' Viglundr's smile grew more genuine as he took a silver-capped horn from the slave. Tilting his head, he took a long swallow of wine. 'Dead,' he repeated, wiping the spillage from around his mouth with the sleeve of his tunic. 'Like all those who try to defy their gods and their kings!'

Beside him, Hjordis bowed her head, hiding her face as tears welled up in her eyes. For an instant, the king smiled, feeling a sense of satisfaction that he had finally broken the headstrong will of an unruly subject. The smile quickly faded as the concerned father stepped down from his throne and placed his arms around his sobbing daughter.

'I want what is best for you and our people,' Viglundr told her. 'You must forget him. He isn't coming back. In time you will warm to Sveinbjorn. He is a great chief among the Aeslings and will give you many fine sons.' The king's rough hands wiped away the tears on Hjordis's cheeks. 'In time you will forget about that vagabond reaver Wulfrik,' he said, his voice soft with compassion.

Loud shouts sounded from the entrance of the hall. Viglundr turned to see what the commotion was, promising dire punishments for whichever drunken oafs had started the row. He began to shout for his bondsmen to break up the fight, then noticed that it was his guards at the heart of the disturbance. The king stared in shock as one of his warriors staggered back, his forehead split open. A second crashed to the floor, bleeding from a deep gash in his side.

Colour drained from Viglundr's face when he saw a furious figure stride past the battered guards. The armoured apparition's eyes scoured the hall with an ire that would have frightened a dragon. Laughter and song died as the revellers became aware of the invader. Horrified gasps rippled around the room as the people of Ormskaro recognised a man their king told them was dead.

The man returned his bloodied sword to its sheath. Angrily he reached over his head, seizing the garland of holly fastened to the archway above the door.

With a savage jerk he ripped the garland and the iron nail fastening it from the stone. Contemptuously he threw it to the floor and crushed it beneath his feet as he marched past the stunned celebrants.

'Wulfrik!' Hjordis cried. Springing to her feet, she pulled away from her father and raced across the now-silent hall. She flung herself into the arms of the returned hero, pressing her lips against his.

The champion forgot his anger for the moment, crushing his love against his chest, returning her kisses with unrestrained passion.

'That is my bride you hold,' a voice snarled.

Wulfrik released Hjordis, turning towards the speaker. His lips pulled back in a feral snarl as for the first time he noticed Sveinbjorn. 'Your bride?' the champion growled. He pushed Hjordis behind him and raised his blood-stained sword. His eyes shifted from the Aesling prince, watching as Sveinbjorn's hersirs began to draw axes from their belts, fanning out across the hall to surround Wulfrik. 'You are a fool if you think to steal from me, born-of-pigs!' the champion spat. He fixed each of the prowling hersirs with his smouldering gaze. 'And I'll send these other fools to attend you in hell if they are idiot enough to stand beside you!'

The Aesling hersirs snarled in anger as they heard Wulfrik's mocking contempt for them. Glaring at the hero, the lordlings spread across the hall, their attention riveted on the defiant hero. Sveinbjorn smirked as he watched his men surround Wulfrik.

'The princess is mine, god-cursed vagabond!' Sveinbjorn shouted. Slowly he drew his own axe from his belt. 'You will beg me for mercy before I finish with you.'

A loud clamour at the entrance of the great hall made Sveinbjorn glance away from Wulfrik. A nervous twinge came to the Aesling's lip when he saw Broendulf standing in the entrance, banging his sword against the boss of a shield. Behind the huscarl was the rest of the *Seafang's* crew, weapons clenched in their fists. Sveinbjorn's hersirs were taken by surprise, muttering anxiously among themselves as they moved away from Wulfrik and slunk back to their prince's side.

'No stomach for a fair fight?' Wulfrik scoffed, watching as the Aeslings retreated from the advance of his own men. Sveinbjorn's bravado faltered as Wulfrik took a step towards him. 'Let's see how much stomach you have,' the hero said, pointing his blade at the prince.

'Enough!' Viglundr's outraged roar echoed through the hall. 'Sveinbjorn is a guest of this court! You will answer if any hurt is done him!'

'Calm yourself, old man,' Wulfrik advised the fuming king. 'I've won one war for you. I can win another just as easily.'

Sveinbjorn backed away as the champion continued to advance. 'I will not cross steel with a common scoundrel,' the prince declared.

'Then I'll butcher you like the swine you are,' Wulfrik grinned. 'It makes no difference to me.'

Viglundr stormed down from his throne, his face crimson with rage. The king shook his fists at Wulfrik. 'I said Sveinbjorn is my guest! You will not touch him!'

Wulfrik snarled at the king. 'Do not think I'll forgive your part in this treachery, dog-licker,' the champion hissed. 'When I am finished with Sveinbjorn…' The hero's words died on his lips as he felt soft fingers close over his own. When he looked into Hjordis's eyes, he could see the entreaty written there. Whatever else he was, whatever he had tried to do, Viglundr was still her father.

Slamming his sword back into its sheath, Wulfrik took Hjordis by the hand and led her from the hall. 'Thank your daughter you still breathe, old man,' he told Viglundr as he stalked away. 'I suggest you bid your guests farewell. If I see an Aesling on the morrow, I'll strike him down, be he swineherd or swine-born.'

CARING NOTHING FOR the displeasure of the king or his court, Wulfrik carried Hjordis back to her chambers. His blood afire from the treachery of Viglundr, it was long into the night before fatigue quieted his passion and he sank down upon the bearskin blanket. Weariness gripped his body, but sleep refused to come to him. His mind dwelled upon the way Viglundr had tried to cheat him. Despite Hjordis, Wulfrik knew the king must pay for his trickery. Once the curse was lifted from him, once Hjordis was his, he would give the king a choice: renounce the crown or try to keep it. He hoped the old man would be stupid enough to try.

Wulfrik flinched as fingers brushed against his cheek, running through his thick beard. He rolled onto his side, staring into the bright eyes of his beloved. His callused hand smoothed her tousled hair away from her face.

'You've been gone a long time,' Hjordis whispered.

The man beside her laughed. 'Peace, woman. I need my strength. I may yet have to kill your betrothed tomorrow.'

The comment brought worry creeping onto the princess's face. Her hand fell against Wulfrik's chest, pressing against his heart. 'You... you wouldn't really have...'

The hero's eyes grew hard. 'Viglundr tried to keep you from me,' he said. 'I'd kill anyone who dared try to come between us, be they king or devil.' His fingers stroked the lobe of Hjordis's tiny ear. 'I have fame and glory enough for a hundred heroes, riches that would make a dragon content, but there's only one thing in this world I want.'

Hjordis drew away, leaning back among the pillows. 'You were gone so very long,' she repeated. 'Every day when you were away, my father pressed me to marry Sveinbjorn. At first he tried to reason with me, then he tried to bribe me, then he pleaded. Finally he threatened. Every day he told me you would never be back, that the gods had taken their revenge. I tried to dismiss his words, tried to keep hope alive. But every day it died a little more inside me. Every day my father's words crept a little closer to my heart...'

'He'll pay,' Wulfrik promised.

'He is still my father,' Hjordis reminded him, fear in her voice.

'And that is the only reason he is still alive,' Wulfrik

said. The warrior shook his head. 'I know too well what it is to cling to hope when all others tell you there is none. It is a pain that cuts deeper than any sword, a wound that never heals.' He smiled reassuringly at Hjordis. 'Until that day when all the naysayers are proven wrong, when the hope you have held so long finally bears fruit.'

The northman rolled across the bed, rummaging through the pile of cast-off armour lying heaped upon the floor. From the heap he lifted the jewelled torc, holding it out so that Hjordis could see the shimmer of the chained rubies.

'This is what I was gone so long to win,' Wulfrik told her. 'Not the head of some southling baron or the heart of some beastkin warlord. This isn't for the gods. This is for me. For us. The Kurgan knows a way to lift my curse. This necklace is the key he needs to work his magic.'

Eyes wide with wonder, her face glowing with excitement, Hjordis reached for Wulfrik's hand. Her fingers closed tight around the torc, as though to assure herself it was real. 'Can this really set us free?' she gasped, almost frightened to even think about such a thing.

'The Kurgan says it will,' Wulfrik assured her. 'He knows what will happen to him if he is wrong.'

Hjordis hugged the warrior, resting her head against his chest. 'Then it is all over,' she said. 'At last, it is really all over.'

'As soon as the shaman performs the ritual,' Wulfrik nodded. 'Then let Viglundr try to keep us apart.'

The woman drew back in alarm. 'He will try,' she

said. 'His mind has set itself upon alliance with the Aeslings. It has become an obsession for him.'

Wulfrik bared his fangs as he heard her warning. 'I'll let no man take you away from me,' he said again. 'If your father thinks I will stand aside and watch another man lay his hands on you...' The warrior's voice quivered with rage. 'I am the only one who will have you.'

'You must be careful,' Hjordis advised, pressing her fingers against his lips. 'There is nothing my father would not try to get his way.'

'I've already killed one king,' Wulfrik muttered. 'Viglundr would be wise to remember that.'

'FOR THE LORD of the Winds, the last breath is given!'

Wulfrik awoke with a start, the voice of his dream thundering through his mind. Again he had seen the apocalyptic vision of a southling town wreathed in fire, its streets littered with the dead. Again he had seen his own body, his chest rent open, his heart lying trampled in the gutter.

Cautiously, he rose from the bed, careful not to disturb Hjordis. Quietly, Wulfrik drew on his armour and stole across the chamber. He did not look back, did not see the princess watching him, her eyes filled with concern.

The hero slipped past the iron-banded door, out into the corridor. Alarm flashed across his face as he observed an armoured figure leaning against the wall, his hand closing about his sword. Recognition made him hesitate, his brow wrinkling in confusion as he found himself staring at Broendulf.

'I thought it best if someone kept watch outside,' Broendulf explained. 'You seemed a bit too preoccupied to notice, but you made a few people angry at the feast.'

'Did any of them try to pay a call while I was asleep?' Wulfrik asked.

'A few,' Broendulf answered. 'I told them you weren't receiving.'

For the first time Wulfrik noticed the red stains on Broendulf's sword and armour. He nodded appreciatively. 'Anyone I should know about?'

'Zarnath, for one,' Broendulf told him. 'The Kurgan wants us to get a new crew together. He says he can't perform the ritual here and needs the *Seafang* to take him to "a place of power", whatever that means.'

'Have Arngeirr begin recruiting men,' Wulfrik said, cursing under his breath. 'No time to bother about the Wolf Forest. Any warrior with a stout heart and a strong back will do – provided they aren't Aeslings,' he added. There was more he would have liked to say, but he would save it for when he saw the shaman. This close to being free from his curse he wouldn't stand for any more of Zarnath's surprises.

'About the Wolf Forest,' Broendulf said. 'There was a messenger from Sveinbjorn. He says the prince will await you there, to settle for once who has the stronger claim on Hjordis.'

Wulfrik smiled when Broendulf gave him the message. 'Sveinbjorn is a bigger fool than I thought. Who does he think built the Wolf Forest? All he's done is make certain I'll kill him!' The champion yawned and stretched his powerful arms. 'First to see what's left over from the feast,' he said, clapping Broendulf on the shoulder. 'Then off to settle with Sveinbjorn. Then to talk with Zarnath about this voyage he's decided we need to make.' He shook his head, cursing again. 'A full morning all round.'

Broendulf watched Wulfrik stalk off down the corridor, his very steps seeming to shake with anger. The huscarl considered that he would not have traded places with Sveinbjorn for all the sand in Araby.

The door beside him suddenly creaked open, startling Broendulf. He spun around to find Hjordis, staring down the hall, watching until Wulfrik disappeared around the corner. Only then did she become aware of the fair-faced huscarl standing beside her. Colour rose to her cheeks and her hands tightened about the bearskin blanket she had wrapped around her body.

'What are you doing here?' she demanded.

'I was standing guard at your door,' Broendulf answered. 'I wanted to be sure you were protected.'

'I assure you I was,' Hjordis said.

'I wanted to be sure, just the same,' the huscarl explained. 'Wulfrik is a mighty warrior, but he forgets himself in battle. He's reckless with the lives of others.'

'I don't need you to tell me about his prowess,' the princess said, her voice sharp as a lash.

'No good will come to you from him,' Broendulf told her. 'There's a terrible doom hanging over his head. One he can't escape.'

'He will escape it,' Hjordis said. 'He will escape it because he is Wulfrik and neither men nor gods will stand in his way. Who are you to question what he can or can't do? Some snippet of a bondsman cast out from my father's service?' Understanding suddenly came into the woman's eyes and she retreated across the threshold of her room, keeping the half-open door between herself and Broendulf. 'Is that it? Did he send you here to try and twist my mind against Wulfrik? What did he promise you for betraying your captain?'

'There's only one thing he could offer me,' Broendulf said. 'And he's already promised that to someone else.' The huscarl reached towards Hjordis. The princess drew back, slamming the door in his face.

'Go away, Broendulf,' Hjordis's voice scolded him from behind the door. 'If I told Wulfrik about this, he would kill you.'

Broendulf put his hand against the closed door. 'It might be better that way,' he said, sadness in his voice.

'Go away, Broendulf,' Hjordis repeated. 'I'll forget what you've said, only go.'

The dejected huscarl turned away from the door. He was under no illusion that he could ever claim Hjordis for his own. The pain of his unspoken love was what had driven him to abandon his post as captain of Viglundr's guard. He had hoped he would find a worthy death joining the crew of the *Seafang*, that by helping to protect the man Hjordis loved he could somehow, in some strange way, earn her affection.

Now he saw how foolish he had been. He had seen

how Wulfrik's curse had hurt Hjordis, but now he saw that even without his strange doom, the man could only bring her suffering. Her father would never allow them to know peace and Wulfrik was too proud to ever compromise. He was a warrior and would never be anything else.

Chapter Eleven

THE BLOODFIELD WAS lost beneath a thick layer of snow when Wulfrik made his way to the training ground. How different it looked from the last time he had been here. The tables where the people of Ormskaro had feasted were all but buried beneath the snow. He could just see the carved headrest of King Viglundr's seat poking through the crust. Somewhere under that white veil was where he had first been approached by Zarnath and heard the shaman's claim that he could lift the curse.

Sigvatr had been beside him then, counselling him against listening to the Kurgan. Had he known his old friend would die in capturing the treasure Zarnath needed, Wulfrik wondered if even his love for Hjordis would have been enough to drive him on. The hero nodded grimly to himself.

Yes, he would have. There was nothing he would not give to free himself from his curse, to end the endless voyages that kept him from his love. Since the gods had visited their punishment upon him, he had been like a dead thing, existing but not truly alive, his heart yearning for the things his curse denied him. A chance to live again, that was worth any risk, any sacrifice.

Wulfrik stared across the snow-covered plateau. He saw the raised platforms and the nest of poles that formed the Wolf Forest poking up through the snow. The deadly spikes were hidden, buried under the crust, but Wulfrik knew they would bite just as keenly unseen. The hero grimaced, a thrill of fear running down his spine. One last battle before Zarnath lifted the curse from him. It would suit the malignant humour of the gods to let him die now when he was so close to escape. His spirit would be damned, a plaything for daemons to torment until the world's ending when all was devoured by the Blood God's hunger.

The hero forced himself to forget such thoughts. Fear would give Sveinbjorn an advantage, perhaps the only one the Aesling needed. He had to concentrate on the fight before him, not the release he would soon obtain.

Sveinbjorn and his hersirs were gathered at the far side of the Wolf Forest, almost twenty in number. The Aeslings had donned heavy cloaks against the cold, but Wulfrik knew they would be wearing armour beneath their furs. Sveinbjorn's men had come dressed for battle this time. Wulfrik grinned fiercely. If it was battle the Aeslings wanted, battle they would have. He turned his head and glanced at the weathered warriors following behind him. He had brought nearly his entire crew with him to the Bloodfield. No more fearsome a body of men existed in Norsca than the bold reavers who sailed upon the *Seafang*; each of his warriors was worth two of Sveinbjorn's. If the prince planned treachery, then he had brought too few to succeed.

Of course, the Aesling had other resources available to him. Standing only a little distance from Sveinbjorn and his hersirs was Viglundr and a dozen of his jarls and bondsmen. Like the Aeslings, they had put on their armour, axes and swords hanging loose beneath their belts. More disturbing to Wulfrik was the sight of a wizened old Sarl clad in sharkskin vestments. His face framed by the open jaws of the shark-head hood, the elder stared at Wulfrik with the single amber eye that gleamed at the centre of his forehead. This was Rundulfr, Ormfell's seer. Wulfrik felt his skin crawl as the mystic's cyclopean eye studied him. Had he come to ensure the fight would be fought fairly and according to tradition, or had Viglundr brought the seer so that his magic might sway the outcome? Wulfrik found himself wishing he had brought Zarnath with him to counter whatever spells Rundulfr might evoke. The hero bared his fangs in a grim smile.

Of course that was assuming the shaman would stay on his side. It occurred to Wulfrik that just as he believed another warlock could discover the secret of the torc, so too Zarnath might take the chance that he could master the *Seafang* without Wulfrik's help.

Wulfrik shook his head. He had to trust the Kurgan a little longer. But he would keep one eye on the shaman just the same.

'So the wife-stealer comes!' Sveinbjorn's voice

called out as Wulfrik approached the gathered Aeslings. 'I had thought you might,' the prince waved his hand through the air, 'get back on your boat and just sail away again.'

'There are men who still need killing here in Ormskaro,' Wulfrik said. 'And Hjordis isn't your wife yet, Aes. Nor will she ever be.' The hero drew his sword from its sheath, laughing when he saw the way Sveinbjorn's eyes were drawn to the skull tied to the hilt. King Torgald had been reckoned a great warrior among the Aeslings. Seeing his skull among Wulfrik's trophies was a reminder to Sveinbjorn of the champion's skill in battle.

'You've agreed to settle this in the Wolf Forest,' Viglundr warned. As the king spoke, his warriors took a step forwards, their axes ready in their hands. 'I will hear no more of this bickering.'

Wulfrik shrugged and turned cold eyes upon the Sarl king. 'It matters not where I kill this vermin,' he said. 'Only that his stink is gone from Ormskaro!' Contemptuously, he turned away from the bristling Aeslings and walked towards the icy ladder leading up to the Wolf Forest.

Haukr hurried after his captain, a heavy southling shield in his hand. He started to hand it to Wulfrik, but the champion brushed him aside. Mockery in his voice, Wulfrik turned from the base of the ladder and addressed Sveinbjorn. 'Give the shield to the prince,' he said. 'I won't need it. I doubt I'll even need my sword. The clumsy worm will probably fall onto the stakes before he takes his second step off the ladder.'

Laughing at the fuming prince, Wulfrik scrambled

up the icy ladder with the nimbleness of a monkey. He was soon upon the narrow platform, staring out across the snow-covered posts. For a man used to climbing into the rigging of a rolling ship upon a stormy sea, the Wolf Forest held no terror. He wondered if Sveinbjorn could boast the same resolve.

Wulfrik turned his head and stared down at the Aesling prince. 'Come along, killer of mice, or has the blood in your veins already turned to water?'

Sveinbjorn glared up at the jeering hero, but made no move towards the other side of the battleground. A sneer curled the prince's lip. 'Me, a prince, lower myself to brawl with some simple sea raider?' he scoffed. 'You really are as stupid as you look!'

Wulfrik bared his fangs, glowering down at the prince. 'What cowardly trickery is this?'

'No trickery,' Viglundr answered. 'Sveinbjorn has challenged you, but has chosen a champion to represent him in battle.'

Wulfrik's eyes narrowed with hate as he realised the deception which had been worked against him. He shifted his gaze from the smirking prince to the far side of the Wolf Forest. The platform shuddered as a huge figure mounted the ladder.

'I would have sent a dog,' Sveinbjorn laughed, 'but I could find none mangy enough to face you.'

Wulfrik's hand tightened about the hilt of his sword. He would make the duplicitous prince eat those words when he crammed the skull of his champion down his throat!

Across the battleground, the Aesling champion finished his climb. Even Wulfrik had seldom seen a more formidable man. His stature was enormous, almost troll-like. His bare arms were so swollen with muscle that they couldn't even hang cleanly against his sides but instead bulged out from his body. A breastplate of blackened steel stretched across his broad chest, its surface pitted and scarred from past battles. A skirt of chainmail hung from his waist, dried human ears fastened to it by hooks. Strips of scaly hide were wrapped about his legs, the tough blue hides of butchered dragon-folk. Iron boots fitted with curved claws encased his feet, sides and soles adorned with sharp spikes so that the warrior could maintain his footing even upon the most treacherous ground. About his head, the fighter wore an ornate helm of bronze, its curled horns twisting upwards from its crown. From the visor of the helm, Wulfrik could see two glowing green eyes watching him hungrily.

Feeling an unaccountable sense of dread, Wulfrik drew the other sword sheathed at his hip and stepped out upon the snow-covered posts. A blade in either hand, he cautiously walked out into the Wolf Forest.

He had only taken a few steps when the eyes of Sveinbjorn's champion changed from green to red. A metallic howl rasped through the steel mask of the Aesling's helm as the huge fighter threw back his head and roared at the winter sky. Then the warrior was dashing across the posts, charging towards Wulfrik with reckless disregard for balance and footing. All that seemed to matter to the fearless champion was closing with his enemy.

Wulfrik braced himself for his enemy's assault. Watching the Aesling leap from post to post, he felt his fear swell. There was something wrong, something hideously unnatural about the warrior, an abnormality that made even a Norscan's skin crawl. As the Aesling closed with him, Wulfrik could see runes burning along the blackened steel of the massive double-headed axe the warrior bore, letters carved in the slithery letters of the Dark Tongue, the language of daemons and sorcerers.

The hulking berserker did not hesitate when he reached Wulfrik, but with an animal snarl he brought his axe chopping down. Wulfrik blocked the murderous blow, catching the descending blade between his crossed swords. The Aesling's strength was that of a titan; Wulfrik could feel the impact of the axe crashing against his blades like a tremor coursing down his arms. His knees were bent by the force of the blow, his entire body straining under the berserker's brawn.

The Aesling's glowing eyes burned in the shadows of his helmet, insane mutterings crawling from behind the steel mask. Flickers of fire danced from the runes set into the berserker's axe, the air turning to steam around the weapon. A chorus of voices clawed at Wulfrik's brain, whispers of madness that fanned the fires of fear growing in his gut. He could feel himself falling into a black abyss, a realm of terror from which there would be no escape.

The Aesling's great strength continued to bear down on Wulfrik. The hero's legs began to buckle; his body began to tremble with the strain of keeping the butchering edge of the axe from cleaving into his chest. He could feel the berserker's daemon-axe chewing into the edge of his sword, biting into the tempered steel. Inch by inch, second by second, Wulfrik knew he was being overwhelmed by Sveinbjorn's champion.

Through Wulfrik's mind flashed the image of a triumphant Sveinbjorn bearing Hjordis to his chambers, lust etched upon the prince's smirking features. He could see old Viglundr rubbing his hands together, chortling greedily over the union of Aesling and Sarl. He could hear the gods laughing at him, mocking his failure as they claimed his damned spirit.

Wulfrik's lips curled back in a snarl. Crimson fury flared through his mind, burning away the whispering daemon-voices. Strength born from rage thundered through his limbs. With a roar, he pressed up against the berserker's axe, his entire body lunging upwards, throwing every ounce of strength in his flesh against the Aesling's steel.

The effort sent the berserker stumbling back, his arms flailing as he struggled to keep hold of his axe. Wulfrik staggered after him, each wobbling step threatening to send him toppling into the snow-covered stakes below. Before the Aesling could recover, Wulfrik's sword flashed out, cleaving through bone and sinew in a scarlet blur. A pained shriek rippled across the Wolf Forest as Wulfrik cut the berserker's hand from his wrist, the severed appendage still locked about the heft of his daemon-axe.

Far from being overcome with pain, the berserker seemed to take strength from his injury. One-handed he brought the massive axe swinging around, slashing it like some monstrous scythe at Wulfrik's head. The hero ducked beneath the murderous sweep of the blade. Before the crouching fighter could draw a breath, the huge axe was swinging back, much lower on its return than it had been before.

Daringly, Wulfrik leapt over the bladed steel. His body trembled as his feet came slamming back down upon the tops of the posts. For a hideous moment, he teetered at the brink of destruction, fighting to recover his balance.

The berserker brought his axe chopping down once more, trying to take advantage of his compromised foe. At the last instant, Wulfrik spun away from the double-axe, shifting his weight towards the left and forcing both of his feet onto the same post.

The axe slammed into the post Wulfrik had been standing on, cleaving deep into the wood. The Aesling struggled to rip the axe free, forgetting for the moment the foe who had so narrowly escaped him.

Wulfrik did not give the berserker time to realise his mistake. Shifting his footing, the hero brought both of his swords slashing into the Aesling's outstretched arm. He felt bone split beneath the blow, saw blood fountain from the hideous wounds. The half-freed axe tumbled from the berserker's weakened grip, burying itself in the snow below.

The Aesling reeled back, blood gushing from his arm. Maddened sounds shuddered from the berserker's helm, his spiked boots clawing at the posts as he staggered away.

Wulfrik surged after the wounded berserker. With the loss of the daemon-axe, the dread that had gripped him was evaporating, the gibbering voices in his mind falling silent. 'After I kill you, I'm going to geld your prince,' Wulfrik hissed at the Aesling.

It was the tone of arrogant confidence in the hero's voice rather than his words that made the berserker cock his armoured head and stare at him with something approaching curiosity. A garbled voice rumbled from beneath the Aesling's helm.

'Fraener... kill... cut... tear... slaughter,' the Aesling's slobbering words hissed.

Wulfrik hung back as he heard the berserker's voice. Fraener had been a great war-chief of the Aeslings, a man who had borne the favour of the gods upon his flesh. He had led his raiders deep into the Wastes, preying upon the Kurgan tribes and looting the ancient dolmens of the beastkin. Surely this crazed mongrel could not be the same man?

The Aesling glared at Wulfrik. He slapped his bleeding arm across his chest. 'Fraener... Fraener...' he repeated. Each time he recited his name, the berserker's voice grew more distinct, more violent. At the same time, his bleeding arm pulsed, swelling and bubbling like boiled porridge.

'Fraener!' the Aesling shrieked in a final scream of primal fury. His bubbling arm split open, the flesh peeling back to expose a wet, dripping claw like the leg of a mammoth spider. Bony spikes rippled along the length of the bloody limb, twitching and throbbing in tandem with the Aesling's breath.

Wulfrik stared in horror at the cackling mutant. If this was Fraener, then the gods had abandoned him somewhere along the way, casting him aside like a broken toy. From a mighty Chosen, marked by the gods with their favour, his mind and body had degenerated into a creature of madness, a debased Forsaken. What trickery had Sveinbjorn used to bring this creature from whatever lonely cave he had hidden himself in, what promises had he made that could stir the mind of a savage maniac?

The Forsaken loped towards Wulfrik, slashing the glistening claw at the hero's neck. Wulfrik dodged aside, growling in pain as he felt the spikes along the dripping limb slash across his cheek. Vengefully, he brought one of his swords slashing across the mutated arm. A filthy brown vapour jetted from the resulting wound, spraying across his face, blinding his eyes.

Unable to see, Wulfrik swung blindly at his foe, trying to direct his attacks at the Forsaken's foul smell. He grinned as he felt one of his blades drive home, sinking into the Aesling's body with a meaty crunch. The next instant, the hero's body was flung through the air, thrown by the powerful impact of the mutant's claw against his chest.

Wulfrik clenched his teeth, expecting any moment to feel the lethal touch of stakes being driven through his flesh. When his body landed, it was with such force that the breath was driven from his lungs. Despite the crushing impact against his chest, he could feel his limbs dangling in the air. Against all odds, he had slammed into one of the posts. Before he could slip off, Wulfrik wrapped his arms and legs about the narrow pole.

There was a red tint to his vision now, but at least some measure of sight had returned to his eyes. Wulfrik struggled to pull himself up onto the post. One of his swords had been knocked from his grip by the violent landing. The other he held so tightly that he could feel his fingers stabbing into his palm. However much it hindered his climb, he would not let the sword go. Unlike the Forsaken, he could not grow a new weapon when he lost his.

Insane muttering and the gory stink of a butchered dog warned Wulfrik of his enemy's approach. Leaping nimbly from post to post, the Forsaken stalked towards him, the spider-like claw quivering eagerly at the mutant's every step. Wulfrik could hear Sveinbjorn and the Aesling hersirs shouting encouragement to the monster, goading him to destroy their enemy.

Despite the cold fear dripping from his brow, Wulfrik forced himself to wait, to bide his time as the Forsaken drew ever closer. From the corner of his eye, he could see the mutant rear back, raising his ghastly arm to deliver the killing blow. The insane mutterings bubbling from the Aesling's helm took on a giggling quality, the imbecilic glee of an idiot child.

Roaring, Wulfrik twisted his body around the post he clung to, spinning so that he faced the Forsaken head-on. The hero's sword licked out like the tongue of a dragon, slashing through the mutant's leg, shearing through the Aesling's ankle. Wulfrik's enemy bleated in alarm, the bleeding stump of his leg waving wildly in the air. Then the mutant toppled, his unbalanced body hurtling down into the stakes beneath the posts. A sickening crunch shuddered through Wulfrik's ears as the Forsaken's bulk impaled itself.

Wulfrik smiled as he started to pull himself up from where he dangled over the side of the post, revelling in the dejected curses he heard rising from Sveinbjorn's men. The prince had arranged a cunning trap for his hated rival. Now he would suffer the price for its failure.

The tone of the Aeslings abruptly changed, curses rising into robust cheers. Instantly, Wulfrik forced his tired arms into a frantic effort, using them to anchor his body against the top of the post. At the same time he kicked out with his legs, swinging them upwards, trying to reach the top of the post closest to him. His boots scraped across the icy wood, then his momentum brought him falling back again. Bending his knees, Wulfrik pressed his feet against the pole and kicked out again. Something strong lashed at his boots as he dangled above the stakes, something that tried to coil around his ankle.

Wulfrik's feet caught on the second pass. His body hanging between the two posts, he risked a glance at the ground below. A sickening sight greeted him. The body of the Forsaken was transfixed upon a half-dozen stakes, the force of his impact driving them through his armour. A green stain was spreading into the snow all around the Aesling, the heat of the ichor causing the snow to sizzle. From the mutant's wounds, long ropey tendrils waved, whipping about in an idiot frenzy. A jagged rent in the Forsaken's armour exposed a toothy maw slobbering and snapping beneath where the man's ribs should have been. A barbed tongue shot out from the ghastly mouth, slicing across the pole supporting Wulfrik's hands, scouring the wood with a deep scar.

The hero turned away from the horrible creature beneath him. Bracing his legs, locking his feet about the sides of the pole they rested on, Wulfrik summoned every scrap of vigour in his powerful arms. He flung his body away from the post, using his legs to help pull himself upright. The Forsaken's barbed tongue flashed out at him again. This time it sheared completely through the post, cutting it clean through and knocking it to the ground. Wulfrik grimaced as he realised how near he had come to following his refuge into destruction.

Crouching upon the top of the pole, feeling it sway and shiver beneath his weight, Wulfrik gazed out across the Wolf Forest. He was almost at the middle of the battlefield, equally distant from either platform. If he made for the platform the Aesling had used to enter the field, he would be able to avoid coming within striking range of the mutant's tongue and the flailing tendrils spilling from his torn flesh. He could escape the monster without any danger.

The hero glared over at the jeering Sveinbjorn and bared his fangs. He wouldn't give the prince the satisfaction of seeing him run.

Wulfrik stared back down at the monstrosity impaled upon the stakes. The Forsaken was struggling to pull himself free, his tendrils coiling around the poles around him, using them as leverage to lift his bulk off the spikes. In a few minutes, the mutant would be free.

Wulfrik had no intention of allowing the Aesling the time he needed. Howling a fierce war cry, closing both hands about the hilt of his sword, the hero leapt from his precarious perch in a savage leap. His boots slammed into the Forsaken's struggling body, thrusting the mutant back upon the stakes, causing more blood and filth to spill across the snow. The Aesling lifted his head, angry croaking echoing from his helm as his glowing eyes gazed upon the man standing upon his chest.

Raising his sword high, Wulfrik brought the blade flashing down, cleaving through the Forsaken's horned helm, hewing through the skull beneath. The twisted body under his feet trembled and thrashed, then fell still.

Wulfrik wiped the Forsaken's filthy blood from his face. Carefully he stepped away from the dead mutant, picking a path through the stakes under the Wolf Forest. Grimly he tore a strip of fur from his cape and began to wipe the monster's gore from the edge of his blade. He wanted his sword keen when he drove it through Sveinbjorn's belly.

The Aesling prince was not gloating now. Fear was in his eyes as he retreated behind the armoured ranks of his hersirs. Their axes rested uneasily in the lordlings' hands. Not a man among them had not seen Fraener's monstrous ability in battle many times before. They regarded the prospect of facing a man powerful enough to kill the Forsaken in single combat as nothing short of suicide. Bonded to fight for the Aesling prince, none of them was eager to die for him.

Viglundr's Sarls marched between the Aeslings and the advancing Wulfrik. The old king stepped out from between his guards, making placating gestures to the infuriated hero.

'You have proven the worth of your claim upon my daughter,' Viglundr said. 'Sveinbjorn's champion is vanquished. There is no need for more bloodshed.'

Wulfrik spat into the snow at Viglundr's feet. 'The hell there isn't,' he snarled, his eyes locked upon Sveinbjorn's pale features.

'You've won, Wulfrik!' Viglundr told him. 'Hjordis is yours!'

'She already was,' Wulfrik corrected him. 'Given to me by your promise. Out of my way, snake-tongue!' he barked at the king. 'I already have half a mind to kill you alongside this Aesling scum. Don't tempt me more!'

'It will mean war,' Viglundr said. 'The Aeslings will avenge their prince!'

'They will try,' Wulfrik said. The hero strode past Viglundr, a terrible light shining in his eyes. The king's warriors stepped nervously from his path. The crew of the *Seafang* watched their captain prowl across the snow, uncertain if he would welcome their help against the Aeslings or curse them for interfering.

Viglundr hastened after the hero. 'Ormskaro cannot stand against the Aeslings,' he hissed in a frightened whisper. 'Even without Torgald and his warriors, they are too strong.'

'For you,' Wulfrik sneered, his eyes never leaving Sveinbjorn. 'Not for me. I've fought one war with these mongrels. I'll fight another just as happily.'

'There's no need,' Viglundr persisted. 'No reason to force them to battle.'

Wulfrik turned his head and stared into the king's face, snorting with contempt at the fear and desperation he saw written across Viglundr's features. 'A wolf without teeth shouldn't lead a pack,' he said. 'Maybe I will kill you when I finish with Sveinbjorn after all.'

'And who would protect my daughter then?' Viglundr asked, his voice dripping with spite.

Wulfrik brandished his sword in the king's face. 'You dare–'

'I am told you must sail away,' Viglundr interrupted him. 'One last voyage before the Kurgan's magic sets you free. How long will you be gone? How long will the gods keep you from Ormskaro after you cheat them? A day? A week? More? And who will keep the Aeslings from tearing down this place when you are gone?'

Slowly, reluctantly, Wulfrik lowered his sword. He smiled coldly at Viglundr. 'Your words are as poisonous as ever,' he said.

'They are only the truth, and you know it.'

The hero gnashed his fangs together, his entire body trembling with rage. Viglundr was right. There was no way to be certain when he would return, no way to protect Hjordis while he was gone. He did not know what strange land Zarnath would need them to sail for in order to work his magic, but he would wager it was no such place as he would take his bride.

He had to be free of his curse. Only then could he defend Hjordis and the kingdom he would wrest from Viglundr's cheating fingers. Until then, he had to set aside his hate. Set it aside, but not forget it.

'Thank the king of the Sarls for your life,' Wulfrik growled to Sveinbjorn behind his guard of hersirs. The hero thrust his sword back into its scabbard and turned his back on the Aeslings. 'Don't be here when I set sail,' he advised as he walked away. 'Or I may decide Torgald's head is lonely.'

Wulfrik marched towards his crew, his voice lifting into a bellow. 'Find Zarnath!' he ordered. 'Bring that Kurgan toad-licker to me!' There were questions he would ask the shaman, questions the mystic would answer, or Wulfrik would flay every inch of skin from the man's hide.

'I'LL STICK THAT sea-rat's head on a spike and leave it for the Crow God!' Sveinbjorn's furious voice echoed from the bare stone walls. 'No man treats me like that and lives!'

Viglundr shook his head as he watched the Aesling prince pace back and forth across the king's council chamber. 'That rug came from an Estalian castle. I'd thank you not to wear it out.'

Sveinbjorn stopped pacing. He stared down at his feet, noting the blue cloth stretched across the floor. A scowl on his face, the prince advanced towards Viglundr's throne. 'Don't think I have forgiven your part in this!' the Aesling shouted.

'What part would that be?' Viglundr said, his voice thin and edged with menace. 'Finding a man who could kill Torgald for you?'

'Torgald's dead,' Sveinbjorn snapped. 'Wulfrik's done what we needed him to do. Now it's time to be rid of the dog!' The prince waved his arms, indicating the small chamber and its sparse adornments. 'Look at you! Hiding away here while he prowls at will through your own palace! You'd think he was already king of the Sarls!'

Anger flared in the icy depths of Viglundr's eyes. 'Wulfrik will never wear my crown,' the king stated.

Sveinbjorn set his hand upon the arm of Viglundr's throne, leaning close to the king. 'Then stop him!' the prince demanded. 'There will be no alliance between our tribes while that man draws breath!'

'Have a care, Sveinbjorn,' Viglundr warned his guest. The king brushed the Aesling's hand from his throne as though swatting a troublesome insect. 'I've removed one Aesling who threatened my plans.'

Sveinbjorn walked away, shaking his finger at the king. 'It's not me who threatens this alliance. It's Wulfrik.'

'I will deal with him,' Viglundr assured the prince.

'How?' Sveinbjorn demanded.

'Not by picking a fight with him and then sending a Forsaken to cut him down,' Viglundr said. 'That man has killed giants and daemons. Do you really think any champion you could set against him would be his equal?'

'Then what? Magic?'

Viglundr shook his head. 'I've tried to order my

sorcerers to use their magic against him already. No matter what tortures I threatened them with, they refused. Rundulfr says that because of his curse, Wulfrik is inviolate. Any sorcerer who uses his magic to kill Wulfrik will inherit his curse. Even a seer doesn't look forward to having his spirit ripped apart by the gods.'

The king laughed as he saw Sveinbjorn slam his fist against the wall in frustration. 'You aren't half as clever as you imagine yourself,' Viglundr chuckled. 'We can't challenge him openly and we can't use magic.' The king's face spread in a cruel grin. 'That still leaves murder.'

Sveinbjorn sneered at the suggestion. 'Even if we found one of our men brave enough, he'd never manage it. That Wulfrik is a daemon with eyes in the back of his head. He'd never let our killer get close enough.'

Viglundr's smile grew. 'One of my men is ready to do the job and Wulfrik will let him close enough to do it. When one plots murder, one should choose an assassin the victim already trusts.' He pointed at an iron-banded door set into the chamber's outer wall. 'Be good enough to admit our friend.'

Sveinbjorn's steps were uncertain as he moved across the room. He kept one hand on his axe when he reached forwards and unlatched the heavy door. The prince cursed and backed away from the doorway after he opened it, drawing his weapon from his belt.

'You!' the prince snarled, glaring at the man who strode into the room.

'Control yourself!' Viglundr ordered the Aesling. 'This man is here by my command.' The king rose from his throne and stepped forwards to greet the fair-faced huscarl.

'Forgive Sveinbjorn,' Viglundr said. 'His pride is still stung by the slight dealt him by your captain. Come inside, Broendulf. We have much to discuss.'

Broendulf bowed and entered the council chamber, closing the heavy door behind him. The huscarl kept his hand closed about the hilt of his own sword and a suspicious eye on the Aesling prince. 'You wished to see me, sire?'

'Indeed,' Viglundr said, motioning for Broendulf to follow him across the room. The king set his arm across the warrior's broad shoulder, at the same time directing a warning glance at Sveinbjorn, a gesture that went unnoticed by the huscarl. 'There is much I would talk over with you.

'Let us start by discussing my daughter...'

Chapter Twelve

WULFRIK'S LIP CURLED back in distaste as he stared out across the deck of the *Seafang*. He could smell the fear rising from the men watching him. Many of them were little more than pups, their faces as smooth as an infant's arse, their axes still carrying the stink of the forge upon them.

'Was this the best you could find?' Wulfrik grumbled.

Beside him, Arngeirr winced and fingered the Estalian flask under his belt. 'The gods were with me to find even these,' he explained. 'Viglundr spread word that you were dead. Most of the men who would have killed to join your crew went back to their homes. The king's huscarls expelled the rest from Ormskaro so that they wouldn't cause any trouble for him. I had to take whoever was left just to get enough men for the oars.'

'These aren't men,' Wulfrik growled. 'These are children.'

'You have yourself to blame,' Broendulf told his captain. He licked his lips nervously as he saw

Wulfrik turn a scowl on him. After a moment, the huscarl decided to speak his mind despite the hero's distemper. 'After the way you treated Sveinbjorn, everyone in Ormskaro is afraid the Aeslings are going to attack. Every man with a family is staying behind to protect them.'

Instead of shouting down Broendulf for his warning, Wulfrik just nodded his head. Sigvatr would have reprimanded him in similar fashion for causing his own troubles. Pride and temper were failings the old warrior had always warned him against, often telling him they were his worst enemies. His mind already sombre after his parting with Hjordis, the hero was more ready to admit his faults than at other times.

'We'll have to make do,' he sighed, stroking his beard as he studied the keen, eager expressions his new crew wore. They might be afraid, but they were also excited. Wulfrik wondered how many of them had never been to sea before, how many of those young eyes had never gazed upon a strange shore.

'There's another way,' Haukr said. 'I've spent some time among the southlings. My father would trade furs in Erengrad when he grew too old for raiding. When a southling captain finds himself in need of a crew, he sends a few of his men to wait outside the taverns with stout clubs and big gunnysacks. A quick crack to the head of a lout already staggering from too much mead and the ship has a new crewman.'

'I'll not sail with any man too much a coward to do so willingly,' snarled Njarvord.

Haukr shot the hairy Baersonling a withering look.

'You're lucky you've never been bashed and stashed, the way you drink.'

The huge warrior's hand curled into a fist and he took a menacing step towards the tattooed reaver. Haukr drew a fat-bladed knife from his boot and backed away from Njarvord. 'Come along, you stupid oaf,' he snarled. 'I'll geld you like a sick mule.'

Broendulf came between the two antagonists, separating them before they could fall upon each other. 'Save it for the voyage back,' he warned them. 'We'll need every man where we're going.'

The huscarl's words had their desired effect. Still glaring at each other, the two warriors stalked off to bark orders at the new crew, setting them to rearranging the supplies piled upon the deck, a chore that had more to do with the surliness of the men snapping orders than any practical purpose.

Wulfrik listened to Broendulf's words, feeling them twist in his gut like Haukr's knife. His men trusted him to lead them into glory. It was why they left their homes and families behind, why they risked their lives fighting alongside him. They knew that he would lead them to victory, that by following him into battle they would find their own path to fame and a heroic death, earn their own places in the sagas.

For the first time, Wulfrik questioned his right to exploit these brave warriors. It was one thing to ask them to die when he fought in the name of the gods. It was another to expect them to die to serve his own ends. True, he intended to reward every man who sailed with him when the curse was broken and he came into his own as king of the Sarls, but it still rested ill with him just the same. Many good men had been lost in the Dark Lands against the dwarfs. The new voyage promised to be no less dangerous.

The hero closed his eyes, picturing again his meeting with Zarnath. His armour still covered in Fraener's blood, Wulfrik had confronted the Kurgan shaman. Surprisingly, the warlock had been forthcoming about the ritual he intended to perform for Wulfrik. The Smile of Sardiss would need to be taken to a site of power. Zarnath would then use his power to draw powerful magics into the torc, giving it a certain polarity that would mask the champion from the sight of the gods. No more would he suffer the visions they sent to him in the night. No longer would he be doomed to wander the world, endlessly killing to appease their capricious whims. He would be free, and when he died the torc's magic would continue to protect his spirit, allowing him to safely enter the halls of his ancestors.

The shaman's words had stirred the hope burning inside Wulfrik's heart. Zarnath was confident his magic would do what he said it would do, showing no fear when the hero threatened a slow death if another nightmare came upon him after the ritual to empower the torc. Perhaps that was because the Kurgan expected even Wulfrik's bold courage to falter when he was told where the torc needed to be taken. The site of power of which Zarnath spoke stood upon the haunted shores of Alfheim, though the shaman had called that sinister land by the strange name of Ulthuan.

Alfheim. The very name was enough to turn a northman's bones to butter. Generations past, the great Erik Redaxe led a fleet of dragonships to the misty shores of that ghostly land. Only a handful of warriors ever returned to tell the tale of that fleet's destruction, of the terrible elf-folk and their powerful magic, of the mighty wyrms that swam the seas around Alfheim and the horrible dragons who flew through its skies. Erik Redaxe's saga did not speak of glory and plunder, but death and ruin.

Wulfrik had been a young boy when Erik Redaxe had led his fleet to destruction, and had listened to the skalds singing the king's tale around the winter fire. The saga the king had made for himself was not one of heroic glory but a testament of tragedy and loss. All his other deeds, all the foes he had vanquished, all the battles he had won, these were forgotten in the reckoning of his life. All that was remembered now was the way he had died, crushed and broken by the sorcery of the elf-folk and their haunted island.

Was that how he would be remembered? Broken by the magic of the elves, all of his victories forgotten, drowned beneath a final ignoble defeat?

It was a thought to quail the stoutest heart. Better to end his days a twisted, mindless creature like Fraener.

Still, Wulfrik refused to abandon the hope that had risen within him. His experience with Sveinbjorn had shown him he was running out of time. He couldn't stave off Viglundr's ambition forever. If he would make Hjordis his own, he had to be free of the curse, and quickly.

A last chance for life. For that, Wulfrik was willing to risk anything, sacrifice anything, challenge anything. If his doom was to die upon the forbidden shores of Alfheim, then he would meet his fate with sword in hand.

The hero turned and regarded the huddled shape of Zarnath sitting at the stern of the ship. The shaman had drawn a heavy seal-fur cape about his lean body, strange symbols stained into the soft fur, runes like none Wulfrik had seen before. The warlock sat with his legs folded beneath him, his hands resting palm-upwards upon his knees. His eyes were open, but there was a dull film over them, blocking out the blue light which normally glowed within them.

Wulfrik repressed a shudder. Sorcerers were eerie enough at the best of times, but Zarnath had become even more so since his return to the *Seafang*. There was an aura of power about him that even Wulfrik could feel. Drawing too close to the shaman made his hair prickle along his arms and rise from the back of his neck. There was an icy chill surrounding the Kurgan and a smell like that of an electrical storm.

Zarnath had warned he would need to prepare himself for the ritual, drawing tremendous powers within himself to ready his spirit for when they reached their destination. There was a practical purpose too, the shaman had said. The magic he was calling upon would shield them from the notice of the elves and their creatures, hiding the *Seafang* and all who sailed upon her from even the mightiest of elf magic.

At least for a time.

The shaman had cautioned that he must not be touched by anyone until after the ritual was completed. Even the briefest nudge would disrupt the power coursing through his body and undo all his preparations. If that happened, Zarnath warned, it would be years before he would be able to attempt the ritual again. Wulfrik had grimly promised the Kurgan that he would not be disturbed, telling his crew that the man who defiled the shaman would die in such a manner that it would sicken even the plague god, Nurgle.

Wulfrik left Zarnath to his meditations. Let the shaman prepare himself in whatever way he needed. His life, as much as Wulfrik's, depended upon the outcome of his ritual.

The hero gazed back over the *Seafang's* deck, then turned his eyes towards Ormskaro. A great crowd had gathered in the snowy streets to watch the famous ship set sail, but Wulfrik paid them scant notice, lifting his gaze instead to the tower of Ormfell. He could just make out the tiny shape waving at him from the roof of the tower, her golden hair rippling around her as the winter wind swept across the fortress.

Wulfrik waved back, his doubts and fears crushed by the resurgence of hope. He would return to her in triumph this time. And not all the monstrous gods of the north would stop him.

THE LITTLE HUT on the hill overlooking Ormskaro was silent as the *Seafang* slid into the icy fjord and made her way towards the sea. The steading of an old freeholder whose fortunes were so small that only a single thrall tilled his fields and a single wife warmed his bed, the small dwelling was seldom disturbed by the people in the town below. Isolated and accessible only by a narrow, treacherous cliffside path, the lonely farm was mostly forgotten by the outside world.

It would be many weeks before anyone wondered about the old freeholder and his household, weeks more before anyone became curious enough to investigate. When they did, they would find the mangled bodies of the old man and his wife lying in their bed. The corpse of the thrall would be under a bench in the hut's cellar, his neck torn through by a single monstrous bite.

There would be no trace of the grisly little creature that had killed the hut's inhabitants. As the *Seafang* sailed from Ormskaro, the gibbering imp was the only thing stirring within the hut, loping through the rooms, blood dripping from its fangs. Around and around it circled the building, snapping at rats and pouncing on mice when they dared to stir from their holes. The imp was tireless in its patrol of the hovel, never relenting in its vigilance.

Only one thing caused it to pause in its routine. As it made the circuit of the hut, the imp would linger near the hearth, staring at a figure seated there in a wicker chair. The endless train of gibberish would fall silent and the imp would tilt its hideous, toad-like head, listening for any sound from the seated man. Eventually, it would decide there was no new command. Mad giggles and lunatic sounds would again spill from the daemon's mouth as it resumed its march.

Upon the chair, the man continued to stare into the cold hearth, his eyes open but unseeing. Except for the concentration gripping his face, he might have passed for one of the corpses scattered about the hut, but no dead thing had ever worn such a mask of malignant purpose.

THE MISTS PARTED. Once more, the *Seafang* returned to mortal seas. Her new crew had borne the hideous ordeal of entering the border-realm with the fierce stoicism of the Norscan tribes, only three of their number succumbing to the whispering wails of the daemons lurking in the fog. Their screams as they leapt into the fog and were devoured had done much to steel the courage of those they left behind. Nothing bolstered a man's valour so much as the prospect of a hideous death should he show weakness.

Wulfrik stared out over the prow of his ship. The shimmering mists girding the dragonship were soon replaced by a grey fog almost as thick. He felt ice tingle along his spine as his eyes struggled to pierce the veil. He recalled stories told about these shores, about tiny islands the elf-folk had cast upon the sea to confound those who would raid their shores. The Shifting Isles, they were called, immense magical rocks that were not anchored in position after the fashion of proper islands but moved about the northern shores of Alfheim with a will of their own. Many a Norscan raider, thinking himself a better warrior than Erik Redaxe, had tried to navigate the Shifting Isles, only to lose his ship when a barren rock suddenly reared up out of the fog where charts insisted there should be only open sea.

Wulfrik dreaded a similar fate for the *Seafang*. To have braved so much and come so far only to wreck his ship upon some elf mage's sorcerous trap would be a pathetic end to his hopes and dreams.

'Sound the bottom,' Wulfrik growled at Arngeirr. The one-legged reaver limped to the side of the longship, dropping a weighted line into the sea. 'The rest of you be ready to push clear from any rocks.' At Wulfrik's command, the crew took up their oars, bracing them to thrust against any obstruction that rose up from the fog to threaten them.

Wulfrik watched the fog swirl about his ship, almost wishing it would drag them back into the spectral border-realm. At least there he would have some idea of what he faced. The hero's mind turned to other stories he had heard about Alfheim. The water around the forbidden island of the elf-folk was said to be infested with terrible monsters. Sailors claimed the spawning waters of the kraken were somewhere off the coast of Alfheim. Others spoke of the pale-skinned merwyrms, the great sea serpents whose coils had crushed the dragonships of Erik Redaxe. There were those who spoke of the megalodon, a shark so huge that it preyed upon whales. Still others whispered of the Black Leviathan, a sea beast so enormous it could swallow a longship with a single snap of its jaws.

'Jokull!' Wulfrik called up to the hunter perched

atop the *Seafang's* mast. 'Keep your eyes on the sea! Shout if you see anything in the water!'

'That will not be necessary,' Zarnath assured the hero. The cloaked shaman made his way effortlessly across the ship's rolling deck, northmen scattering at his approach. Wulfrik's awful threat was still fresh in every man's mind.

'Do you think the sea monsters will shun the flesh of a Kurgan any less than that of a Norscan?' Wulfrik snarled, irritated by the placid, unworried expression on Zarnath's face.

'My magic will hide us from them,' Zarnath stated. 'You need not fear any beast of the Great Western Ocean. Nor need you fear the Shifting Isles.' The shaman lifted one of his arms, waving his hand through the air. In response to his gesture, the fog rolled back, parting as though cut by a blade. As the veil drifted back, the men aboard the ship muttered in awe. Beyond the fog were mighty cliffs, white-capped waves crashing about their rocky base. For hundreds of feet, like a grey wall, the cliffs towered above the sea.

'Behold! The cliffs of Cothique!' Zarnath exclaimed proudly. He smiled as he turned to Wulfrik. 'Atop that wall lies the land of Ulthuan and the site of power that will set you free.'

Wulfrik studied the menacing cliffs. 'You will have earned your price, warlock,' he told Zarnath. 'No coward could call himself master of the *Seafang*. No coward would venture to a place such as this.'

'But first we must break the curse,' Zarnath reminded the hero.

Wulfrik's hand tightened about the jewelled torc, reassuring himself that it was still safe. 'Indeed, Kurgan,' Wulfrik said. 'Let us finish this.' Turning away from the prow, the *Seafang's* captain bellowed at her crew. 'Set oars, men! Before another sun rises, I will feel the soil of Alfheim beneath my boots or I will hear the cries of the valkyries in my ears as they bear my crew to their ancestors!'

THE SEAFANG SAT at anchor beside the sheer face of the grey cliffs. Arngeirr had suggested trying to find a less imposing spot to make their ascent, a sentiment echoed by others of the crew. Zarnath, however, had cautioned against roving too far. The elves had many settlements along the coast of Cothique and each sported its own complement of sleek warships. The shaman's magic could hide them from the notice of the elves, but there was no sense in tempting fate recklessly.

Staring up at the fearsome cliff, Wulfrik was sorely tempted to give in to his grumbling crew. It was only Zarnath's insistence that the site of power they needed to reach was near the top of the cliff which hardened the champion's resolve. More than the risk of elven warships, it was the threat of delay that set his mind to making the dangerous climb. How much time they had already lost travelling into the borderrealm, how much more they would lose on the voyage back were questions that tormented him; he would not add to his lost days any more than he could help.

'Jokull.' Wulfrik beckoned the wiry hunter down

from his perch atop the mast. The northman hastily scrambled down to the deck, joining his captain at the prow. Wulfrik turned his eyes from the cliff, then stared at Jokull. His jaw set, his decision made, the champion handed a thick coil of rope to the hunter.

Jokull studied the cliff, his eyes roving across the jagged stone. He glanced over at Arngeirr, gesturing for the reaver to hand him his flask of kvas. Gasping from the fiery liquor, the hunter thrust the flask back into Arngeirr's hands, his face flushed with the warm rush of alcohol through his body. Slipping the coil of rope over his shoulder, Jokull climbed onto the *Seafang*'s gunwale. Bracing his feet, the hunter leapt at the cliff beside the ship. The tentacle which served him for an arm whipped about, slithering into a gap in the stone, catching fast in the crevice.

Supported by the hold his tentacle-arm had secured, Jokull began to scale the cliff face, inching his way towards the plateau above. The men on the deck of the *Seafang* watched his gradual progress with admiration. Even for the mountain-climbing Norscans, Jokull's feat was impressive.

Hours passed before Jokull reached the top of the cliff. The hunter waved down to his comrades on the ship far below. Soon the rope was cascading over the side, dropping down like some immense vine. Njarvord leaned over the *Seafang*'s gunwale to fish the end of the line from the sea. Savagely he pulled at the rope, testing its strength. Whatever Jokull had found to anchor it to above held firm. Satisfied, the hairy Baersonling handed the rope over to Wulfrik.

'Twenty men with the ship,' Wulfrik told his crew.

'The rest with me. Kaetill is in charge until I return.' The hero tightened his grip on the rope and moved towards the *Seafang's* gunwale. A sudden thought made him turn around, his eyes fixing on Zarnath's robed figure. Grimly, Wulfrik held the rope towards the shaman. 'You first, sorcerer,' he said. 'I'd hate to leave you behind.'

Zarnath's lip curled back in sardonic amusement. The Kurgan made no move to take the rope from Wulfrik. Instead, he strode to the side of the longship. With surprising agility, he leapt onto the gunwale, and from there he flung himself at the cliff. The northmen watched in amazement as the shaman latched onto the sheer cliff face. Like some immense lizard, he scurried up the rocks, seeming to glide over them with only the briefest contact of his hands against the stone.

'We should have had him take the rope up,' observed Haukr, his voice low with awed respect. If any of the men had forgotten the shaman's magic, they were witnessing a stark reminder of it now.

'I don't think I'd trust him to tie it,' Wulfrik said. Fangs gleamed as his face twisted into a snarl. 'And I damn well think I don't want him up there while I'm climbing.'

Without another word, Wulfrik jumped over the side of his ship, his armoured body splashing through the sea until his momentum brought him swinging against the face of the cliff. Setting his boots against the rock, wrapping the heavy rope through his arms, the northman began the arduous climb to the top.

Broendulf used a bill-hook to retrieve the end of the rope from the sea. He watched Wulfrik scaling up the cliff for a moment, then turned to the rest of the crew. 'Come along, you dogs!' he barked. 'We need to beat the Kurgan before he decides to cut the rope!'

Cursing all sorcerers and outlanders, the northmen followed their captain. They couldn't keep the fear from their eyes as they glanced at Zarnath's lizard-crawl, watching the shaman draw steadily closer to the top. It was a hopeless race, but the stoic Norscans were determined to run it anyway. Dying because of treachery was better than living because of cowardice.

With all eyes upon the cliff and the men struggling up its face, no one was left to watch the sea, or to observe something stirring beneath the waves.

IT WAS A good land, Wulfrik decided as he cast his gaze across the rolling plains of Alfheim. Everything was green and vibrant, even when winter gripped Norsca in its icy claws. The hero wasn't sure if it was some caprice of latitude that made the island flourish or the powerful magics of the elf-folk that kept the ravages of snow and frost from their shores. It didn't matter. It was enough to see with his own eyes this enchanted realm. For a moment, he could even forget the grim purpose that had brought him here.

The plains stretched away in a great prairie of swaying grass, the green sea broken only by occasional islands of darker hue, isolated stands of trees, great ashes and oaks taller and mightier than any tree Wulfrik had ever seen. Wild flowers of every colour and description added to the beauty of the plains. The northmen could see a stream cutting through the landscape, its waters so clear and pure that they might have been made of glass.

Crowding close upon the prairie were a range of mountains equalled only by those upon which the Norscans had hunted the dread yhetee. The mighty Annulii Mountains, their slopes lush with thick forests of pine, their peaks shrouded in cloud. A nimbus of light, pulsating and crackling with aethyric energies, shimmered about the heights of the mountains. Wulfrik was reminded of the aurora which could be seen glowing in the northern skies of his homeland, an eerie manifestation of the raw power of his gods.

Wulfrik turned his face from the mountains and the eerie display of magical energies coruscating about their peaks. The sudden reminder of his gods made him question what he was trying to do. He could almost hear Sigvatr's voice cautioning him against defying his curse and in doing so challenging the gods. Seeing the northern aurora repeated here in the land of the elf-folk made him think of something Agnarr had once told him. The eyes of the gods were everywhere, always watching. It was never a question of if the gods *could* see a man's deeds, but whether they *would* choose to see.

Would the gods choose to see him now, stealing through the plains of Alfheim, searching for the place that would allow him to escape his curse? Was it nothing but some cruel game with which the gods were amusing themselves? In the moment of triumph, as he reached his hand out to seize his destiny, would the gods snatch it from him like a cruel father wresting a toy from a child's hand? Had he come so far only to fail?

The hero looked aside, hiding the doubt he felt within as he stared into the faces of his warriors. He could see the fear there, the anxiety running through their hearts. All of them had heard the saga of Erik Redaxe and the terrible doom that had claimed his fleet. They knew how terrible the elf-folk were to invaders and that from their wrath there could be little chance of escape.

Yet still they followed him, these sons of Norsca. Sarls and Baersonlings, Vargs and Graelings, Aeslings and Bjornlings, whatever their tribe, they followed him. They trusted Wulfrik to lead them to glory, to victories that would be worthy of the sagas. Even here, in the supernatural realm of the elf-folk, pride and courage would not make them hide their faces. They would face their doom and spit in the eye of death even as it reached out its bony claws to claim them. Wulfrik admired their acceptance of fate, but he would not share it. He would cheat his own doom and if he had to use these men to do so, then so it would be.

'Where is this place you must cast your spell?' Wulfrik asked Zarnath as he turned his back to the mountains.

The shaman didn't appear to hear Wulfrik at first, his eyes instead roving across the landscape, seemingly overwhelmed by the peaceful beauty of the prairie. When the hulking champion took a step towards him, however, Zarnath was instantly alert, springing back, his hands clutching the seal-fur cloak tight about him.

'Your touch will profane me!' the shaman warned, his voice raised into a shriek. 'The ritual won't work if you defile me!'

'The ritual will work,' Wulfrik said. 'Or you'll never be master of the *Seafang*. Indeed, your bones will probably remain here for the elf-folk to bury.'

Zarnath scowled at the threat, but held his peace. He knew how dangerously thin Wulfrik's temper had grown the nearer they came to the end of his quest. The hero was becoming more suspicious and paranoid with each passing breath. There had been a moment, atop the cliff, when he had thought Wulfrik would try to seize him and throw him into the sea, convinced the shaman had intended to cut the rope when he reached the top.

The shaman turned his scowl into a smile, trying to reassure Wulfrik. He pointed a thin hand towards one of the clusters of trees dotting the plains. 'There,' Zarnath said. 'I can sense the power I need to draw upon coming from among that copse.'

Wulfrik glanced at the stand of trees, then back at the shaman. The copse looked like any other bunch of trees scattered across the landscape. 'You are certain?' he asked, his voice a low growl.

Before the Kurgan could answer, Jokull's voice was raised in alarm. The hunter gestured with his hand at something off to the left of Wulfrik and his men. Every warrior turned his eye towards whatever Jokull had spotted. It took only a moment to recognise riders galloping across the meadows. Even from such a distance, the northmen could see the lean, powerful build of the horses and the knights who rode upon them. Sunlight glimmered off the sharp points of their lances, reflected from the polished plates of silvered helms and armour. Following their progress, the men could see a structure towards which the knights were advancing. It was a tall, slender building crafted from some strange yellow-hued marble. It didn't seem to rise from the ground so much as flow from it, every contour of its delicate architecture crafted to blend into the aesthetics of the plains.

'Elf-folk,' Njarvord grumbled, fingering his axe. The other warriors muttered fearfully and drew their own weapons.

'They go to report to their kings,' Broendulf said. 'We must return to the *Seafang* before they can bring an army against us.'

Wulfrik turned on the frightened huscarl. 'Any man who tries to go back to the sea will get a taste of my steel.' Sheepishly, the fair-faced huscarl lowered his head.

'There is no need for fear,' Zarnath insisted. 'My magic hides us from their eyes. If it were not so, they would have caught us upon the cliffs and shot us full of arrows before we ever set foot in Ulthuan.'

'The warlock's spells protect us,' muttered Tjorvi. 'I feel safer already.'

'Safe or not,' Wulfrik snarled, 'no man leaves here until we have done what we came here to do.' The hero drew both swords from his belt, brandishing them over his head to emphasise his point.

'Lead the way, sorcerer,' Wulfrik told Zarnath.

Bowing his head, the shaman led the warriors across the plains towards the dark copse and their captain's doom.

Chapter Thirteen

Raised voices greeted the northmen as they crept into the shadows of the copse. Standing among the trees, Wulfrik could not decide if they were natural growth or had been planted in some complex pattern by the elf-folk long ago. There was something unnatural about the trees, a deformity about them that made his flesh crawl. Not the sort of corruption as had afflicted Fraener, but a more subtle kind of change, a sorcerous enhancement that had altered the trees from root to branch. It wasn't the change that upset Wulfrik's sensibilities, but the way the magic had been so seamlessly blended into the trees. A man could feel the alteration, but he could not see it.

The voices were no less strange to the ears of the Norscans. They were sombre and piercing, with a musical quality to them that made the men recall tales of sirens and harpies who could lure a longship to wreck itself with only the power of their song. Nothing human ever spoke in such melodious tones, even the little songbirds the Arabyans kept never sang with such beauty.

Wulfrik grew tense, certain that for all the melody within them, the voices were some kind of alarm, that whatever power lurked within the copse was aware of the invaders and was warning the elf-folk of their presence.

Zarnath tried to calm the hero and his warriors. 'Those are the voices of the elves,' the shaman told them. 'It is they who are singing, thanking the land for keeping them safe from their enemies – both element and man.'

'They should sing louder,' Njarvord growled, a bloodthirsty gleam in his eye. It had been far too long since the Baersonling had killed something.

The shaman chuckled at the remark. 'Even if they did, my magic would hide us from them.' For an instant, a troubled expression flickered across the Kurgan's face, a look which was equal parts doubt and guilt. Zarnath quickly composed himself. 'We must press on,' he told Wulfrik. 'The very heart of the grove. The magic will be at its most powerful there. Strong enough to break even a curse from the gods.'

Wulfrik smiled. 'If this works, warlock, I shall give you a dozen ships like the *Seafang* and a thousand men to crew them! You shall be acclaimed the mightiest sorcerer in all Norsca!'

Zarnath bowed his head in acknowledgement of the honour Wulfrik paid him. 'We must hurry then, to claim our due.'

The marauders marched through the glade. There was no question now that the trees grew in a pattern, forming a great spiral that wound itself tighter and tighter as it drew towards the centre. The voices grew louder as the men pressed deeper into the copse, the sense of magic becoming so strong that the breath of the warriors turned to frost. Closer and closer the Norscans approached the centre, Zarnath's voice snapping at them like a whip when the oppressive feeling of the glade caused them to hesitate. Wulfrik echoed the shaman's orders, urging his men on.

Soon there will be an end to it, Wulfrik thought, and the curse will be behind me. Then I will take my place as king of the Sarls with Hjordis beside me and after me my son will become High King of all Norsca.

Jokull hissed a warning from his place at the head of the column, motioning for the northmen to halt their march. Scurrying back through the ranks of warriors, the hunter made his report to Wulfrik. 'The path opens into a clearing ahead. A great stone stands at its centre, not unlike the dolmens reared by the Kurgan tribes,' he added, casting a suspicious glance at Zarnath.

'A menhir,' explained the shaman. 'Erected by the elves to mark the lines of magic flowing through Ulthuan and help channel their energies back into the vortex.'

The hunter shrugged at Zarnath's explanation. 'Whatever it is, you can see it glowing with light wherever the shadow of a tree falls upon it. The entire surface of the thing is etched with strange runes...'

Wulfrik seized the hunter by his tunic, lifting him from the ground. 'You try to frighten us with stories of glowing rocks!' he snarled, his fangs bared.

'No! No!' Jokull protested. 'There are people surrounding the stone! Elf-folk!'

Wulfrik released the hunter. 'How many? How are they armed?'

'Thirty or forty,' the hunter answered after a moment of consideration. 'I saw no armour and no weapons. They seemed to me to be women, she-elves.'

A greedy laugh rumbled up from Haukr's tattooed face and he clapped his hands together. 'Elf wenches! Those should be worth twice their weight in silver if we get them back to Ormskaro alive!'

'They'd swallow their own tongues before sailing with you, Haukr,' said Arngeirr.

Haukr scowled at the one-legged reaver's advice. 'Some sort of bit would be in order then,' he said, rubbing his chin as he considered the idea.

Zarnath saw the way Haukr's avaricious proposal was taking hold of the northmen. They sailed with Wulfrik to share in his glory, but none of them was an altruist. A bit of plunder, even living plunder, was a welcome bonus.

The shaman's eyes narrowed with contempt. He turned to Wulfrik, but when he spoke his voice was loud enough for all the marauders to hear. 'You must take no chances with these elves! They are witches, harnessing their magic through the menhir! Allow them a moment's breath and they will cast a spell on you!'

Wulfrik rounded on his men, glaring at them like a rabid troll. 'You heard the sorcerer!' he snapped. 'No prisoners. No mercy. We fall upon the elf-folk and kill them all. If any man allows one to escape, he pays for his mistake with his heart.' The hero motioned with his sword, gesturing at his warriors. 'Spread through the trees, Jokull will show you where. Every man chooses his own prey. When I begin the attack, find your elf and kill her.'

The northmen scattered along the path, forming a perimeter around the clearing. Fists tightened about axes and swords as each warrior took his place. They positioned themselves in the narrow gaps between the trees, their eyes fixing upon the kneeling elves they saw gathered around the menhir.

Wulfrik took his place at the forefront of the ambush, pressing close against the trunk of a towering oak growing near the spot where the spiral path opened into the clearing. The melodious sound of the elven voices filled his ears, tugging at his heart. There was sorrow and anguish in that song, a desperate pleading in the cadence of the strange lyrics. He thought there was hope there too, a hope nourished long after it should have been allowed to die, a pathetic entreaty to uncaring gods for succour and solace. The Norscan gazed into the clearing, observing the elf women as they knelt before the ancient menhir. They were thin, delicate creatures, as fine and fragile as the porcelain dolls crafted by the southlings. Their lean bodies were wrapped in shifts of silver thread, the flowing locks of their golden hair bound in caskets of diamond wire. Sandals of ivory and ruby clung to their tiny feet and rings of sapphire and jade shone upon their fingers. Somehow, the northman did not find the display of jewels and wealth ostentatious or gaudy, every diamond and every ruby combined to complement the intrinsic grace of the she-elves. Wulfrik felt his determination waver as he contemplated the beauty of these creatures. Panic seized him as he remembered Zarnath's warning about witchcraft and magic.

Roaring, Wulfrik exploded into the clearing, leaping over an earthen mound to pounce upon the elf he had marked as the first to feel his sword. Strangely, the elves did not react to his savage charge or his fierce war cry. Only when his raised sword came slashing down, cleaving through the dainty neck of a kneeling elf, did the elves awaken to their danger. As the blood of Wulfrik's first victim sprayed across the menhir, the others leapt to their feet, screaming in shock and horror as the other marauders came rushing at them from the trees. The warriors surged over the low earthen mounds surrounding the clearing, leaping over them as easily as their captain had. Naked steel gleamed in the sun as the northmen fell upon the elves.

The massacre was as swift as it was brutal. None of the she-elves escaped the clearing, but died in their dozens around the menhir. The last to fall did not even try to flee, but bowed their heads and waited for the axes of the northmen with what dignity they could still command.

Wulfrik gazed across the slaughter, wiping elven blood from his blades. His men prowled among the bodies, killing the wounded, ripping jewels from the bodies of the dead. The echoes of the elf song continued to sound in Wulfrik's mind, a mournful dirge that whispered to him of dreams denied and dead. The hero shook his head, trying to drive the sounds away. The elf-folk were a fading people, doomed to oblivion. Men would not share their fate. He would not share their fate.

The champion pulled the Smile of Sardiss from his belt, watching it gleam in the glow of the menhir. Soon he would be free. Then he would return to this ghostly land and give the elf-folk reason to cry in the twilight of their kingdom.

Harsh laughter boomed like thunder through the clearing. The northmen turned to find Zarnath glaring at them, his eyes burning like pits of azure flame. 'Blood-crazed barbarians!' the shaman howled. 'You have sown the seeds of your own destruction!' He gestured with a claw-like hand at the butchered she-elves. 'These were no witches, but elf-wives come to pray to their gods for fertility! Such wrath as the warriors of Ulthuan will visit upon you for this outrage will make the very heavens cringe in horror!'

Zarnath's words faded into another peal of caustic laughter. The marauders stared fearfully at him, wondering if the magic of this place had overwhelmed his mind and driven him mad. Sane or otherwise, Wulfrik would not be mocked by the shaman, not after all that had been promised to him.

'You share our doom then, sorcerer,' Wulfrik snarled, stalking towards Zarnath. In one hand he still held the torc, in the other he gripped his sword. 'Without me you will never master the *Seafang* and without the ship you will never leave Alfheim!' He raised his fist, shaking the torc at the shaman.

'Keep your promise, Kurgan! Free me of my curse!'

Zarnath's face twisted into a sneer of loathing and contempt. 'Be damned to your Dark Gods and their thousand hells!' he spat. 'It is you who are trapped here, doomed and damned by your own deeds! Rot, barbarian! Fester in the soil of Ulthuan until your bones are dust and your name forgotten!'

Fury seized the hero. Like a panther, he sprang at the mocking shaman. His sword slashed at Zarnath's head, the heavy blade cleaving through the Kurgan's face. Wulfrik stumbled and crashed to the ground as his body lost balance. Instead of striking flesh and bone, his sword encountered only empty air.

'Keep your devil-ship, barbarian,' Zarnath hissed. 'I do not need it to leave this place, because I was never here!'

Wulfrik lifted his face from the dust, his eyes glaring murder at the Kurgan. Angrily he shook the Smile of Sardiss at Zarnath. 'All a lie!' the hero raged. 'From the first!'

Zarnath lifted his hand, pointing at the sky overhead. A flare of light exploded from his fingers, rocketing through the air. High above the trees, the light blew apart in a great starburst, burning like a second sun over the copse. 'Every elf in Cothique will see that,' the shaman laughed. 'You will not escape the armies of Ulthuan as you did those of the fire dwarfs!'

From the ground, Wulfrik leapt at the mocking sorcerer, lunging at him like an enraged tiger. Zarnath's body seemed to fold around the hero's outstretched arms, collapsing as Wulfrik's drive bowled him to the ground. But when the Norscan stared at the mass beneath him, he found he had caught nothing more than the shaman's seal-fur cloak. Of the man who had worn it, there wasn't any trace.

'A wraith,' gasped Haukr, eyes bulging with fright. 'All this time, he was nothing but a ghost!'

'He was real enough before,' Njarvord growled. 'Real enough to turn tail and run when that dwarf sorcerer was after him.'

'It was a sending,' Broendulf told them. 'Zarnath kept his body back in Norsca and only sent his spirit along with us, wrapped in that magic cloak. That was why he insisted no one touch him. There wasn't anything there to touch.' The huscarl stared intently at his captain, watching as Wulfrik slowly rose to his feet. The hero made no move to address his crew, simply glaring down at the empty cloak on the ground.

Carefully, Broendulf approached Wulfrik. The huscarl knew he could easily strike down his chief while his mind was lost to the immensity of the betrayal that had robbed him of his dreams. Broendulf, however, wasn't willing to forsake his own life to eliminate that of his captain. Zarnath might not need the *Seafang* to escape from Alfheim, but the rest of them did.

'Wulfrik,' Broendulf carefully addressed his captain. 'That cur told the truth about one thing. The elf-folk will be coming here and they will avenge what we've done this day. We have to get back to the *Seafang*.'

The hero turned his head, staring into Broendulf's

face. The fair-faced Sarl had never seen a more piteous look of despair than that which clouded the eyes of Wulfrik at that moment. It was like looking into the eyes of something already dead.

'All a lie!' the champion moaned.

The northman's cry seemed to ripple across the clearing, echoing strangely from the trees and the glowing menhir. Broendulf turned away from his dazed chieftain to find the source of the weird echoes. His blood turned to ice as he saw strange misty shapes rising from the earthen mounds. His horror was echoed in the frightened howls of the other warriors. As a man, they backed away from the weird mist, their skin prickling from a spectral chill.

From each of the mounds, a column of mist slowly drifted towards the Norscans. There was something hideously suggestive about the shapeless masses, something elusive yet familiar. Each of the six foot pillars of grey fog lingered above the pools of blood splashed throughout the clearing. As each patch of mist hovered over the blood, it became less translucent, more a thing of substance than shadow. Form began to replace shapelessness, cloudy wisps of fog becoming lean arms and thin faces. Before the stunned eyes of the northmen, the mists became phantom figures, deathly elves draped in shrouds, ancient armour clinging to their emaciated bodies.

The face of each ghost was a mask of silent, inhuman rage, its dead eyes burning with the fury of the grave. The earthen mounds surrounding the clearing were barrows, the tombs of fallen elves. When the northmen had spilled blood so near the menhir, they had drawn the spirits of the elves from their biers. Now they closed upon the murderers to wreak vengeance for their slaughtered descendants. Zarnath's projection had fled back to Norsca too quickly to appreciate the immediacy of the trap he had set for Wulfrik and his crew.

One of the new crewmen, a brawny whaler from Ormskaro, mustered his courage, determined to prove his valour to his comrades and his gods. Raising his axe on high, bellowing like a rampaging ogre, the marauder charged the ghost nearest to him. In the blink of an eye, a phantom sword appeared in the apparition's bony claw. The marauder's axe passed harmlessly through the ghost, but when the spirit stabbed its blade into his breast, the northman screamed in agony. His flesh blackened where the sword struck him, rotting from his bones even as he tried to back away. He was dead before he could raise his axe for a second blow.

'Kharnath's blood!' Haukr swore, retreating from the advancing ghosts. 'How can we fight what we can't even touch!'

'Like the drowned legions of Mermedus,' Tjorvi shuddered. The slippery Graeling had his back to the menhir, his eyes darting about, looking for any gap between the ghosts he could exploit to reach the shelter of the trees.

Another of the new recruits from Ormskaro shrieked as a ghost cut him down. The man's destruction seemed to energise the other ghosts. Like an onrushing tide, they swept towards the men, their swords stabbing through bodies, leaving withered husks lying on the ground.

'Hopeless or no, they don't take me without a fight!' Njarvord cursed. The hairy Baersonling gnashed his teeth, glaring at the nearest of the phantoms. Before he could rush into the midst of the ghosts, he felt Jokull's hand on his shoulder, pulling him back. The hunter gestured towards Arngeirr. Like the rest of them, the one-legged reaver was beset by the apparitions. However, his kraken-tooth sword was proving more effective than steel. When he struck the ghosts, their misty bodies flew apart, drifting away across the clearing. The hope that he was doing the ghosts any lasting damage was quickly banished. The scattered mists soon reformed into spectral elves. Arngeirr could fend off the ghosts, but he couldn't destroy them.

Relentlessly, the ghosts pushed the northmen back. Broendulf grabbed Wulfrik's arm, intending to pull him from the path of the advancing spirits. The hero angrily wrested free from his grip. For an instant, the huscarl thought Wulfrik was going to split his skull with his sword.

'All a lie!' the champion growled at Broendulf.

'Are you going to die here then, and let the dog get away with cheating you?' Broendulf growled back.

Wulfrik's face became livid, the rage boiling within his eyes burning away the despair that had filled them. 'All a lie!' the hero roared, hurling the Smile of Sardiss at the glowing menhir. The torc struck the standing stone, shattering into a hundred pieces, the shards scattering across the clearing.

A stagnant, mephitic stench rose from the shards of the shattered torc. The power contained within Khorakk's talisman was freed by its impact against the enchanted menhir. Like crimson smoke, it slithered across the clearing, lingering over the bodies of the slain as the elven spectres had done. The ghosts withdrew from the red smoke much as the northmen had recoiled from the approach of the phantoms. Their retreat, however, was not quick enough.

From the midst of the smoke a great hairy arm struck out, the black talons on its hand lancing through one of the ghosts. The spectre uttered an anguished wail as the claw shredded its essence, scattering its ghostly form. A barking, snorting sound rumbled from the cloud, the hungry grumble of something bestial and monstrous.

The ghosts forgot about the northmen, converging upon the red smoke and the thing lurking within it. Their phantom swords lashed out, cleaving through the smoke, evoking pained howls from the lurker. The smoke rippled away from the spectres, smashing into one of the men from Ormskaro. The Sarl shrieked as three hairy arms, lanky and segmented like the limbs of a spider, shot out of the smoke and tore his body into bloody sections. Ugly, slobbering sounds came from the midst of the smoke as the thing inside greedily devoured the man it had slaughtered. The cloud of smoke swelled, growing larger as the beast gorged itself. The ghosts pursuing it hesitated, something like fright passing across their dead faces.

Masters of a sinister magic, there was no saying

what sort of daemon the dwarfs of Zharr Naggrund had bound into the Smile of Sardiss, but it was such a thing as to make even a phantom know fear.

Wulfrik did not care what the thing hiding in the red smoke was. It was enough that it would keep the ghosts busy while his men escaped. Roused from his despair by Broendulf's words, a new purpose filled the hero's heart in place of the hope that had so cruelly been crushed. Revenge. He would find Zarnath and he would make of the treacherous shaman an end that would make even the gods tremble.

'Away, you dogs!' Wulfrik called to his crew. 'Stop gawking and take to your heels! The daemon will kill you just as quick as the ghosts!' As if to prove the hero's words, the red smoke slammed into another of the Sarls clustered about the menhir, tearing him apart in the same grisly fashion as his comrade.

'Away!' Wulfrik barked again. He grinned fiercely as his warriors rushed past him, racing into the forest. The hero lingered a moment, soaking in the spectacle of the butchered elf-wives and his slaughtered men, of the wailing ghosts and the raging daemon. Of the crimson shards of the torc strewn about the clearing.

'We've a ship to sail,' Wulfrik growled through clenched fangs, 'and a Kurgan to kill.'

THE MARAUDERS RACED through the forest, eager to put as much distance between themselves and the haunted clearing as possible. More than before, the trees seemed to regard them with some awful awareness of their own, hostile and malignant.

Unconsciously, the northmen kept to the path winding through the grove, unwilling to chance pushing their way through the trees. At every turn, they expected to see the ghosts barring their way or encounter the crimson daemon still eager to glut its hunger.

When trouble came, it came from neither phantom nor fiend.

A Sarl suddenly cried out, toppling to the ground, an arrow through his neck. From the shadows, more arrows came whistling down, lodging into the bodies of men with chilling accuracy. Warriors crumpled to the ground before they could even draw their axes, their bodies looking like pin-cushions as arrow after arrow stabbed into their flesh.

Had their attackers been less wrathful, they could have slaughtered Wulfrik's entire warband. Instead, the ambushers vented their fury, loosing arrows into the same target over and over.

'In the trees!' Jokull shouted. The hunter loosed one of his own arrows into the darkness overhead. A thin wail greeted his shot, and a lean body hurtled down from the branches to slam into the ground. It was the body of an elf, that of a warrior wearing breastplate and helm over his green tunic and robes. A yew bow fell from the elf's dead fingers.

Zarnath's flare had alerted the elves in the tower. With incredible speed they had dispatched scouts to investigate and defend the elf-wives praying in the grove. Hearing the sounds of men running through the woods, the elves had hidden themselves in the trees. It was easy enough for them to guess they were too late to save their wives: every one of Wulfrik's warriors was carrying loot ripped from the dead she-elves. Now they would wreak a terrible revenge upon the barbarian invaders.

Jokull had only a second to revel in the accuracy of his archery. A dozen arrows thumped into his body, striking him with such speed that they might have been loosed from a single bow. The hunter's bloody body slumped against the trunk of a tree, his tentacle writhing against his chest as life drained out of him.

Wulfrik snarled in impotent wrath. The elves were picking his men off one by one and there was nothing the northmen could do to fight back. The trees offered some cover, his marauders forgetting their repugnance in their eagerness to avoid the arrows of their foes. But there was no real shelter to be had in the wood. He could hear the branches overhead creaking as the elves nimbly sprang from one perch to another, circling around the warriors to strike them from behind.

Staying in the copse was death. The prairie would be worse: the grass and wildflowers would offer absolutely no protection from the elven bowmen, but at least it offered a chance to reach the *Seafang* and escape.

'Dogs of Norsca!' Wulfrik shouted to his men. 'Follow me and live, stay here and die!'

The hero didn't wait to see how many of his men abandoned their cover to follow him. He was too busy sprinting down the path, weaving from side to side as he ran, trying to thwart the marksmanship of the elves. Arrows whistled past his ear, stabbing into the earth around him. Pain flared through his body as one of the missiles cut across his arm, leaving a bloody gash along his shoulder. Behind him, he could hear northmen crying out in agony as other arrows found their mark.

Bright sunlight welcomed Wulfrik when he emerged from the copse. The men following him cheered as they felt the warmth of day shining down on them, banishing the supernatural chill of the sacred grove from their bones. From the depths of the forest, the screams of the men who had clung to the cover of the trees rang out as the elves continued to whittle away at them.

Wulfrik dismissed the wretches from his mind. They had made their choice, now they would suffer for it. The gods favoured the bold. The best of his crew were still with him. They would be enough to sail the *Seafang* and voyage back to Norsca and vengeance.

The hero studied the winded, panting warriors behind him. Almost every man had at least one elven arrow stuck in his flesh; only a half-dozen of the score who had managed to escape the forest looked unscathed. Every man cast frightened glances back into the trees.

'They won't stay in there long,' he snarled at his warriors. 'As soon as they finish off the men we left behind, they'll be howling at our heels!' Wulfrik turned and pointed his sword across the plains, towards the distant cliff on the horizon. 'We won't be safe until the *Seafang* is under our feet again and we are gone from this accursed land!'

Tired, wounded, the northmen nevertheless jogged after Wulfrik as he set out over the prairie. At every step, each man expected to feel an arrow slam into his back. With nowhere to hide and only open ground between them and the sea, there was no question of eluding the elves when they emerged from the forest and began their pursuit. The only uncertainty was how long it would take their enemies to catch them.

Resigned to their doom, the northmen loped through the grassy meadows. The landscape that had filled them with admiration only hours ago now seemed to them as bleak and unforgiving as the wastes of the Dark Lands, as pitiless as the Mountains of Mourn. There seemed no end to the rolling plains, the cliffs drawing no nearer no matter how strenuously they strived to reach them. The worst of the crew's wounded fell as they ran, slumping wearily to the ground. No thought was given to helping them; each man had to save his strength for himself. The abandoned men did not curse their comrades, but instead turned their faces back to the copse and drew their axes. At least they would have steel in their fists when they entered the halls of their ancestors.

Wulfrik ignored the pulsing pain in his arm as he ran, was deaf to the sound of injured men collapsing behind him. Only the cliff and the sea mattered now, reaching the *Seafang* and showing Zarnath that his trap had failed.

The hero held up his arm, motioning his warriors to halt. Wulfrik glared across the meadows, watching as seven riders galloped towards the northmen, the sun glistening from their tall silvery helms and long lances. Elf knights, waiting to cut off the retreat of the men who had escaped from the grove! Wulfrik cursed. Caught in the open, the armoured cavalry would cut the marauders down as easily as the bowmen.

'What do we do?' Tjorvi demanded, panic in his voice.

Wulfrik gave the Graeling a contemptuous glance. 'We hold our ground, unless you want to go back to the grove.'

Before the northmen, the galloping knights lowered their lances. The ground shuddered as they spurred their powerful warhorses into a charge. The marauders could see the stern, merciless expressions on the faces of the elves. No quarter would be given. The knights would ride them down like animals.

Wulfrik bared his fangs and braced himself for the attack. 'Any man who fails to slay three knights is a mongrel unfit to lick the arse of a maggot!' he growled at his men.

'Kill these bastards and prove to the gods your fathers weren't southling thralls!'

Chapter Fourteen

THE ELF KNIGHTS gave voice to a weird exultation, a cry as melodious as a harp and biting as a whip. There was neither doubt nor hesitance in the riders as they bore down upon the northmen. Masters of saddle and blade, hardened by centuries of warfare, the knights had only contempt for the barbarians who stood before them. Many of the elves had been there when Erik Redaxe's army had been slaughtered by the hosts of Cothique and Chrace. They remembered that battle now as they charged Wulfrik's men, confident that these wounded, weary marauders would be easy prey.

Several of the Sarl warriors were indeed trampled by the knights, their bodies torn and mangled by their lances. But the elves did not strike with impunity. The horde of Erik Redaxe had looked to their king for leadership and in that moment of need, he had failed them. Wulfrik was made of sterner stuff than the vanquished king.

As the knights rode down his crew, Wulfrik sprang from the ground, his sword lashing out, the blade hacking into the arm of an elven rider. The bright, silvery ithilmar mail withstood the sharp edge of the hero's sword, but the bone within was not so unyielding. The crushing impact of Wulfrik's blow snapped the rider's arm like a twig. The elf cried out in shock, his lance falling from a suddenly nerveless hand. Before the elf could recover from his surprise, Wulfrik's other sword came flashing out at him. The left-hand blade glanced across the horn of the elf's saddle, stabbing deep into the neck of the horse he rode.

Wulfrik jumped back as the injured warhorse reared up, its hooves pawing the air, blood spurting from where the northman's sword was buried in its neck. The knight struggled to recover control of his wounded steed. Almost he succeeded, such was his mastery over the beast, but before he could wheel the warhorse around, Njarvord rushed at him from the other side, smashing into the horse's flank with his shoulder. The Baersonling's berserk charge and the fury of his impact against the horse caused the animal to lose its footing.

Whinnying in terror, beast and elf fell. The knight struggled to pull himself from beneath his thrashing steed, but before he could, Njarvord was upon him, driving his axe into the knight's face. The sharp, patrician features of the knight lost their ethereal beauty as the axe's spike stabbed over and again into his face.

A second knight, seeing the destruction of his comrade, charged Njarvord. The Baersonling had only just turned away from his victim to face the sound of pounding hooves when the knight's lance crunched through his ribs, exploding from his back in a welter of gore. Impaled upon the knight's lance, the northman howled in pain, blood and froth bubbling from his mouth.

The elf's horse reared back, the man impaled upon the knight's lance lifted into the air by the motion. The knight kicked out with his armoured boot to push Njarvord's body from his weapon. The smack of a boot in his belly roused the Norscan, giving his mind something more than pain to consider. Njarvord glared at the elf, spitting blood at the haughty knight as he moved to kick the marauder a second time. Clenching his teeth, Njarvord closed one hand around the shaft of the lance. Screaming his agony, the warrior pulled his body down the lance, feeling his bones crack as he pressed the shaft deeper into his flesh. Angrily, Njarvord shook his head, struggling to defy the pain. Trembling with the effort, he raised his other arm, the cleaving edge of his axe gleaming in the sun.

Horror crawled onto the elf's face. In a thousand years, the elf knight had never seen such mindless, murderous determination. Panicked, he kicked his boot into Njarvord's body, raking his thighs with his spurs. The warhorse reared again, its legs flailing at the impaled northman. Njarvord defied every effort to knock him loose. Shrieking a war cry that would have deafened the grim gods of the north, he forced his body another foot down the lance and brought his axe swinging around to cleave the elf asunder.

Belatedly, the knight abandoned his lance, casting

it and the man impaled upon it from his grasp. The move caused Njarvord's axe to miss its target. Within reach of the elf, the marauder's blow would have torn even an ithilmar breastplate. Instead, the strike crunched into the skull of the warhorse, splitting it down to the jaw. The beast dropped as though smashed flat by the fist of a giant, crashing to the ground, crushing the dying mass of its killer beneath its own bulk.

The elf knight tried to squirm out of the saddle as his steed died beneath him. With an inhuman display of grace and agility, he lifted himself from the back of his warhorse and sprang to the ground. Instantly, his battle-hardened reflexes were in motion, an ithilmar blade flashing from its scabbard to parry the strike of a Norscan sword. However, even the elf's reflexes were not enough to fend off Wulfrik's second blade. The hero's sword smashed into the knight's back, just above the join between cuirass and mail skirt. The elf flopped to the earth, his spine severed. He tried to slash his blade across the champion's belly as Wulfrik loomed over the wounded knight. The northman's boot smashed down upon the elf's hand, breaking every finger as he ground his heel savagely against the prisoned flesh. The elf's cry of pain was silenced in a bloody gargle as Wulfrik stabbed the point of his sword into the knight's neck.

Wulfrik turned away from the dead elf, shaking the knight's blood from his sword, his eyes hungry for enemies to slay. He found four knights galloping across the plains, heading away towards the grove. Behind them they left three of their number. Arngeirr had cut the legs out from under a warhorse, the kraken-tooth sword shearing clean through flesh and bone. The dismounted knight had been finished off by a blow from Broendulf's sword.

However, the knights had wreaked havoc with their charge just the same. In addition to Njarvord, seven northmen were lying dead in the grass. Only ten of the marauders were still standing with Wulfrik. He could almost read the thoughts of the elf riders. They had lost almost half their number, but they had destroyed half of the invaders with that charge. The price was high, but with their blood roused by the massacre of their wives, the elves might not care how many of their own fell to prevent the invaders from escaping.

Wulfrik turned his head and snarled at his surviving crew. 'Gather the bodies,' he snapped. 'Build a barricade against their next charge.' He watched his men only long enough to make sure they were following his orders, then returned his attention to the knights. As he had predicted, they were wheeling about, making ready for another charge. Then, suddenly, they stopped. Wulfrik saw one of the knights turn and look behind him. Faintly he could hear the rider shout something. The hero's keen eyes could see movement in the grass. It could be one of the wounded men the marauders had left behind trying to crawl his way to the cliff, but somehow he doubted it. When he saw the knights lean back in their saddles, adopting an almost relaxed posture, he was certain of it. There would be no charge now. The knights were afraid of trampling their own people as they crept through the tall grass.

'Down!' Wulfrik snarled, diving behind the gory wreck of the horse that had crushed Njarvord. Not all of the other northmen were quick to understand the immediacy of their captain's howl. Two Sarls struggling to move the corpse of Arngeirr's horse, and a third Sarl trying to shift the body of an elf knight; these were caught in the open when the reason for Wulfrik's warning manifested itself.

Several hundred yards from where the northmen made their stand, bowmen suddenly rose from the grass. With lethal precision, the elves loosed a volley of arrows at the warriors, dozens of shafts falling upon the men in a murderous rain. The Sarls caught without cover shrieked as the arrows slammed into them, crumpling to the earth like broken toys.

Wulfrik pressed his shoulder against the horse carcass he hid behind, forcing it up onto its side, using it like a shield against the incoming arrows. The morbid bulwark shuddered as it was struck again and again, but none of the missiles stabbed deep enough to strike the man himself. He risked a quick look past the rump of the warhorse, watching as the elves dropped back down into the grass.

'More to starboard!' Arngeirr shouted. Frantically, the northmen shifted their grisly shields as a second band of archers rose from the tall grass and sent a volley at them. More screams sounded as one of the Sarls was hit, a shaft lodged in his hip. He flopped out from behind the pile of Norscan dead he had used for shelter, rolling across the ground in agony. A second arrow silenced him, smashing clean through his forehead.

'Scum! Curseling swine!'

Wulfrik felt steel press into his collar, felt blood gushing down his shoulder. He rolled onto his back, kicking out with his boot. A blade flashed before his eyes. He heard the sound of metal sinking into flesh as the blade hacked into the horse carcass. It had missed his neck by a hairsbreadth, but for the impact of his boot against the body of his assailant, it would have struck true.

Tjorvi ripped his axe from the dead horse, at the same time slashing his knife at Wulfrik, the hero's blood dripping from its steel. The Graeling's face was livid with rage, the merciless fury of a man overwhelmed by fear. 'We trusted you to lead us to glory!' Tjorvi hissed. 'Instead you bring us only death!'

The furious warrior lunged at Wulfrik. Wulfrik swatted aside Tjorvi's axe, prepared to do the same with the man's knife when his keen ears caught the whistle of arrows in the air. He tried to throw himself flat, but was too late to avoid all of the missiles hurtling down upon the northmen. Pain flashed through his body as an arrow slashed across the side of his head, gouging a deep furrow in his scalp. A second crunched into the meat of his leg, a third punched through his forearm.

Shielded from the arrows by his foe, Tjorvi sprang at the stricken champion. His knife bit across Wulfrik's hand, forcing him to drop one of his swords. His axe smacked against the hero's chest, shattering one of the trophy skulls he wore, denting the steel of his breastplate.

Snarling like a cornered wolf, the chieftain brought

the pommel of his sword smashing into Tjorvi's face. The raging warrior staggered back, spitting teeth from the pulped mash of a broken jaw. Wulfrik lunged after him, but fell as his injured leg collapsed beneath his weight. Tjorvi grinned through the ruin of his mouth as he saw his enemy's weakness.

Broendulf watched the crazed Graeling close upon Wulfrik once more. It would be easy to leave the hero to the killer. Viglundr and Sveinbjorn would not care who killed Wulfrik, just so long as he was no longer an obstacle to their plans. Broendulf would be able to return to Norsca and claim Hjordis for himself. There was no way to evoke the *Seafang's* magic without Wulfrik, but a new thought entered the huscarl's mind. Even without magic, the *Seafang* was still a ship, a ship that could still make the voyage across the Great Western Ocean.

Broendulf had half-risen from his cover, intending to stop Tjorvi. Now he hesitated. He could have Hjordis and without any risk to himself. It was the sort of cruel scheme that would have made Viglundr proud. To Broendulf, however, it smacked too greatly of treachery. The example of Zarnath showed him the kind of man who practised such deceit. He loved Hjordis too much to win her through such craven ways. He would earn her love, not steal it.

The huscarl began to leave his shelter for the second time when he found that Wulfrik didn't need his help. Tjorvi had rushed the fallen hero, chopping his axe at his foe's head. In the same instant, Wulfrik's sword flashed out, cutting into Tjorvi's calf. The sneaky Graeling reeled back, shrieking in pain.

Before he could get away, Wulfrik reared up from the ground, pouncing on the murderous marauder.

Wulfrik's injured arm coiled about Tjorvi's torso, spinning him around. The arm holding Tjorvi's axe was pinned against the warrior's side, but the hand with the knife slashed at the champion, slicing across his cheek. Wulfrik roared at the wiry betrayer, using his own anger to fight the pain throbbing through his ravaged body. Tjorvi refused to relent, frantic to free himself from the hero's crushing grip. He clenched his legs together, pinning Wulfrik's sword between them before the champion could wrench it free from his calf. Tjorvi's knife slashed again at Wulfrik's head, cutting his ear, all but sawing it from the side of his skull.

Wulfrik's eyes blazed hatefully at the back of Tjorvi's head. He smiled cruelly as he crushed the Graeling closer to his body. 'This time I use you as my shield,' he growled at the man.

Tjorvi screamed as another volley of elf arrows came raining down upon the northmen. His body twisted and writhed in Wulfrik's clutch as missile after missile slammed into it. When no more arrows struck the Graeling, Wulfrik tossed the arrow-riddled corpse aside and collapsed to the ground.

'They're moving!' Haukr shouted to his comrades when a new volley failed to manifest. 'Trying to get in close!'

'They mean to get prisoners,' Arngeirr cursed. The reaver clenched his fist about his sword. 'Khorne grant the cowards come close enough to cut!'

Broendulf carefully raised his head, staring out over the grassy plains. He couldn't see any sign of the elves beyond the four knights who were still sitting atop their horses far back towards the copse. It didn't mean they weren't there, though. The huscarl had heard it said an elf could hide himself in an empty room with only dust and sunbeams for company.

'We could make a break for it now,' Haukr suggested. The tattooed warrior grimaced when he made a quick count of his remaining comrades. Except for Arngeirr and Broendulf, he was alone. He had hoped for a few more bodies to stay between himself and the elf arrows.

'Maybe the chief has some ideas,' Broendulf countered. Like Haukr, he had small appetite for an arrow in his back.

The surviving marauders scrambled to the side of their fallen chief. Wulfrik bared his fangs at them, swinging his bloody sword as they approached. 'Back, jackals!' the hero snarled, his eyes passing over each of them, lingering upon Broendulf. The huscarl felt a sense of guilt rush through him. Had Wulfrik seen him hesitate against Tjorvi?

'We've sailed with you longer than that cur!' Arngeirr snapped, spitting on Tjorvi's body. 'Do we look eager to pick your bones?'

Wulfrik glowered at his men. Again, Broendulf had the feeling the hero's eyes lingered on him longer than the others. 'No man knows another. Not that well.' He laid his sword across his lap. Turning to his injured arm, he seized the arrow lodged in his flesh, breaking the shaft with one twist of his hand.

'Even if we did,' Haukr groaned, 'we'd never be able to sail the *Seafang* without you.'

Broendulf grinned despite himself. Haukr was making the same mistake he had, fixating upon the ship's magic and forgetting that it was still a ship. He shook his head in disgust at himself. What did it matter if they could sail the ship? They would never make it back to the *Seafang*. Not with the elves waiting to stick them full of arrows!

Gingerly, Wulfrik felt the wreckage of the ear Tjorvi had tried to saw away. He lowered his hand, sniffing the blood coating his fingers. 'Arngeirr,' he said, 'give me that southling flask you carry.' Puzzled, but obedient, the reaver pulled the dented tin bottle from his belt and offered it to the chieftain. Wulfrik held it beside his head, shifting his arm when he remembered one of his ears was gone. He shook the flask, listening as its contents sloshed against the sides. 'Mead?' the hero asked.

'Kvas,' Arngeirr answered.

Wulfrik grinned and turned his attention to Haukr and Broendulf. 'Rummage among our dead,' he told them. 'Get anything that looks like it will burn good.' He cast a wary glance at the tall grass around them. 'Don't touch any of the elf-folk,' he advised. While the warriors hurried to follow the hero's orders, Wulfrik drew two jagged pieces of flint from a bag tied to his boot. He set them on the ground, waiting for his men to bring him the strange plunder he had requested.

As he tried to remove Njarvord's bloodied shirt, Haukr passed near one of the dead knights. His eyes settled upon the rings decorating the elf's lean fingers. He cast a glance back at Wulfrik. Seeing his chieftain was occupied with the litter Arngeirr and Broendulf had already brought him, a sly smile crept onto his face.

Like a striking weasel, Haukr reached for the dead elf's hands. Before he could touch the cold, dead flesh, pain flared through his chest. He stared in confusion at the arrow piercing his breast, skewering his lung like a salmon upon a fisherman's spear. Groaning, he slumped to his knees, then crashed headfirst across the feet of the dead knight.

'I said don't touch the elf-folk,' Wulfrik muttered, glancing up from his labour. The unseen bowmen were content to leave the Norscans alone while they crept closer, but they would not suffer their dead to be defiled. In their position, any Norscan worthy of the name would do the same.

Wulfrik grinned admiringly at his handiwork. Arrayed about him were ten little bundles, each a knot of cloth bound around a few arrows. The arrows would give the bundles weight and rigidity, allowing them to be thrown farther. As for the cloth, the hero upended Arngeirr's flask over the bundles, dousing them in the pungent kvas, trying to ration it between them. In the end, the small flask had only enough alcohol in it to treat six of the improvised missiles.

Wulfrik scowled and ran his hand through the grass around him. Ideally, it should be much drier. He could only hope it would burn the way he needed it to. Otherwise his plan would never work.

Behind the cover of the dead horses, Wulfrik set to

work with his flints, sending sparks flying from the jagged stones as he slid them against each other. Soon, a knot of kvas-soaked rag tied round a single arrow caught fire. Wulfrik held the tiny torch in his hand and gestured with it at the tall grass around them.

'Now we give the elf-folk something to think about,' Wulfrik told his men. Touching the torch to one of the bundles, Wulfrik rose to his feet and hurled the fiery missile far out into the grass. Immediately, arrows came shooting towards the northmen in response, but the warriors were already back against the side of the slaughtered horse.

'The Hung kill mammoths this way,' Wulfrik said. 'I'm not sure it will work so well upon elf-folk, but I only need to keep them busy while we get back to the *Seafang*.' The hero lit another bundle and threw it out into the grass opposite where he had thrown the other one. A few arrows shot at him in response, once again slamming into the carcass of the warhorse.

The three men watched with satisfaction as smoke began to fill the air. The fire wasn't spreading very quickly through the grass; it wasn't dry like that upon the steppes where the Hung hunted mammoths. There was little chance of surrounding the elves in a ring of fire and burning them to death, in any event. Wulfrik had hoped only to drive the elves back with his fires. However, the strange grass of Ulthuan had a quality about it that served his purposes almost as well. Slow to take fire, the grass gave off an inordinate amount of smoke. Perhaps elves could see through smoke, but Wulfrik doubted it.

Wulfrik started to light a third bundle when Arngeirr reached to take the torch from him. 'Leave it to me,' the reaver said. 'I'll keep them busy while you get back to the ship.' He tapped his bone leg. 'I wouldn't make it in any event. Even with an arrow in yours, I'd slow you down.'

Wulfrik nodded slowly and released the torch to Arngeirr. 'Hold them back as long as you can,' he told the warrior. He glanced at Broendulf. 'Are you staying with him, or me?'

Broendulf smiled sadly at the one-legged whaler. 'I want to see Norsca again,' he apologised.

Arngeirr simply shrugged, accepting the lonely doom he had chosen. 'Just find that crook-tongued Kurgan rat,' he said. 'That way I can hold my head proudly in Valhal.'

'Aye,' Wulfrik promised. 'That is one oath even the gods won't stop me from keeping.' His eyes narrowed as he regarded Broendulf. 'Keep before me, Sarl,' he warned. 'I saw you when Tjorvi was trying to cut my throat. It seems to me you were thinking about helping him. Why didn't you?'

Broendulf glared back at the chieftain, all of the jealousy in his heart rising to fill his eyes with the coldest hate. 'I want to get back to Norsca,' he said.

Wulfrik snorted his contempt for the huscarl's words. 'Then you are a coward and a traitor,' he spat.

'When we get back to Ormskaro, I will show you who is a coward,' Broendulf growled.

The hero laughed at Broendulf's words. 'If the daemons of the border-realm are hungry, you will never see Ormskaro.' Wulfrik waved his hand, impatiently motioning for the huscarl to precede him across the plains. He half-expected the Sarl's body to sprout a dozen arrows as he loped through the grass, his body bent in a half-crouch. When nothing happened, Wulfrik hurried after Broendulf.

For some time, the two warriors had the benefit of the smoke to hide them from the elves. Eventually, however, Arngeirr could set no new fires. The elves were a sharp-witted people. They would figure out what was happening. When they did, they would be on Wulfrik's trail again.

He only hoped to be close enough to the sea by that time to have a real chance of escape. Broendulf wanted to see Ormskaro again. Wulfrik's hopes were even more modest. He only wanted to see the *Seafang* one last time.

'WHAT DO WE DO NOW!' Broendulf raged, smashing his fist against his side in impotent fury. Another arrow clattered off the stones near his feet.

Wulfrik smiled coldly at the blond Sarl. 'The dragon or the elves,' he told Broendulf. 'The gods leave us small choice, but at least the serpent won't make a game of killing us.'

Wulfrik did not wait to see what effect, if any, his logic had upon the other Norscan. Clenching the blade of his sword between his fangs, the warrior flung himself over the side of the cliff.

The waters of the Great Western Ocean closed about Wulfrik like a grave shroud. He felt his body plunge deep into the briny depths, the weight of his armour dragging him down. The chill of the sea numbed his flesh, seeping into his bones, enticing him to abandon himself to the oblivion of the lightless deep. He could hear the pressure around him pounding against his skull, becoming more intense with each passing instant.

No! He would not die this way! If he was fated to die, he would perish in battle, not smothered like some sickly infant by the sea. Clenching his fangs, exerting his prodigious strength, Wulfrik clawed his way upwards, fighting the drag of his own body as he strived to escape the embrace of the deep.

Gasping, the northman's head broke the waves. His flailing arms caught hold of a shattered length of beam bobbing upon the surface. Wulfrik clutched it to him, clinging to it like a babe to its mother's teat.

All around Wulfrik, the shattered wreckage of the *Seafang* floated, pounding against the cliffs of Cothique with each surge of the tide. A few ragged bodies, all that remained of the crew he had left behind, sagged across the splintered husk of his ship, their blood clouding the water around them. As he watched, one of the bodies was dragged under by some scavenger of the sea, vanishing into the black depths that had so nearly claimed him.

A seething hiss, like the steaming breath of a volcano, shuddered through the air. Wulfrik lifted his eyes, watching as the source of the sound reared up from the sea. A tremendous scaly neck split the waves, rising like some mighty pillar from the deep. More massive than even the giant trees of the elf-folk's sacred grove, the huge neck was coated in an armour of blue scales as big and thick as shields, the pale throat covered in a leathery skin crusted with barnacles and parasitic fish. Atop the monstrous neck was a gigantic wedge-shaped head with tremendous jaws filled with sword-like fangs. Spray jetted from the nostrils above the jaws, reeking of the brine and the bottom. Huge eyes, big as cartwheels and lustrous as amber stared from the scaly face, pupils narrowed to angry slits in the uncomfortable light of the surface world. A reptilian stink rose from the immense beast, filling Wulfrik's nose with a draconic reek.

Many were the sailors' stories of sea serpents and their predations. They were the terrors of the sea, monsters to evoke horror in even the most hardened corsair and most jaded pirate. As Wulfrik gazed up at the merwyrm, however, only one emotion burned in his heart. This mindless reptile had destroyed the greatest ship in the world. *His* ship. For that, the beast would pay.

'Down here, you eel-rutting crab-stain!' Wulfrik roared at the serpent. He grinned fiercely as the merwyrm's eyes focussed on him. Another steaming hiss rippled from the monster's jaws. It swung its head aside as something crashed into the water beside it. Wulfrik cursed the dumb beast. He didn't care if Broendulf survived his jump or drowned; all that bothered him was the distraction the huscarl had caused. Wulfrik tore one of the trophies hanging from his chest off its chain. Fingers curled in the sockets of the skull, he hurled the macabre missile at the merwyrm.

The sea serpent snapped around, one eye dripping

tears from where the skull had struck it. The merwyrm's hiss had a definitive note of anger to it now. Wulfrik glared back at the monster.

'Go ahead, fish-faced dung-sucker,' he snarled at it as the merwyrm clashed its jaws together. 'From inside or out, I'm going to cut that ship-cracking gizzard!'

Like a thunderbolt hurled by an angry god, the merwyrm struck at Wulfrik. Its vision impaired by the tears clouding its bruised eye, the serpent's jaws plunged into the water beside the Norscan. The impact of the huge monster's body slamming into the sea hurled Wulfrik and his refuge high into the air, borne upon a violent wave. As the beam swung away from the merwyrm, Wulfrik threw himself from his refuge, diving for the gigantic neck only a few feet from him.

The chieftain's sword bit deep into the scaly flesh, treacle-like blood spurting from the wound. Wulfrik wrapped his injured arm about the hilt of his blade, using it to anchor him to the serpent's side. With his good hand, he drew a saw-toothed dagger and plunged it into the merwyrm's neck, slashing through the leathery skin to gouge the flesh within.

The merwyrm's body undulated through the waves, continuing the downward plunge initiated by its foiled strike. Again, Wulfrik felt the cold waters of the sea close above his head. Panic thundered through his mind, but the hero refused to release his hold on the serpent. The water became black with blood as the northman's dagger sank repeatedly into its body.

The reptile's body suddenly shuddered, its lethargic nervous system at last registering the wounds Wulfrik was inflicting upon it. The serpent thrashed about, lashing its body like a great whip. The man clinging to its scaly hide tightened his grip, holding fast as the beast's wild undulations threatened to rip him loose. Crazed with pain now, the merwyrm sought to sink back into the black depths. Wulfrik's lungs burned for want of air, his head pounding with the mounting pressure as the merwyrm bore him with it into the deep.

Resolutely, with the vicious fatalism of his race, Wulfrik continued to stab his knife into the merwyrm's flesh. Death could crush him in its bony fist and choke the last breath from his body, but he would leave his mark upon the monster that destroyed his ship.

Bubbles exploded from the merwyrm's mouth as a pained roar rumbled from its throat. Maddened by the violence of Wulfrik's attack, the confused serpent rolled its body through the water, churning through the sea like a mammoth corkscrew. Disorientated, even its instincts overcome with anguish, the merwyrm swam for the surface again, unable to understand it had changed direction.

As the merwyrm's head broke the surface, Wulfrik expelled the foul air from his lungs and drew a fresh breath into his body. His head was spinning from the wild movement of the serpent, the world rotating crazily before his dazed eyes. Even the most potent beer brewed by the dwarfs of Kraka Drak had never stricken his senses so brutally. Yet it took no great skill to strike a scaly neck the size of a longship. The hero continued to hack away at the reptile, determined to avenge the *Seafang*.

The merwyrm's agonised howl dislodged stones from the cliff above. The reptile lashed out at the falling rocks, its dull intelligence connecting the motion with the pain it suffered. The wedge-like head struck, smashing its snout against the unyielding face of the cliff, its scales scraping against the jagged stone.

This time even Wulfrik's strength could not maintain his grip. The pained thrashings of the merwyrm as it whipped its body across the waves dislodged both marauder and sword from its neck, flinging them across the waves like a stone skipping across the surface of a pond. Bleeding from the dozens of cuts the hero had inflicted, fangs cracked by its crazed assault on the cliff, its side gouged by the jagged rocks, the merwyrm hissed its fury to the hated sun. It dived back beneath the waves, its serpentine coils plunging after it, retreating back into the darkness of the bottom to lick its wounds.

Bruised and battered by his battle, half-dead from the pressure and cold of the ocean deeps, Wulfrik flailed through the churning water. Desperately, he wrapped his arms around a chunk of floating debris, struggling to keep himself afloat. The hero coughed, vomiting the mouthfuls of water he had inhaled. In his travels, he had come close to death many times, but rarely closer than in his efforts to kill a merwyrm single-handed.

Wulfrik, face dark with reptilian blood, looked

towards the spot where the merwyrm had disappeared beneath the waves.

'Coward!' Wulfrik spat between coughs. 'Come back and fight like a snake!'

Chapter Fifteen

WULFRIK CLUNG TO the floating spar, his eyes still glaring at the spot where the merwyrm had submerged. The hero knew it was madness, but he wished the monster would return to finish their battle. Better death in the belly of a serpent than by drowning. The spirits of drowned men never entered the halls of their ancestors but were instead cast into chains by Mermedus, the grisly Lord of the Deeps. Wulfrik smiled grimly to himself. He wondered if Mermedus would contest ownership of Wulfrik's spirit with the Dark Gods who had cast their curse upon him, or would the bottom-feeder quietly withdraw his claim?

The hero cast his gaze upwards, scowling at the cliff looming overhead. He could see armoured heads peering over the side, staring at him with vengeful eyes. That was another option, of course. He could climb back up to the cliff and face the elves. The prospect of battle and sending a last few enemies into the afterworld appealed to Wulfrik, but the possibility of falling into the hands of the elf-folk alive didn't. A prisoner could count upon no mercy from the elves, not after what Wulfrik's marauders had done. Even a hero might turn coward under the torturer's knife. Wulfrik would not shame his ancestors by spending his last hours screaming and begging for death.

A splash to the chieftain's left brought his attention away from the elves. He almost expected to see the merwyrm's scaly head rising from the sea. Wulfrik was disappointed to find that the source of the sound was nothing more than a man.

'Tzeentch watches over traitors,' Wulfrik growled as Broendulf came swimming towards him. Lacking the hero's prodigious strength, the huscarl had divested himself of his armour, letting it sink into the depths while he remained afloat. Even so, Broendulf hadn't fought a merwyrm only minutes before. He was in a more fit condition than the battered, weary Wulfrik. That would count for more in a fight than the armour bound about the hero's body.

Broendulf's eyes studied Wulfrik, seeming to reach the same conclusion about the hero's condition. A thin smile worked onto the Sarl's face. 'Where's the serpent?' he asked.

Wulfrik coughed as he tried to laugh. 'I let it go,' he said. 'Too big to take back as a trophy anyway.' The hero's eyes hardened as the huscarl swam over to the floating spar, his hand tightening about the hilt of his sword.

Broendulf did not try to hide the hate in his own eyes. With everything brought to ruin by the destruction of the *Seafang*, there was no sense in trying to deceive Wulfrik that he was anything but the hero's enemy. 'What do we do now?' He glanced away from Wulfrik, back up the cliff at the elf warriors. 'We might climb back up and give an accounting of ourselves before the end.'

'Those of us with swords might,' Wulfrik said.

Broendulf grimaced at the chieftain's words. Along with his armour, he had lost his blade. A Norscan feared one kind of death, a death that took him without steel in his hand. 'There must be another way,' the Sarl said, his words sounding empty even to himself.

'We could swim around here until the elf-folk get tired of waiting and decide to sink us with arrows,' Wulfrik growled. 'Or else maybe they'll send for one of their sorcerers and have him call back the merwyrm.' The hero chuckled grimly at his own morbid jest. Then his eyes grew hard again. 'Why?' he demanded, his voice low and full of menace.

'Why what?' Broendulf asked, returning Wulfrik's tone in kind.

'It wasn't fear that made you turn on me,' Wulfrik said. 'I can see that in your eyes just as cleanly as I can see your hate. What made you turn on me?'

Broendulf shook his head, scowling at the hero. 'What does it matter now? You have a sword. Cut me down and let the gods judge my reasons.'

'Were you in league with the Kurgan?' Wulfrik growled. Broendulf could see the champion's knuckles turning white as they closed still tighter about the grip of his sword.

'Crow God rot your nethers!' Broendulf snapped.

The huscarl half-lifted himself from the water as he lunged for the champion. Wulfrik lifted his arm, smashing the flat of his blade across the Sarl's face. Before Broendulf could recover from the stunning blow, Wulfrik's other arm was wrapped around his throat, holding him fast against the hero's chest. Savagely, Wulfrik held the huscarl's head under water, allowing him to rise only when he was on the very brink of drowning.

Sputtering, gasping for breath, the huscarl flailed about in Wulfrik's mighty grip. The champion snarled into Broendulf's ear. 'Where's Zarnath? Where's that bastard gone?'

Broendulf shook his head, trying to cough an answer. Wulfrik didn't wait that long, dunking his head back under the waves. This time, the huscarl was certain the hero intended to drown him. Spots swirled through his vision, his lungs turned to fire, and still Wulfrik held him under.

'Tell me where the Kurgan has gone or by all your back-stabbing ancestors you'll wear the chains of Mermedus!'

Wulfrik started to dunk Broendulf down. The huscarl slapped desperately at the champion, gasping out hurried words. 'Hjordis! Hjordis!' he cried.

Wulfrik pulled his captive up by his hair, spinning him around and glowering into Broendulf's bleeding face. 'What do you mean?' he demanded.

'It was for Hjordis,' Broendulf sputtered, feeling more weak and ashamed with every word. 'I wanted to kill you for Hjordis. I had no part in Zarnath's trickery.'

The champion grinned at the pathetic confession. He raised his sword, pressing the point against Broendulf's throat, bringing a bead of blood from the Sarl's pale flesh. 'She would have nothing to do with a half-man like you,' Wulfrik scoffed. 'You die not only as a traitor, but an idiot as well!'

Broendulf glared defiantly at Wulfrik. 'She would have been mine,' he hissed. 'King Viglundr promised her to me.'

Mention of the king's name made Wulfrik hesitate. His eyes narrowed with renewed suspicion. 'Viglundr?'

'Yes, Viglundr,' Broendulf snarled. 'He promised Hjordis would be mine if I killed you.'

Wulfrik laughed at the firmness with which Broendulf spoke. 'You are twice an idiot then. Viglundr wants Hjordis for Sveinbjorn, not some wastrel huscarl.'

'Sveinbjorn would marry her,' Broendulf said, 'but it would be marriage in name only. In everything else, I would be husband to Hjordis.' The Sarl bristled at the mocking disbelief he saw on Wulfrik's face. 'Sveinbjorn needed a man for his wife because he cannot sire heirs for himself.'

Harsh laughter rolled from Wulfrik's fanged mouth, startling even the glowering elves on the cliff above. 'Three times an idiot!' he barked. 'No heirs? Sveinbjorn of the Aeslings? That cur has so many bastards and half-kin to his credit half of his tribe can call him uncle and the other half knows him as father!'

If Wulfrik had smashed the flat of his sword across

the huscarl's face again, Broendulf could have been no more stunned than he was by what he heard. He felt as though the bottom had dropped out from his stomach and a hand of ice closed across his chest. Viglundr had tricked him! He'd exploited Broendulf's love for his own underhanded purposes. No doubt Sveinbjorn had killers ready and waiting for him when he returned to Ormskaro to 'reward' him for the service he had done the Aesling prince.

'I'll see them both dead!' Broendulf growled through clenched teeth.

'That seems unlikely,' Wulfrik said. He released Broendulf from his grasp, pushing him away.

Broendulf glared at the fanged champion. 'And how likely is it you'll get revenge on Zarnath? We've both been deceived and there's nothing we can do about it.' The huscarl shook his fist at the elf warriors watching them from the cliff. 'Finish it, you spineless she-whelps!'

'They still have a mind to take us alive,' Wulfrik told Broendulf. The hero nodded his head towards the north. Faintly, a long, sleek ship with a swan-like prow was gliding across the sea, sailing in their direction. An elf warship, and neither man needed to be told what foes she sailed against.

Hopeless, yet Wulfrik's face bore a fierce smile as he turned his head from the approaching warship. Savagely, he raked his palm across the bare edge of his sword. 'Stay and amuse the elf-folk,' the hero growled at Broendulf, 'but I mean to cheat them if I can.'

Broendulf watched in confusion as Wulfrik pushed

off from the spar, swimming with broad strokes towards a bit of the *Seafang's* wreckage. Understanding dawned on him when he noticed the dragon face carved upon the floating debris: the longship's broken prow, and upon it the enchanted figurehead which was the focus of the *Seafang's* magic! Cold horror surged through the huscarl's body. Frantic, he threw himself into the waves, desperately trying to catch up to Wulfrik before it was too late.

Ahead of the two men, the elf warship drew steadily closer, armoured warriors standing upon the decks, silver nets at the ready, pikes and bludgeons close at hand. Broendulf could almost smell the hate rolling off the elves, a fury colder and more intense than anything merely human. The elf-folk would indulge that hate for a very long time if they took any captives. In the matter of vengeance, they were not so far removed from their corsair kin. Khaine was yet among the gods of Ulthuan.

Wulfrik barked in triumph as he gained the broken figurehead. Victoriously he raised his hand over his head, clenching his fist so that blood bubbled between his fingers. Defiantly he glared at the bewildered elves upon the decks of the warship. Some of them, perhaps sensing the mighty magic Wulfrik would soon evoke, began to nock arrows to their bows. But it was too late to stop what the hero had begun.

The Norscan's bloody hand smacked against the forehead of the wooden dragon. Greedily the carved reptile drank the hero's offering. Wulfrik threw back his head and laughed as mist began to swirl about him, blotting out the cliffs of Cothique and the elven warship. The half-world of the border-realm stretched out its phantom fingers, drawing Wulfrik and the broken figurehead beyond the world of mortals.

Broendulf screamed in terror, throwing his failing strength in one last tremendous effort. The huscarl's body surged through the waves, lunging into the mist and the fading Wulfrik.

Darkness engulfed the wooden dragon, a grey shadow that seemed to devour the entire world with jaws of mist and fangs of nightmare. Gibbering things shrieked and howled, clawing at the boundary between flesh and nothingness – the tatters of Old Night coalescing into daemon spirits, struggling to emerge from their realm of oblivion. The chill of the void and timeless evil seeped through the veil, slithering across mortal flesh like the coils of a deathly serpent. A stench, cloying, redolent with sin and slaughter, saturated the air, drowning the senses at every breath.

Broendulf found each hideous sensation more comforting than the last. It meant he had won his desperate race. He had reached the figurehead before Wulfrik's blood could send it back into the border-realm. He had escaped the fury of the elf-folk and left the horrors of Alfheim behind. They were going home now, back to Ormskaro.

Back to Hjordis.

'The gods decided to spare you,' Wulfrik said, watching Broendulf from where he clutched the broken figurehead. 'I wonder if the daemons of the void will be so timid.'

Broendulf glared back at the menacing chieftain. 'The daemons are drawn to violence,' he told Wulfrik. 'Attack and they will destroy us both. Then how will you stop Sveinbjorn?'

'I will kill the Aesling,' Wulfrik said. 'But Hjordis will be mine, not yours.'

'She will be Sveinbjorn's if we die here,' Broendulf warned. 'And Viglundr will be rewarded for all of his treachery.'

Wulfrik gnashed his fangs together, his eyes blazing with such fury that some of the daemons pawing at the fog drew back in fear. 'There is another traitor who will pay!' he growled. 'And not even the wergild of the gods will keep my hand from his throat!'

Broendulf nodded in grim agreement. Zarnath had lured all of them to Alfheim to die. The huscarl was not about to forgive the shaman such trickery. Perhaps his reasons were not as great as the betrayal Wulfrik felt, but he would see the Kurgan dead for his murderous deceit.

'A truce then?' Wulfrik suggested. 'Until Zarnath and the other enemies we share are dead?'

Broendulf scowled. 'This thing between us can only end in blood,' he said.

'Who says different? When the Kurgan is dead, we will meet in the Wolf Forest.' Wulfrik spat into his hand, pressing it over his heart. 'May I forsake the love of my woman if I break this oath,' he told Broendulf.

The huscarl repeated Wulfrik's solemn gesture. 'I

make the same vow, before the eyes of the gods. When we return to Ormskaro, I will help you seek the shaman and protect Hjordis from her father's deceptions.'

'Zarnath first,' Wulfrik growled. 'I'll have no peace until he has paid for toying with me. Whichever nameless hell he has hidden himself in, I will find him! Not all the daemons of the pit will keep me from vengeance!'

The arrogant oath caused a chorus of angry shrieks and yowls to emanate from the darkness beyond the mist. The two warriors watched in alarm as a tide of clawing, snarling blackness tore at the thin barrier separating them from the nothingness between worlds. In shreds and tatters, the mist began to break apart. Immense, long-fingered hands thrust themselves through the veil, stretching towards the mortal flickers who dared to mock the hunger of daemons.

Wulfrik slashed his sword across the knuckle of one hairy hand, boiling ichor spilling from the wound. The daemon yelped in pain, its arm shooting back into the blackness of the void. Other hands quickly took its place, pawing and scratching at the men, slowly ripping the rents in the veil wider.

Before the daemons could fully penetrate the barrier, a great thunder boomed through the blackness, a sound like the raucous screech of a vulture or the cry of a monstrous hawk. The frenzied daemons froze at the tumult of that shivering cry, their claws only inches from the ashen faces of the northmen.

The shriek echoed across the void once more. This time sparks of light blazed through the darkness, brilliant swirls of fire that scintillated like gemstones of every colour and hue. Like angry stars, the lights swarmed about the shattered veil, driving off the hungry daemons, sending them skulking back into the shadows of the void. A third time the deafening screech roared through the border-realm. In response, the chromatic spheres of light began to lose their lustre, fading until they merged with the darkness.

'The feathers of the Raven God,' Broendulf gasped in awe as he watched the last of the lights burn away. 'The gods themselves guard our way back to Ormskaro.'

'If the Raven God wants to help, let him guide me to Zarnath,' Wulfrik snarled, unmoved by the miracle he had witnessed. 'Otherwise let him stay out of my way!'

From the darkness, it seemed the raucous shriek sounded one last time, faint and distant.

Broendulf could not shake the impression there was now a note of mocking amusement in the screeching cry.

THE MISTS PARTED, the darkness faded, replaced by a dim star-swept sky. It was not the sky Broendulf had expected to see, the stars positioned at angles never seen from the streets of Ormskaro and the fjords of Norsca. The constellations rose in places which could be seen only from seas far to the south and lands far from Norsca's icy shores.

Panic seized the huscarl and his hand fell to his belt, reaching for the sword he had let sink into the cold waters of Alfheim. He calmed slightly when he became aware that his surroundings were no longer those of Ulthuan's haunted seas. The water flowing about him lacked the briny tang of the ocean, and the breeze sighing through the air did not smell of the sea. Wherever the *Seafang's* broken figurehead had brought them, it was far inland. Gazing about him, Broendulf could make out the lights of a settlement burning above the black bulk of the shore. He could see the tops of towers and temples outlined against the sky.

'Where are we?' the fair-faced Sarl growled at Wulfrik. 'This isn't Ormskaro!'

The hero was silent for a moment, just as confused as his companion. When he had placed his bleeding hand upon the figurehead, the fjord of Ormskaro was the only destination in his mind. By all rights, it should be the jagged peaks of Norsca's mountains and the bonfires of Sarl fishermen greeting them. Instead, his keen eyes saw the stone walls of a strange city rising from the shore, his nose filled with the reek of cabbage and manure which he always associated with the communities of the southlings. They weren't in Norsca. The power of the *Seafang* had brought them to the Empire instead!

Wulfrik thought about that for a time, wondering why the magic had only brought them halfway home. Then a boisterous peal of laughter rumbled from his throat as he realised the answer. Broendulf stared at his captain, wondering if the cursed hero's mind had finally snapped.

'Who goes there?' a hard voice called from the

darkness, the words spoken in the guttural Reikspiel of the Empire. The two northmen could hear a small boat sliding through the water near them.

Broendulf's eyes could not pierce the night so well that the boat and its occupants were anything more than a dark shape looming over the water. With their wolf-keen sharpness, Wulfrik could see the boat quite well. It was too big for a fisherman's keel, too wide for a ship's longboat and too small for a trading vessel. The smell of steel and oil which rose from the occupants told him they were well equipped for such a small boat, and equipped for trouble bigger than a struggling marlin. He could hear the rattle of mail armour as the boat rowed towards them.

'Play dead, or you will be,' Wulfrik whispered to Broendulf. He matched deeds to words, resting his head across his arm and letting his body sag in the water. Broendulf followed his example.

'Over here!' one of the men in the boat shouted. His vision wasn't quite as sharp as that of Wulfrik but years of prowling the rivers of the Empire by night had made them more sensitive than those of common men. He saw the floating hulk of the figurehead and the two bodies draped across it.

The other men in the boat weren't so blessed with night vision as their comrade, however. A lantern soon blazed into life, casting its light over the river, surrounding the little boat in a halo of illumination. The riverwardens preferred to hunt their prey – smugglers and pirates – in the dark, using their ears to detect their quarry. Only when certain of a catch did they light their lamps.

'Manann's beard!' one of the riverwardens exclaimed when he saw the two bodies. Almost unconsciously he pulled the lantern back, recoiling from the grisly sight. His sergeant, a man hardened by both more years and experience, took hold of the arm gripping the lantern and pulled it straight once more.

'Hrmph,' the sergeant grunted. 'Looks like these ones had a falling out with their mates. No honour among thieves, even when they sail the Reik.' He nodded as he considered the two bodies. 'Fish them in, Hans,' he told one of the riverwardens. 'Even dead, someone might recognise them and give us an idea who their mates were.'

The boat pulled alongside the carved dragon and the two bodies draped over it. The riverwardens muttered among themselves when they saw the strange carving, but a few sharp words from their sergeant had them moving. The river pirates had many strange rituals peculiar to themselves. Tossing a few unwanted comrades into the Reik tied to a wooden dragon was a new one to him, but not one that he found terribly surprising.

'Look at him!' exclaimed one of the riverwardens as his boathook gripped Broendulf's shirt and he started to raise the Sarl from the water. 'He's big as an ogre! Someone help me get him into the boat!'

'Not seen his like before,' one of the men helping pull Broendulf into the boat said. 'Think he's a Middenlander?'

'Kislevite, more like,' spat a third riverwarden, straining to lift the huscarl's leg into the boat. 'Even in Middenheim they don't wear rags like this. Smells like they didn't even finish scraping the meat off the hide when they made this fellow's trousers!'

While most of the boat's crew helped lift Broendulf from the water, a lone riverwarden investigated the second body clinging to the figurehead. His eyes widened in surprise when he saw that the other man wore armour, an unusual affectation for a river pirate. He wondered if perhaps the man had been a marine hired to protect some merchantman who had ended up on the wrong side of a pirate sword. The riverwarden reached down to raise the body's head from the water, curious to see if the face belonged to anyone he might recognise.

As soon as the riverwarden's hand closed about Wulfrik's scalplock, the northman sprang into life. His armoured hand closed about the southling's wrist, jerking him into the river before he had time to scream.

The loud splash of the riverwarden sinking into the Reik startled the other men in the boat. They swung around, their attention diverted for the moment from the hulking body they had just lowered over the gunwale. It was a mistake they would not live long enough to regret. Instantly their backs were to him, the 'dead' bulk of Broendulf thrashed into life. Powerful legs kicked out, smashing into the riverwardens with all the bone-crushing fury of a wild mule. The huscarl's enormous arms shot up, wrapping about the neck of the man with the boathook. A savage twist snapped the southling's neck. Broendulf let the twitching carcass topple into the river.

In the meantime, Wulfrik was lunging up from the river, seizing the side of the boat in one powerful fist. One of the riverwardens, the man who held the lantern, jabbed at the northman's hand with a short sword. Wulfrik shifted his grasp, sliding his hand along the edge of the gunwale a second before the short sword crunched into the damp imprint of his previous handhold. The young riverwarden was screaming in terror, staring with gaping eyes at the fanged northman glaring back at him. To the youth, Wulfrik looked like nothing less than some malevolent daemon of the Reik come to steal his soul.

Wulfrik settled for the southling's life, stabbing him in the neck as he frantically tried to free his short sword from the boat's side. The hero tossed his own sword into the bottom of the boat and planted both hands upon the gunwale. It took a superhuman effort for the northman to lift his armoured body from the river, the wood beneath his hands starting to splinter as his massive weight pressed upon them. Only a man whose flesh had been warped by the Dark Gods and whose spirit burned with bloodlust could have managed such a feat. Wulfrik the Worldwalker was such a man.

The hero dropped into the bottom of the boat, the planks creaking beneath his boots. He caught up his sword just as the sergeant of the riverwardens came rushing towards him, thrusting at him with a barbed pike. Accustomed to fending off smugglers and pirates whose only drive was escape, the riverwarden underestimated the nature of his foe. As the pike grated across Wulfrik's breastplate, the northman struck back at the sergeant, his sword flashing so near the man's face he could feel air sweep against his nose.

The sergeant recoiled in horror, eyes going wide as he noticed the skull dangling from the hilt of Wulfrik's sword, the other skulls fastened to his belt and armour. Realisation that he fought something more than a river pirate struck the soldier as solidly as one of Broendulf's kicks. His flesh turned clammy and his stomach went sour as the idea formed in the river-warden's mind that his foe was something far darker. This stretch of the River Reik was far from the great seas, but not so far that stories of Norscan raiders and their savage brutality had not reached the ears of even the lowest peasant.

Calling upon Sigmar, patron god of all men of the Empire, the sergeant thrust his pike at Wulfrik. The barbed point stabbed into the northman's leg, almost in the exact spot where the elf arrow had struck him. Wulfrik howled in pain, his sword smashing down, crunching through the wooden shaft of the pike. The sergeant staggered back, trying to recover his balance.

Maddened with pain, Wulfrik pounced on the retreating riverwarden. He crushed the sergeant beneath his armoured bulk, smashing him across the bottom of the boat. The soldier screamed and flailed under the furious northman, battering at him with the broken length of the pike. Wulfrik ripped the crude club from the sergeant's hand as though he were a child, then broke the man's wrist when he grabbed for the knife in his belt.

Snarling the name of Khorne, lord of blood and slaughter, Wulfrik pressed the edge of his sword against the riverwarden's face, slowly sawing through the screaming man's flesh. It was some time before the screaming stopped.

Wulfrik rose from the dead riverwarden, brushing blood and teeth from his armour. He cast his gaze across the patrol boat. Only one other man still stood amidst the gory charnel house. One of Broendulf's hands clutched a wound in his side. The other clenched a southling sword in its fist.

'Put that away before I forget our agreement,' Wulfrik warned the injured huscarl. He smiled at Broendulf. 'You didn't stab me in the back when I was killing the master of this scow. I don't think you'll do so now.'

Broendulf nodded, lowering the captured sword. 'These are southlings,' he said. 'Why did the magic bring us into southling waters instead of Ormskaro?'

Wulfrik thrust his own sword back into its sheath. Coldly he reached down and grabbed the bloodied tunic of the sergeant, lifting the mutilated man from the belly of the boat. 'We are here because I wanted to be here,' he told Broendulf. Callously, he tossed the body of the sergeant into the river.

'What?' Broendulf demanded, anger rising in his voice. 'Why not Ormskaro? Why here? Where is this place?'

'I don't know,' Wulfrik shrugged, reaching down to grab the body of another riverwarden. 'That is, I don't know the name of this place.'

'Then where are we?' Broendulf persisted.

Fangs gleamed from Wulfrik's savage smile. 'This is where Zarnath has fled to,' he answered, his voice never more like the hungry growl of a wolf.

Broendulf shook his head in disbelief. 'That doesn't make sense,' he protested. 'How can the magic bring us somewhere without a name?'

Wulfrik tossed the body of the riverwarden into the Reik. 'I didn't want to find a place. I wanted to find a man.' He pressed a finger to his head. 'In here I wanted to find Zarnath more than return to Ormskaro like a whipped dog. The *Seafang* took me where I wanted to be most. To the place where Zarnath has hidden himself. I can smell his stink in the wind,' the hero added, closing his eyes.

'This is madness!' Broendulf said. 'Why would a Kurgan hide among southlings?'

'Because he isn't a Kurgan!' Wulfrik snapped, his eyes burning with hate. 'Everything he told us was just another of his lies! An illusion to cover his tracks! A trick to save himself.'

'Who is he then?' Broendulf asked.

Wulfrik clenched his fist, glowering at the distant lights of the settlement stretching across the bank of the river. 'A southling wizard who thinks he can cheat the gods by playing with my dreams,' he hissed. 'Now he will share my nightmares!' He turned his gaze on Broendulf. 'Help me lift the dragon into this scow,' he ordered the huscarl.

Broendulf limped to Wulfrik's side, straining with the hero to raise the wooden figurehead from the river. Gasping, panting for breath, he sank down on one of the boat's benches when the labour was finished. 'Now what will you do?' the Sarl wondered, gesturing at the *Seafang's* figurehead.

Seemingly oblivious to injury or fatigue, Wulfrik prowled across the little boat, hoisting the bodies of the other riverwardens over the side, wiping the blood from the vessel with strips torn from its sail. 'I will return to Ormskaro,' he said. 'I will make that scoundrel Viglundr raise up such a fleet as Norsca has never seen. Then I will come back here and burn this city to cinders and offer every living thing within its walls to the gods!'

Broendulf could hear the fanatical determination in the hero's voice. Despite everything, he found himself believing Wulfrik could do just what he promised. He would force the treacherous king of the Sarls to raise the men and ships he needed. He would sail across the Sea of Claws and batter his way through the fortresses of Marienburg. He would sweep past the fleets of the Empire and bring his army here, to this place, this refuge where Zarnath had fled.

The huscarl stirred from his thoughts as he noticed Wulfrik turn towards him. The hero had finished his morbid cleansing of the patrol boat, removing the bodies and most of the blood, eliminating the fodder that would draw daemons from the border-realm even more swiftly than the presence of living men. Blood dripped from Wulfrik's palm where he had reopened the cut across his hand.

'Out,' the hero snarled at Broendulf. The huscarl started to reach for the stolen southling sword in his belt, but Wulfrik's bloody hand closed about his wrist, pinning it in place. 'You're staying here.' Wulfrik exerted pressure, forcing Broendulf to stop struggling and listen to him. 'You've seen Zarnath. You know what he looks like. Whatever disguise he wore as a Kurgan, he won't be able to hide those eyes of his. Find him! Watch him! Don't let him run! The gods shrivel your bones if you do!'

Wulfrik gripped Broendulf's shoulder, lifting him and pitching him into the river with a single fluid motion. The huscarl struggled up from the cold embrace of the Reik, his head breaking the surface just in time to see Wulfrik press his bloody hand against the wooden dragon and watch as spectral mists gathered to engulf the little boat.

Broendulf waited until the mists had cleared and Wulfrik was gone. Turning from the vanished boat, the huscarl began swimming towards shore. He would do as Wulfrik had ordered. He would find the shaman and see that he did not escape. But when the hero returned, there would be a reckoning between them.

By all his ancestors and the gods, Broendulf would settle with Wulfrik.

Chapter Sixteen

DEATH CAME TO the huscarl without warning or preamble. One moment he stood upon the weathered battlements of Ormfell, staring out across the sprawl of Ormskaro, watching the light of the moons shimmering across the cold waters of the fjord. In the next breath, he was lying upon his back, gasping out his life while blood gushed from a gash that split him from belly to groin. Fiercely, the dying warrior tried to pull the axe from his belt, his last impulse even in death a savage urge to strike back at his killer.

Wulfrik waited until the huscarl was still, then returned his gory knife to its sheath and climbed over the worn battlement to drop onto the roof of Ormfell. It had taken the wounded hero two hours to make the climb up the side of the tower, a climb even the boldest Norscans would have baulked at. The ancient walls of the tower were almost sheer, the stone crumbling and treacherous. Not for a chest of gold would even a brave man consider such a reckless climb. Wulfrik, however, was after something more precious to him than gold. And he would not be denied.

None had seen the little boat emerge from the fog, nor watched as Wulfrik rowed the tiny craft onto the beach of Ormskaro. A fisherman had seen him as he hid the *Seafang's* figurehead beneath a pile of worn wool sails, but Wulfrik had ensured the old man would never tell anyone what he had seen. A drunken warrior fumbling about in the pathway behind a mead hall had been the only other man to stumble onto Wulfrik. Like the old man, the warrior would not spread word that the hero had returned.

The hero took the axe from the dead huscarl's fingers, lifted the iron helm from the Sarl's head and made his way across the roof. He paused at the trapdoor, his nose flaring as he drank in the smells rising from the tower below. Fangs gleamed in the moonlight as the marauder smiled. Sinking the toe of his boot under the trap, he kicked the door open with a savage thrust. Before the opened door could smash down upon the roof, Wulfrik was already leaping down the hole.

One hand hooked about the side of the wooden ladder, the wild chieftain hurtled the fifteen feet between the roof and the corridor below. He landed with a bone-jarring crash at the bottom of the ladder, his injured leg threatening to buckle beneath him. Wulfrik gasped in pain as he landed, putting a note of fear into his voice.

There were two men in the corridor. They spun about, axes at the ready when they heard Wulfrik make his violent descent. By the gloom of torchlight, however, all they took notice of were the familiar axe in the hero's hands and the iron helmet which enclosed his head. Like the rest of Ormskaro, they thought it impossible to climb the walls of Ormfell. Suspecting nothing, the two warriors laughed and approached the northman huddled at the base of the ladder.

'Seeing ghosts, Orfi?' joked one of the Sarl warriors. 'I told you you couldn't hold your mead!'

The banter fell silent when the warrior came close enough to see the eyes burning from the iron mask of the helm and the full red beard beneath. He opened his mouth to shout a warning, but his voice collapsed in a liquid gurgle as Wulfrik brought the stolen axe hewing into the man's side. Mail links snapped and ribs splintered beneath the hero's mighty blow. The Sarl crashed to the floor, thrashing as blood filled his lungs.

Wulfrik snarled and turned away from his first victim. The other guard was overcome by fear, perhaps aware of who it was he faced. The Sarl turned, running down the hall. Before he could shout an alarm, Wulfrik threw the heavy battleaxe at the fleeing man. The weapon smashed into the warrior's back, crunching through armour and flesh. The man stumbled, groping futilely at the axe, trying to pull it free. He took a few staggering steps, then sagged weakly against the wall.

Wulfrik stalked past the two men he had killed. A new scent was in his nose now, a smell imprinted upon the deepest recesses of his heart. Long, lonely nights he had spent with only that scent to offer him solace. There was a lock of golden hair even now in a bag around his neck that bore that scent. For a moment, violence and vengeance were forgotten. Dead hope flamed into terrible life within his heart. The most desperate dreams are those which die hardest.

Another smell struck Wulfrik's senses and his lips curled back in a feral growl. The hero knew that smell too. Sveinbjorn. The Aesling prince was still in the tower.

The hero quickened his pace, sprinting down the silent halls of Ormfell like a wolf on the prowl. He hesitated when he heard voices coming from behind closed doors, and lingered to listen to some of the muffled conversations. What he heard sent slivers of fire racing through his veins. Wulfrik's death had again become accepted fact in Ormskaro, announced by the sole survivor of the hero's last expedition: the Kurgan shaman Zarnath. He had related the death of Wulfrik and his crew before announcing his own departure from Norsca. The shaman had taken pains to make it clear he was returning to his own people far to the north in the Wastes.

A last ploy in case Wulfrik should make it back from Alfheim. The hero clenched his fists in silent fury. Zarnath hoped he would go racing off looking for him among the Kurgans. Without the *Seafang*, it would be a quest that would consume a man's lifetime. But the supposed shaman had made a mistake when he reckoned upon the destruction of Wulfrik's ship and its magic. He also hadn't considered that Wulfrik's hate would lead him to the traitor's true homeland, the Empire.

Vengeance! It was a truer dream to cling to than the

hope Zarnath had betrayed. When Wulfrik caught the filthy sorcerer, he would cut out the liar's heart and make a present of it to Hjordis. As much as himself, Zarnath's crooked promises had betrayed her. She deserved to taste the bitter fruit of revenge. It was all they had left now.

Wulfrik suddenly froze in his steps. Quickly he pressed himself against the stone wall, peering around the corner to watch the hallway. Almost he had walked straight into a guard, so distracted was he by his thoughts of revenge. Now he studied the man lurking in the corridor, and with each observation, the hero felt his anger swell. The guard was no Sarl huscarl, but an Aesling hersir. His axe was leaning against the wall beside him. The guard was turned away from Wulfrik, with his ear pressed against the panel of a door.

For a moment, Wulfrik watched the spying hersir. So content was the guard upon his snooping that he didn't hear the marauder step away from the wall and creep down the corridor towards him. The first the spy was aware of Wulfrik was when the hero's powerful arms coiled about his neck and crushed his windpipe. Wulfrik waited until the choking hersir was dead before tossing the guard aside like a sack of meal.

Curiosity made Wulfrik press his ear to the door. He listened and a cold light grew in his eyes. The sounds coming from beyond the door were not unfamiliar to him. At least one of the voices wasn't.

If a blood-crazed troll had struck the door it might not have been propelled with such violence. The heavy oak panel crashed inwards, torn from its hinges, the twisted debris of its lock clattering across the floor. Gasps of shock and alarm rose from the huge bed sitting in the middle of the room. A brawny figure leapt from the nest of blankets and furs, lunging for a sword lying upon a chest against the wall.

He never reached the weapon. Before he had taken more than a few steps, Wulfrik was upon him. The hero's fist smashed into the naked man's face, knocking teeth from his jaw. The man shrieked in outrage, lashing out with his own fist. Wulfrik caught Sveinbjorn's hand in his own. Exerting all of his ferocious strength, the hero broke Sveinbjorn's fingers, driving the wailing prince to his knees.

'Wulfrik!' a shrill voice cried. The hero looked away from the whimpering prince, his eyes locking on the comely shape that rose from the bed. For a moment, he almost forgot Sveinbjorn and Zarnath, almost forgot the cruel curse laid upon him by the gods. He drank in the bare, curvaceous body descending to the floor like an Arabyan lost in the desert setting upon the cool embrace of an oasis. The scent he knew so well, the golden hair he kept about his neck, the smooth ivory skin…

Savagely, Wulfrik brought his knee smashing into Sveinbjorn's face. The prince's nose cracked under the impact and he flopped to the floor. Wulfrik kicked him in the ribs, glaring at the faint red marks left by his hands upon Hjordis's pale flesh.

Hjordis stood a little away from the furious hero, shock and wonder written across her face. She fumbled at the bed behind her, dragging a bearskin away to wrap about her nude frame. 'Wulfrik?' she said again, a note of doubt in her voice.

'Wulfrik,' the hero told her. 'Not a ghost,' he added, delivering another savage kick to Sveinbjorn's ribs.

The stunned princess rushed to him, oblivious as she dropped the bearskin and trampled it beneath her feet. 'The Kurgan said you were dead!' she cried, tears streaming down her face. She caught at Wulfrik, trying to press herself against him. 'Oh, he said you were dead!'

Wulfrik's face twisted with revulsion. Sternly he gripped the woman's arm, pulling her from him. 'You stink of Aesling,' he growled, kicking Sveinbjorn once more.

Hjordis retreated from the glowering hero, her face going almost white with horror. 'They said you were dead...'

'You didn't take long to replace me,' Wulfrik snarled. 'And with scum like this,' he snapped, burying his boot in Sveinbjorn's gut. The prince rolled over onto his back, gagging as vomit spilled from his bloody mouth.

Hjordis's lips trembled as she stared at Wulfrik. 'It wasn't like that,' she said, shaking her head. 'My father... when he heard you were dead...'

'All this time,' Wulfrik said, his voice quaking with emotion, 'through all the battles and suffering, one thing kept me going. That was knowing you were waiting for me here! Knowing that however far I fell, however many friends I led to their deaths, I could count upon your love!' He pounded his fist against his chest. 'That long, I had something! That long I was still a man, whatever hell the gods cursed me to!'

'Do you really think I love *that*!' Hjordis sobbed, pointing a finger at Sveinbjorn. 'It was you, *is* you! Only you! When I thought you were dead, I went out of my mind with grief. I wept for you from dawn until the dying of the night.'

Wulfrik's face curled back in a sneer. 'Yes, I'm sure. Just lying in here with Sveinbjorn weeping and rutting and weeping, sniffing about his legs like a bitch in heat!'

'No!' shrieked the princess, colour rising into her cheeks. 'It wasn't like that! When they thought you were gone, when the Kurgan swore you were dead, my father demanded I marry Sveinbjorn! I wanted no part of him! I wanted only you!'

'Seems you've had more than a part of him,' Wulfrik snarled.

'My father forced me into it!' Hjordis cried. She turned her back to Wulfrik, displaying the scarred flesh across her shoulders and sides, the marks of a whip.

In an instant, Wulfrik felt a surge of compassion rise within him. Almost he went to take her in his arms. The smell of Sveinbjorn's scent on her held him back. The memory of Sigvatr lying dead in the Dark Lands flashed through his mind. 'Men have died in shame for a lie,' Wulfrik told her. 'You don't know the meaning of suffering.'

Wulfrik swung around, the sword flashing from its sheath. He pounced on Sveinbjorn as the prince made a scramble for the door, crushing the Aesling to the floor. Wulfrik buried his knee in the man's back, wrapped his fingers in the prince's hair and savagely pulled his head back. The steel of Wulfrik's sword rested against Sveinbjorn's neck. The skull of King Torgald seemed to grin at its son's predicament.

'Don't kill him!'

The shout came from King Viglundr. The old Sarl led a score of warriors, an equal mix of huscarls and hersirs, across the shattered threshold. Wulfrik simply smiled back at the king and his entourage, baring his fangs in a vicious snarl.

'I was going to pay a call on you,' Wulfrik said. He pulled back on Sveinbjorn's hair, forcing a cry from the prince. 'Once I was finished here.'

Viglundr's face was white with terror. 'Don't kill him, Wulfrik!' the king pleaded. 'It will mean war with the Aeslings! You can name your price! Your weight in gold! The best warriors in my house! I'll even give you Hjordis!'

Wulfrik cast a sideways glance at the princess, his eyes like chips of ice as he gazed on her. 'Damaged goods,' the marauder said. 'I didn't come here to bargain like a beggar.' Angrily, Wulfrik released Sveinbjorn, kicking the prince away from him. While Sveinbjorn scrambled across the floor to the safety of Viglundr's bodyguard, Wulfrik dipped his hand into his belt, removing a small leather pouch.

'I came here to make a proposition,' he told Viglundr. Haughtily, Wulfrik dashed the pouch to the floor, spilling its contents across the room. The men around the king gasped in amazement as they saw a fortune in sparkling gemstones dancing before their eyes. Wulfrik had taken it from Tjorvi after killing the murderous Graeling. The gems had been plucked from the dresses of the massacred elf-wives, but there was no way for the men scrambling to gather them up to know that.

'Treasure from the southlings,' Wulfrik boasted. 'Rubies, sapphires and diamonds! A fortune for any man willing to reach out his hand and take it!'

Viglundr stared in awe as one of his huscarls poured gems into the king's outstretched hand. He shook his head in disbelief. 'The southlings have no such wealth,' Viglundr said. 'Many times have I raided their towns and cities. Never have I seen stones such as these!'

'You call me liar, Viglundr?' Wulfrik growled, menace in his voice. 'Of course you never saw wealth such as this! Where have you raided? Along the coast, sacking places plundered dry by generations of Norscans. The real treasure lies far from the sea, deep in the heart of the Empire!'

'And the great Wulfrik has sailed to such places,' scoffed Sveinbjorn. 'He has fought his way past the fortresses of Marienburg and the fleets of the southlings with only a single longship!'

'No, Aesling,' Wulfrik said. 'There is no need to squander the strength of my warriors so far from the treasure. Not with a ship such as the *Seafang*, which can sail upon the seas of the gods and come out again where I will.'

The statement brought excited murmurs from the assembled warriors. They had all heard of the *Seafang*'s magic from the longship's crew, though the ship's captain had been careful to keep the exact manner of the magic a secret. They knew Wulfrik spoke true about sailing seas beyond the mortal world.

'What do you propose?' Viglundr asked.

'I need a bigger ship to haul away the plunder I intend to capture,' Wulfrik said. 'You will build me a new hull, a new *Seafang*. It will be the greatest ship in all Norsca, forty benches and no less.'

'You would need to cut down the Trolltree to find timber to lay down such a keel,' Viglundr grumbled.

'Then set men to hunting the Trolltree,' Wulfrik ordered. 'Surely there are some among the Sarls with spine enough for such a quest. If not, lend me the men and I will hunt down the beast.'

'It would take fifty warriors to kill the Trolltree,' sneered Sveinbjorn. 'And you'd have to set fire to it, making its timber worthless for building a ship.'

Viglundr rubbed his fingers across the gems in his hand. 'I'll send a hundred warriors then, and they'll not set fire to the monster or I'll feed their children to the eels.'

The king's eyes narrowed, fairly glowing with avarice. 'It will take more than a handful of gems to pay for the risk I put my warriors in. You must agree to the wergild for those the Trolltree slays.'

'Any ship and any man who wishes may sail with the *Seafang*,' Wulfrik told the king. 'I will lead them to the richest southling settlements and they may plunder them until their holds are filled with such wealth as to make even the gods envious!'

Sveinbjorn could see from Viglundr's expression that Wulfrik's words had won the king over. Seething with hate, the prince tore a sword from the clutch of a hersir and rounded on the hero. 'This is a trick!' the Aesling shouted. 'He is playing us for fools! What does a man cursed by the gods care for gold?'

Viglundr stared from the gems in his hand back to Wulfrik. 'Sveinbjorn raises a point,' the king said. 'What does a man cursed by the gods need wealth for?'

Wulfrik's voice became a low hiss, dripping with a hate far deeper than Sveinbjorn's. 'I was betrayed by Zarnath. The Kurgan left me to die in Alfheim after using lies and trickery to lead me there. He has returned to his people. I will need warriors and ships to find him. To get them, I need gold.'

Viglundr nodded. There was no fakery in the hate he heard in Wulfrik's voice or the murder burning in his eyes. However much reason he had to feel betrayed by Viglundr and Sveinbjorn, he wanted Zarnath's blood even more. 'I will help you,' the king decided. 'I will send my warriors to fell the Trolltree. I will set my shipwrights to building this new *Seafang*. I will send out word and gather the best ships and crews among the Sarls and the Aeslings.' The king smiled and gestured at Wulfrik's many wounds. 'I will send the best vitki in Ormskaro to tend your injuries.' A crafty look came across Viglundr's face. 'In return, I want the dragon's share of the treasure and your oath that you will renounce your claim upon Hjordis and never again darken Ormskaro with your presence.'

'By the Axe of Kharnath and the wings of Tchar,' Wulfrik said, spitting on the floor to cement his oath.

He heard the woman standing behind him gasp in disbelief as he spoke the words. 'Remember, Viglundr, I am the only one who can command the *Seafang's* magic. I wouldn't suggest any treachery. At least not until the treasure is safely back in Ormskaro.'

'Of course not,' Viglundr agreed. 'You will be as safe as my own daughter until your return.' The king motioned for his warriors to withdraw from the room. Sveinbjorn advanced towards Hjordis but halted when he found Wulfrik standing in his way.

'Where are you going, Aesling?'

Sveinbjorn's face went crimson with fury. 'I go to fetch my wife!' he roared. Before the prince could raise his sword, Wulfrik's blade smashed across his fingers, striking with the flat of the weapon. Sveinbjorn barked out in pain, the sword clattering to the floor.

'Now you have a matching pair,' Wulfrik told the prince, gesturing at the broken fingers of his other hand. 'I'll send the vitki to visit you after he looks after my hurts.'

'My wife, damn you!' Sveinbjorn snarled.

Wulfrik glanced back at Hjordis. He could see the anxious appeal in her eyes. 'Find some she-goat to warm your sleep,' Wulfrik told the prince. 'I keep Hjordis with me. Viglundr said I would be as safe as his own daughter. If she is with me, then whatever misfortune might overtake me will happen to her first.'

Sveinbjorn did not mistake the threat in Wulfrik's voice. Scowling, but subdued, the Aesling prince stalked from the room. The hero watched him go, laughing at the man's back.

'I've watched ratkin retreat with more dignity,' he laughed. Wulfrik turned as he heard Hjordis come up behind him. He felt a sting of pain as he saw the anguish on the woman's face, the fright in her eyes.

'He will try to kill you, whatever my father says,' Hjordis warned. She could feel Wulfrik wince as she laid her hands on his shoulders. 'Don't trust them. Either of them.'

'I am not such a fool,' Wulfrik said. He shrugged from beneath Hjordis's hands.

'Is my touch so unpleasant?' the princess asked, her voice quivering with despair.

Wulfrik stared at her, part of him wanting to seize her in his arms. The smell of Sveinbjorn on her skin drew him away. 'There is a time for love,' the marauder said. 'In the midst of my enemies, under their own roof, I can't afford any distraction. No matter how pleasant.'

Tears streamed down Hjordis's face. 'You don't mean that,' she said. 'You don't want me. You think I'm some kind of unclean thing.'

Frowning, Wulfrik turned to the bed, piling some of the furs on the floor. 'You need your sleep,' he advised. 'I'll stay on the floor and wait for the vitki. Or Sveinbjorn's killers, if they come first,' he added, patting the bare steel of his sword.

'Tell me you still love me,' Hjordis demanded, her jaw set, her eyes imploring. 'Tell me there is still hope for us.'

Wulfrik took her hands in his and stared hard into

her eyes. 'I will tell you this. Those who have betrayed us will pay for it.' He bared his fangs, his eyes looking not upon Hjordis or the room around them, but focussed instead upon a distant town deep within the Empire. 'All of them will pay,' Wulfrik snarled.

FROM A HIGH cliff, Wulfrik and Viglundr watched as the Sarl woodsmen made ready their trap. It had taken many weeks for hunters to find the tracks of the Trolltree and a week more to find an ideal place to confront the monster. Once, the sagas said, there were many creatures like the Trolltree lurking in the deep forests of Norsca. They made war against the first men, slaughtering them without mercy when they sought timber to build their homes and their ships. In despair, the men cried out to the gods and mighty Tchar brought to them the gift of fire with which to make war against the treeblood. With fire and axe the Norscans scoured the treeblood from the land and claimed the forests for their own. The few treeblood who survived had retreated into the oldest, most impenetrable of the forests, there to brood upon the victory of man and allow the memory to turn them mad with the thirst of revenge.

Some of the greatest heroes of the sagas had earned their names felling these monstrous survivors, using their wooden bones to build their mead halls. Over time, tales of the treeblood dwindled. Now, it was said, the Trolltree was the last. Last because it was the mightiest and most monstrous of its kind. Many bold warriors had dared enter the Trolltree's forest only to be discovered months later, their innards strewn through the branches. Any man who trespassed into the Trolltree's domain courted death; any man who took timber from the haunted wood threatened to bring doom to his entire village, for the Trolltree would stir from its forest to avenge a fallen tree.

Wulfrik grinned as he watched the Sarls at work. There was a deeper purpose moving them than simple obedience to their king. They had lived their lives in fear of the Trolltree, and some of them had seen their villages devastated by the monster. There was a feeling of retribution that burned in each woodsman's breast as he laboured, a thirst for vengeance that Wulfrik could empathise with. It was only right that the seeds of his own revenge should grow from that of other men.

The plan was Wulfrik's, adapted from the tactics used by the Hung nomads when they hunted mammoths. The game Wulfrik intended to bring down was bigger than any mammoth, but so too was the scale of the trap. No, the hero was confident they would be able to bring down their quarry. The question was, could they make it stay down?

Sveinbjorn claimed it was a fool's errand, doomed to fail. He'd kept his Aeslings with him in Ormskaro. It was a mistake on the prince's part. Whether motivated from genuine fear or resentment of Wulfrik, Sveinbjorn had upset the Sarls by taking no hand in the hunt. They would remember the arrogant disdain with which Sveinbjorn had dismissed their vendetta. When the Trolltree fell, they would remember it was Wulfrik, not Sveinbjorn who brought them their triumph.

The Sarls would never accept Sveinbjorn as their king now. Wulfrik knew that, even if the Aesling prince was too proud and bitter to see it for himself. Since Wulfrik's return, Hjordis had been quite vocal in decrying Sveinbjorn as a weakling who had won her unfairly. The very legitimacy of the prince's claim on her had come into question, and opinion already favoured the hero Wulfrik over the usurper Sveinbjorn.

Viglundr was the real enigma. Wulfrik was certain the cunning old king knew what was going on, yet he made no move to stop it. Thoughts of rich treasures had clouded the king's judgement. Or perhaps he felt secure enough in his own position to undo whatever damage Hjordis and Wulfrik caused Sveinbjorn. After all, Sveinbjorn had stayed behind while the Sarls hunted the Trolltree. Viglundr had not.

A cold smile worked onto Wulfrik's face as he glanced at Viglundr. The old king would bide his time. He would wait until the riches Wulfrik had promised him were safely in Ormskaro before he made his move. When that time came, Viglundr would learn he was too late. And then Wulfrik would take from the treacherous old king everything he possessed.

The cry of a shrike echoed from the clearing below. Wulfrik waved down to the hunter who had made the cry. The trap was complete. Now it was time to set the bait. The hero raised both fists over his head. In answer to the gesture, dozens of Sarls drew axes and rushed a stand of saplings growing along the southern edge of the clearing. Ruthlessly, they hacked away at the trees, sending slivers of wood dancing in every direction. Other northmen gathered the chunks of wood, dropping them into cauldrons of boiling water. Soon the pungent aroma of sap was thick about the clearing.

For hours the woodsmen attacked the saplings, laying into the trees with as much violence and noise as they could. The smell of sap continued to thicken, hugging the ground as a faint breeze sent it crawling into the forest. From the cliff, Wulfrik and Viglundr listened to the northmen work, their eyes never leaving the deep woods.

Wulfrik saw the first sign that their trap had worked. A faint movement of the distant treetops was the first warning. Only the hero's animal-keen eyes saw the motion, but soon other scouts became aware that something gigantic was making its way through the forest. The sound of ponderous footfalls and snapping branches increased, becoming audible to the woodsmen in the clearing. Fear was in their faces as they scrambled for cover, but not a man among them cried out. Afraid though they were, none of them wanted to be remembered as the man who warned the Trolltree.

Branches continued to snap and creak until it seemed the entire forest was in motion. There was no mistaking the wild, frantic motion of the trees now, as though a mighty gale swept through them. The ground rumbled from the impact of tremendous feet, booming like a titan's drum.

It was no imagination but an eerie reality that the trees at the edge of the clearing parted, leaning away to allow the monster to emerge from the forest. The beast crawled forwards on all fours like some great and terrible hound. Its immense body was covered in bark, split and cracked and hoary with age. When it was clear of the trees, the beast lurched upwards, standing upon its hind legs in crude semblance of a man, though a man built of wood rather than flesh. A gash-like mouth, with jagged splinters for teeth and yellow moss for gums, yawned from the middle of the thing's torso. Great pits which burned with something like marsh-fire served it as eyes. Immense arms studded with thorn-like branches dangled from what passed for its shoulders, each hand ending in a crooked finger of timber and a hooked talon of gnarled wood.

There was no need for Wulfrik to stare down at the Trolltree. The wooden monster stood one hundred and fifty feet, even without anything that might be called a head rising from its broad shoulders. Even the tallest tree in its forest was a dwarf compared to the giant treeblood. Only by crawling through the forest had the ancient monster managed to hide itself.

Now it had no interest in hiding. Wulfrik felt the hair rise on his neck as the Trolltree's glowing eyes passed across him, as he felt the creature's primordial hate sear into him. There was wisdom in that gaze, timeless and inhuman, but it was a wisdom that had become rotten with loneliness and hate.

The Trolltree swung away from its silent contemplation of Wulfrik, glaring down at the fallen saplings and the boiling cauldrons. Though the monster's gash-like mouth did not move, a great groan sighed up from the treeman, an anguished cry of pain and mourning.

Wulfrik expected the Trolltree to be drawn to the fallen trees. Instead the monster swung back towards him, its fiery eyes narrowed to smouldering embers. Slowly, clumsily, it raised one of its immense arms.

'Look out!' Wulfrik roared, pushing Viglundr away. The king scrambled through the rocks as the Trolltree's clawed hand came crashing down. The talons dug deep into the cliff, shearing several feet from its face as the treeman pulled its arm back.

Coughing from the dust the impact had stirred, his face bleeding from shards of rock thrown up by the Trolltree's fist, Wulfrik struck at the monster. His sword cracked against the Trolltree's hand, chewing into the wood, causing bright red sap to bubble into the gash.

'Now! Now!' Wulfrik howled.

In the clearing below, northmen erupted from the bushes, hurling axes at the Trolltree. The monster turned towards them as the blades bit home, chips of wood flying from its legs and back. The warriors whooped war cries and jeers at the treeman, fleeing as it took a shuddering step after them. One man, slower than the others, screamed as the Trolltree caught him in its claws. The timber fingers closed in a brutal vice about the struggling warrior, crushing him to pulp before letting the mutilated remains drip back to earth.

'That's it!' Wulfrik grinned as he watched the

monster pursue the Sarls. 'A little more, you dumb damn brute!'

The Trolltree's steps became faster as it lurched after the fleeing warriors, building momentum like some living avalanche with each yard it travelled. The cries of the men became screams of terror as the treeman closed upon them.

Then the monster's foot crashed through the thin skin of sticks and leaves covering the pit Wulfrik's men had spent most of the day digging. The marshfires in the Trolltree's face widened with surprise as it found itself toppling forwards. A cloud of dust exploded from the pit as the treeman crashed.

Instantly, other warriors were in action, leaping from the bushes, each man carrying a heavy chain. They charged at the fallen monster, thrusting axes and jagged spears into its wooden skin, the heft of each weapon attached to one of the chains. In a short time, the treeman's body was pitted by dozens of blades, burdened with yards of heavy chain. As the Trolltree struggled to rise from the pit, its powerful exertions pulled on the chains. Massive boulders to which the chains had been anchored were dragged from the bushes. Some of the Sarls wailed in horror at this display of the Trolltree's awful strength; others cursed and rushed to burden the monster with still more chain.

Eventually, the weight of steel and stone binding it was too great even for the Trolltree's strength. The monster's thrashings became little more than a frenzied rocking back and forth in its pit. A few warriors, too near the feet of the beast, were ripped apart when thick roots whipped out from the treeblood, but the northmen quickly learned to stay clear of the beast's feet. Instead they clambered atop the prone monster's chest, chopping away at it with axes, cracking its bark with hammer and spike.

Wulfrik marched across the clearing and stared into the Trolltree's burning eyes. He felt a sense of regret that he could not have faced this beast on more equal terms. It would have been a battle unequalled in the sagas. He could pity this creature, ancient beyond its time, lurking forgotten and abandoned in a world that had passed it by. Better to die with purpose than to linger lost and alone with nothing to love and nothing to love it in return.

The hero watched the Trolltree's eyes flicker and wink out. The great beast's body shivered and was still. There was an unaccountable sense of sadness in the air as the treeblood died, the sorrow that marks the passing of something which shall never be seen again. It was some time before the Sarls rallied from their melancholy and the immensity of their accomplishment dawned upon them. Cheers thundered through the wood. Some cheered Viglundr. Most cheered Wulfrik.

'Be careful with the beast's carcass!' Wulfrik ordered when the cheering had faded to a low roar. 'This timber is mine and I'll crack the skull of any man who abuses it!'

Wulfrik smiled as men clambered over the Trolltree's body, this time not to kill but to cut. Like butchers at a hunt, carpenters and shipwrights scrambled over the body, using saws and axes to section the mighty carcass. The Trolltree's wooden flesh would form the ribs of a new *Seafang*; its backbone would be the keel of Wulfrik's ship.

'You have your monster,' Viglundr said when he joined Wulfrik beside the dead Trolltree. 'When do I get my treasure?'

Wulfrik did not look at the king when he answered, seeing instead the image of an Empire town and a man who pretended to be a Kurgan.

'Soon,' Wulfrik promised. 'I am as eager to strike against the southlings as any man in Ormskaro.'

Chapter Seventeen

LUDWIG STOSSEL STARED for the thousandth time into the cold ball of crystal, trying to force it to show him what he desired to learn. But the artefact that had served him so faithfully for twenty years persisted in remaining stubbornly silent. It was a silence that the wizard found profoundly disturbing.

He turned away from the mahogany table, casting a black silk cloth over the frustrating crystal sphere. At first he had been willing to accept the sphere's silence as evidence that he had succeeded, that the threat to his life and soul was gone. Even the wisest prognosticator of the Celestial College could not see into the realm of death itself. Morr guarded his gardens too fiercely for any wizard to pierce that veil, though the wizards of the Amethyst Order had some skill at evoking spirits from the otherworld.

Stossel stared gloomily about his laboratory, gazing at the shelves of arcane tomes and the tables littered with magical paraphernalia. He had wrested many secrets from his studies, secrets unknown even to the masters of his order. He had learned how to send his spirit striding across the land while leaving his body safely behind. He had discovered the art of assuming another countenance so perfectly that he could fool even another wizard. He had learned to disguise his spells so that they drew faintly upon all the winds of magic, and in so doing did not leave the telltale aura of Azyr, the blue wind. He had learned the ritual to summon Grylikh, his powerful familiar.

The astromancer regarded Grylikh on his golden perch. No longer needing the fearsome aspect it had adopted in Norsca, the familiar wore the less frightening shape of a marble-hued shrike. The bird cocked its head and returned Stossel's scrutiny with an air of expectancy. It would obey whatever orders he gave it. The problem was, Stossel had no idea what to do.

Many years ago he had discovered the death that awaited him. He would die by the hand of a barbarian named Wulfrik, his soul to be fed to Tzeentch, the ghastly Dark God of Sorcery. It was the kind of fate that would chill the blood of Sigmar himself. But an astromancer knew how easily the threads of fate could be altered. There was not one future, but many. And by acting at the right time, a man who had foreseen that future could change it.

Stossel had acted first by sending Grylikh to watch Ormskaro. Through the crystal, he had seen Wulfrik return to the settlement again and again to rest and refit his ship. He had seen the barbarian take counsel with the seer Agnarr. It was here that Stossel caused his familiar to keep watch. The seer had never suspected the gibbering imp he captured and set in a cage was actually a spy and, when the time came, an assassin.

When Grylikh heard Wulfrik describe a dream to the seer which meant Stossel was the barbarian's next victim, the knowledge was instantly conveyed to its master. It had taken powerful spells to speed the astromancer to Ormskaro, to strike at Wulfrik before it was too late.

It was unthinkable to strike Wulfrik directly. To do so would shift the barbarian's curse onto himself and place his own life in thrall to the Ruinous Powers. If he would escape the marauder's sword, he had to be cunning. He had to lead Wulfrik to his death but take no direct hand in it.

Stossel used his magic to become Zarnath the Kurgan, and in this guise he had played upon Wulfrik's deepest desires. He'd led the barbarian and his crew to the deadliest places the wizard could think of. Somehow, he had survived the Dark Lands and the degenerate dwarfs of that fell place. Leading Wulfrik to Ulthuan, Stossel had hoped to destroy both the man and his devil-ship.

Somehow, both Wulfrik and his ship had survived. Where they were, what they were doing, Stossel did not know. His crystal refused to show him either Wulfrik or the *Seafang*. Even Ormskaro was blocked from his sight. He had seen other signs, though. He had seen an exodus of Norse warriors and raiders journeying into the lands of the Sarls. He had seen the gathering of a great fleet written upon the stars. War was brewing in the icy north.

The astromancer knew where the battle would be

fought. Only circumstance had caused him to make the discovery, to learn both that Wulfrik was alive and that the barbarian was after him. He had been called to attend Baron Kruger, Lord Protector of the town of Wisborg – another of the baron's attempts to prevent his wife's infidelities. So convinced was Baron Kruger of the baroness's indiscretions that it always came as a shock to him when Stossel couldn't give him any forewarning. One look at his wife, however, was enough to convince a rational man that the baron's fears were groundless.

Upon entering the castle, however, it was Stossel who received a shock. A prisoner was locked in stocks in the courtyard. A prisoner the astromancer was horrified to recognise. The man was Broendulf, a member of the *Seafang's* crew!

Stossel overcame his shock long enough to discover that Broendulf had been in Wisborg for at least a week, posing as a sailor from Middenland. He'd been arrested for starting a brawl in one of the taverns and sending no less than five men to the healers and two others to the priests of Morr. The fact that their prisoner was a Norscan barbarian came as a surprise to Baron Kruger and the reeve of Wisborg, one it took a great amount of persuasion to get them to accept.

Stossel felt like ripping his beard out by its roots every time he thought about Baron Kruger's disbelief. The baron's response to his warning had been lethargic at best. It was harvest season. Bringing all the farmers into the walls of the town would mean losing the better part of the crop. Moreover, there were the traders to think about, buying up supplies of wheat and barley to sustain Altdorf through the winter. Kruger needed something more than a Norscan vagabond and a wizard's unfounded fears to warrant sealing up Wisborg. Grudgingly, he had sent messages out to neighbouring towns and even a man to Altdorf to advise that there might be trouble threatening Wisborg, but he'd couched it in such vague terms that the peril might be as minor as weevils or as nebulous as underfolk sightings.

Wulfrik was coming. Stossel knew it as firmly as he knew anything. The question wasn't if, but when. The wizard stepped to the narrow window of his laboratory. Rising above the town, the astromancer's tower gave him a good view of Wisborg. He frowned as he stared out across the tile roofs and watched the little plumes of smoke rising from chimneypots. He could see children playing in the streets, drovers moving their stock to the docks, farmers bringing their crops to market. The smell of baking bread rose to fill his nose.

Stossel wondered if he would ever see Wisborg like this again. His presence had caused a terrible doom to hang over the heads of every inhabitant of the town. It was too late now to run, to try to lead the menace away. The astromancer might save himself that way, at least for a time, but Wisborg's danger would remain.

'No,' the astromancer said, turning away from the window. 'The only thing to do is stay and fight. Even if the baron refuses to listen, I *know* what is coming and will be ready for it.' He sighed and shook his head. 'Perhaps that is what I should have done from the start instead of trying to trick fate.'

On its perch, Grylikh hopped from one foot to the other, sharing the wizard's agitation. But the bird's eyes were not on Stossel. They stared instead past him, past the window, at the black waters of the River Reik.

THE MISTS PARTED slowly as the *Seafang* emerged once more from the border-realm. Wulfrik ran an admiring hand along the gunwale of his new ship. It was the finest he'd ever set foot upon, sleek as a merwyrm and powerful as a behemoth. The spine of the Trolltree made for an impressive keel, and a ship that boasted forty-three benches. The tall mast was fitted into a kerling fashioned from the treeblood's foot, the woollen sail sewn with runes to speed the wind and draw the favour of the gods.

Wulfrik looked out across his crew, hungry warriors drawn from across the length and breadth of Norsca by the promise of plunder and the prospect of battle. Eighty-six men sat upon their sea chests, rowing the *Seafang* against the slow current of the river. There were another hundred and forty standing at the ready, shields slung across their arms. These men had proven their courage during the frightening passage through the border-realm, prepared to defend the rowers from the daemons of the void. The eight who had been found to be cowards were strangled during the passage – even now some of the crew were pitching their stripped bodies into the river. Wulfrik would suffer no cowards on this voyage.

Ahead, through the darkness, Wulfrik could see the familiar towers of Zarnath's refuge. The gods had shown favour to him by letting the *Seafang* return under cover of night. The hero only hoped they would continue to favour him. Man for man, the southlings were weak, as weak as their simpering gods. But the southlings had a strength the northmen lacked: numbers. Given a chance, the Empire could muster armies even the greatest High King had never imagined.

Wulfrik didn't want to give them that chance. At least not until he was ready.

The hero turned away from the prow of his ship, glancing back at the darkness sternwards. He could see the last shreds of fog dissipating. He waited until he was certain the mists were completely gone, then turned to his helmsman.

'Cut the chains,' Wulfrik told him.

The helmsman, a snaggletoothed Varg named Skafhogg, barked orders to the warriors nearest him. Great axes snapped into the staples binding dozens of thick chains to the *Seafang's* hull. The chains flew into the river with a splash. In response, lights flickered all along the river. Wulfrik counted each light as it blazed into life, knowing them to be torches wielded by the captains of the other longships, letting him know their position and their safe passage through the border-realm. The hero's fierce grin grew with each light. Attached to the *Seafang* by the chains, the entire fleet had entered the fog. Twenty ships had passed safely through the mists, leaving only three behind with the daemons. The gods continued to favour Wulfrik.

He only hoped Sveinbjorn hadn't been on one of the ships lost in the mists. He didn't want the Aesling prince to die just yet. Wulfrik needed him alive just a little longer.

Wulfrik watched as the longships dropped oars and began to knife their way across the river. They could see the prize Wulfrik had promised them, the lights of the southling town burning even at this late hour.

When the ships were only a league from the town, their decks suddenly blazed into life, hundreds of torches lit almost in unison. Great horns bellowed out across the waves, rolling like thunder against the stone walls of the town. The warriors onboard the ships crashed axes against shields, lifting their voices in a fierce cry that became a deafening tumult.

'Khorne!' they roared, invoking the sacred battle-name of Kharnath the Blood God, Lord of Battles. 'Khorne!' they howled until it seemed the walls must fall from the violence in their voices alone. 'Khorne!' they shrieked as they gnashed their teeth and bit their shields.

The Norscan fleet landed upon the riverbank, grinding small fishing skiffs beneath their hulls, splintering ramshackle piers into kindling before their prows. The ships had barely stopped moving before northmen were hurling themselves over the sides, charging through the river and onto the shore.

Bells rang through the walled town. Light now blazed from every quarter of Wisborg as the alarm was sounded. Archers scrambled onto the walls, hastily pulling armour over their shoulders as they climbed into the watchtowers and gatehouse. The screams of women and children echoed from the streets as panic set in.

The northmen formed themselves into a series of wedges, a serrated phalanx known as the swine-array. Thick shields interlaced with each other, protecting the warriors from the marksmen on the walls. Like the fangs of some great beast, the northmen advanced towards Wisborg. Behind them, other warriors removed timber from the holds of their ships, hurriedly constructing a palisade to guard their vessels from attack.

Arrows clattered against the shields as the marauders stalked towards the walls. A few hunters among the northmen returned the fire, popping up from the midst of the shield wall to loose their own arrows at the archers.

When the shield wall was only fifty yards from the walls, the northmen came to a halt. With the crash of blades against shields, the shouts and war cries fell silent. The front ranks of warriors parted, allowing their hulking leader to emerge.

Wulfrik glared up at the walls, fairly daring any bowman to shoot him. None of the southlings rose to the challenge of his threatening stare, nervously watching him from behind their stone ramparts, each man promising himself he would wait until the hero took another step before loosing an arrow at him.

'Men of the Empire!' Wulfrik called out, his voice like the roar of a lion. 'I would have words with your leader!' He waved his sword through the air,

Torgald's head bouncing upon its tether. 'Fetch him, that I may speak with him!'

'I am Baron Udo Kruger!' a sharp voice rose from behind the fortified face of the gatehouse. 'Wisborg is under my protection and I have no words to waste with heretic scum!'

Wulfrik laughed at the baron's rebuke. 'Protect your town then! I only came here to see your wife and my children!'

There was an inarticulate screech of outrage from within the gatehouse. Wulfrik retreated back to the safety of the shield wall as dozens of arrows came shooting down at him. A few of the northmen cried out as handguns were discharged and shot punched through their shields.

'Let me in, Kruger!' Wulfrik yelled. 'It's not right to keep the baroness waiting!'

Wulfrik smiled as he heard the baron shrieking in fury, calling for armour, demanding his knights saddle their warhorses. From his tone, it seemed he wouldn't be swayed by his advisors or his officers. He was determined to answer the challenge Wulfrik had hurled upon him, the insult the Gift of Tongues had torn from Kruger's mind and placed on the hero's lips.

THE NORTHMEN BEAT their shields and called upon the name of Khorne, working their blood up into a fury of battlelust while they waited for Baron Kruger to sally forth from the walls. A punishing fusillade of arrows, bolts and bullets had come shooting down from the walls, but the heavy shields of the marauders prevented many casualties. More devastating had been the cannon the southlings had wheeled up onto the battlements and fired into the swine-array, blasting a score of northmen into heaps of mangled flesh in an instant. Before the cannon crew could fire again, one of the seers Wulfrik had brought from Ormskaro unleashed a nimbus of black cloud about their heads, causing their flesh to melt off their bones like hot wax and detonating the supply of gunpowder beside the cannon. The resulting explosion removed thirty feet of battlement and set fire to some of the buildings close to the wall. Since then, the southlings had shown no interest in bringing more cannon onto the walls.

The clarion call of trumpets gave the northmen warning before the gates of the city were flung open. But there was no warning when a shower of burning stone plummeted down upon their heads. Sections of the phalanx shattered as warriors were set afire by the flaming stones, as the tiny meteors ripped through shields and armour. As the formation shattered around him, Wulfrik glared up at the gatehouse. He remembered seeing similar magic worked by Zarnath against the dwarfs. Now he found himself staring at a bearded southling dressed in elaborate robes of midnight-blue. There was only one thing that harkened back to the Kurgan shaman: the wizard's glowing eyes.

Wulfrik bared his fangs and would have charged the walls despite the shower of fiery magic and the hail of arrows. Only the thunder of hooves clattering across the lowered gate snapped him from his thoughts of revenge. He watched as Baron Kruger and forty horsemen came galloping out from behind the walls, lances lowered.

'Loose the hounds!' Wulfrik roared. The command brought some semblance of order to his reeling warriors. The northmen formed up ranks again, locking their shields together in a fortified barrier against the tide of snapping, snarling fury which came loping from the direction of the longships. Dozens of warhounds, bred by the northmen for size and ferocity, twisted by the powers of the gods into ghastly monstrosities, charged full into Baron Kruger and his knights. The smell of the great hounds excited the horses, causing them to falter at the worst moment. The momentum of their charge lost, the baron and his men were forced to defend themselves from the mutant hounds, stabbing at them with lances, kicking at them with the hooves of their steeds.

The northmen quickly followed the charge of the warhounds, pouncing upon the embattled knights, dragging them down from their saddles, braining them with axes and flails.

A sharp cry of fury drew Wulfrik's attention. The hero watched as Baron Kruger fought free from the hounds, skewering one on his lance, crushing the head of a second with the iron-shod hooves of his warhorse. Mouthing a stream of obscenities, the baron came charging at his enemy, tossing aside his lance and drawing his sword.

The hero stood his ground before the massive destrier and the enraged knight upon its back. At the last instant he ducked aside, rolling away from the deadly sweep of the baron's sword and ending the manoeuvre at the opposite side of his foe. Wulfrik slashed his blade into the breast of Baron Kruger's horse just behind its steel barding, dropping the beast like a stone and trapping the armoured nobleman beneath its weight. He kicked the sword from the baron's hand as the noble tried to stab him in the gut. Scowling at the pinned baron, Wulfrik shook his shaggy head.

'Don't make my dogs sick,' the marauder growled, ripping the helmet from the baron's head. He turned his back to the screaming man, rushing to join the tide of northmen streaming through the open gates of Wisborg.

STOSSEL WATCHED WITH mounting horror as the warhounds were set loose, their crazed rush spoiling the charge of Baron Kruger and his knights. Loudest among the voices advising the baron against such a reckless sally, warning him that it was the witchery of Wulfrik's voice that goaded him to such madness, the astromancer could now only watch in frustration as his fears were realised. What use was foresight if no one would listen?

The wizard prepared to send another shower of meteors streaming down into the marauders. Kruger and his knights were finished, but it was still possible to keep the northmen from entering Wisborg. Behind him, he could hear the commander of the gatehouse ordering the gate drawn up. Like Stossel, he realised the baron and his men were lost.

Suddenly the commander's words disintegrated

into a wail of pain and a wet, slurping noise like a toothless ogre licking its lips. The interior of the gatehouse became as cold as ice and Stossel could smell the reek of dark magic in the air. He turned to find the commander wreathed in fire, but the purple flames were not burning him. The havoc the witchfire was working upon the man's body was far more ghastly. Before Stossel's eyes, the soldier's flesh was curdling, running off his bones and reshaping itself into flopping tentacles and snapping pincers. New eyes sprouted from the stricken man's knees and a slobbering mouth tore open across his spine, a cluster of snake-like tongues flapping obscenely along his dislocated shoulders.

The commander's body swelled with the raw magical power being siphoned into it, his very substance being corrupted by the essence of Chaos. One of the archers in the gatehouse shrieked in horror, the sound drawing the mutated commander's attention. An arm with too many joints in it reached for the soldier, impaling him upon a finger that was like a bony spear.

Stossel's eyes glowed with power as he unleashed a stream of starfire into the abomination's face. Skin blistered and peeled beneath the fury of the spell, eyes bursting from the cosmic heat the wizard had evoked, but the thing refused to die. Spawned from Chaos, the mindless, wretched horror howled through the wreckage of its head and undulated towards the nearest soldier.

The wizard sent another blast of cosmic fire into the beast, but with as little effect as before. Soldiers charged it as the thing that had been their commander lashed out with clawed tentacles and spiked flippers. One man cried out as his head was crushed in a pincer-like appendage, and another laughed madly as he stabbed the abomination's flank over and over again with a halberd.

A creeping trickle of fear rolled down the astromancer's spine as he realised the commander hadn't closed the gates before the foul magic of the northmen struck him down.

'Forget the monster!' Stossel shouted. 'Close the gate!'

The wizard threw open one of the steel shutters, staring down at the gateway. Already it was choked with ravening marauders. Stossel closed his eyes, focussing upon the scene with his wizard's sight. He pointed his hand at the gateway and made a sweeping gesture. A tremendous wind crashed down upon the northmen, driving them to their knees, hurling them back across the shoreline.

Stossel coughed, wiping perspiration from his brow. Blood trickled from his nose, his body shivering with the tremendous toll the spell had taken from him. He would not be able to loose another such storm upon the barbarians. Even as the thought occurred to him, he could see enraged northmen rising to their feet, charging once more for the entrance to Wisborg.

'Close the gates!' Stossel cried out again.

The soldiers had the slobbering hulk that had been their commander pinned in one corner of the gatehouse. At the wizard's shout, two men left the cordon around the monster and scrambled to the windlass that controlled the gates.

The soldiers never reached their goal. Once more, the stink of sorcery filled the air and a man's body was enveloped in twisting, mutating fire. The soldier beside him ran his sword through the changing abomination, intending to end its hideous new life before it began. Instead, the spell that had enveloped his comrade spread to engulf him as well. The bodies of the two soldiers seemed to flow together, merging into an almost shapeless mass of bubbling skin and blinking eyes.

Stossel peered from the window again, this time gazing away from the gate. He found what he expected to see, one of the Norscan seers leaning over a pile of animal bones, working his obscene magic against the men in the gatehouse. The astromancer felt his blood boil at the sight of the heretic sorcerer gleefully inflicting such atrocities.

The wizard's anger took the shape of a spear of lightning, crackling down from the night sky. The Norscan seer looked up, his clawed hands waving wildly in a desperate effort to ward himself against Stossel's magic. The effort failed and the seer's body leapt ten feet in the air as the lightning sizzled through him, vaporising his innards and leaving his blackened husk smoking on the ground.

Inside the gatehouse, the second abomination was lurching across the room towards the first. Some of the soldiers broke off from their efforts to contain the first spawn, fleeing down the stairs to the street below. A few stubbornly tried to hold back both beasts.

Even if he had the strength, there was nothing Stossel could have done to save the embattled soldiers. Any spell powerful enough to affect the Chaos spawn would incinerate the men he was trying to help. The wizard turned his back on the ghastly scene, trying to block the screams of the doomed men from his mind. He needed every bit of concentration now. There was no room for guilt and pity in his thoughts.

With the spawn between himself and the stairs, Stossel's only avenue of escape was the window. A bigger man could never have squeezed himself through the narrow opening, but the astromancer had the lean, scrawny build common to scholars and ascetics, men who took pains to feed their minds but often forgot their bodies. Holding his breath, he squirmed out onto the narrow ledge.

Shouts from the northman horde told that his exodus had not gone unnoticed. Arrows and throwing axes flashed through the air as the marauders trained their fury upon the fleeing wizard. The brooch of star-stone Stossel wore upon his cloak blazed with energy as the missiles provoked its lambent magic into life. A spectral wind whipped around the wizard, scattering the arrows and axes like chaff.

The wizard ignored the thwarted attack. The talisman would only defend him for a limited time and he had to focus his thoughts if he would be away before one of the Norse sorcerers took an interest in him. His magical powers already taxed, he doubted if he would be a match for even one of the savage warlocks.

Stossel spread his arms, his cloak and robes

fanning out around him like the wings of a great bat. The wizard stepped away from the window, out into empty air. Instead of falling, the astromancer's body lifted into the sky, twinkling lights flickering all around him as the Wind of Azyr bore him aloft. More arrows and axes rose from the horde as the wizard soared above them. The ring on Stossel's left hand glowed as its energies were evoked, warding the wizard against the hostile magic being directed against him. He smiled coldly as a cluster of northmen exploded into a cloud of crackling ashes, victims of the spell his ring had caused to ricochet back upon the barbarians.

It was tempting fate to linger any longer over the battlefield. Stossel pictured his tower in his mind and his body flew out over the besieged town. If he would do his people any good, he had to replenish his power. There were things in his laboratory, ghastly secret things any sane wizard shunned. He had discovered the method of their creation in one of the old books Grylikh had found for him. There was a price to be paid for evoking such forces, a price of blood.

If it would stop Wulfrik, then Stossel knew he had to pay that price. Wisborg was doomed unless the northmen could be vanquished.

Stossel had brought this doom upon the town. Whatever it cost him, he knew he had to save whatever was left to be saved.

THE NORTHMEN RUSHED into the narrow passageway between the outer and inner gates. Both portals were still open, Wulfrik's challenge to Baron Kruger and the magic of his seers had seen to that. The passageway was only a dozen yards long, and roughly as wide, but the southlings had made it a killing field. Murder holes bored into the roof above them, arrow slits cut into the walls to either side, and before them a barricade of broken wagons and piled furniture from which riflemen fired into the very faces of the attackers.

Against the assault of weaker foes, the brutal defence would have thrown the enemy back. The northmen, however, would not be denied. Like beasts scenting blood, they would not relent until they fed the hunger burning within them. They knew the eyes of their gods were upon them, judging their strength, testing their courage. The northmen did not court death, but they accepted it when it came. To fall with sword in hand was their destiny, either here in Wisborg or on some other battlefield. They feared the shame of defeat more than the kiss of the valkyries.

Molten lead poured down upon the northmen from the holes in the ceiling, so they used their shields to deflect the boiling metal. Arrows whistled from the slits in the walls, so they piled the bodies of their dead against the holes so that the hidden archers couldn't strike at them. The bullets of the gunners tore through shields and ripped through armour, so they propped their shrieking wounded before them and used their flesh as a living barrier against the defenders of the barricade.

Foot by foot, the northmen closed upon the

barricade. When they heard the gunners retreat from their positions, the marauders flung aside the bodies of their mangled comrades. In a great wave of armour and muscle, the northmen crashed against the mass of piled furniture and broken wagons. The barricade shuddered under their assault, grinding against the flagstones of the street as it lurched outwards from beneath the gate.

Soldiers rushed at the barricade, hurling flasks of oil at the piled debris. Other soldiers raced to fling torches into the oil. Flames soon licked about the barricade as the wood began to burn.

Still the northmen would not be denied. The warriors pushing against the barricade tried to retreat from the flames, but the press of bodies behind them left them nowhere to flee. If they did not want to burn, they had to bull their way through the fiery barrier.

In failing to drive back the marauders, the fires set by the soldiers actually helped their enemies. Weakened by the flames, the charred wagons and smouldering wreckage splintered apart under the furious assault of the Norscans. After three mighty efforts, the barricade crumbled. Hulking northmen, their beards singed, their hide leggings and fur cloaks smoking, came leaping through the flames, axes gleaming red in the flickering light. To the defenders of Wisborg, the scene was like watching the mouth of hell spit out a legion of blood-mad daemons.

'You are men of the Empire!' a fierce voice shouted. 'You are the children of Sigmar! Do not fear the heathen beast! Drive it back into the abyss with its black masters!'

Wulfrik charged through the flames, his eyes glaring at the town around him. The gateway opened into a market square, a wide plaza fronted by several tall buildings and with a half-dozen streets snaking away from it in every direction. Stalls and carts had been tipped over to form improvised defences for archers and gunners. More marksmen were perched upon rooftops, raining death down upon the northmen. Across the centre of the square was a wall of spears and shields barring the marauders from gaining the side-streets and running amok through the town.

'Formation!' Wulfrik bellowed, watching with disgust as blood-crazed warriors rushed pell-mell at the southling spearmen only to be cut down by bullets and arrows. 'Shields!' he roared, ripping a massive panel of wood and steel from the burning body of a marauder at his feet. 'The gods spit on any man who dies without the blood of ten southlings on his blade!'

A horn sounded. The northmen emerging from the gateway no longer raced across the square in berserk fury but instead closed ranks, forming once more the fang-like wedges of their broken phalanx. The arrows of the archers clattered harmlessly against the thick shields, only the bullets of the gunners capable of striking the men sheltering behind them. And the gunners were too few, their weapons to slow to re-arm, to turn back the horde.

The northmen surged forwards in a great body, their boots causing the flagstones to shiver beneath them. Again axes clattered against shields, again the marauders shouted the name of the Blood God. 'Khorne!' they yelled, flecks of blood flying from their lips, froth and foam trickling down their beards.

The wedges of the Norscans smashed into the defensive line of the southlings like a typhoon pounding against a crumbling shore. From the first impact the soldiers of the Empire were staggered, struggling to retain their cohesion. Militiamen, unaccustomed to a pitched battle against anything more serious than scraggly herds of beastmen raiding farms or bandits preying upon travellers, they were forced to rely upon their training rather than experience.

Spears stabbed at the northmen in the automatic, precise fashion of the drillyard, only to be deflected by the shields of the marauders or caught by the hooked beaks of their axes. Some of the soldiers staggered forwards as their weapons were ripped from their hands, breaking the defensive line. Others quickly stepped into their place from the rear ranks, holding desperately to the hope that they could hold their ground and keep back the Norscans.

Training and discipline were not enough, however. Each northman had the experience of a life spent hunting and fighting in the icy wilds of Norsca behind him. Each of the marauders towered over the militiamen, bodies hardened by lives of ceaseless toil and endless war. When they brought their shields smashing against those of the southlings, it was the soldiers who were pushed back. When the soldiers tried to press back, the northmen remained as fixed as a mountain.

There was another difference between the enemies. The southlings had been taught to shun and despise the wicked gods of the north, but they had also been taught to fear them. As the soldiers heard the marauders invoke the dread name of the Blood God, that fear returned to them. The northmen did not share the same feeling when they heard the southlings call upon their own god. To the Norscans, Sigmar and all the gods of the south weren't even things to be shunned, simply mocked and jeered. They felt no fear when they heard the name of Sigmar.

That changed when a half-dozen Norscans were suddenly flung through the air. An instant later, four others were sent flying, scattered like leaves before a storm. A mighty voice, the same voice that had rallied the southlings before, shouted down the howls of the marauders, drowning their fierce war cries.

'I am his hammer!' the voice thundered. 'I am his fist! I am the eye that judges and the wrath that punishes!'

The northmen backed away, recoiling from the imposing figure who strode from the ranks of the soldiers. He was a tall man, garbed in heavy armour and white robes. In his steel gauntlets he held an immense warhammer gilt in gold and wreathed in a nimbus of blinding light. The man's face was hard and severe, his bald pate branded with the symbol of a twin-tailed comet. Fires seemed to burn beneath the man's flesh, and with every step he appeared to swell with power. One marauder, slower than the rest in retreating, was thrown through the air by a sweep of the warhammer. He landed in a battered mess, his shield dented into a concave disk that was embedded in his ribs.

'By the might of Sigmar!' the warrior priest bellowed. 'I shall scour this place of the heathen, the heretic and the witch-folk!'

The marauders fell silent at the priest's fury, cringing back like whipped dogs. From their cowed ranks, Wulfrik emerged.

The hero stared at the priest with an air of unconcern, as though he had not just watched the Sigmarite swat a dozen of his warriors like flies. The priest glared coldly at Wulfrik as the champion took his measure, pacing slowly back and forth in the gap that had been created between the lines.

Finally, Wulfrik stopped. He bared his fangs in a sardonic grin and gestured with his sword at the warrior priest's forehead.

'In Norsca,' Wulfrik said, his words spoken in precise Reikspiel, 'we call that sign the Serpent's Tongue.' He spat on the ground and stared hard into the priest's eyes. 'Those who wear that symbol are the lowest perverts in the cult of Slaanesh.'

Chapter Eighteen

WULFRIK WAS FLUNG through the air as the warrior priest's hammer came crashing down into the flagstones beside him, missing the hero by a hairsbreadth. Shards of rock tore the northman's face sending blood trickling into his beard. He landed with a brutal impact against the shields of his own warriors, knocking several men to their backs as he smashed against them. He could feel the spikes on one hersir's shield bite into his back, gouging his armour and pricking the flesh beneath. Angrily, Wulfrik leapt back to his feet, stalking towards the grim armoured priest.

'My father had a hammer like that,' Wulfrik sneered at the priest. 'Maybe he took it from your father after he got tired of listening to him beg for mercy…'

The priest lunged at Wulfrik, an inarticulate snarl of rage flying from his lips. The massive warhammer, its head smouldering with wisps of orange flame, came hurtling down with the fury of a thunderclap. Wulfrik sprang away from the mighty blow, rolling across the ground as the hammer pulverised the flagstones.

Better prepared for the might of the priest's hammer this time, Wulfrik was able to arrest his momentum before smashing into his own men. The hero glared at the southling priest from above the rim of his shield. Every eye was now upon their fight, those of the invading northmen and those of the southling soldiers. To the victor of this contest would go Wisborg and all within its walls.

'We used that hammer to club swine,' Wulfrik said. 'It wasn't fit for killing men...'

'Heathen filth! Still your blasphemies!' the warrior priest roared. Again, the hammer came swinging towards Wulfrik, its head now glowing like iron in a forge. This time the hammer struck Wulfrik's shield, crumpling it like a sheet of tin. The marauder was tossed through the air, smashing into the abandoned carts and stands of the marketplace. Glass shattered and wood splintered as the armoured warrior ploughed through the stall.

'So are the proudest of the ungodly smote down by the wrath of Sigmar!' the warrior priest's voice thundered across the ranks of the awed northmen. The marauders began to back away from this fearsome southling with the divine fury of his god burning in his eyes and blazing from his hammer. The soldiers defending the square cheered, marching forwards to aid the priest in driving the invaders back to their ships.

Suddenly, the retreat of the northmen stopped. Marauders pointed with their axes, muttering excitedly as they watched something rise from the wreckage of the stalls. The warrior priest turned his head, his jaw clenching in anger as he saw his enemy regain his feet.

Wulfrik wiped blood from his mouth and spat a broken fang into the street. 'My mother spanks harder than that,' the hero growled, kicking aside a splintered cart and marching towards the priest. With every step he took, more of the northmen began to beat their shields. By the time he was close enough to engage his foe, the tumult had risen to an almost deafening din.

Wulfrik cast the dented shield at the priest's feet, then drew the second sword from his belt. A blade in either hand, he closed upon his enemy.

The enraged priest sprang to the attack first. Gripping his hammer in both hands, he brought the heavy weapon hurtling downwards in an overhead strike, intending to drive Wulfrik's head into the ground like a nail. The burning hammer looked like a bolt of sun-fire as it came crashing down.

Again, the agile hero avoided the Sigmarite's furious assault. Goaded into a zealous fury, the warrior priest had forsaken craft and cunning, relying upon strength, power and conviction to maul his enemy.

The hammer smashed into the ground, once more gouging a crater in the flagstones. Wulfrik was thrown from his feet by the tremulous impact, but this time he was not batted about the square by the resultant shock wave. The instant the priest's hammer was in motion, Wulfrik struck out with one of his swords. He did not strike for his enemy, however, but drove the point of his blade deep between the cobblestones. Maintaining a fierce grip about the weapon, Wulfrik held his ground.

As the warrior priest rose from his vicious attack, Wulfrik was in motion. Using the sword as a fulcrum, the hero brought his entire body swinging around. His heavy boots smashed into the Sigmarite's belly, knocking the wind out of him and throwing him to the ground. Immediately, Wulfrik sprang atop his foe, releasing his hold on the sword embedded in the flagstones and bringing the other smashing down.

The priest cried out in agony as Wulfrik's sword slashed his hand, forcing the hammer from his grip. The warhammer rolled away from the stunned priest, the divine glow winking out the instant it struck the ground. A wild cheer rose from the massed ranks of the northmen. Stunned silence was the only sound among the despairing line of soldiers.

Roaring and beating their shields, the marauders lunged across the square to face the soldiers once more. What missile fire continued to assail them was sporadic and hurried, causing few injuries. The fangs of the Norscan phalanx crashed against the shields of the southling line. At first, the line held, but soon it began to buckle as the axes of the exultant marauders cut down the frantic soldiers. Once the first wedge was driven into the line, it quickly fell, the routed soldiers fleeing down side-streets and alleys, trying to find any hole in which to hide from the rage of the northmen.

In the market square, Wulfrik brought the hilt of his sword smashing down into the side of the priest's head, driving consciousness from him. The hero rose from his vanquished foe and grinned triumphantly as he watched his warriors pursuing the retreating soldiers. The wails of southling townsfolk, the screams of southling women, rose from the streets as the marauders began to sack Wisborg.

'Strike me with your daemon's hammer?' a sharp voice snarled. Wulfrik caught a jagged harpoon as it was being thrust at the unconscious priest. With a twist of his powerful hand, the hero snapped the heft of the weapon.

The harpoon wielder staggered back. Blood streaked his face, but not enough to hide the features of Sveinbjorn, prince of the Aeslings. He glared at Wulfrik, his entire body trembling with outrage. 'No man strikes an Aesling in battle and lives!' the prince spat.

Wulfrik returned the prince's furious stare with a cold look. 'This one does,' the hero said, pointing his blade at the prostrate priest.

Sveinbjorn smiled as he heard Wulfrik's words. He glanced from side to side as a group of Aesling hersirs slowly closed around the hero. The prince straightened up, puffing out his chest in an arrogant display of authority. 'I say he dies.'

'This one is mine,' Wulfrik snarled back. 'Take him from me... if you can.'

Sveinbjorn's grin grew wider. He motioned for his warriors to finish encircling Wulfrik. More than he wanted the priest's blood, he wanted the hero's head.

The prince's smile died when he felt a blade against his throat. He looked nervously aside and saw the imposing figure of Jarl Tostig of the Graelings beside him. The sword against his throat was that of the jarl. Other Graelings and warriors from several other tribes were closing upon Sveinbjorn's hersirs.

'Wulfrik is the only one who can command the *Seafang*,' Tostig told Sveinbjorn. 'Kill him and you strand us here, far from the sea and deep in enemy lands.'

'I will not be denied!' Sveinbjorn growled. 'If he will not give me the southling, then I demand wergild!'

'You may have the finest steed in this town,' Wulfrik laughed. 'Then you will just need someone to teach you how to ride.'

Sveinbjorn glared at the champion, but knew Tostig and the others would kill him if he didn't accept the jibe. Besides, the jarl was right. Wulfrik was their only sure way back to Norsca. Once they were safely back in the fjord of Ormskaro, then would be the time to settle with the hero and make him answer for all of his insults.

'I'll go look for my horse,' Sveinbjorn said, his voice like a whip. He motioned for his hersirs to back down. Pausing only to glower at Wulfrik, the prince led his men down one of the darkened streets of Wisborg.

Wulfrik watched the prince slink away. Sveinbjorn was at a disadvantage. Wulfrik knew when the prince would strike at him. The prince could not say the same.

The hero turned to watch the stream of northmen pouring through the broken gates to ravage the town. He held up his fist, calling out as he recognised men from the *Seafang*'s crew among the warriors.

'Helreginn!' he barked out, drawing the attention of a huge warrior encased in black armour. The hulking Norscan approached his captain, the eyes behind the sockets of his skull-faced helm glancing down at the priest's body.

'A rare prize,' Wulfrik told the warrior. 'I'm trusting you to keep it for me.'

Helreginn nodded his head, his armoured hands running across the heft of his axe. 'Alive?' the warrior's metallic voice rattled from behind the steel teeth of his mask.

'So long as he is fit to ride a horse, make what sport you will with him,' Wulfrik said.

Helreginn nodded again. He removed a strip of dried eelskin from his belt and knelt beside the fallen priest, binding his hands together.

Wulfrik turned away from Helreginn and his prisoner. The hero's eyes drank in the sight of his conquest, watching the blood pooling about the dead soldiers, seeing flames lick up into the night as the northmen put Wisborg to the torch. Screams echoed from every quarter, the shrieks of the vanquished and the war cries of the conquerors. Above the stench of fire and flame, Wulfrik could pick out the bitter tang of blood and death. But it was another scent that caused the hero to leave the square, sprinting down one of the narrow side-streets.

He passed marauders looting shops and plundering homes, warriors cutting down ragged knots of militiamen, warhounds worrying mangled bodies with savage fangs. He saw a raven-haired southling woman flailing in the clutch of a brawny Aesling, helpless to stop him swinging her babe by its ankle and spattering its brains against the cobblestone street. He watched as a feral Baersonling, his body twisted into a shaggy thing more bear than man, gorged himself upon the gutted husk of an ox in the shattered window of a clothier's shop. He observed a pair of Sarl reavers lumbering down the street, burdened by the still-smoking bulk of an iron stove.

There was no fight left in Wisborg. The town was broken. Those who could would flee.

Wulfrik hastened his pace, following the faint scent that drew him after it. He had to find Zarnath before the wizard could escape. He knew that after coming so close, he might never get another chance at his betrayer.

THE WIZARD'S SCENT led Wulfrik to the very heart of Wisborg. Organised resistance in the town to the northmen had collapsed, and those southlings the hero encountered as he made his way through the chaotic streets were either too frightened to pose any danger to him or too dead to pose a threat to anyone ever again. The greater hazards were the fires his jubilant men were setting. The flames spread quickly through the town, entire blocks becoming raging infernos in a matter of minutes. There was small chance of restraining the marauders, however. Their blood afire from the thrill of battle, their brains swimming in the beer and wine they found in the shops and homes they ransacked, little short of a personal appearance by the Skulltaker would bring discipline back to the raiders.

Wulfrik found that the wizard's smell was thickest about the castle rising from the centre of the town. Ancient seat of the Krugers, the town had been built around the fortification until at last growing large and prosperous enough to warrant its own walls. What few defenders Wisborg had left were clustered inside the castle, firing guns and loosing arrows from its battlements. A large force of northmen howled outside the walls, making efforts to assail it with ladders and grapples. So far, the efforts of the soldiers had been enough to drive off these attacks.

A more formidable assault was being planned, however. Wulfrik found Skafhogg and several men from the *Seafang's* crew stealing to the castle gates, employing a shield wall to protect them from missile fire. The hideous helmsman had a devious mind as crooked as his body. Clearly Skafhogg remembered the destruction on the town walls when the seers used their magic to ignite the cannon and its ammunition. The northmen had captured another battery somewhere in the town. Unfamiliar with the weapon itself, they had an idea about how to use the gunpowder to bring down the gate.

The southlings on the walls cried out in horror when they realised what Skafhogg was doing. They began to hurl stones down upon the Norscans, trying to drive them away from the gate. The northmen threw lewd remarks back at the soldiers, refusing to be driven from their labour.

When the last barrel was placed, the northmen scrambled away from the gate, taking refuge in the shattered windows of the townhouses facing the keep. One of the crewmen, a one-eyed Skaeling named Lopt, strode boldly towards the brick causeway before the gate. Bullets and arrows glanced from Lopt's steel armour, each piece marked in blood with the skull-rune. The Skaeling ignored the soldiers firing at him. Coldly he raised his leathery hand to his breast, tapping it against his heart. Then he stretched his hand towards the barrels. A ghastly mouth opened in his palm and from between its fangs jetted a stream of molten fire. The liquid flame crashed about the barrels, igniting the blackpowder. An instant later, all of Wisborg was rocked by a tremendous explosion.

The castle was lost in a cloud of dust and smoke. Even before the echoes of the explosion subsided, Wulfrik was charging at the place where the gate had stood, leaping across the great crater the explosion had ripped from the ground when it blew the gatehouse to smithereens. All around him he could hear the war whoops and bloodthirsty howls of his warriors as they rushed to invade this last bastion of defiance. A stunned soldier, banging his hand against his helm in an effort to clear his ringing ears, staggered out of the smoke towards Wulfrik. The hero cut him down before he was even aware of the northman's presence. A second soldier, vainly trying to arm a crossbow broken in the explosion, at least had time to scream before the hero's blade took his life.

Marauders streamed through the broken wall, springing to stairways and ladders to reach the stunned defenders on the ramparts. Those northmen more concerned with loot than battle raced for the keep itself and whatever wealth Baron Kruger had bled from his township. Wulfrik saw a grotesquely obese woman dressed in a rich purple gown and with her breast covered in glittering necklaces come stumbling from the keep. She was screaming at the marauders, begging them to take her jewels and spare her life. A Sarl axeman silenced her wails, making it clear the northmen would have both.

'Should have known you'd join us here, Wulfrik,' Skafhogg said as he came loping through the smoke and saw his captain. 'Where do you think the southlings have hidden their treasure?'

Wulfrik smiled at his helmsman and gestured with his bloody sword at the keep. 'Be sure to tap the walls and rip open anything that sounds hollow,' he advised. He caught the snaggletoothed warrior's arm before he could move. 'Make sure the best gets aboard the *Seafang*.'

'Wulfrik?' a haggard voice coughed. The hero turned from his helmsman, looking about the courtyard until his eyes settled upon a ragged figure imprisoned in a set of wooden stocks. The prisoner had been a large, powerful man once, but hot irons had torn his muscles, pincers had removed his eyes and hammers had broken his teeth. Still, there was something familiar about the prisoner.

Wulfrik approached the prisoner, studying his tortured frame. No one would think Broendulf fair again.

'Wulfrik?' the captive called, seeming to sense the hero's nearness despite the hollow pits where his eyes should be.

The hero kept his silence, thinking instead upon the pact he had made with Broendulf. Like all his other dreams, it was a hollow mockery of what it should be. Something that was not worth the winning.

'By the blood of Kharnath!' Broendulf cried. 'Let me die with a blade in my hand!'

Wulfrik glanced over at Skafhogg, then back at Broendulf. Savagely, he drove the point of his sword into the captive's brain. 'Call to your own gods, southling,' Wulfrik spat. 'Those of the north will not hear you.'

Skafhogg grunted in amusement at the callous execution. Wulfrik wiped Broendulf's blood from his sword and pointed to the keep. 'Take whatever we can carry. I want the *Seafang's* holds filled to bursting. We wouldn't want to disappoint Sveinbjorn.' The comment brought a cruel smile onto Skafhogg's face. Wulfrik turned away, facing the tall narrow tower at the western corner of the courtyard. It was about the tower that Zarnath's scent was strongest.

'I'll be in here if you need me,' Wulfrik told his helmsman, a tone of such malignance in his voice that Skafhogg wouldn't have dared disturb the hero if the Emperor and all his armies appeared outside the walls of Wisborg.

There was the promise of death in Wulfrik's voice. Death that would be slow and horrible for the man who had been marked for destruction.

Stossel crouched upon the floor of his laboratory, a circle drawn in his own blood marking the floor all around him. Seven candles, black as midnight and crafted from the fat of murderers, smouldered at the tips of the star the wizard had scribed in the middle of the circle. He stared at the hideous symbol, feeling its dark energies saturating the air. Even if he survived this night, there would be no hiding this transgression into the black arts. If the witch hunters did not come for him, then the astromancers would dispatch a magister vigilant to make him answer for his crimes.

The wizard was resigned to his fate. He had seen the tragedy that resulted from trying to run from the future. All his efforts to escape from his hunter had led to destruction. He felt no remorse for the Norscans who had perished upon the voyages he had tricked Wulfrik into making, even less for the degenerate dwarfs who had been slaughtered by the northmen. He regretted the elves who had died because of his trickery, but in his desperation he had seen no other way to destroy Wulfrik. Now it was the innocents of his own lands who died because of his failures, their screams which filled the air.

No, Ludwig Stossel had earned death many times over. But if he could obliterate the monstrous champion of the Dark Gods, if he could strike down Wulfrik before he died, then perhaps he might redeem some small measure of worth for his blackened soul.

His breath haggard with the effort of the profane ritual, Stossel lifted his eyes to his familiar. Grylikh was hopping excitedly about its perch, its keen eyes watching the wizard's every motion. He wondered for a moment at his familiar's energy, puzzling over the reason it did not share the fatigue which taxed his own spirit.

Stossel dismissed the imp's erratic behaviour, concentrating instead upon the complex hieroglyphs he now summoned from memory. Far below him, he could hear the door to his tower being smashed open. He knew who it was that came to violate his sanctum. The wizard had gambled his soul on this last effort to destroy his enemy and atone for the evil he had brought upon Wisborg. Now he would see if his gamble had paid off.

Eerie figures shimmered in the air before Stossel as the astromancer spoke the ancient syllables of each name-picture which formed in his mind. The spectral hieroglyphs fractured into wisps of energy as the next was spoken. The strands of power slithered about the laboratory, flitting around the legs of tables, crawling up the sides of chairs before finally draining into a fist-sized diamond locked within a setting of obsidian.

At first the diamond glowed only slightly, but as more and more magical energy flowed into it, the pallid gem began to give off an amber pulse of light. Faster and faster the pulses came and with them there sounded a dull pounding, like the beat of a hammer against stone.

The obsidian shape in which the diamond was set had stood in shadow when the astromancer began his ritual. Now, by the amber pulses of light, it stood revealed, a monstrous, man-like shape ten feet tall. The statue's physique was that of a powerfully athletic youth, its only raiment a loincloth of obsidian. However its head was a grisly mockery of life, a jackal's skull crowned with a golden headdress.

Stossel had created the ghastly statue in mimicry of the ushabti crafted by the ancient liche-priests of Khemri. Grylikh had led him to the ritual to construct the guardian statue, hidden deep within an old treatise on the vanished kingdoms of Nehekhara. The imp had also found for him the scroll which related the spell to give the statue motion and motivation.

Despite the horror of what he had done, Stossel felt a sense of pride as the throb of the ushabti's diamond heart pulsed through the tower. He spoke the name-sign which would give his creation motion, awed when the obsidian statue took a quaking step across the laboratory. Quickly he berated himself for such arrogance. It was the same ignorant thrill of power he'd felt as a youth receiving his first portents, the jubilation of an apprentice evoking his first rainstorm, never appreciating the power he wielded.

This was evil magic, black sorcery of the foulest stripe. It belonged to the world of necromancy and daemonology, not the refined schools of wizardry. The seductive power of what he had done only added to Stossel's repugnance. He understood now why the witch hunters were ever distrustful of wizards. It was so easy for them to be overwhelmed by the power they could command.

Stossel wondered if even destroying Wulfrik could justify this being he had created. Could the destruction of one evil ever condone the birth of another?

The wizard turned a questioning glance at Grylikh, but the shrike simply continued to hop about on its perch, offering neither approval nor condemnation.

Then the door of the laboratory came crashing inwards. Stossel looked at the crazed warrior standing in the doorway, his armour soaked in the blood of innocent men. All moral qualms vanished from his mind as the wizard stared at Wulfrik.

'Kiiiillll,' the astromancer hissed. 'Kiiiilll hiii-immm.'

WULFRIK BASHED IN the oak door, the last barrier between himself and Zarnath's stink. He stood at the top of the spiral staircase that coiled its way through the wizard's tower and glared across the dark laboratory, lips curling from his fangs as he saw the sorcerer sitting upon the floor. Eagerly, the hero's fingers tightened about his sword.

Before the Norscan could charge across the room and deal death to his betrayer, a huge shape lurched out from the shadows. Wulfrik's body grew tense as he watched the mighty ushabti step into the centre of the chamber, barring his path to Zarnath. There was no life in the empty sockets of the carved skull that served it for a face, no mind locked within its stone body. There was nothing at all within this hulking automaton which the Gift of Tongues could goad into reckless fury; he might as soon curse the sea as cast insult upon the golem-beast.

Wulfrik heard Zarnath's hissed command. In response, the ushabti slowly turned, reaching to one of the walls, its stone hands tearing a massive greatsword and an equally enormous siege shield from where they were bolted to the wall. In the monster's hands, the huge two-handed sword looked as slim as the silver-steel blades of the elf-folk, the massive siege shield little bigger than a buckler in the statue's grip.

Armed now, the ushabti lumbered forwards to carry out the command of its master. Wulfrik did not wait for the monstrous statue to attack. Howling like a maddened beast, the northman leapt across one of the wooden tables scattered throughout the wizard's laboratory. A sword in either hand, he lashed out at the automaton, eager to remove this last obstacle between him and his revenge.

With surprising quickness, the ushabti met Wulfrik's attack. It raised its sword in a quick parry, nearly ripping the sword from the hero's right hand. Wulfrik's other blade clanged against the bronze plate of the siege shield, inflicting no more hurt to it than a scratch across its painted face. The ushabti stomped forwards, flinging the northman away as it exerted its stony strength.

Reeling away from the statue, Wulfrik felt his back slam against one of the tables. Quickly he rolled aside as the ushabti brought its sword swinging around, shearing through the bottles and alembics standing upon the table, sending shards of glass and strangely coloured vapours flying about the chamber. He drove at the statue's side, trying to strike it before the monster could recover, but again found the heavy siege shield raised against his blades.

Wulfrik dodged away as the ushabti swung towards

him, its massive sword slashing down in a cleaving arc. This time when he swatted it aside, he did lose one of his own weapons, the impact of the ushabti's blow pulsing through his left arm, stunning the nerves into numbness. His sword clattered across the floor as it fell from his deadened grip.

The ushabti gave no sign of satisfaction at partially disarming its enemy, but continued to press Wulfrik with the same slavish obedience. Its shield warded off a strike from his remaining sword, its own blade coming flashing down in a brutal arc that passed close enough to the hero that he could feel air swish across his throat.

The hero kicked a stool at the ushabti, then flipped across a table as the monster stormed after him. Its stone legs crunched through the wooden stool, obliterating the obstruction, but at the cost of some of the statue's coordination. When the ushabti brought its sword slashing down at the man slipping around the table, the edge slammed instead into the oak surface, gouging a deep rent in the wood.

For an instant, the automaton's weapon was trapped. Before it could rip the blade free, Wulfrik brought his own sword slashing across its hand. The volcanic glass of its fingers was shattered by the ferocious impact. The ushabti reeled away, holding its broken hand in the air.

Wulfrik leapt atop the table, intending to force his advantage. Before he could swing his blade at the ushabti's skull, the marauder dived to the floor, the heavy siege shield slicing through the air as the statue flung it at him. The shield slammed into the shelves against the wall, shattering bottles, flinging books and jars across the floor and sending the mummified husk of a swamp lizard plummeting down the stairway.

Before Wulfrik could scramble from cover, the statue was ripping its sword free from the table with its good hand. The jackal-skull grinned at the northman as the ushabti swatted the obstacle aside and closed upon him. The hero tried to parry the downward thrust of its blade, but the impact of the blow brought him to his knees. The statue struck at him with the stone club of its injured hand, the jagged obsidian edges shearing through his armour. Wulfrik cried out in pain as twisted links of mail bit into his flesh.

Dodging another sweep of the automaton's sword, Wulfrik stumbled upon the debris littering the floor. The ushabti rushed him, its sword striking sparks from the wall as Wulfrik ducked beneath its murderous edge.

Wulfrik staggered away from the remorseless statue, driven back to the doorway from which he had started. He glared into the dead visage of the ushabti, enraged that his death should be brought at the hands of a thing unable to recognise its accomplishment.

A croaking caw diverted his attention for an instant from the monster. Wulfrik's eyes darted to the floor, shocked to see a black bird hopping about the debris. His shock turned to a grim smile when he saw the object the bird was so interested in. It was a metal flask with a gromril stopper. The Gift of Tongues didn't allow Wulfrik to read the archaic letters scrawled across its surface, but he didn't need to read the flask to know what was inside it. The smell of its contents was too strong even for metal to hold captive. It was a smell no warrior of Norsca could ever forget.

The ushabti lunged at him once more, sword slashing at his darting body. This time Wulfrik did not retreat from the monster, but instead sprang past it, rolling along the floor. The black bird hastily retreated as the northman's violent slide brought him within reach of the metal flask. The sizzling trickle streaming from the dislodged stopper and burning little pits in the floor told Wulfrik the arcane symbols had not lied about its contents. Few things were more caustic than troll bile.

The jackal-headed statue swung towards Wulfrik, raising its heavy sword to cut the northman in half. He snarled back at the ushabti, knocking the stopper free with the edge of his sword and splashing the flask's contents across the monster's chest.

Smoke rose from the obsidian statue as the troll bile ate into it. The ushabti staggered back, shaking its head from side to side in an almost human gesture of disorientation. The massive diamond continued to pulse in the centre of its chest – even troll bile could work no more harm than an ugly discolouration upon diamond – but the obsidian around it grew brittle and cracked apart.

The monster took a few more stumbling steps, then flailed its arms as it reached the top of the stairway. The ushabti fought to retain its balance, a fight it seemed about to win until the diamond suddenly dropped from its chest. Instantly, the statue became a lifeless hulk of stone. Without motion or motivation, it toppled backwards, pitching headlong down the stairway, its body cracking apart as it plummeted from the tower.

Wulfrik rose to his feet, kicking the glowing diamond across the floor. Sparing only a single wary glance at the stairway to assure himself that the automaton showed no sign of returning, he turned his eyes on the wizard squatting in his circle of candles and blood.

The wizard looked far different from when he had appeared to Wulfrik as the Kurgan shaman Zarnath, but the astromancer had neglected to mask his scent as thoroughly as he had his face. Wulfrik would not be deceived. This was the man he had led an army halfway around the world to kill.

Stossel recoiled from Wulfrik's approach. Gone was the might of his magic, drained from him by the hurried spells unleashed by him during the battle, his vitality further sapped by the desperate animation of the ushabti. Barely a hint of blue light glowed in his hollow eyes now, his body withered into an almost fleshless skeleton, the colour drained from his skin. Strands of hair fell from his beard as he raised his terrified eyes to the advancing northman.

Wulfrik glared at the pathetic wretch, his gaze as merciless as a winter storm.

The wizard turned frantic eyes to the perch of his familiar. Grylikh was still there, hopping excitedly from one foot to the other, but the imp was anything but diminished by its master's distress. If anything, it had grown in size, swelling with power. Stossel sensed something terrible in the creature and for the first time wondered exactly what it was he had conjured up from the old grimoire to serve him.

Grylikh cawed at Stossel, and the familiar's shape shifted from that of a shrike into the sleek shadowy form of a raven, a single multi-faceted eye burning at the centre of its face. The black beak seemed to smile at him, the sardonic grin of a patient trickster.

An armoured fist smashed into the wizard's face, sprawling him across the floor. Too weak to even lift a hand to defend himself, Stossel could only whimper as Wulfrik loomed over him. The northman's face was so twisted with hate that it seemed scarcely human. It did not take a prognosticator to read death in the marauder's blazing eyes.

'You favour birds, Zarnath?' Wulfrik snarled as he seized the wizard's robe and lifted him from the floor. The astromancer pawed feebly at his assailant, trying to hold him back. The pommel of Wulfrik's sword buried itself in Stossel's gut, sending him crashing back to the floor again.

Wulfrik glared down at the prone wizard. Slowly he sheathed his sword and drew a dagger from his belt. He marched towards Stossel, driving his boot into the astromancer's side, flipping him onto his belly.

'Since you like birds so much, traitor,' Wulfrik hissed, 'I will make you one.'

Stossel cried out as Wulfrik stomped a boot into the small of his back. It was the first of the wizard's screams.

It was not the last.

An hour later, Wulfrik crouched beside the gasping, simpering ruin that had once been Ludwig Stossel, renowned astromancer of Wisborg, magister of the Celestial Order. A man who had learned the secret ways of magic and bound them to his service. A man who had peered into the future and tried to shape it to fit his needs. Prophet and mystic, Stossel had long trespassed in the domains of the gods, believing his foresight placed him beyond their power.

Wulfrik wiped the dying man's blood from his hands, using the torn tatters of the wizard's own robes to cleanse himself. He nodded with satisfaction as he studied his work. It had taken every ounce of his will to restrain himself from killing Stossel outright. Now he savoured the obscene spectacle he had created.

The tribes of Norsca called it the blood eagle, a torture reserved for their most hated enemies. It was a gruesome tradition that stretched back into the mists of legend. Wulfrik could think of no better doom to bestow upon the man who had lied so cruelly to him, who had held everything he dreamed of before his eyes and then snatched it away even as he reached for it. The traitor could be thankful the northman could only kill him once.

First Wulfrik had flayed the skin from Stossel's back, exposing the meat and muscle beneath. He cut the ribs from the wizard's spine, bending them outwards until they broke. Then, with the most delicate care, he reached into the traitor's body, lifting out the pulsing lungs and laying them upon the shoulders.

Like the gory wings of a hellsent fury, Stossel's lungs shivered against his shoulders as his mutilated body struggled to draw breath.

The hero watched his betrayer die inch by inch, his eyes locked on Stossel's mangled flesh with the intensity of a basilisk's stare. Wulfrik savoured each agonised breath the wizard took, delighted in every tortured sob that choked past his lips, relished every pained shiver of his limbs. Like all delights, Wulfrik knew the wizard's torment must end, but he would glut his soul upon it while he could.

The cyclopean raven, the only other spectator to Stossel's suffering, flitted excitedly through the room, sometimes landing to hop in the pools of blood leaking from the wizard. Wulfrik let the morbid creature be. Ravens were the messengers of Tzeentch and to see one so visibly bearing the mark of the Great Mutator was a doubly noble blessing. Indeed, the wizard's renegade pet seemed to take as much glee from its master's suffering as the northman did.

Eventually, Stossel's ruined body began to fail. Wulfrik frowned when he heard the first ragged shudder from the wizard's throat. Grylikh croaked angrily, ruffling its feathers and flying onto its perch. The raven's grisly eye stared hatefully at the expiring wizard.

Wulfrik, however, knew there was one thing more he had to do. Standing over Stossel, the hero brought his brawny hands slapping down upon the wizard's exposed lungs. While the tortured body beneath him thrashed wildly as it at last suffocated, the northman lifted his head, staring past the ceiling, staring at the invisible thrones of his gods.

'To Tzeentch, Lord of Fate, Changer of the Ways, I give the last breath of this offering.'

As Wulfrik spoke, the death rattle sounded from Stossel's throat. The wizard's last exhalation became a shimmering streak of light as it left his body, rising in pulsating strands of luminescence from the mutilated corpse. The northman could see tiny figures moving within the lights, a thousand scenes playing out within the wizard's breath. Flashes of another life, Stossel's life, captured within the traitor's final breath.

Wulfrik looked away from the dizzying spectacle of events, feeling his brain ache from the bombardment of stimulation. Grylikh, however, was not so timid, its multi-faceted eye riveted upon the strands of light. Cawing happily, the raven flew down amid the lights, snapping them from the air as though they were locusts, crushing each in its beak before eagerly devouring them.

The hero left the daemon to gorge itself upon Stossel's soul. Sombrely, he made his way through the wreckage of the laboratory. There was much he still had to do. Zarnath had been at the top of his list of traitors he would see dead, but he was not the only one. With the shaman and Broendulf gone, it would be Sveinbjorn's turn next.

The Aesling prince would wait until they were back in Norscan waters before trying to destroy Wulfrik.

Wulfrik would not be so patient.

Epilogue

SILVER, SLAVES AND gold. Wulfrik cast his gaze across the shore as the Norscans loaded the wealth of Wisborg into the holds of their longships. There were many sour looks directed at the *Seafang* by the marauders. The riches they had plundered from the town were respectable, but a far cry from the dazzling fortune they had been led to expect after Wulfrik's display with the elven jewels back in Ormskaro.

Jarl Tostig and Than Canute, two of the most powerful chieftains who had set out upon the voyage, were especially bitter in their scrutiny of Wulfrik and his ship. Theirs had been the loudest voices urging a return to Norsca to divide such loot as they had taken in Wisborg. It would not be much, parted among so many, but it would at least pay for the warriors they had lost taking the town.

Wulfrik had proposed a different strategy. He would lead the fleet further down the Reik, to still greater and more wealthy cities, ripe for the plunderer's sword. The hero's offer had been met with enthusiasm by most of the marauders, if not their chieftains. In order to appease their own men, Tostig and Canute and the other leaders agreed to follow Wulfrik to another town and see if its coffers were more rewarding than those of Wisborg.

It was Jarl Tostig, full of venomous suspicion, who demanded that Wulfrik allow one of the other chiefs aboard the *Seafang* to ensure the veracity of the hero's promise. Not willing to put his own neck at risk, Tostig suggested the one man among all the leaders who could be counted upon to be no friend of the Wanderer's. Surprisingly, Sveinbjorn had made only a feeble effort to back out of the hole Tostig had put him in.

There was only one reason Sveinbjorn would be willing to sail on Wulfrik's ship. Tostig was right to worry about treachery, but he should have spared some of his suspicions for Sveinbjorn while he was trying to guard against trickery.

The hero grinned at the level of callous ambition and greed the Aesling prince possessed. He knew Sveinbjorn had bribed men from his crew to sneak treasure from the other longships into the *Seafang's* hold. He knew the prince had conspired to smuggle extra passengers aboard, hidden among the southling captives. Two dozen of Sveinbjorn's most loyal hersirs could cause a great deal of trouble, given the chance.

As the last longship was loaded and the fleet took sail, Wulfrik was not surprised when he saw Skafhogg and Helreginn leading Sveinbjorn across the deck. There was a look of smug triumph on the prince's face as he approached, the expression of the cat who has gobbled up the songbird.

'You have a fine ship,' Sveinbjorn said, running an appreciative hand along the *Seafang's* rail. 'I have never seen a vessel with such a splendid shape, such rugged beauty.'

'I have already noted your eye for beauty,' Wulfrik growled. 'A foolish man might say we share the same tastes. I'd have to nail his tongue to the mast.'

Sveinbjorn chuckled at the thinly veiled threat. The way he moved his hand along the rail took on a languid, suggestive flair, as though tracing its way up a supple leg of ivory skin to squeeze the smooth thigh above. Sveinbjorn laughed again when he saw by the smouldering anger in Wulfrik's eyes that the hero appreciated the gesture.

'I would like to have a ship such as this,' Sveinbjorn said. Other men from the *Seafang's* crew now began to rise from their benches to approach the prow and their captain. Wulfrik could see the five hersirs Sveinbjorn had openly brought aboard with him as a bodyguard among the men closing upon him.

Wulfrik curled his lip and sneered at the Aesling prince. 'You wouldn't know how to handle a ship like this. I am told you don't perform well with things of quality, be they ships or women.'

Outrage flared across Sveinbjorn's face as the barb struck his ears. His hand fell to the hilt of his sword and started to draw it from his belt. Then the oily smile was back on his face. 'I know you don't like to share,' Sveinbjorn told him. 'So I'm not going to ask you to. Hjordis is mine, and so is this ship.'

'You can't command her magic,' Wulfrik said, his tone as friendly as an open grave.

'But you can!' Sveinbjorn snarled, pointing his fist at the hero. He glanced aside, nodding his head, motioning for the crew to tighten the circle around their captain. 'You can, and you will! By Shornaal's teat, you'll guide this ship where I tell you or I'll geld you and stake your manhood on a briar thorn. A small briar thorn.'

Wulfrik eyed the warriors surrounding him, making no move towards his weapons. 'You've planned this quite well,' he said. 'But in a rather predictable fashion. Tell me, how much of my treasure did you promise my crew if they betrayed me?'

Skafhogg pulled an ugly, crook-bladed knife from his boot, letting sunlight dance across its menacing edge. 'A quarter of the plunder is ours when we deliver this ship to Prince Sveinbjorn.'

Sveinbjorn giggled vindictively as he listened to the *Seafang's* helmsman pronounce Wulfrik's defeat. The hero was nothing without his ship. He would be lost to the terrible doom the gods had set upon him. His only hope now was to grovel before his enemy and beg Sveinbjorn for mercy.

Wulfrik's next words caused the Aesling to almost choke upon his laughter.

'Tell the prince what I promised you when we return to Norsca,' the chieftain said.

'You offered us everything in the hold,' Skafhogg declared. 'Every coin, every keg, every thrall. All of it when we deliver Sveinbjorn to you.'

Before the prince could react, Skafhogg's knife was pressed against his throat. Helreginn drove his spiked mace full into the skull of the closest hersir.

Other crewmen swiftly dragged down the remaining Aeslings on deck.

Wulfrik smiled coldly at the shocked Sveinbjorn. 'You're a poor haggler,' he said, baring his fangs. He noticed the colour drain from the prince's face as the crew began throwing the bodies of his guards into the river. 'Don't fret after your men in the hold. They've already been dealt with.'

Sweat streamed down Sveinbjorn's face, his lips turning almost colourless. 'You don't dare kill me!' he yelled. 'It will mean war! Ormskaro will burn!'

The hero rounded on Sveinbjorn, smashing his fist into the nose he had broken in Hjordis's bedchamber. Except for Skafhogg's support, the prince would have collapsed from the vicious strike.

'It'll be war,' Wulfrik agreed. He turned his eyes from Sveinbjorn and snapped commands to his crew. 'Remove this pig's armour and helm! Lopt! You look slippery enough to pass for this scum at a distance! Put his armour on and strut about the decks like you own this ship! Olav! Remove my standard from the stern and put up Sveinbjorn's banner!'

Wulfrik turned his eyes back on the bewildered Sveinbjorn. 'The *Seafang's* hold is filled to bursting, and with more treasure than either you or I could have acquired fairly. I'm guessing a fair amount of that plunder belongs to Tostig and Canute and the others. What was your plan, Sveinbjorn? Have me send the *Seafang* into the mists and cut the chains? We safely sail back to Norsca while everyone else gets eaten by the daemons? Or maybe the ships loyal to you and Viglundr make it back too?'

The shocked expression on Sveinbjorn's face told Wulfrik his guess had hit very near the mark. 'A good plan,' the hero grunted. 'But I've made a few changes to it.' He looked away again to bark further orders to his crew. 'Bring my priest and the prince's prize horse up from the hold!'

'I'll call the fog and enter the border-realm,' Wulfrik told Sveinbjorn. 'But I have an errand to deal with first.'

The bound Sigmarite priest was hauled onto deck, battered by his ordeal but with his spirit unbroken. He glared at his captors and when his eyes fell upon Wulfrik, there was a gleam of raw hate in them. The chieftain was pleased to see his prisoner so defiant and filled with rage. He intended to use those qualities.

Wulfrik stalked across the deck until he stood before the warrior priest. He met the southling's hate with an arrogant sneer. 'I have decided to let you live, false-father,' he told the Sigmarite.

'Then you are stupid as well as obscene,' the priest snarled back, making a powerful effort to raise his bound arms.

Wulfrik laughed at the priest's malignance. He reached up and took the bridle of the sleek riding horse his crew had brought up from the hold. 'I do not fear your Sigmar and I do not fear your Emperor. I am sending you to tell him to bring all his armies here and face me, if the dog has the stomach for battle. If he doesn't, tell him I will take ten thousand pounds of silver as payment not to put his villages to the sword. Next time I will ask for more. Do you think you can remember all that?'

The warrior priest was smiling now. 'I will happily take your message to Altdorf, barbarian. You will wait here for the Emperor's answer?'

'We will be near, upriver or down,' Wulfrik answered. 'If your Emperor looks, he will find us.'

'Yes, he will,' the priest promised as a pair of marauders lifted him onto the back of Sveinbjorn's horse and tied him to the saddle.

The hero smiled at the southling's remark. 'Row to the other bank!' he told his crew. 'We have a messenger to set ashore.'

Wulfrik marched back across the deck to the bow of the ship where Skafhogg continued to hold Sveinbjorn prisoner. He passed Lopt, the pretend-prince cutting a prideful figure as he swaggered about the ship. There was small chance anyone watching from the other longships would think they were watching anyone but the Aesling prince.

There was confusion on the real Sveinbjorn's face when Wulfrik returned to the *Seafang's* bow.

'I told you I made some changes to your plan,' Wulfrik explained. 'I won't abandon good fighting men to daemons. The chains will be cut, but they will be cut *before* we enter the fog. The fleet will be stranded here, in the land of the southlings. My messenger will see that the wrath of the Empire is focussed here. He will send his ships and his armies looking for me. The men I leave behind will have to fight if they will ever see Norsca again. But the gods favour the strong. Some of them may make it back. But they won't do it soon.'

Sveinbjorn gasped as he understood the horrible

consequences of what Wulfrik had done. If any of those men returned to Norsca, they would say that it was Sveinbjorn, not Wulfrik, who had abandoned them. Even worse, they would think he had betrayed them to the southlings! The sagas would brand him the blackest traitor since Dletch Ogrefeeder!

'No! Wulfrik!' Sveinbjorn pleaded. 'Kill me! Torture me! But leave me my name! I can give you gold!'

'I want no gold,' Wulfrik said. 'I meant what I said when I told my crew everything in the hold was theirs.' The hero waved his hand, motioning for a few of his crew to come near. Each of the three men carried an object in his hands. One held a metal pipe, a second bore a torch. The third carried a small wooden box. 'Not everything,' Wulfrik corrected himself. 'I saved a little something for you.'

Sveinbjorn thrashed about in Skafhogg's grip, trying to break free. The snaggletoothed warrior kept him pinned against the deck, helping the crew hold him down as Wulfrik took hold of the box. He opened the lid and quickly jabbed his armoured hand inside. When his hand emerged from the box, a slender, sinuous shape dangled from it, whipping coils about his wrist.

The prince looked with renewed terror at the metal pipe and burning torch. He knew what was coming. The most insulting death a Norscan could offer an enemy, a shameful death that even the Crow God would shun.

'You can have Hjordis!' Sveinbjorn cried.

Wulfrik took the pipe from one of the warriors with his free hand. He cast a cold gaze upon the pleading Aesling. 'She's not yours to give!' he hissed. Skafhogg shifted his hold, forcing Sveinbjorn's jaw open so that Wulfrik could insert the end of the pipe in the prince's mouth. When the pipe was in place, Wulfrik sent the snake he held in his other hand slithering down the open end. To encourage its progress, the torch was used to heat the metal and drive the viper down Sveinbjorn's throat.

'So passes the next king of Ormskaro,' Wulfrik said. 'We will take his body back to the halls of his fathers and let them know of the passing of Sveinbjorn Snakebelly.

'And then there will be war.'

SILENCE REIGNED IN the darkened halls of Ormfell. Whispers of war were on the wind, rumours of rebellion among the jarls and thanes. No more did the walls of the tower echo with the laughter of midnight feasts, the song of harper and skald. A pall had descended upon Ormskaro, the darkest it had known since the death of King Torgald.

Viglundr sat alone in his empty council chamber, sullenly drinking a goblet of Bretonnian wine. With his most trusted jarls breaking faith with him, forming alliances among themselves to crown a new king, Viglundr was suspicious of his own huscarls. He would not end his days because of a twilight visitation and a cup of molten lead poured down his ear. If the Sarls wanted a new king, then they would fight the old one to do it.

Viglundr sloshed the wine around in his cup, staring sourly at the rich red liquid. Jackals! Vultures!

The upstart chieftains thought Ormskaro was weak, thought this was their chance to slake their own ambitions. They knew many of Viglundr's warriors had sailed away with Sveinbjorn and Wulfrik.

They would learn! When the fleet returned, its holds stuffed with treasure, Viglundr would be the wealthiest king in Norsca. He would hire armies to put down the rebellious chiefs, he would have sorcerers wither their lands and trolls devour their herds! Their children would be cast in chains and sold to the Kurgans! He would make of them an example that would horrify…

A shadow fell upon Viglundr's throne, stirring the king from his thoughts. He looked up in fright, his hand reaching for the sword at his side. All thought of fight vanished when he saw something fall to the floor at his feet. Viglundr gazed in open-mouthed horror at the decapitated head of Sveinbjorn, the features battered and swollen by poison.

'I brought your son-in-law back to you,' Wulfrik told the king as he stepped out from the shadows. 'Somebody put a snake in his belly.'

Viglundr continued to stare into Sveinbjorn's cold features. 'What have you done?' the king gasped.

Wulfrik took another step towards the throne, an icy smile on his scarred face. 'He had some idea of stealing my ship as well as my woman. I had some ideas of my own about that. I left the rest of the ships in the Empire to fare as they will. If the gods are kind, a few of them might make it back to Ormskaro in a year.'

The king reeled at Wulfrik's words, staggering back,

collapsing against the foot of his throne, his sword clattering to the floor. Sveinbjorn dead meant war with the Aeslings, and just when his own chieftains were giving him trouble. Loss of the fleet would bring those tribes that had sent ships on the voyage seeking wergild for them, at a time when Viglundr would need every ounce of silver to hire mercenaries.

'They're saying Sveinbjorn took control of the *Seafang* and it was he who cut the chains and abandoned the fleet. They say he even betrayed them to the southlings,' Wulfrik said. 'Of course, they say that only after my crew had told them that was what happened. The Aeslings will, of course, insist the treachery was your idea.'

Viglundr raised a trembling hand to his forehead. 'You have brought ruin to Ormskaro,' he croaked. 'The tribes will descend upon my city like vengeful wolves.'

'It will be amusing to see who comes for your blood first,' agreed Wulfrik.

Viglundr lifted himself to his feet, supporting his shivering body by leaning against the side of his throne. 'You have made your point,' he told the hero. 'Everything I hold I owe to your sword. You defeated King Torgald. You made everything possible. I accept that. I was wrong to try to cheat you.'

'I fought one war for you,' Wulfrik said, turning to walk away. 'That was when I didn't know better.'

'Wait!' pleaded the king. 'You can't forget Hjordis! If my city suffers, then she will suffer! Help me, and she is yours!'

Wulfrik's eyes were empty, like those of a dead

thing, when he turned and stared back at Viglundr. 'Pray to the gods, king,' the hero said. 'You have nothing left to offer me.'

The marauder didn't tarry to listen to Viglundr's increasingly desperate cries. The king was already a dead man, but before he went slinking into the halls of his ancestors, he would see everything he had built, that his fathers had built, come crashing down. Ormskaro would burn. It would make such a bonfire as to blind the gods themselves.

A ONE-EYED RAVEN circled the *Seafang* as Wulfrik's longship slipped through the fjord of Ormskaro for the last time. The crew sat with sombre faces upon their benches, not a man among them daring to make a sound.

In the bow of the ship, Wulfrik stood, his hair whipping about him in the wind. He held a bundle of bloodied silk in his hands, his face raised to the sky, his keen eyes peering at the dark clouds, trying to see the visages of his gods. The champion's eyes were devoid of warmth, as icy as when he had last gazed upon Viglundr.

Slowly, he reached into the makeshift bundle, lifting from within a gory strip of flesh.

'To Khorne, the face I would have kissed,' Wulfrik called out, his solemn words rolling across the waves. He flung the tatter of soft pale skin into the sea and reached into the bundle for another offering.

'To Slaanesh, the heart I would have cherished. To Nurgle the belly I would have filled with sons and daughters.'

As he made each offering, Wulfrik cast another ghastly prize into the sea. Finally the bag was empty. Slowly, reluctantly, the chieftain removed a lock of golden hair from his belt. He stared sadly at it for a time, then cast it into the sea to join the other offerings.

'To Tzeentch, the last hope of love,' he said, feeling the bitter pain of his loss pulsing through his body.

Wulfrik stared out across the sea, watching the horizon where dark clouds met darker waters. He could feel the might of his gods. Everything he had suffered would have come to him even without the curse. Viglundr would still have stolen Hjordis from him, gifting her to that Aesling pig Sveinbjorn. His love would still have been betrayed and defiled, the stink of another man on her flesh, the taste of another man on her lips.

What he had thought a curse had in fact been a blessing. Because of the curse, he had been given the tools to destroy his betrayers. Without the power of the *Seafang* he would never have been able to tempt and trap wily schemers like Viglundr and Sveinbjorn. Without the fame and glory of being the Worldwalker, he would never have gained the loyalty of men like Njarvord and Arngeirr, Jokull and Skafhogg. Without the lies of Zarnath, the pieces would never have come together.

The gods had helped him, now Wulfrik would serve them. There would be no more attempts to escape his doom. He would sail the Great Western Ocean and the fog between worlds and he would strike down the sacrifices demanded of him by the gods.

Overhead, the raven cawed, gradually turning in its flight, soaring back towards the icy mountains of Norsca.

Its work was done.

The gods had their champion now and for all eternity.

ABOUT THE AUTHOR

C. L. Werner was a diseased servant of the Horned Rat long before his first story in *Inferno!* magazine. His Black Library credits include the Chaos Wastes books *Palace of the Plague Lord* and *Blood for the Blood God*, *Mathias Thulmann: Witch Hunter*, *Runefang* and the Brunner the Bounty Hunter trilogy. Currently living in the American south-west, he continues to write stories of mayhem and madness set in the Warhammer World.

Visit the author's website at
www.vermintime.com

SWORD OF JUSTICE ~ CHRIS WRAIGHT

WARHAMMER HEROES

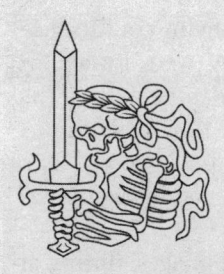

An extract from Sword of Justice
by Chris Wraight

SCHWARZHELM READIED HIMSELF as Raghram came at him. The doombull was massive. The musk around him was thick and cloying. Beneath his hooves, spoor clung to the rock, stinking. The wide bull-mouth bellowed. The axe swung, spraying rain. On either side of him, the Knights Panther took up their positions against the doombull's entourage of gors. The elite troops of the two armies came together on the slopes of the Bastion, and the fury of the storm above was but an echo of the savagery of their encounter.

Schwarzhelm met the onslaught full on, blunting the full force of the charge. Coarse iron clashed with pure steel, sending sparks spinning into the shadows. The blow was heavy, far heavier than that of a man. Schwarzhelm judged it carefully, dousing the momentum without aiming to stop it. When the moment was right, he withdrew the blade, sprang aside and plunged a stabbing blow at the monster's flank. It connected, and black blood pumped down the beast's twisted legs.

On either side of him, Schwarzhelm could sense the presence of the knights. They were locked in combat with the gors. Dimly, right at the edge of his vision, he could see the ebb and flow of battle. A knight would fall, pierced with a cruel horn-tip. Or a beast would stumble, its chest opened by an Imperial blade. It was finely balanced.

But these were just the ghosts of images, flitting at the periphery. Ahead of him, roaring its rage, the doombull came again. Again the axe fell, again it was parried. Schwarzhelm wielded the sword expertly, making play of its speed and keenness. As it worked, the failing light flashed from the steel.

Schwarzhelm let the Rechtstahl guide his hand. He was a master swordsman, second only to one other in the entire Empire, but you could not wield a holy blade as if you owned it. The sword was its own master, and he was but the most recent of its stewards. Only after half a lifetime of wielding it did he understand some of its secrets. Most would never be uncovered.

Raghram maintained the charge and the axe swung like a blacksmith's hammer. In the massive, bunched arms of the doombull, it looked like a child's toy. Schwarzhelm saw the feint coming and angled the sword to parry. At the last moment, he shifted his weight. The blades clashed once more. Feeling the camber of the slope beneath his feet, adjusting for the force of the attack, he pushed back.

His arms took the full momentum of the doombull's weight. For an instant, Schwarzhelm was right up against the monster. The ruined face was above his. The eyes, kindled with a deep-delved fire, blazed at him. Strings of saliva drooled down from the tooth-filled jaw. Raghram wanted to feast. He was drunk on bloodlust.

Then Schwarzhelm's foot slipped. The rock was icy with surface water and he felt his armoured sabaton slide on the stone. The axe weighed down, the blade-edge hovering over his torso.

Schwarzhelm gritted his teeth, pushing against the weight. The power of the doombull was crushing, suffocating. But Schwarzhelm was no ordinary man. Tempered by a lifetime of war, his sinews had been hardened against the full range of horrors in the Old World. He'd stared into the rage-addled faces of greenskin warlords, the horror-drenched gaze of Chaos champions, the cruel and inscrutable eyes of the elves. All had met the same fate. This would be no different.

He twisted out of the encounter, arching his body to deflect the secondary blow, using the power of the beast to drag it forward. He could still sense the battle raging around him. There was no way of telling who was winning. All his attention was bent on the monster before him. This was the fulcrum of the battle. If he failed now, then they all died.

He pulled back, but Raghram was upon him. The axe swung down again. The obvious choice was to step back, evade the curve. But the Rechtstahl seemed to draw him on. Inured to hesitation, Schwarzhelm plunged inside the arc of the axe, crouching low. He was within the grasp of the beast. Twisting the blade in both hands, he brought the tip up. With a savage lunge, he thrust it upwards, aiming beneath the doombull's ribcage.

The tip pierced its flesh, driving deep. Fresh blood coursed over his face, hot and rancid. The doombull roared afresh and pulled back. Schwarzhelm withdrew the blade, ducking under flailing fingers, feeling the monster nearly grasp him. He pulled back again, feeling his breathing become more rapid. There was no fatigue, no weariness, but the sheer power of the beast was impressive. He would need to do more than stab at it. From somewhere, the killing blow would need to be found.

Now the creature was wary. It lowered its head. The horns dripped with rain. The axe hung low against the ground. When it growled, the earth seemed to reverberate in warped sympathy. Schwarzhelm held his position, sword raised. His eyes shone in the dark. Every movement his opponent made, every inflection, needed to be observed. He would wait. The Rechtstahl felt light in his hands. On either side, the savage cries of battle still raged. His knights were holding their ground. No gor would get to him while any of them could still wield a blade. The duel would be undisturbed.

Raghram charged again. Even as the hooves pushed against the rock, Schwarzhelm could see the energy exerted. The muscles in the goat-shaped thighs bunched, powering the massive creature forward. The head stayed low, trailing long lines of blood-flecked drool. As the doombull moved, its horns swayed.

Schwarzhelm adjusted his stance. His armour

suddenly felt like scant protection. Keeping his eyes on the swaying axe-blade, he braced for impact.

It was like being hit by a storm. A human, however strong, had no chance of halting such a monster. It was all Schwarzhelm could do not to get knocked from his feet. Bringing all the power he could to bear, he traded vicious blows from the axe with the Rechtstahl, giving ground with every one. Raghram let slip a crooked smile as it advanced. Deep within that deranged face, something like amusement had emerged. He was being toyed with.

Schwarzhelm leaped back, clearing half a yard of space, and let the Rechtstahl fly back in a savage backhanded arc. If it had connected, it would have spilled the monster's guts across the Bastion floor. But Raghram was too old and wily for that. With a deceptive grace, it evaded the stroke, its momentum unbroken.

This was dangerous. Schwarzhelm felt his balance compromised, but there was no room to retreat. The axe blade hammered down, and he barely parried it. His blade shivered as the full force of the axe landed on it, and he felt the power ripple through his body.

He gave ground again, losing the initiative. Raghram filled the void, hacking at his adversary even as it roared in triumph.

Then the axe got through. Whether it was skill or luck, the doombull's blade cut past Schwarzhelm's defence. It landed heavily against his right shoulder, driving deep into the metal of the pauldron. He felt the plate stove inwards. An instant later sharp pain bloomed out, and he staggered back from the blow.

Raghram leapt up. The axe was raised, and a look of scorn played across the bull-face. Schwarzhelm raised his sword in defence, watching the advance of the monster carefully. The doombull came on quickly. Too quickly. In its eagerness to land the killing blow, its axe blade was held too far out.

Schwarzhelm swept his sword up, twisting it in his hands as he did so. He left his torso unguarded. That was intended. The manoeuvre was about speed. Raghram reacted, but slowly. The Rechtstahl cut a glittering path through the air. Its point sliced across the beast's face, pulling the flesh from the bone and throwing it high into the storm-tossed air.

Raghram staggered backwards, a lurid gash scored across its mighty cheek and forehead. The great creature lolled, stumbled and rocked backwards, blinded by its own blood.

Schwarzhelm recovered his footing. The Rechtstahl glistened eagerly. Taking the blade in both hands, he surged forward. The tip passed clean between the beast's protruding ribs, deep into the unholy torso and into the animal's heart.

Raghram screamed, and the last veils of shadow around it ripped away. The sudden lurch nearly wrenched the blade from Schwarzhelm's grip, but he hung on, twisting the sword further into the monster's innards. It bit deep, searing the tainted flesh like a branding iron on horsehide. The doombull attempted to respond, flailing its axe around, searching for the killer blow.

But its coordination was gone. Slowly, agonisingly, the pumping of the mighty heart ebbed. The light in its